THE

Sun Collective

THE

Sun Collective

Charles Baxter

Pantheon Books, New York

All rights reserved. Published in the United States by Pantheon Books, a division of Penguin Random House LLC, New York, and distributed in Canada by Penguin Random House Canada Limited, Toronto.

Pantheon Books and colophon are registered trademarks of Penguin Random House LLC.

Grateful acknowledgment is made to The Permissions Company, LLC on behalf of BOA Editions, Ltd., for permission to reprint an excerpt from "On the Lawn at the Villa" from *The Owner of the House: New Collected Poems 1940–2001* by Louis Simpson. Copyright © 1963, 2001 by Louis Simpson. Reprinted by permission of The Permissions Company, LLC on behalf of BOA Editions, Ltd. (boaeditions.org).

Library of Congress Cataloging-in-Publication Data
Names: Baxter, Charles, [date] author.
Title: The sun collective : a novel / Charles Baxter.
Description: First edition. New York : Pantheon Books, 2020
Identifiers: LCCN 2019050883 (print). LCCN 2019050884 (ebook).
ISBN 9781524748852 (hardcover). ISBN 9781524748869 (ebook)
Classification: LCC PS3552.A854 S86 2020 (print) | LCC PS3552.A854 (ebook) | DDC 813/.54—dc23
LC record available at lccn.loc.gov/2019050883
LC ebook record available at lccn.loc.gov/2019050884

www.pantheonbooks.com

Jacket photograph by Wenbin/Moment/Getty Images
Jacket design by Tyler Comrie

Printed in the United States of America
First Edition
2 4 6 8 9 7 5 3 1

For Daniel,

Hannah, Isaac,

and Julia Baxter

It's complicated, being an American,
Having the money and the bad conscience, both at the same time.
Perhaps, after all, this is not the right subject for a poem.

—*Louis Simpson,*
"ON THE LAWN AT THE VILLA"

Part One

- I -

SOON AFTER HE BOARDED THE BLUE LINE LIGHT RAIL AT THE DOWN-
town Minneapolis station, keeping an eye out for his son, who had
deliberately gone missing and was living on the streets, Brettigan
checked the available space, saw two empty seats next to each other
at the far end of the car, and aimed himself in their direction as the
doors chimed shut. Having taken the one on the aisle, he removed his
Minnesota Twins baseball cap and placed it beside him so that no one
would drop down there. The translucent advertising sheath attached
to the outside of the train car was filtering the sun and gave his hands
a bruised discoloration, as if he'd been in a fistfight.

A young couple shadowed him onto the train and sat down in the
seats opposite his own.

A man of retirement age, Brettigan wore an expression of studied
neutrality whenever he found himself in public. He had the look
of someone who possessed important secret information and who
needed to fade into the background to avoid exposure. On his ring
finger he wore a loose-fitting gold wedding band thickened with adhesive tape to secure it. Despite his age, he still had a full head of graying
hair, rather bushy eyebrows, and penetrating blue eyes. Deep lines
creased his face. With his khakis and cotton sports shirt, he gave an
appearance of informality, but he sat as straight as a child who has
been told not to slouch, and he gazed out the grimy window with
the uneasy intelligence of someone who has few illusions to comfort
him.

Last week on this commuter train there had been an incident. A woman whose baby was in a stroller had pitched and rolled her way to the seat directly in front of him. Brettigan had been close to the window, near enough to hear her panting. From time to time she had uttered soft groans. Every few seconds, she would nod and say, "Uh-huh," as if in conversation with a ghost companion. When an old man had walked past and leaned down to pat her stroller-bound infant on the head, the woman had started to shout, "Don't you touch my baby!" She pointed at the aging passenger, who, alarmed, hurried out the doors at the train's next stop. Then she had glared at Brettigan, still sitting there behind her. Collecting himself, Brettigan had pretended to stare at the landscape outside. Where he looked apparently didn't matter. "Don't nobody touch my baby!" she cried out suddenly in Brettigan's direction. She smelled of wine. Her baby probably smelled of wine. The whole car smelled of wine and beer and Red Bull.

But this morning the train had apparently been steam-cleaned, and the usual professional-managerial types—suited, accessorized, and iPhoned—were seated nearby, tapping out messages, talking into their Bluetooths, or reading *The Wall Street Journal*. Very few Victims of Capitalism were on the train today. Most people thought of them as the homeless, or vagrants, or the deinstitutionalized mad—one of Brettigan's friends preferred to call them "scum"—but for Brettigan they were the Vs of C, that generously proportioned sector of the economy that had never had a single foothold on the ladder of success and who were lying on the ground anywhere they could fall unmolested. In midsummer you'd find them on the train rumbling out to the Utopia Mall, a terminal point where they would not disembark but stay right where they were, collapsed in heaps, half-asleep and therefore semi-alert, until the train started up again and returned to downtown Minneapolis. They had no purchases; they consumed nothing but air and food scraps. Even the tattered clothes they wore seemed borrowed from somewhere. Back and forth the trains would go, carrying their somnolent human freight.

Whenever Brettigan exchanged glances with one of these people, he tried to make his face express compassion and kindliness. They looked back at him with sodden indifference or hatred.

Months before at home, in the grip of insomnia, Brettigan had found himself watching a late-night movie that had apparently started a few minutes before he tuned in. An early talkie, statically photographed in old-style black-and-white and therefore comforting, the movie had pleasingly slow narrative rhythms, easily comprehended, or so it seemed at first. The film's plot appeared to be deadpan fantasy: seven passengers dressed in formal evening attire were conversing in the lounge of a transatlantic ocean liner. The camera seemed to be stuck in one place, and the sound recording was rudimentary, but that was okay because the movie had quite obviously been adapted from a stage play, and the characters on the screen were as bewildered by the plot as Brettigan was. What were they doing on this ocean liner? No one seemed to have any idea. They kept asking themselves how they had gotten there. None of them could remember booking passage on this ship or by what means they had boarded. Perhaps a joke was being played on them. Where were they going?

They were all dead, of course, and the ocean liner was taking them to the realm of shadows, and the movie was called *Outward Bound,* by someone named Sutton Vane (Brettigan had found this out by Googling the title once he had discovered it), and he thought of the movie whenever he was on the light rail here in Minneapolis or the New York City subway on those occasions when he visited his brother in Brooklyn. Judging by the appearance of their riders, one would think that the late-evening subway trains were populated almost exclusively by the dead or by people who wanted to be dead. Something about public transportation—you could also see it on the coaches in Amtrak train cars—had a narcotic effect and seemed to render the passengers half-alive, their heads flung back in comatose slumber. They didn't appear to be asleep as much as anesthetized, lifeless, unticketed, and whenever he saw Victims of Capitalism in a heap in a corner somewhere, he remembered *Outward Bound* and the journey they were all on.

Sometimes one of the Victims of Capitalism would awaken, and, weighed down with God, would start to shout inspired prophecy. "Look at my wounds," someone had once commanded him on the A Train, though without specifying any location. Here in Minneapolis, a rider had paced up and down the car asking, "Where's Duluth?"

A retired structural engineer and bridge designer, Brettigan observed the traffic backed up on Hiawatha and noted, as he always did, the Sabo Pedestrian Bridge with its inclined tower and slender concrete deck. It had the appearance of an outer-space structure painstakingly transported to Earth. He thanked the gods that he had not been involved in its design, given the failure of two of the cables thanks to wind-induced fatigue cracking at the anchorages a few years after the bridge had opened. The cables had fallen onto the bridge deck below; fortunately, no one had been hurt.

Now the light rail passed by several abandoned grain elevators, as blindingly white as the abstract geometries of a Charles Sheeler painting. At Thirty-eighth Street a well-tailored gentleman boarded. He wore a three-piece suit, a trench coat, and a soft black trilby hat. That hat made him appear as if he were in costume. He trailed a small suitcase on wheels. His glasses consisted of small tinted circles on thin gold frames, and some property in the lenses reflected light in such a way as to make his eyes nearly invisible. Standing in the aisle next to Brettigan, bathed in soapy blue sunshine, he looked down, smiled, and asked if the seat next to Brettigan's, the one on which Brettigan's baseball cap lay, was taken.

"No, not at all," Brettigan said, picking up his cap and putting it on. "Please sit."

The man dropped down in slow motion next to Brettigan, lifting the crease in his trousers in an old-fashioned gesture. "Thank you kindly," the man said. He had a trace of a southern accent.

A few moments passed. The man cleared his throat. "Thank you," he repeated, looking straight ahead before checking his pocket watch, like the White Rabbit in Wonderland.

"You have a plane to catch?" Brettigan asked, making a social effort.

"Yes, you could say that," the man said.

"Where to?" Brettigan asked, trying to keep his questions on this side of politeness, the starchy affability one attempts with strangers.

"Paris," the man said. "I'm goin' to a conference."

"Ah," Brettigan said.

"And you?" the man asked. "Where might you be goin'?" He turned to glance at Brettigan, but behind the lenses the man's eyes remained invisible. Maybe he didn't have eyes. Maybe he had something else.

"Oh, me?" Brettigan shook his head. "I'm . . . headed out to the mall to get some exercise. I'll meet with some friends out there, and then we'll walk around until we tire. It's air-conditioned, and although I don't particularly care for—"

"Yes," the man said, agreeably interrupting him. "I've seen them. I should say, I've seen walkin' around people like you. But tell me, why don't you stroll around the lakes in the city? Or the parks? Outdoors? I myself enjoy the city's recreational locales this time of the year. Birds, and . . ." The man thought for a moment. "Trees." The stranger wore cologne, Brettigan noticed. The scent was like autumn—aromatic burnt leaves. And the man's accent faded in and out as if he were imitating a southerner without actually being one himself.

"I have a medical condition," Brettigan informed him, "so I need to stay out of high temperatures, and therefore I—"

"Go out to the mall," the man said, interrupting again.

"Yes." Who *was* this character, prying into his early-morning life and finishing his sentences for him? "So," Brettigan said, doing his best to take control of the situation, "if you don't mind my asking, what conference are you going to?"

Rather quickly and as if by magic, the man reached into his pocket and drew out a business card before handing it to Brettigan.

DR. ARVER L. JEFFERSON, M.D.

PSYCHOANALYTIC AND
ASSOCIATED THERAPIES

Member: Midwest Institute of Proton-Analytics

The doctor's email address and phone numbers had been printed at the bottom of the card, but the ink was smudged and mostly illegible.

"I've never heard of proton-analytics," Brettigan observed, putting the card into his shirt pocket. "What is it?"

The doctor drew in a long breath. "I'll give you an example. You see that man over there?" he asked, nodding in the direction of the young couple who had followed Brettigan onto the train. The man wore earbuds, and a stack of pamphlets lay in his lap. The woman seemed to be studying both Brettigan and the doctor. "Yes," the doctor affirmed, "*that* one. As soon as I get off this train, he will ask you for money. He will test you. He will beg you for somethin', anything. You must give him a dollar at least. Do you know the legend of *Notre seigneur en pauvre,* our Lord in rags?"

"No."

"It's a French-Canadian legend of Jesus," the doctor said with low-level excitement as he warmed to his subject, "and in this legend Jesus is dressed as a beggar and is roaming the Earth, testing the generosity of everyone he meets. It's a spot quiz for your salvation. You could think of that man over there as Jesus. I recommend that you do so. Did you say that you have a medical condition?"

Brettigan nodded.

"The airport is coming up soon, and I shall have to be on my way," the doctor informed Brettigan. "But I will tell you another legend that grew up among my people in the South. This one will help you, I guarantee. It will help you personally. Here is what you must do. What I have for you is a cure, a cure for afflictions." The doctor now seemed nervously energized and was enunciating his words with care, as if he were speaking to a child with disabilities. "Find a mirror, the largest one that you can easily carry, let's say a hand mirror, and take that mirror to a creek or even better to a flowing stream or best of all a river, and here is what you must do. You must lower the mirror into the water."

As he spoke, the doctor's hands moved in the air in front of him, pantomiming, or so it seemed to Brettigan, a vigorous form of washing.

"The water has to flow over the mirror or the cure won't work, and once you have the water streaming over the glass, you wash your reflected face in the mirror. Not your *actual* face, but your mirrored face in the water. Holding the mirror so as not to lose it, you wash your face, your reflected face, your face in the mirror, and you will get well, you will recover, and, renewed, you will prosper. I give you my personal guarantee. Really, I promise you, you *will* get better, freed from all your afflictions. This is an ancient cure. It is proven. It is so. There is a vast literature to this effect."

The little recital sounded like nonsense to Brettigan, but even non-sense can serve a purpose sometimes.

The train entered a long tunnel, and the sudden change in air pressure caused Brettigan's eardrums to pop as soon as he swallowed. He saw his own reflection in the window and was startled. Across the aisle, the half-sleeping young man wearing earbuds sat up and rubbed his face. In his lap, the collection of pamphlets appeared to levitate. Next to the young man, the woman gazed fixedly at the tunnel before taking out her flip phone and tapping a message into it.

"I must go now," the doctor said, standing up and gazing at Brettigan one last time. His opaque lenses gave the doctor the appearance of a walking oracle. "Enjoy your walk, and do as I say. You will get better, I guarantee. You will be saved." As he turned, his glasses reflected the sun. "Perhaps you shall see me again, and you can tell me how you got well."

The doors of the train opened, accompanied by a two-note electronic chime, and the doctor hurried out, pulling his suitcase and checking his pocket watch, and as he exited, Brettigan thought he heard the doctor say, "You never told me your name," but he might have imagined those words, tossed into the air behind the black trilby hat in the general tumult of passengers rushing out toward the terminal where the TSA would soon examine them for concealed weapons and malevolent intent.

Now the light rail car was mostly empty. Brettigan counted only a dozen or so passengers, including the young man and woman still sitting across the aisle from him—the man who, the doctor had predicted, would soon ask him for money. In preparation for this request, Brettigan reached into his wallet and opened it, taking out a five-dollar bill, which he folded into his palm. The young man watched him do so without interest and then went back to straightening and fussing with his pile of pamphlets. As the train erupted from the tunnel into the sunlight, Brettigan waited to be asked for money, to be put to the test, to be saved by *Notre seigneur en pauvre,* but the young man had turned his head to observe the landscape of hotels and businesses passing by, and Brettigan, clutching his money, realized that he wouldn't be tested today, nor would he be saved.

2

THE CODGERS CLUB, A GROUP OF RETIREES ALSO KNOWN AS "THE THUN-
dering Herd"—a schoolteacher, a pediatrician, a morose mechanic,
and a man who seemed to have spent his life as a successful high-
society drug dealer and who was now noted for his dapper outfits,
impeccable manners, and straight talk—were all waiting for Brettigan
near the Utopia Mall food court, in front of a shuttered Asian fast-
food outlet, the peculiarly named Slow Boat to China. They had all
been in high school together and through the years had remained
semi-friends.

"Look who's here," the pediatrician said, wagging a fat finger
in Brettigan's direction. "You're late." The pediatrician, the oldest
morbidly obese person Brettigan knew, was lovable and soft-spoken,
although this morning his speech was interrupted by a coughing fit
with broken chords of phlegmy notes scattered up and down the
scale. "What," he coughed, "happened to you?"

"I met someone," Brettigan announced, smiling down at his assembled aging acquaintances. "I met someone on the light rail." Chaz,
the drug dealer, was drinking his usual herbal tea from a thermos
and seemed preoccupied. He gazed in the direction of the Mountain
Music store, which, because of the early hour, was also shuttered, all
its guitars and banjos under lock and key.

"You met someone?" Celia, the schoolteacher, asked. She was a
smoker, and her breath smelled like an ashtray. "So? Why'd that make
you late? Did this person slow down the train?"

"This someone," Ken, the mechanic, inquired gloomily, "was she beautiful?"

"Well, no," Brettigan told them. "It was a doctor. He. He was a doctor. He said he was a doctor. I have his business card right here somewhere. This guy gave me a cure for everything and told me that a French-Canadian version of Jesus would give me a test this morning for my salvation." Brettigan scratched a mosquito bite on his forehead. "But there was no test. Jesus didn't show up."

"Oh, *that* guy?" The drug dealer was suddenly alert and paying close attention. "The physiognomist? With the trilby hat and the glasses?" Brettigan nodded. "I know him," the drug dealer said, without elaborating.

"He didn't mention anything about physiognomy. His card said he was a psychoanalyst."

The drug dealer shrugged. "No, it didn't say that. Guy's a four-flusher. He calls on Jesus, but guess what, Jesus ain't coming. That's all I know." He took another swig of his herbal tea. "No Jesus today, no Jesus yesterday, no Jesus tomorrow. Jesus has left the building." He smiled. "Did he want to give you a cure for old age? He does that. Fountain of Youth type thing. No such cure. I have news for him: old age is lethal. No one survives it."

"Okay. Forget Jesus. Let's get going," the schoolteacher said, rising with some difficulty to her feet, supported by her cane whose ivory handle was carved in the shape of a cocker spaniel. "You guys. Who's got the stopwatch?"

"We already talked about this," the mechanic said, sounding impatient. His face was a succession of masks. He really had no face of his own. "We're not using the damn stopwatch. This is not a race, for heaven's sake. We are not competing. How many times do I have to say that? I refuse to be pressured. I told you all this only last week."

"Well, it may not be a race, but don't forget that the Hungry Dumpster is always gaining on us," the drug dealer said, raising his finger in the air to make his point.

"Chaz, stop with the metaphors. I hate them," the schoolteacher said. "All right. No stopwatch? Fine. But we agreed that we needed to pick up the pace, didn't we? I thought we had agreed about that."

"You agreed," the mechanic said. "You agreed with yourself. You can break free from us any time you want." He made another face, this one for exasperation. "I won't mind."

"We all seem rather irritable this morning," Brettigan observed. "We need to exercise. Come on. Let's go."

AS HE WALKED, BRETTIGAN CONTEMPLATED HIS ENVIRONMENT, AS HE always did. A dream palace owned by Canadians, the largest of its kind in the United States, the Utopia Mall had no windows to the outdoors and no visible clocks to note the time of day, producing in the visitor a disorienting spatial-temporal rupture. You didn't know where you were or what time it was, and after a while you might forget why you had come there and who you were. The mall didn't look like a shopping center so much as a casino that had somehow taken the form of a labyrinth. The mall had a center, but the Thundering Herd had disagreed about where it was located and what could be found there and whether trapped spirits resided at its core. Constructed in the early 1990s, the mall contained millions of square feet of retail space, and untold visitors annually. One of these visitors, his hands crossed over his chest in an X so that his right hand grasped his left shoulder and the left hand the right shoulder, a look of sheer mad terror on his face with Thorazine-associated tongue waggings, was now headed toward Brettigan, who stepped out of the man's way just before the stranger tottered off in no particular direction.

"Look at that American. A wack job. Haven't seen *him* before," the drug dealer said, giving Brettigan a slight nudge in the ribs. "And believe me, I've seen most of them and done business with them."

The Thundering Herd accelerated slightly as they made the turn past a bicycle store, once called Pedalphilia until protests from the community caused it to be renamed A Bicycle Built for You, and an audio outlet, Unbound Sound. Behind the gated window was a statue of a god, Prometheus, wearing headphones and chained to a rock. Next door was a seafood restaurant, The Prawnbroker. Brettigan felt a twinge in his knee. Would there ever be an end to the cutesy marketing names? No. Among other things, retail capitalism was all about disguises—Jack the Ripper wearing a clown mask. Most of the stores were still closed and would not open for another hour. This time of day, the light seemed to have been artificially sweetened, and from a distant source, music of no particular character or expressivity dribbled downward over everybody.

Ahead of him, Brettigan saw the red-haired and freckled young man who'd been sitting across from him on the light rail, making odd zigzag motions as he sauntered forward, first toward another shuttered store, Shirtz-and-Shooz!, then toward the courtyard, where he seemed to be inspecting the floor while beside him his girlfriend opened up her flip phone before tapping out more text messages. She had a determined, unhesitating stride. Her hair was done up and covered with a red scarf, and periodically she would look over at the young man as if seeking cues from him, and as she did, her eyes narrowed, giving Brettigan the impression that the two of them were engaged in some sort of clandestine activity, though perhaps what he was witnessing was just love, clandestine in its own way. They had all the raggedy charisma of youth and its attendant health. They seemed to be up to something, but Brettigan couldn't tell what their mission was. The boy still clutched his stack of pamphlets tightly, and the Thundering Herd moved on past them, turning another corner in front of Hare Today, a sports outlet for runners, and My Back Pages, a bookstore. The food court lay ahead of them at the end of their first circular lap. At its center was a coffee shop, Caf Fiend.

Beside Brettigan, Elijah, the pediatrician, huffed and puffed. Brettigan could see tiny beads of sweat on the old man's brow. "How's Alma?" the pediatrician asked. "And any sign lately of your son?"

"Tim? Sometimes I think I see him everywhere, in every street person. His friend Rusk told me that he's around. He's not missing, exactly. More like misplaced. Alma's okay. How's Susan?"

"Sometimes," Elijah said. "Sometimes I don't have an opinion. *Forty years* we've been married. Can you imagine? I can, because I lived it. Our history says that we're married, you know what I mean? And sometimes we're not? We have a connection, fine, we have it, and then it's gone, dissolved, and we're strangers. No ties holding us together at all, bingo, we're staring at each other—who *is* that? What is she doing, having breakfast, and talking to me and making no sense? She gets strange, like from Mars. Well, I get strange, too. Of course, I love her, and everything."

"Right."

The pediatrician looked up. "This place is like a cathedral."

"It is?"

"Sure. Look at how high it goes. It's awe-inspiring. The gods live here."

"They do?"

"I'm pretty sure—" His thought was broken off by what sounded like an explosion at the other side of the mall.

"Terrorists!" the drug dealer announced excitedly, pointing in no particular direction. "Let's go see the mayhem. Come on." He picked up his own pace and seemed to be herding the group toward the source of the noise. "They probably have their assault rifles out right now." He thought for a moment. "We'll stop them. We'll be heroes. We're old and have got nothing to lose. This is our time. Let's roll."

When they rounded the next corner, past a Minnesota-themed restaurant, Cry of the Loon, they saw that some workmen up on a scaffolding had inadvertently dropped a piece of equipment whose crash landing on the floor had been the source of the noise. The equipment resembled a mechanical squid that was now in its death throes ejecting bile or ink. While several other workmen rushed toward the scene with maintenance equipment—mops, pails, and another machine with a long tube apparently designed to suck up anything in its path—the Thundering Herd stopped and gazed at the mess that was almost instantaneously being cleaned up and obliterated by this group of men, all of them speaking excited Spanish.

"They should do this at night," the mechanic said. "This is for the janitorial staff. They don't do this kind of work in the daytime. Somebody could've been hurt, with that falling gizmo."

"I guess it's emergency maintenance," the drug dealer said, sounding disappointed.

"Look." Brettigan gestured toward a shaded corner where several sheets of thick paper had been deposited. At that moment he realized that the boy and his girlfriend, the ones he had seen on the light rail, had been walking around the mall unobtrusively dropping these pieces of paper here and there in the corners. Nobody in his group of friends seemed particularly interested in Brettigan's discovery. Ignoring him, they had set off again. He went over to pick up one of the sheets, and even from a few feet away, he could see that the top of each one contained a headline printed in bold lettering.

A Survival Manifesto!!!

Well, those two were just unripe kids, entering the age of death metal, all-night sex, and three-exclamation-point manifestos. They would get over it. They would calm down. Everyone did, eventually. And the mall's silent and mostly invisible security staff would pick up their pamphlets soon and if possible escort the kids to a holding jail in the mall's sub-basement where they would fester and age. Brettigan folded the sheet of paper. He then forced it down into his pocket next to the business card he had acquired from the doctor and set off to catch up with the Thundering Herd.

3

THE TELEPHONE WAS RINGING WHEN BRETTIGAN RETURNED THROUGH the back door. He let it peal away while he wiped his shoes on the unwelcome mat, a novelty item he had once acquired with the words GO AWAY in raised rubber lettering on it. Alma had not bothered to answer the phone either—that is, if she happened to be home. He wondered where his wife was. She hadn't told him whether she'd be running errands, so he called her name, but the house answered with a returning moment of silence before he was greeted at the entryway by the dog and the cat, Woland and Behemoth. Reaching down, he scratched the dog behind the ears and patted the cat on the head. The dog closed his eyes with pleasure, and the cat answered his gesture by raising her tail, giving him a quick meow. As if he'd just heard something at the front of the house, the dog trotted off, trailed by the cat.

They were inseparable, those two, and presented a queasy-making cornball spectacle. After his daughter had grown up and left the house, and after their son, Timothy, had found some temporary gainful employment as an actor, Brettigan and his wife needed help filling the hours. After considering the matter, they found at the Humane Society a nondescript mongrel puppy and an equally nondescript mongrel kitten, both from the slums. They were the offspring of shiftless vagrant animals. These two pets would be employed to keep Brettigan and his wife company, provide them with caretaking responsibilities, and populate the empty nest with themselves. After seeing to their vaccinations and the subsequent neutering and spaying, Alma set up the foundlings in different geographical sectors of the house.

Thinking that the dog and the cat would never get along, Brettigan house-trained the puppy in the back hallway and the kitten in the front rooms, giving her the living area and the half-bath, where her litter box was located under the sink. If she so desired, she could sit on the front windowsill and contemplate the birds she would kill if she were ever allowed outdoors.

The arrangement had not lasted for long. The two animals had both raced through any open door to get together and to mix it up, with the dog squeak-growling merrily, rolling onto his back while the cat pounced on him or pretended to swat him. The dog nipped at the cat, but as they grew, their play seemed to turn into affectionate and almost surreptitiously loving behavior, as if they were shameful traitors to their species.

The scenes of their interactions grew treaclier and more sentimental by the day, a living pet-kitsch greeting card. The two began to groom each other, licking each other's faces, sleeping with each other, the cat curled up against and sometimes on top of the dog, her head on his belly. *Aww, so cute,* their friends would say before launching into predictable sermons about how *if dogs and cats could get along, why couldn't* et cetera. Having decided that such dog and cat behavior could not last and was against nature, Brettigan and his wife let the two animals spend their days together until the inevitable moment when they would discover that they hated each other and were incompatible. After the war—barking, snarling, spitting—would come mediation, the divorce, and the division of playthings.

But now, fully grown and immune to criticism, the two creatures followed each other around in their own Peaceable Kingdom. When the dog went out for a walk, the cat would yowl piteously until he returned. When the cat spent two days at the vet, the dog moped around the house, not eating, whimpering at night, and searching the corners. Upon the cat's return, the dog ran mad circles around the house, leaping on sofas, barking happily, his orderly life restored.

The two did not share all interests. The cat watched snobbishly indifferent and bored when the dog chased after a ball, and the dog had no interest in studying birds or in killing and eating the mice in the basement. Watching the cat do her predatory work, the dog yawned.

IN THE KITCHEN, INHABITING THE LOUD SILENCE LEFT BEHIND BY THE no-longer-ringing telephone, Brettigan poured a cup of burnt coffee from the little electric percolator on the counter next to the radio permanently tuned to NPR. When she was out running errands, Alma left the radio on to deter break-ins. Burglars hated NPR, she believed. Today the radio was off. Brettigan called out, "You home?" given the possibility that she was upstairs and had not heard him. The silence he received in return convinced him that he could go to the back den and play the piano for a while, without bothering her. She didn't like his playing. They were both musicians, but she had developed a distaste for music, especially his.

He emptied his pockets onto the kitchen counter. The manifesto uncurled a bit, opening itself like a flower.

At the piano, he felt a stinging of notes in A minor play themselves, doodling down and then upward as a sort of introduction before an odd bluesy tune interrupted the chords he had been vamping around with. The tune started in his right hand before moving to his left, sounding vaguely like an absentminded jazz pianist remembering Bill Evans but as Bill Evans, debilitated and in a cocaine haze, might have remembered Debussy. All of Brettigan's music was filled with memories of other music.

Brettigan was grateful that he was an ordinary musician and not great. Greatness entailed a broken soul and too much suffering. He played nothing too severe. He loved pensive abstraction, the poetry of turning away, of mulling it over, of driving through the city at two a.m., only a few lights burning, only the night crew still awake, the night watchman at his post waiting for dawn and humming a tuneless tune to keep himself company. "The only music you're good at is nocturnes," one of his piano teachers had said. "That's all you can really do."

As Brettigan thought about his son's childhood, his fingers broke into a melancholy tango. Timothy was never very far away from his thoughts whenever he sat at the keyboard.

This time, the tune began to stretch itself over several measures, and as he tried it out, Brettigan felt the leisurely melancholy of the key of A minor, a satisfying Where-have-they-all-gone? feeling, and he could feel himself doing his best to avoid the tug of C major, that white-bread, midwestern, let's-all-be-happy-right-now key, A-minor's first cousin with the smiley face, a really *major* major, so he dropped his left hand two octaves down and added a soft low tremolo. Jesus Christ, where did *that* come from? That death rattle, death ringing the doorbell? Someone buried and waking up underground and speaking with music instead of words?

He heard the front door open, then the sound of Alma walking into the kitchen. He heard her put down a grocery bag.

"Bloody hell?" his wife cried.

"Welcome home," he said loudly enough to be heard over the chords he was determined to play. Bah boom. The end.

From the kitchen came sounds of struggle. She had ripped the grocery bag, and fresh fruits and vegetables and lettuce and asparagus—Brettigan knew their sounds—were being scattered onto the counter and into the crisper, accompanied by spousal mutterings rising to an irritated half-bark that summoned both the dog and the cat to observe her.

"So you'll never guess what I . . ." she was saying halfway across the house, the second half of the sentence drowned out by distance. She sometimes mumbled in order to force him to move to where she was. He lowered the lid over the piano keys before making his way back into the kitchen.

"Hi," he said. Alma was putting the last of her purchases, a bottle of oregano, into the spice rack. He kissed her tentatively and shyly to test her mood. It was unsettled. The heat and the humidity outside had caused her hair to curl and coil so that the silver strands looked like miniature bedsprings. Her cheek was damp and salty.

"Did you see him?"

"I never see him."

"All the same, I think he's around, I can sense it."

"Yes. He's here somewhere. Everyone says so. He'll show up sooner or later."

"I hope you're right. He'd better. You know that church, the one on Blaisdell? You'll never guess what I saw as I was coming back from back there," she said.

"You were at church? You've converted to something? You're a Muslim now?" He smiled. "You'll have to start wearing that thing, the thing women wear, Muslim women, what do they call it, that thing?"

"A niqab." She was not amused.

"That's it. A niqab. With a little slit for eyes. A makeover. You'll look all mysterious, just your eyes floating around the house, the rest of you hidden from view."

She turned around to pretend-glare at him, a preface to her own irony in combat with his irony and to the underlining that she gave to certain words. "No, Harry, I was *not* at church and I did *not* convert to Islam and I am *not* wearing a niqab. I was driving. To get our *groceries*. To *feed* us. To provide us with *something for dinner* this very evening. Do you want to hear my story or not?" She offered him a halfhearted expression in which love and irritability were equally mixed and fighting it out.

"Sure," he said, "I'm always eager to hear your stories, you know that—I mean, hey, what have we got? Your stories and nothing but time." Her hair was a bit . . . disarrayed, a few strands falling over her forehead, which reminded him of the way she had looked— what? Forty years ago, when they were still young and she had the most beautiful eyes he'd ever seen, deep and soulful, and she was so beautiful in every possible way that she was just out of his league, untouchable in her grace, but she had loved him anyway back then and still contained a memory of that love, now, buried deep within her somewhere.

"So there was this wrecking company," she said, a curl bouncing against the middle of her forehead, "on Blaisdell, and you know that church there, the Blessed Church of the Fiery Holy Smoking Bleeding Heart of Jesus?"

"Old building? Red stone exterior?" He reached for the celery before she took the stalks away from him.

"You shouldn't eat that without cleaning it. Um, the church, yes, that's the one," she said. "So there I was, sitting in my car, stalled in traffic, nothing moving including me." She paused for dramatic emphasis.

"You were sitting in your car, nothing moving including you," he echoed.

"Yes," she said. "And do you know what they were doing? What those *men* were doing? Take a guess."

"Demolishing the church?" Brettigan said. "Wrecking ball? Dust and debris? Big lifting hook and crane? Spectators? Asbestos dust? Cancer?"

"Yes," she said. "How'd you know?"

"It was in the paper."

"Well, I hadn't been informed. No one had told *me*. And I was, I was sitting in the car, and, you know, I—I couldn't breathe. Took the air out of me."

"The air . . . what're you talking about?"

"Oh, come on, Harold. Let's try to keep up with the conversation here. Let's pay attention. Give me my due. I was using a metaphor. I couldn't, I'm saying I couldn't breathe."

"I love you, Alma. And I always give you your due. How come you couldn't breathe?"

"Oh, do you give me my due? *Well*," she responded with an increasingly argumentative tone, as she turned away from him, holding some fresh broccoli and waving it around like a whisk broom. "Be that as it may. There I was, in the car, not moving, the street all trafficked up."

"And?"

"And they had this wrecking ball, and this particular wrecking ball was smashing into, what do you call them, the turrets, those little towers, smashing into that old red church brick. Bang. Crash." Alma waved her arm with the broccoli back and forth, pantomiming wreckage.

"The old must make way for the new," Brettigan said quietly. "Dem's the conditions that prevail."

"In that case, we're sunk. Personally," his wife said. "That place was beautiful, Harry. I loved driving past it."

"Right, okay, yes. But we weren't members. You weren't, I wasn't. The Burning Heart of Jesus had to burn without you, all those years. We didn't contribute, and we can't complain."

"You bet I can complain. I'm complaining now. That's what I'm doing. Can't you understand anything? It gave me a moment."

"A moment? In the car?"

"Yes." She turned her face slightly away from his and put her hand on the kitchen counter. "They were so happy doing their demolishing, those *men* in their yellow hard hats over their hard heads, bent to their work, so serious. So officious. With their awful destruction machines. You boys are so proud of your machines."

"No," Brettigan said. "Include me out of that." He could see her eyes beginning to tear up, so he put his hand on her shoulder. "Okay, I'm sorry," he said as gently as he could. It was an all-purpose apology. When you aged, all the small destructions began to add up. They were like paper cuts, and they hurt everywhere. After a while, you couldn't stand it, and then, who knows, you might have a good day, and all the paper cuts healed, for a while.

"All the old things," she said quietly. She glanced out the window at the backyard bird feeder, and Brettigan followed her gaze to see a blue jay, large and bullying, eating the seeds and the suet. The smaller birds, the sparrows, had gathered on the ground for the husks. "I know I'm being sentimental but I can't help it. Do you know what's going up there?"

"Where the church was?"

"Are you even listening to me? What do you think I was talking about?" She wiped her eyes free of tears with her forearms.

He hated to say it even though he knew. "Yes, I read about it. One of those franchise gyms. I think it's called 'Gopher Fit.' For Minnesota, the Gopher State." He waited. "Or 'Go For It.' Or 'Gopher It.' I don't remember. Anyway it's a fitness place. The church of fitness. Gophers are involved."

"Sometimes I can't bear it," Alma said quietly. "Any of it."

"I know. But we have to." He debated inwardly whether to embrace her from behind, and he did, but he could tell—from the knowledge about her that he had accumulated in their long marriage—that the embrace could not comfort her and was an annoyance. She stiffened for a micro-moment. Nevertheless, he held her still. She smelled of lavender, from her soap, and he thought of her fleetingly as a boat and himself as her harbor.

"And how was your morning, Harry?" she asked. "And all those senile geezer friends of yours?"

"Well," he said. "A man, a doctor, well, he *said* he was a doctor, spoke to me on the train. He gave me a cure for everything. *Everything.* You name it, he had the cure. And then there was a young couple at the mall, dropping pamphlets here and there. They were very cute."

"You can't do that, dear," Alma said, pulling away from him. "Pamphlets at the mall? It's illegal. And also, it's, what do they call it, an anachronism. People use the internet now to broadcast their mad opinions. Anyhow, that mall won't let you do that. It's private property, that place."

"Okay." He watched her floating away from him across the kitchen. "I picked up one. It's over there on the counter."

"This one?" She peered at it.

"Yup."

"Oh, goodness," she said, reading it. "This is all whoopee stuff." Brettigan let her read it, and slowly she passed the pamphlet over to him. He bent down and raised his head slightly so that he could see the print through his bifocals. The print was large and thick, and the pamphlet showed signs of haste.

A Survival Manifesto!!!

The world has gone mad and we must put a stop to its self-extinction. You are all dying and may not know it. The love of accumulation is killing us and turning us into shadows. What comes after Postcapitalism? The dreaded *something* that they are keeping behind the barbed wire electrical curtain. As Martin Luther King Jr. said, "Something is wrong with capitalism." And we know what.

Stop bad love. Bomb this bad love and get right with your hearts. Bomb the power. Bomb the plate glass, bomb the store dummies, bomb the consumers, bomb the bankers, the business-men, the hucksters, bomb the oligarchs, the thieves. The Mall is a disease. Do not be silent. Silence kills. Speak up. Remember the words:

I once was lost but now I'm found
Was blind, but now I see.

Let us open our hearts. Let us brush the snow from our lips. Let us breathe in suffering and exhale charity. Let us be humble and leave this evil place and put good where there has been only its absence. Love one another. Consumption consumes us. Do not let them use God against us again. Love God, love Moham-med, love the Buddha. Befriend the poor. Do not wait. Love them right now. Love all the colors of humanity. Come to our meetings. Let us know how you live. Peace

—The Sun Collective of Minnesota ☛ ✷
www.suncollectiverevolution.com
4201 Roosevelt Avenue NE

"Oh, those people?" Alma said. "I love those people. Harry, I've told you about them, don't you remember?" He stared at her. "You never pay attention to me. I even went over there once. They sit around and talk and make plans. They're extremely chaotic, but they do things. It's very sweet."

The manifesto had cheered her up, Brettigan could see, the Earth-improvement project, all the desperate remedies.

4

HE HAD ONCE COMMITTED A MURDER.

The trouble was, he couldn't remember whom he had murdered or how exactly he had gone about doing it. One morning he had awakened bathed in sweat, his heart thumping like an engine about to seize up. Alma slept peacefully next to him, breathing through her mouth with delicate snores. The chalk outline of his victim, pointedly clear in his dream, had now faded away. How could you be a murderer if you couldn't remember the specifics of your crime?

And how had the murder occurred? The dream-memory had involved not a gun but a knife, infinitely sharp, sharper than a surgeon's scalpel. Despite the gaps in the narrative, Brettigan did remember how blood seemed to be spurting everywhere, and the inner exposed body parts of his victim, and the screaming. He remembered the terrible baritone roar, the rattling, gurgling outburst of a man in his last moments dying under protest, the light going out in his eyes.

But who was the victim? And where did the rage come from? He couldn't remember. You don't expect a man like Brettigan to be a murderer. It wouldn't fit his profile stored up in all the algorithms that were forming slowly, like sea slugs, on everybody, inside the godlike computers that no one could unplug. Here he was, a virtuous man, a retired structural engineer, a bridge designer who'd volunteered in soup kitchens, tutored disadvantaged children, raised a beautiful daughter and a handsome son, driven them to softball games, soccer games, attended their piano recitals, helped them with homework, walked his daughter down the aisle at her wedding, paid everyone's tuition—a model citizen! Hardly a blemish visible anywhere! If anyone was qualified for the role of devoted father and faithful husband, he'd be at the front of the line.

And yet his dreams: his dreams would send him to the electric chair. Or the gas chamber. Which they didn't have anymore. But they did have potassium chloride and would enthusiastically inject it into him.

"You, Harold, a *murderer*? That's a laugh. You're harmless. Always have been," Alma had said when Brettigan told her his dreams. She yawned, lying next to him, and treated him to a patronizing chuckle. "You're the most harmless person I ever met." And she kissed him on the cheek before getting up to take her shower.

"Not *that* harmless," he muttered. "I'm capable."

WEEKS LATER IN A BOOKSTORE, IDLY PAGING THROUGH A COLLECTION of European and African aphorisms and fables, he had come upon this passage, planted squarely in the middle of the page.

> *In mid-life a man wakes up believing that he has committed a murder. He cannot, however, remember who his victim was or what method he has employed to do the killing. Despite his forgetfulness, for years the man is weighed down by the memory of his crime; his guilt becomes ineradicable and leads to his physical decline. On his deathbed he is visited by the angel of God, who tells him that his only victim was himself and that he has murdered his true self for the sake of the life he has actually led.*

It sounded like one of Kafka's parables or a story by Henry James. (Brettigan had in his early twenties been a reader of fiction but in middle age grew to despise it; fiction was like quicksand, dragging you down.) He didn't care who had written this quaint parable with its lethal, accurate truth. Stealthily, he closed the book and replaced it on the bookstore display table. No one would ever know that this book had found him out. No one had seen him reading it. The other customers—that lady, over there, in the threadbare flower-pattern print dress, who was trying to memorize a recipe in an unpurchased cookbook, or that man reading a guide to explosives—they were all oblivious to him. The book, with its fables and aphorisms, had his number and was selling for $24.95. He had checked the price. Somebody had stolen his dreams and had put them into this book. The unconscious never takes a vacation. And capitalism sniffs out your secrets. It knows all of them by now and has lists with your name on them matched to a facial recognition file.

Wherever you go online, the Big Computer knows what you want before you want it. It's ready for you and waits patiently, humming. It knows where you will be tomorrow and what you will be doing, and it carefully calibrates the shame you carry with you in hopes that you will buy something to restore your peace of mind.

HE HAD HAD, HE FELT, A LUCKY LIFE OF GOOD FORTUNE AND PRIVILEGE, and if the sun was setting on people like him, middle-class white guys, well, okay. His only real cause for disquiet had been Timothy, their gifted boy. As the younger of their two children, he'd been born with an uncanny talent for mimicry, beginning at age six with imitations of his sister, Virginia, whose whine he could duplicate so accurately that if you were in the next room over or down the hall, you'd think she was speaking in her usual wheedling way. She dropped little pauses in her sentences and rushed her verbs and nouns together, and Timothy had somehow trained himself to parrot those habits too, so much so that the imitations gradually became distracting and weird, as Brettigan and his wife waited for Timothy to sound like himself. As he grew, the voices proliferated: he could sound like film stars or rock musicians or politicians or panhandlers or his parents. He could be anybody, but when he was himself, when the disguises disappeared and the masks fell, he seemed not to be present and accounted for. And he had a magician's gift for vanishing, almost on the spot. He was there; you saw him; you looked away, and when you turned back, he was gone.

He had gravitated toward the theater, his natural home. He was astonishingly good-looking and had a handsome man's indifference to engaging in intimate conversation and to exerting himself in courtship. In high school he played the Stage Manager in *Our Town* with a perfect New Hampshire accent. At the university he played the Gentleman Caller in *The Glass Menagerie* and Sir Fopling Flutter in *The Man of Mode* and Rosalind in an all-nonbinary *As You Like It* and King Creon in *Antigone* and Deeley in Pinter's *Old Times.* Whenever he came home for visits, he sat in the living room staring at his iPhone screen, or he disappeared into the basement, where he memorized his next part. Conversations seemed to cost him a great deal of effort, and he never asked polite questions and could not feign interests that he did not have. Emotionally, he was always somewhere else, flirting with oblivion, a place where his parents could not find him.

He had many girlfriends, all of whom were initially delighted to be in his company and who thought they could turn his habitual half-smile and easygoing affability into a grin that signified love. But the half-smile was frozen in place, as was the affability, and the pleasant, speculative expression on his face never varied much in mixed company. Some coolness resided at his center, a little pinpoint of ice. He could be wonderfully wicked and entertaining, though it all felt scripted, and not by him, so the discouraged girlfriends drifted away from him or were discarded, confounded by his glacial surface and their own inability to melt it.

He had no cruelty in him, just an emotional absentmindedness that seemed to be part of his character.

After earning a BFA in acting, there he was, in Chicago, a star, playing the lead in Brecht's *The Resistible Rise of Arturo Ui.* And there he was, again, as Dr. Astrov in *Uncle Vanya.* And he would return to Minneapolis, he told his parents, for the role of Estragon in *Waiting for Godot,* but then something happened to him, a mystery he refused to explain. There had been a girlfriend to whom a calamity had occurred. "I need to become a person," he told his father over the phone. There was an urgency in his voice that Brettigan had never heard before. What sort of person? The question encountered a silence. He claimed that he would live on the streets for a time, "as an experiment." What sort of experiment? He would not explain.

He moved from apartment to apartment, sometimes telling his family and friends where he was. But then he became unreachable, unlocatable. At first he had called his parents to say he was all right, but he was going to "de-phone"; then he let his cell phone service lapse. He was somewhere here in the city, drifting, though no one seemed to know exactly where. One of Brettigan's friends claimed to have seen Timothy sitting in front of the luggage carousels at the airport, sitting there unmoving, minute after minute. When asked whether he was meeting anyone getting off a flight, Timothy had said, "No. I just like to see families reunited. I like to see happiness. Don't you?"

And once Brettigan had seen a bearded man on a city bus who might have been his son, but the man got off before his father could reach him. At other times Timothy seemed to be over there, on the other side of the street, ambling without destination, studying the sidewalk, distantly walking away, like an urban ghost who gave you glimpses of himself before dematerializing. He was only visible out of the corner of the eye—fleetingly, in a crowd leaving a stadium, or in the distance on an escalator, at the ballpark eight sections over, or in the backseat of a taxi speeding away.

You couldn't report him because he wasn't really missing. He was here somewhere. And now his mother dropped in on churches, the ones with their doors open, and cathedrals, Quaker meetinghouses, basilicas, synagogues, Kingdom Halls, chapels, mosques, storefronts, and meditation centers, sneaking in quietly and sitting in the back, surveying those who sat and prayed, trying to imagine him back into existence as a happy solid citizen in one of these congregations, but half-seeing him, instead, on street corners, on benches, with the ragged and rusted-out street people with their staring empty eyes.

He will turn up someday.

Only God knew where he was. And another question: Where had *God* gone to?

- 5 -

ACROSS THE WAY IN MINNEHAHA PARK, SEATED AT A PICNIC TABLE underneath the shade of a large maple tree but still visible to Brettigan and his wife, a young couple, accompanied by a toddler, were smoking cigarettes and unwrapping their sandwiches while their daughter played nearby with a half-inflated yellow balloon. As Brettigan watched, the man transferred his cigarette to his left hand, inhaled, then took a bite out of his sandwich, and as he chewed and talked, cigarette smoke emerged from his mouth. The woman spoke to him, and he laughed softly without smiling, a married laugh, whereupon more cigarette smoke issued from his mouth and nose as if his head were on fire. He could smoke and eat sandwiches and laugh at the same time. How strange people were!

A cool front had descended from Canada, so the day was unexpectedly mild, with high wisps of clouds, and as Brettigan unwrapped his own sandwich, a bologna-and-lettuce-and-cheese concoction sprinkled with a few drops of mild green Tabasco, he felt a yearning for a deviled egg as a marker of summer. He put the sandwich aside and peered into the cooler.

"Hey," he said. "Where are you?" His glasses slid lower on his nose, a result of sweat and the thinning effects of age.

"Where are you what?" Alma asked. "And what *who*?"

"I was talking to the deviled eggs," Brettigan said, "which aren't here. Which I thought we had packed. Which . . . I want to eat them."

"They're not hiding," Alma told him. "They're absent and forgotten."

"Forgotten by whom?"

"By me," she said. "In the kitchen, where I made them and left them behind, all freshly wrapped up in waxed paper on the counter. I can almost see them this very minute." After reaching into the cooler and pulling out a bottle of white wine, she poured a drink for him in a plastic cup. "Sorry, Harry. It's another modest senior moment. Here," she said. "Have some wine. Drink up. You'll forget what I forgot, those eggs. Isn't it a beautiful day?" She examined the sky. "It's one of the most beautiful days ever."

Last night, rain had fallen for an hour, and today the air seemed to have been washed clean and somehow sanitized. Beyond the picnic table where the eating-and-smoking man and his wife were sitting, other couples and families sat or strolled in Seurat-like calm. In the distance was a sun-bleached playground, where little kids clambered over tubular structures. Other kids, shouting with glee, sat in swings pushed by their parents. As Brettigan bit into his sandwich, he had a thought: *History has stopped today. History is powerless here.*

"What are you thinking?" Alma asked. "You have that look you get." She put her hand on his shoulder.

"The weather. I was thinking about the weather."

"No, you weren't. Your face had that faraway mask. You look like that when you have thoughts."

"I was thinking about nothing. It was very pleasant."

"Over there." Alma pointed at something behind her husband. He turned to see: off on the other side of the picnic area, a guy in jeans and a T-shirt was blowing soap bubbles, and a young woman, similarly clothed, was dancing around, popping the bubbles with her fingers and occasionally leaping up to pop them with her bare feet. She was remarkably agile, and her movements resembled those of a martial artist. A third person, seated at a nearby picnic table, oddly dressed in clothes too heavy for the weather, was observing them.

"Sweet as a couple of bunnies," Alma said, removing her hand from her husband's shoulder and nervously touching a brown spot on her forearm. "Too cute for words."

Brettigan had always had a weakness for picnics, for summer and its long, drawn-out days, for laziness and the sweet languor that accompanied it. During the summer, time stretched out to accommodate whatever you needed to do, particularly when you didn't need to do anything, and you were occupied watching the runner at second base, and the count was three-and-two, and the home team was losing, and no one, absolutely no one, really cared. You ate your salt-in-the-shell peanuts and waited for something to happen. Chewing his sandwich, he remembered the two years before he and Alma had had children, and they had paraded around the house naked and had gone on camping trips and had made love outdoors as if it were summer all year long. Their honeymoon lasted for quite a blissful period, and they had thought themselves very daring in those days, before they settled in to the hard labor of parenthood.

Having finished his sandwich, Brettigan bit into a carrot.

"You're daydreaming," Alma said. "You're having one of those fantasies of yours." No one could say that she didn't know him. She'd always had a rather frightening ability to access his thoughts and say them aloud before he could. Did all longtime married couples share each other's thoughts? She put her hand on his arm and gave his open palm a brief involuntary caress. "We were like that. You didn't miss out on anything."

Something about the two young people, especially the girl popping the soap bubbles, seemed familiar, but Brettigan couldn't quite place them. Young people were beginning to look generic to him. What individuality they had didn't matter anymore.

"They haven't done anything we didn't do," Alma told him with a trace of pride in her voice. "We were once beautiful, too. Don't forget that. I'm sorry I said you were harmless. That was unkind."

"Do we know those two?" he asked.

"They look like anybody," she said. "Finish your carrots, Harold. I want to walk somewhere." She closed her eyes and tilted her head so that the sun bathed her face, as if she were taking a shower in it. Her expression radiated a transitory peacefulness.

After he put his paper napkin and the waxed paper wrapping back into the cooler, he took his wife's hand with a slight upward pressure, encouraging her to stand. She smiled and nodded before rising. They were both expert at these little marital pantomimes and enjoyed occasions of semi-comical tenderness. She asked, "Should we leave all this here?" meaning the cooler and the tablecloth and the cups of wine, and he nodded and escorted her onto the sidewalk that angled in toward the pavilion. All at once he drew back. "No, wait," he said.

"What is it?"

"I just thought of somebody I haven't thought of for . . . I don't know. Forty years. Longer. Decades."

"Who?"

"Give me a minute."

"Harry, what is it?"

Feeling himself caught and hooked in a memory, he returned to the picnic bench. His surroundings had rather suddenly become abstract: the park that had been painted by Seurat was now splattered by Jackson Pollock, and Brettigan felt himself pulled out to sea by a tidal wave of memory.

WHEN HE'D BEEN A BOY AND THE WORLD HAD SEEMED IMPOSSIBLY large, his parents had hired a woman to clean the house, an affable German-American named Mrs. Schimmelpfennig from a nearby farm community. She cleaned other houses in town, singing German school songs as she dusted and swept. She walked around in an aromatic lemon cloud from the furniture polish she applied to the tables and chairs.

She'd owned an old two-story house with a wide front porch, and she did occasional babysitting and had taken care of Brettigan on a few occasions when his parents were out. She enjoyed teaching him songs in German. While she sang, he'd been fascinated by her watery blue eyes and uncombed fairy-tale brown hair. He could remember the German sounds but couldn't quite remember what she had told him they meant.

Abends, will ich schlafen gehn,
vierzehn Engel um mich stehn:
zwei zu meinen Häupten,
zwei zu meinen Füssen,
zwei zu meiner Rechten,
zwei zu meiner Linken,
zweie, die mich decken,
zweie, die mich wecken,
zweie, die mich weisen
zu Himmels Paradeisen.

NOW HE REMEMBERED, AND OUT OF SOME RESOURCE OF SPONTANEITY he suddenly knew its meaning, the German words no longer a barrier but a portal to that moment when you went to bed and were about to go to sleep with the help of angels who would transport you to heaven. Its equivalent in English was "Matthew, Mark, Luke, and John, bless the bed that I lie on." Sitting in the park with Alma looking down at him, Brettigan felt the German words slide through him, accompanied by Mrs. Schimmelpfennig's quavering voice in the summer air as a visitation.

"Zu Himmels Paradeisen," he said now, glancing at Alma. She observed him warily.

"I worry when you lapse into German. Are you okay now?"

"I think so," he told her. "I just had a memory of a babysitter I once had."

"Oh, that one? The one who was murdered by a drifter?"

"Yes, that one. How'd you know?"

"I'm omniscient," she said, sitting down next to him and massaging his back. "I'm the eye at the top of the pyramid. What haven't you told me by now? Nothing. Everything you have to tell me, you've told." She took his hand. She had the stern but encouraging expression of a grade school teacher. Brettigan noticed that she had a small purple stain on her blouse from the plum she had just eaten. "Let's go for a walk," she said, pointing in the direction of Minnehaha Falls and the creek that drained into the Mississippi.

He stood up, took his wife's hand again, and nodded. Over there, under the shade of a maple tree, the young couple now sat at a table.

Past the park pavilion where children were gathered to buy ice cream at a concession window, their shrieks and cries echoing against the concrete, Brettigan and his wife monitored each other for balance as they walked forward, before descending the stairs leading to the base of the falls. Hearing birdsong, they both looked up to see a female cardinal hovering in the air above them and then landing on a branch, and above the cardinal . . . what *was* that? A hot-air balloon with rainbow colors on one side and a bearded man's face on the other floated silently overhead, seemingly aloof and imperturbable.

"Look," he said, as they stopped halfway down the stairs. He pointed at the balloon. "Aren't there power lines around here?"

"Who's the guy?"

"Who's the guy who?"

"On the balloon. The face. It's like an ad for something." She held her head back, her right hand at her forehead, shielding her eyes from the sun.

Brettigan took off his glasses, breathed on the lenses before cleaning them on his shirtfront, wiped the sweat off his nose, and put the glasses back on as he said, "Jesus. That's who it is."

"That's not Jesus," Alma told him. "That's the man on those, those cigarette papers. The ones you used to roll joints with. Remember? That guy? I can't think of the brand. It's been too long."

"Zig-Zag," Brettigan said loudly, still gazing at the hot-air balloon now drifting away in a northerly direction, obscured by trees. "Zig-Zag cigarette papers." He thought for a moment. "What's a hot-air balloon doing here? We're close to the airport. That has to be completely illegal."

"No." Instead of shaking her head, she nodded. "It's a good omen, don't you think? That balloon? Come on." She led him down the remaining steps, and they stood watching the falls for a few minutes before they turned and without speaking advanced down the pathway alongside the creek. Behind them and then on each side, the birds cried and sang as if they were announcing some important breaking news in bird-bulletins, some wonderful or terrible event that was about to happen and whose preview they had already seen.

Overhead, the illegal hot-air balloon advertising cigarette papers having drifted away, the trees on either side of Minnehaha Creek formed a canopy producing a shade so thick that Brettigan seemed to see dots of shadow wherever he turned his head, as one does with the onset of fever. Alongside Brettigan and his wife, the flowing water chuckled, and the still air had a supersaturated vegetative aroma with something angry and sour in it like the oxygen in a locker room after a losing game. A sparrow hopped from a maple tree to a blighted cedar, following them, it seemed, with interest. From a great distance came a low, thundering sound, the roar of an airplane clearing its throat, and the air moved, though not with wind, as the branches of the neighboring maples and poplars began to gesticulate in their direction—some kind of sign language, Brettigan suddenly thought, conveying secret information.

Alma turned to her left, took her hand from his, and, bending down, riffled her fingers in the creek water. "It's not that cold," she said, standing up and retaking his left hand in hers, the water from the creek and now from her hand wetting his fingers. They walked past a few other couples and some scattered children toward a slight leftward bend in the creek where a gap in the trees produced a thick rivulet of vertical sunlight, and after advancing into it, they were alone, standing in the brilliance produced by the absence above them both. Alma knelt, putting both hands in the flowing water, and Brettigan knelt down beside her. From his shirt pocket he removed a small hand mirror.

"What's that?" she asked, nodding at it, the question directed not so much at the mirror's existence as at its function. "You brought a mirror?"

"Take a look," Brettigan said. Lowering the glass into the creek's flowing water, he angled it so that he saw her face reflected, darkened and tinted by the moving current, which at first altered her expression so that she seemed to smile and produced a shimmering outline to her face, as if what he saw there had entered a time tunnel, a wormhole extended to the shadow side of an alternative universe where a previous Alma lived, no longer his wife but instead an anonymous beauty in blue jeans and penny loafers whom he had met at a college mixer in the university's student union when he had walked up to her and said, "Wanna dance?" extending his hand as the bad local band had lurched into the opening chords of "Wild Horses." She had nodded gamely before they nervously and urgently strolled toward the middle of the room where in the obscurity produced by the other dancers they would not be noticed. Instead of staggering around to the song's shuffling lust-drugged rhythms, the anonymous girl who she then was had unexpectedly fallen into his arms as a refuge, before reaching around him in a clutching embrace as if she had known him all her life or somehow understood that she would know him for the rest of it, as was true now and would be forever.

It was her face from that dance that he saw gazing back at him from the hand mirror he had lowered into the flowing water of Minnehaha Creek, and now, with his sunhat fixed to the top of his head to protect his skin from the ultraviolet rays that inspired squamous cell cancers that were probably already taking root there, he drew his hand across the image of her nineteen-year-old face, touching the image, caressing it and washing it as she looked at him from the puzzled distance of forty-five years ago, and she smiled uncertainly, not exactly wanting to be a girl again, not now, not ever. Please stop. No, she didn't want to be back there, her eyes said; she had been there, she had been young once, and now she wanted their precious daily lives unaltered, and she wanted Timothy, her son, to be safe and to be aboveground, somehow. This trick, this magic, had something decidedly terrible in it. The Fountain of Youth flowed only in one direction, toward you, with poison. You had to drink the poison to make it work. And as it did its work, it erased you. "What are you doing?" she cried out.

Brettigan turned to see Alma closing her eyes and then shaking her head to clear her thoughts, the age lines in her cheeks reinstated, the liver spots on the backs of her hands reappearing as soon as he looked down at them and as the music from the bad local band playing "Wild Horses" faded away. Turning her head slowly toward him, she said, "Something is wrong," as she tried to stand up. In the static humming silence, the song of the birds now began to intrude, the show they had quieted themselves to watch being over.

"What is it?" he asked.

She stood momentarily before staggering a few steps backward, out of the direct rays of the sun. "I don't feel well," she told him, slurring the words. She bent, tilted, toward him. "Oh, Harry," she said. He couldn't help himself: he turned to the left to see the mirror he had abandoned in Minnehaha Creek, but of course Alma's face wasn't there anymore. It was beside him, her jaw working in spasmodic up-and-down movements. Seeming to recognize the trouble she was in, she raised her left arm around his neck, and she slurred, "Mister, do you love me?"

After decades of being married to him, she had apparently forgotten his name.

Brettigan grasped her hand and lowered his right arm to her waist, feeling her weight falling against him, as if she could no longer support herself. At first she seemed capable of walking, but as he retraced their steps up alongside the creek bank, he noticed that her steps had grown more uncertain, more like the steps of a toddler, less balanced. After a minute, her feet were stumbling in the sand, leaving the trace of dragged lines. *Where were the other visitors to the park? The people who might help?* They were gone, all of them. They always disappeared when you needed them. Alma's weight fell against him. She muttered unintelligible words.

"Help!" he cried. Then louder, "Someone please help!"

He reached into his pocket for his cell phone, but as he touched a collection of furry, linty coins, he remembered that he'd left it behind at home on the dresser: in his mind's eye he saw it residing there, charging up, useless. With each passing moment, Alma's deadweight was growing deader. Brettigan cried out for help again, and this time the two young people he'd seen earlier blowing and popping soap bubbles appeared from behind a tree almost as if they'd been hiding there, but, no: behind the tree was an open field where they'd been congregating.

"Here," the young man said. He drew Alma's right arm around his neck, and together he and Brettigan brought her up the stairs, back to the picnic tables where they had been before. The young woman had taken out her cell and was now talking to the 911 operator, describing Alma's symptoms.

When they reached the shady spot where they'd been before, Brettigan and the young man lowered Alma to a sitting position. All at once she opened her eyes and said, "What just happened?"

"You fainted," Brettigan said to her, sitting beside her, holding her hand. "I thought you'd had a stroke." He noticed absently his wife's hand, to which, in all his confusion and panic, he had held firm.

"Well, maybe I did." Turning toward her husband, she asked, "Who are you?" When he gave her a stricken expression, she said, "Kidding!" Pivoting in the direction of the young man, she said, "And you? Who are you?"

"Ludlow," he told her. The boy's face had a triumphant, transparent absence of guile: from his straw-blond hair, to the blue eyes, and the vague affability visible in his open, brilliantly white smile—he looked like an actor in a toothpaste commercial—and the tattoo on his left arm that said, YOU'RE WELCOME! he appeared to have no agendas, hidden or otherwise, except to enjoy himself in the company of people who were as guileless as he himself was. He gave off an aura of sloppy and slightly unintelligent benevolence: an adult child, a plaything, someone's toy. "My name's Ludlow."

"Unusual name," Alma said, patting away the dampness from her forehead with a hankie she had produced from somewhere. "And you?" she asked the young woman. "Who might you be?"

"He's Ludlow because he's a Luddite," the young woman said, rather sharply. Brettigan quickly examined her. She, too, had blondish hair—Minnesota had a contagion of these stubborn blondes; they were everywhere—and she carried herself with an upright, regal bearing, the perfect posture of a ballet dancer, but her eyes had none of Ludlow's guilelessness. Instead, she projected a quiet, commanding authority on the cool side of the spectrum, as if she were accustomed to giving orders and having them followed and in addition always kept a trove of carefully considered punishments ready to be deployed whenever correction might be necessary.

"Didn't I see you last week?" Brettigan asked her, as the EMS siren became audible from the distance, drawing up in the nearest possible spot, the siren's wail abruptly silenced as the medics hopped out and ran in the direction that a third man, who was formally dressed, had indicated. "I saw you at the mall. I read your pamphlet. You're the Sun Collective. You want to befriend the poor."

"No," she said, "that wasn't us. That was somebody else. But, yeah, we're part of that, too. Everybody is a child of the sun. Including you. Both of you."

AND THEN EVERYONE WAS TALKING AT ONCE: THE EMS TECHNICIANS were speaking to Alma, holding three fingers in front of her and asking her to count them, taking her pulse and her blood pressure, inquiring if she felt light-headed and could stand up or would be more comfortable lying down, while Brettigan described his wife's fainting fit and made an effort to explain why he hadn't let her sit by the creek but had, instead, tried to make her walk back to the picnic area in the fireman's carry he'd used; and the young woman, seemingly oblivious to the medical emergency taking place in front of her, said to Ludlow, "What now?" while he doggedly grinned at her as if he didn't understand English; and meanwhile a small crowd had gathered and then dispersed.

After a few minutes, the EMS guys asked Alma to stand, and she did. She announced that she felt fine. With a few blunt but polite phrases, she refused to be taken anywhere for further observation. She had had a little episode, she said, and she wished to be left alone now. "Thank you," she said to the two EMS technicians, one of whom was speaking to someone else on a headset, "and now please go in peace."

Go in peace? She must still be out of it. She never used such phrases.

But there still remained documents to sign. Both Brettigan and his wife had to apply their signatures to them, agreeing to this and that, and as they did so, the young woman glanced down to witness it. She interrupted what she was saying to Ludlow and turned to Brettigan.

"So it says here you're Harold Brettigan," she said, "and so you're Alma, his wife," locking eyes with the two of them, taking them in. Instead of saying, "Nice to meet you," or some other clichéd civility, she lowered her head to study her fingernails. All she seemed to want were their names, stripped of pleasantries.

"And who might you be?"

"Christina," the young woman said, after a hesitation. "Brettigan, Brettigan, hmm: Is your son the actor? I saw him once years ago, in Chicago."

"Really? You did? Well, everyone has a name," Alma remarked, "and that's ours, and that's his."

"Okay, and thank you for your help," Brettigan said. After having walked arm in arm with Alma back to their picnic table, he began now to gather up their picnic things: the slippery, sweating, chilled wine bottle, whose exterior moisture seemed excessive; the brown picnic hamper with its remnants of sandwiches; the uneaten peaches and cookies; the paper napkins folded into halves. As he put the odds and ends back into the basket, Brettigan glanced over at his wife, who was smiling in no particular direction: first at the trees, then at the sky, in a kind of outdoors charm offensive. But it was a smile without an audience. A mood had come over her, as if she were thinking of a topic that she would not broach just yet; nevertheless, she had the look of someone who is preparing an announcement of the greatest possible importance.

"Come to the meetings, if you want to find out about the Sun Collective," the girl said. "Haven't we seen your wife there? Yes, we think so. And now we want to see you."

"Right."

"We can help. We're under our own instructions to help. To help *you. To help everybody.* You would love us."

"No kidding. You're sure? Help who?"

"You. Your wife. Come meet us. Meet Wye."

"Wye?"

"Yeah. You could say that he's the ambassador to old people like you."

After turning away at the mild insult, Brettigan noticed a mere moment later that the boy, Ludlow, and the girl, Christina, both had seemingly dematerialized. They appeared and vanished without warning, having some sort of spectral means of transportation, or as if he had left his theater seat and entered the lobby, only to return to find the primary actors gone.

"Come on," Brettigan said, grasping the picnic basket with his left hand and taking Alma's hand with his right. "Dear, let's go home."

Behind them, the birds, once again, grew suddenly quiet, as if taken aback for a second time.

AFTER HAVING ACCOMPANIED ALMA UP THE STAIRS TO THEIR BEDROOM, where he thought she would take a nap, Brettigan was emptying the picnic basket in the kitchen, where the deviled eggs wrapped in waxed paper were still out there on the counter, when he heard his wife's voice from the second floor: she was speaking—almost singing—in a high, unnatural register, her sentences interrupted by pauses and by deep laughter, the exceptionally lively half of a conversation apparently going on with someone whose cleverness was inspiring her to new heights of gleeful agreement. To whom could she possibly be speaking? What was going on? Surely it must be their daughter. But Brettigan had never heard Alma talking to Virginia in this excited and almost adolescent manner, at least not since their daughter had grown up and acquired a husband and formed a family of her own. Alma took a mature, measured tone with her daughter. Perhaps she was speaking to one of their two grandchildren. Nor had she ever spoken to Timothy that way. He hadn't heard that quality in his wife's voice in years, and he struggled to think of the proper word for it. *Delighted.* As of someone who's being flirtatious. Someone who, caught by surprise and love, might be having an affair.

He lifted the receiver of the kitchen's landline telephone to eavesdrop and was met with a dial tone.

After removing his shoes in the mudroom by the back door, he took the stairs one by one, skipping the step fifth from the bottom, whose prominent creak would announce his movements up toward her. What was he doing, spying on her like this? Surreptitiously, with neither of them bothering to have secrets from each other anymore? At this age, they had outgrown shame and therefore possessed nothing worth hiding and had almost nothing left to reveal except for the specific content of their dreams. The whole boatload of their lives was all out there in the open, all of it. Nevertheless, he felt in his bones, all the way down to the roots of his soul, that at this moment he must be watchful. He felt the hairs at the back of his neck standing up: *Something is going on here, and you don't know what it is, do you?*

No, he thought, *I don't.*

Reaching the top of the stairs, he stood next to the linen closet, easing his way toward the bedroom without being detected. Just past the doorway, he saw his wife, who sat at the edge of the bed, her back to him, the dog and the cat positioned in front of her by the window, both of them fixedly staring at her. The dog sat on the floor, and the cat was perched on the windowsill. Brettigan felt a cold breeze start at the top of his head and travel electrically downward. The dog, sensing Brettigan's presence, raised his muzzle and gave Brettigan a brief, irritated look.

Meanwhile, Alma continued to speak animatedly, waving her hands in the air as if she were grasping little flags and watching a motorcade pass by. To the dog, she said, "I felt a bolt of God's lightning, right on the very spot," and then she paused, not speaking, during which time she turned her face toward the cat. For several seconds, she sat quietly in a posture of listening, nodding in assent. *Listening to the cat!* That was it! She was—Brettigan couldn't quite believe it—carrying on a conversation with their two household pets, both of whom were apparently making assertions with which she found herself in total agreement.

For a moment, Brettigan thought of the future: the parade of doctors and neurologists, the expensive tests for stroke, the rehabilitations, the MRIs. After all, she was hearing voices now, animal voices. The doctors would put a stop to it; that was their job. Science demanded it. Well, yes, but he too had heard Mrs. Schimmelpfennig's voice and a bad local band from decades ago. He and his wife were hearing things in tandem.

The dog, with an odd movement, seemed to indicate to Alma that Brettigan was standing behind her, and accordingly she turned to see him, and when she did, she smiled broadly and happily, her eyes wet with tears. In his entire life, and during their long marriage, he had rarely seen his wife so happy, so transported with gaiety.

She was so happy, she was no longer herself. She seemed to be someone else entirely.

"Oh, Harry," she cried out, joy spreading across her face, "the most wonderful thing has happened."

 Part Two

- 6 -

ONE EVENING THE PREVIOUS WINTER, CHRISTINA HAD GLANCED IN THE mirror above the sink, and what looked back at her was this grimacing female gargoyle, only without horns. There she was, in the ladies' bathroom at the yoga studio, trying to give the appearance of a slightly down-market Junior League solid citizen, but when she turned the old-fashioned porcelain faucet handle labeled COLD to wash the gargoyle weirdness off her face, hot water came streaming out, so hot that she couldn't put her hands in it to normalize herself. Yet another prank of the gods. They were always on the job, setting traps, laughing up there on Olympus, spewing lava-scented spooge over everybody. When you needed cold water to straighten yourself out, you got the opposite. From curiosity, she tried the faucet labeled HOT, and of course cold water gurgled into the sink, which was irony, or something.

Christina dipped her hands in the cold water labeled HOT and in slo-mo bent over to splash it on her cheeks and eyes and forehead, which still hurt from the door she had walked into a few hours ago. She didn't quite have a handle on this drug that her downstairs friend Lucille had given her. A designer concoction purportedly from a basement chemical laboratory in Memphis operated by a genius misfit albino dropout from MIT, it blew things pleasingly out of proportion and produced temporary blackouts, during which you were in two places at once, and sometimes in both the present and the future. Also, it conferred on its users a feeling of blessedness that lasted for an hour, depending on the weight of your past sins. Under its effects, you tended to lie down on the floor, unless you were levitating. Its street name was BT, "Blue Telephone," in honor of its blue-black exterior coating. She'd had it before, in Chicago, but its effects were getting more specialized, more targeted to warping spacetime. There was no Operator once you swallowed it, however, though there were plenty of messages, such as "You are a total genius," and "Everybody loves you and thinks you're beautiful." And the other one: "Why did you *ever* worry about *anything*? Paradise is here, now!" A brushfire of undifferentiated acceptance and love spread out over her interior landscapes, spitting up hot coals of joy.

People said it was like a haphazard combination of LSD and crystal meth and heroin and psilocybin, but with the sight-and-sound dial turned down to manageable levels, but they were so wrong: it wasn't, it had *nothing* to do with LSD or meth or heroin or manageability; it was made of invented vagabond molecules meant to rip a hole in quantum fields. It would dement you but in a good way.

Her high, however, was making her slightly more unsteady than she would have liked: right now, her thoughts had grown marquee-gigantic and were appearing on a jumbotron overlooking a huge empty stadium, which was her mind.

Another woman dressed in tank top and tights, hair snarled in an unkempt ponytail, very homecoming-queen-on-a-bender, came into the ladies' bathroom and looked at Christina with a split second of quasi-sympathy before racing into the toilet stall, from which ugly sounds emerged.

Christina dried her hands on a . . . what was *that*? An old roller towel? Did they still *have* those anymore? Who made them? The same company that made manual typewriters and vacuum tubes? She pulled it down and dried her face on the cloth, and when she stepped backward, she saw that the towel had streaks of blue from her eyeliner, and the blue streaks seemed to be forming into words and sentences, and the sentences were speaking aloud, criticizing her, finding fault. Water from somewhere was dousing the sparklers of joy.

Very untrustworthy, this drug. Also: the warm, you-have-a-fan-base feeling, the everybody-loves-you feeling, the highlight-reel feel-ing, all of them were creeping away and leaving behind a skid-row emptiness with several blocks of tenements and trash can fires and no plumbing and rats crouching over stale sandwiches.

Time to return to the yoga studio. Time to straighten up. The ses-sion would begin in a few minutes. She would have to look normal. No more *thoughts,* not now, and no more *voices.* She would have to get her mind back inside her head, pronto, like toothpaste back into the whatchamacallit, the tube. No more conversations on the Blue Telephone. Got to hang that receiver up right now.

But what a relief it was to be stupid for a while.

Walking out of the ladies' room, she made her way down the corridor, floating an inch or two above the surface of the floor, inas-much as the soles of her feet were numb, to the entryway outside the studio. Two benches were arrayed on either side and, underneath the benches, discarded shoes. They were multitudinous. All the begin-ning, middle, and end-stage yogis had left their footwear out here in the hall, as if somehow the shoes were safe from theft, because anyway you couldn't take them into the studio on your feet. That was a rule, being barefoot, the first one in a long list.

Christina gazed down at the shoes. They reminded her of the shoe bin at Goodwill, where the Authorities of Charity kept in the center's northeast corner a big gray box of harvested unmatched shoes for mismatched feet. Looking at all the footwear now outside the studio, mostly women's sneakers and running shoes and one pair of hiking boots, she began to cry, because . . . well, because they had been *left behind,* and it was exactly like an orphanage, except of shoes. Also the brogues, sandals, clogs, sneakers, oxfords, ballet flats, and wedge pumps were huddled down there on the ground, mewling. She dried her eyes on her sleeve. Things were getting a bit out of hand. A soup-çon too much Blue Telephone was coursing through her bloodstream for her own good, the jumbotron was blowing a few cherry bombs here and there, sorrow was being thrown around like inkblots splat-tered on the studio wall, invisible people were sobbing, and perhaps the time had arrived to sober up and straighten out.

She set her shoulders, slipped off her sneakers, and strode with a thoughtful, determined air into the yoga studio carrying her yoga mat, which had materialized from somewhere.

IN THE DIM LIGHT FROM OVERHEAD AND FROM THE STREETLIGHTS outside on Third Avenue, Christina unrolled her mat on the wood-slatted floor and began her stretching exercises. The streetlights gave the room a golden crepuscular glow that caused everyone to radiate with a warm physical aura as if they were lit from the inside. Yoga studios always had this apparitional sexiness, this heat; you could feel it. On either side of Christina and in front of her were the solid-citizen-in-tights brigade, the svelte young women who looked as if they could command the world with their power and strength and suppleness and beauty, and then there were the guys, always in the minority, typically rather wiry and stubble-bearded and New Agey and lacking authority, but given to the occasional sidelong wolfish predatory glance, especially when upside down.

Directly ahead of her was someone she'd never seen here before. When he turned, she got a good look at him. He was quite noticeable: he wore sweatpants and an orange T-shirt with some sinister cartoon robot on it, and on his left bicep was a tattoo that said YOU'RE WELCOME! in Baskerville typeface—Christina knew her fonts—and above the sweatpants and the shirt and the pleasingly broad working-man's back was a face that . . . well, you didn't see eager faces like that often anymore, at least not on men. He possessed two raffish blue eyes, widely separated, and, below the high cheekbones, what used to be called a strong jaw, but the sum total of this face was that of an innocent warrior, a boy in a man's body, because the eyes looked out at the world with a warrior's fierceness but were also blank, as if he didn't know what he was fighting for and possibly didn't care. Maybe he was looking around for someone who would lead him into battle, someone who could give him some sensible orders to follow.

She thought: *I want that man in my army.*

But then he boldly stared in her direction for a moment, more knight than pawn, and very nonprotocol for yoga sessions, before raising his arms above his head, a stretch but also a display, an invitation, a come-and-get-it. With the supreme confidence of immaturity combined with male beauty, he turned around and gave her a view of his back before getting down on the floor to do a left twist with his left leg bent. Despite his strength he seemed unsteady, as if he hadn't had a meal all day. He was trembling and doing his best to cover it up; the Blue Telephone, though fading away, helped Christina see within him, through his skin to the wall behind him. With sudden X-ray vision, she noted his frailty; she could see it through his solid musculature. She could see the hunger in his bone marrow.

The yoga teacher entered the room, greeted everybody, rang her little Buddha bell, and started the session after lighting a candle. Concentrating on her poses and slightly hypnotized by the enforced, strained peacefulness of a yoga workout, Christina momentarily forgot about the boy warrior until in the middle of a handstand, his body propped up against a wall, he seemed about to fall, not a controlled fall but a collapse. Waving back and forth like a reed in a high wind, he tipped backward, and at that moment the residual effect of the drug she had taken caused the jumbotron to light up in some lower region of Christina's consciousness, and she got to her feet and stood over him as he slowly crumpled into a non-yoga position on the floor.

The staticky thought occurred to her, as if broadcast in shortwave from an asteroid, that this guy was weakened by malnutrition, and he was here to be picked up, in every possible sense. Or maybe it was all an act. You couldn't tell with people like him.

The instructor hurried over to him and asked if he was all right, and the boy said, "Affirmative," in that faux-military way that Christina's teenage brothers used to employ when they were hurt and wanted to sound tough. But he didn't move. He just lay there, seemingly paralyzed, and the other students stared over at him with steely Zen detachment. Nor did the yoga instructor seem eager to help out. Something had to be done. Something always had to be done. Christina took his hand and raised him up.

"Thank you," he said. He gave her a flash of a smile. "You're being useful, aren't you?" he asked.

"Yes. Are you okay?"

He dusted himself off, and Christina noticed that his large hands were trembling. The instructor, after doing a quick once-over of the boy, had returned to her place at the head of the class.

"What's the story?" Christina asked, as quietly as she could.

"Well, okay. I could use a meal, that's my story."

They were murmuring to each other, their faces very close together, the way intimate friends might talk.

"So, all right, I get it. You're hungry." For a moment she considered whether she would make some kind of move, and as she did, the Blue Telephone, in its last gasp broadcasting from the future, the final long-distance call before the click of termination, said to her that no harm could come to her from this boy-man, because after all, look at him, see how harmless he was? Like a water lily? And besides, wasn't she, Christina, an adventurer? Wasn't she the most fearless person she knew, across all the genders and ages and continents? And didn't she despise the ruinous dull comforts of routine? She *did* despise them, every day. "Let's get out of here."

Together they stepped around the other contorted bodies on the floor belonging to people who were now taking no notice of this particular situation: a couple exiting the dim room together. Just a mere yoga pickup. The oblivious, well-maintained, recently cleansed, low-fat bodies moved into a collective Downward Dog as Christina and the boy opened the studio door, and they exited, Christina going first. In the hallway outside, the boy slipped some white athletic socks onto his big feet and then searched around the floor in the mess of assorted discarded footwear until he found his battered running shoes, scrawled over with words in Magic Marker: SUN on the side of the left shoe and LIGHT on the right. Christina cracked a micro-smirk to herself as she found her own tennis shoes and her winter jacket, while the boy put on his gray hoodie and a backpack that had been hanging on a hook. He had no gloves; Christina looked down and saw that his hands, flecked with paint, were chapped with tiny lesions. Anyone could take control of this guy at any time, she could see. He wasn't clueless so much as stupefied by his own masculinity, like the rest of them.

"Anything you want?" she asked him, making sure that the question was sufficiently open-ended to give him a moment's pause.

"A beer," he said, gazing at the floor. Now he was wearing blue jeans. Where had they come from?

"How about a beer and a hamburger?"

"Okay."

Minutes later, crossing the street to a restaurant, the Monte Carlo, she checked out his progress over the snow-covered sidewalk and the curb. Once again, he seemed ready to fall from hunger or exhaustion or sheer absentmindedness. Christina kept her hand extended slightly in his direction in case he happened to stumble into her. He seemed to be listening to extraterrestrial conversations and had no inkling of where he was going, swaddled in a very private and comfortable fog. Wherever he was, he wasn't quite here.

Inside the restaurant, standing next to each other, they both took in the glass shelves of liquor bottles behind the bar. These shelves, bathed in light, row upon row, rose to the stamped-tin ceiling like an altar of decorative temptations presided over by the priestly bespectacled bartender drying glasses with a soiled towel. As they were led to a booth, Christina felt her hand brushing against the boy's thigh and was startled by how hard the quadriceps muscle was underneath the cloth. After being seated across the table from him, she said, "So. Have you thought of a name by now?"

"For what?"

"For yourself."

"Yeah, I have. What's *your* name?"

"Kristin," she said, and when she saw the smiling disbelief on his face, she said, "No, you're right. I lied. It's Christina. But wait. What if we did without names, you and me? Or what if I gave you a name, and you took it, and then that was your name from then on, as if I had baptized you or something? That would be so, I dunno, *transgressive*."

"Are you always like this?"

"Yes. No. Anyway, I mean, I'm sitting here, and I'm, well, I'm looking at you, and I'm thinking that you look like a Josh or a Matt, you know, one of those one-syllable names that doesn't, uh, really signify anything. Like Slim, on fat people?" The server came by and gave them the menus, which the boy didn't look at. "Because," she continued, "I have a feeling that you're not really one-syllabled . . ."

"Cut it out," the boy said. "You're nervous. And your nervousness is making *me* nervous. Because, here's the thing: which is, we're strangers, and I'm hungry. I haven't eaten for a while. Plus I'm feeling light-headed, and maybe you noticed a few minutes ago across the street that I started to pass out. So here you are doing this flirty routine with names like we're on a date, which, so far as I know, we aren't, and meanwhile I'm fucking *starving*, whatever your name is. This is . . . whatever. And I'd like to have a meal and then I'd like to get some sleep, and after that, well, if we're okay with each other, I don't know."

"How come you haven't eaten in so long?" she asked.

"Because I'm a revolutionary," he told her with apparent seriousness and looked her straight in the eyes at such length that she eventually turned away.

FOR A FEW MINUTES THEY SAT SILENTLY LIKE THE STRANGERS THEY were until his beer arrived; he gulped it down, and when his salad and his cheeseburger were delivered to the table—the burger so thickened with tomatoes, lettuce, cheese, and pickles that it seemed too awkwardly constructed to bite into—he devoured them quickly and without speaking. She herself dipped a spoon daintily into a bowl of chicken noodle soup. Finally he wiped his mouth and leaned back, suppressing a belch, and he smiled. "I'm Ludlow," he said, extending his hand. She took his hand, feeling her own hand nestled inside the chapped skin clutching hers with a tight muscular grip, and he held on to her for a fraction of a second too long.

"What kind of name is that? I'm Christina, in case you weren't listening a minute ago."

"Do you have a car?" he asked. *"Christina?* You look like the sort of person who would have a car. An old beat-up Volvo that your dad gave you? An old rusty Plymouth?"

"No. An old beat-up Saab," she said. "It's blood-clot-colored."

"Uh-huh." He nodded. He continued to smile in a slightly menacing way. All the possible adjectives about him—*insolent, overconfident*—washed against her: whatever it was he possessed, he had *something* on her, some power that simultaneously drew her toward him and repelled her, but he wouldn't offer the next topic of conversation and seemed instead to be enjoying her uneasy silence. Possibly he wasn't as subservient as she thought he might be. "Because I could use a ride," he said at last. "I could always take the bus, but I'd rather have a ride if you'd give it to me. To where I'm staying, I mean."

"Where's that?"

"You could say I'm housesitting."

"But you're really not?"

"No," he said. "Do you really want to know? So, okay. I was staying with a friend, sleeping on his sofa, but he kicked me out for various reasons I won't go into now. So the past few weeks, I've been breaking into houses whose owners are away on vacation or gone for the winter. You'd be surprised how many people in Minnesota leave their houses and go south once it gets cold. 'Snowbirds,' they call them. Hundreds of them, thousands. Houses without security systems are empty for *weeks* all over this city, though you have to know where to look, which I do. The very rich, those one-percenters, they have silent alarms, and the poor never go anywhere. It's the middle you have to scope out, recent money, carelessness. Middle-classers. Where they live, the city is *vacant.* You want a free room? Easy-peasy: no lights on at eight o'clock, no lights on at bedtime. Besides, one job I had, I installed security systems, and I know what they look like. So in I go, and I house-sit for them; they just don't know I'm doing it. I leave the house exactly the way I found it, except better. I take care of their valuables. I never steal because I don't want what they have. I polish the silver and clean up. If there are dirty dishes in the sink, I scrub them spotless and put them away. The owners usually turn the heat down when they leave, but the electricity stays on, and anyway I don't need much of that. All I need is enough light to read by. I'm a temporary tenant, on *principle,* mostly because I'm a temporary sort of guy—you know: here today and Guatemala. If I get a hint that someone's coming back, like the paper suddenly gets delivered on the front stoop one morning, I find another place to stay. Anyway, daytimes I'm out, I'm working."

"But what if—?"

"That? That's only happened once. This person came home, an old woman, kind of bent over and deaf, her gray hair in a ponytail, dropping her suitcases in the front hallway, the foyer. No, excuse me, the foy-*yeh.* I'd seen her from the, you know, upstairs window as she was getting out of a Yellow Cab. When she came in, grandmotherly type, very lonely and giving off those lonesome radio signals, she called out, 'Hello?' as if she guessed somebody was there, upstairs, but no one was in her house but me, and I left through the back door before she knew I'd been sleeping in her bed like the big bad wolf."

"Stealthy."

"That's me," he said. "I'm covert. But the thing is, I got the feeling that she really wanted *somebody* to be right there in her house, to greet her, hand her a cup of hot tea, ask her how her flight home had been, any unexpected turbulence, that sort of thing, and how was it down there in Tampa or wherever she'd been. Somebody, even a stranger, to greet her. To care about her a little, I would—well, care enough to ask how she was, and to wait for an answer. Not a wolf, but, you know, a messenger. So I almost did that. I almost stayed. I almost gave her a cup of hot tea. Chamomile, which I had spotted in her pantry."

"You're a very strange person," Christina told him.

"And I *could* have done it," he said, "I could have welcomed her back into her house and she wouldn't have screamed, because you can tell by just looking at me that I'm a good person, I'm like the very best person you've ever met. I'm a bright angel; I'm a messenger from that place that's just past heaven, and I make visitations. I give off light. I'm very radiant. I got the spirit moving around in me like a critical mass, like an atomic pile, glowing like that. I'll show you. Finish your soup and we'll do a visitation. I'm serious. Come on."

"Come on where?"

"Finish your soup and pay the bill, and we'll get into your blood-clot-colored Saab, and I'll show you."

Christina glanced up at the server, who looked back at her with a bored expression on her face that seemed to say she had observed every kind of behavior here, and Christina nodded inwardly, having decided that this person, this Ludlow, was harmless. She felt herself thawing a bit in his presence, and when the bill came, she paid it.

7

BEHIND THEM A FULL MOON HAD RISEN OVER THE SNOW-ENCRUSTED streets, and after she started the car and pulled out of the restaurant's parking lot, with Ludlow slumped down on the passenger side, gazing with indifference at the lighted shops they passed, Christina saw that little dots of white crystals, the snowflakes that were harmless individually but treacherous when gathered into an army, were beginning to descend rapidly from the sky, obliterating the moon, and melting instantaneously on the front windshield before refreezing as ice. The snow had been unpredicted by the weatherpersons, or maybe she hadn't been paying attention. Well, no one understood anything about weather anymore; weather was moody when it wasn't overtly psychotic. "Turn left," Ludlow said, and she did as he had instructed her, the left-turn signal's tick-tock sounding like a heart monitor. The car fishtailed slightly down an empty street bordered on each side by warehouses that were gradually disappearing in the ever-increasing whiteness dropping all over them, all over everything. Minnesota winter weather could be like a series of lethal practical jokes. You walked out of the house, you fell down on the ice, you broke your leg, you got pneumonia. Ha ha ha. She turned up the blower for the defroster, and the windshield wipers scumbled over the glass with a sound like automotive flatulence—"wiper farts," people called it. After another direction from Ludlow, she saw that they were passing Loring Park, whose pond was frozen, and whose geese, disconsolate, were huddled together under a tree.

"Turn here again, left," Ludlow said, his eyes mostly closed, as if he were navigating the car through some dreamworld he had managed to externalize onto the city's grid, and as they made their way up Lowry Hill, the front-wheel-drive tires beginning to spin, he said, "Now go straight for a while." His head was flung back. "So, Christina," he said. "Tell me about yourself. What do you do? Do you do anything?"

Christina's hands were gripping the steering wheel. She was finding it hard to think. "I'm sort of between things," she told him. The blood-clot-colored Saab advanced through the snow that was growing thicker now and gradually obliterating the bars and restaurants on either side of the street. "In college I was in critical theory and had a sort of cultural-studies major," she told him, "and maybe like you, I was *very* political. You know: action-feminism, the environment, neighborhood organizing. I needed alternatives. I wanted to wake people up." She said that she had gone on to graduate school for a while and had been interested in the purer forms of critical theory, but she had made a mistake: she had proposed a deconstruction of the Gettysburg Address. "I said that you can't really establish an argument if your foundational word is *hallowed*. The argument gets unstable real fast." There was more academic-style outrage, this time higher in the chain of command. She was asked to take a leave of absence.

She decided not to tell him about her relationships. After all, she didn't know him that well. Also, she still felt completely unspooled, thanks to the drug. "So I got myself here in Minneapolis and then I went to work as a receptionist in a bank out in the suburbs," Christina continued. It was supposed to be a temporary job, but they had liked her out there, and they wanted to keep her and were begging her to stay on permanently. At a bank! As a receptionist! And they wanted to train her to be a loan officer! Talk about a sellout. You could *smell* the cancer in there. "But it pays the bills," Christina said sadly, after taking another right turn into a residential area whose homes were occasionally visible behind the scrim of snow. "I have a fortune in student loans to pay back. I mean, really, all I want to do is save the world. I want to be helpful somehow. That's not much. How about you?" she asked.

He started talking, but Christina was concentrating so hard on not hitting the parked cars on the street and not sliding helplessly through icy intersections that she caught only dribs and drabs of what he was telling her. He'd grown up on a dairy farm out in the middle of nowhere North Dakota, it seemed. The closest town had been settled in the nineteenth century by Finns and Swedes, refugees from their own countries and then from the copper mines in northern Michigan, where the work conditions had turned them into emotional Marxists—they hadn't actually read Marx but they knew what Marx meant, knew it *emotionally,* and believed it. Most of the businesses in town were co-ops. The community itself was somewhat insular, agrarian-based, and a weird hybrid of individualistic and communitarian principles. Everyone knew everybody else and had opinions about their fellow citizens that could not be changed by circumstances.

As a smart kid from the sticks, he'd gotten a free ride and a full scholarship to the university, here in the cities. There, he'd taken a class on the reformist tradition, taught by this unbelievably brilliant and charismatic guy, a lecturer, whose name—Christina didn't quite catch the next phrase—had once been Wyenakowski or something unsayable like that, though everyone called him "Wye" or sometimes "Why." And this Professor Wye had, sort of surreptitiously, off the books, helped others to organize a neighborhood working group, a local anarchic-or-something cadre that would—

"Watch *out!*" he said, interrupting himself, although his eyes were closed, as a snow-covered dog ran quickly in front of them before disappearing into the white. "I just realized something. You're *entirely* stoned. You were macro-stoned when you took me out of there and you were stoned when you bought me dinner, and you're stoned now." Christina nodded, halfheartedly. "What're you on?"

"Blue Telephone," she admitted in a blitzed whisper that sounded like a dog slurping at its water bowl.

"Oh, *that* shit? Damn. Women really like that drug. It makes them feel like princesses in the pre-pumpkin phase. Lifts you up, spins you around, then drops you down. Messes up your quantum fields, if you want that. What I heard was, it—it'll fuck up your here-and-now and you'll live permanently in today or tomorrow-plus-today. Two places at once, both bad. You're not careful, you'll end up like Schrödinger's cat."

"Well, I—"

Languidly, and speaking slowly, he interrupted her. He was quite the interrupter. "You should get yourself cleaned up," he said, speaking over her and all at once sounding calmly preemptive, as if he had taken off his former personality and changed into a new one. "Drugs are just an admission of defeat and make you into a passive-voice person and a Keyhoteeist. 'I got fired,'" he said, raising his voice in falsetto mockery to sound like a ruined child. "'I was *abducted*. I was demoted. I was disrespected. I was *abused*.'" He lowered his voice to its baritone rumble. "Well, no. This is what I'm saying to you. You gotta wise up. The oligarchs love it when you use the passive voice in any form whatsoever. That's their first victory over us. Drugs induce the passive voice," he said, too loudly, as all around them the snow blew down thickly, and Christina wondered what a Keyhotecist was and why she had ever bothered to help get this guy up from the floor of the yoga studio, bought him a meal, and given him a ride home. "Every victim has got to be a willing accomplice to his victimization, even grammatically, don't you *know* that?" he asked. "Unless they're subalterns. Or . . . well, it's complicated. That's Politics 101. I have an idea: you should take boxing lessons. You should learn to punch. You could start with me. You could hit me as hard as you can. I wouldn't mind. Stop here."

Christina put her foot on the brake pedal, an action that had no appreciable effect on the car, which slid gracefully down the street, its wheels locked, until it seemed to change its mind and slowly decelerated as it came gradually to rest, the engine humming quietly, in a massive descent of snow, a white curtain on all sides.

"You need to learn how to punch," Ludlow told her. "I mean, I shouldn't give advice, being a guy, but, hey. You gotta get tough and learn how to fight. Reverse roles, you know? Women getting tougher and men getting, I don't know, more . . . what's the word I'm looking for? This is my stop. This is where I get out." He put his hand on the door latch.

"Where are we?" Christina said. "And what gives you the right to tell me what women should or shouldn't do? Jesus. I can't see anything."

"We are where we are," he said. He opened the door after reaching for his backpack. Christina wondered momentarily whether he would invite her in and then remembered that he was your basic breaker-and-enterer and a dangerous romantic prospect. He *did* have that outlaw glamour, and in a certain light, he was very good-looking and not particularly stupid in any of the customary masculine styles. Then she waited to see whether he would ask her for her phone number. Maybe he was de-telephoned. He stepped out into a drift as high as his midcalf.

She asked, "Is this your . . ."

"This is where I get out."

"What if . . . ?" she started to ask but once again was unable to finish the sentence.

"Don't worry," he said, poking his head inside the car. "I know how to find you. I know where you are. I got radar. It's—I always know where you are. You send out signals." He closed the door and was almost immediately obliterated by the snow as he walked away.

INCHING FORWARD, THE CAR CLEARED AN INTERSECTION AND CHUGGED down another block, while Christina peered out at the blanketed landscape and asked herself whether she and the car would make it home. All at once, the snow began to let up, as if Ludlow's presence had been an inspiration for its descent, and Christina saw to her left a city park with a baseball diamond and a playground. In the center of the playground were a swing set and a snow-covered climbing structure. Christina looked more closely, unsure of what she was seeing. There, suddenly illuminated by a parting of clouds and full moonlight, were two children in snowsuits on the swings, rising up in high arcs and then falling backward and up again, back and forth, playing in the silvered midnight dark. But something was wrong: listening to the two kids' muffled cries of happiness, the only sound in the winter air except for the car's interior fan blowing warm air onto her ankles and the engine's intermittent rumble, she realized that their swings, as high as they were, *were in slow motion*. How, propelled so slowly, could they rise at all? One child swung backward, and at the top point of the arc, seemed to stop. The other child, on a forward arc, also ceased to move. In the frigid air, time itself had been frozen. She couldn't breathe. Christina looked at the clock in the car, whose second hand stayed right where it was.

It had to be the drug. She was still ratcheting back and forth in spacetime. She wasn't quite where she was. Ludlow had maybe come to her from the future and then returned to it.

She pressed her foot to the accelerator, and the car gamely inched forward down the street, past the playground where time had stopped, and onto Hennepin Avenue, where a snowplow in front of her escorted her homeward. She found herself shaking, though not from cold.

8

THE NEXT MORNING, TWO DOORS DOWN FROM THE ENTRANCE TO THE bank where Christina worked, a man wearing a heavy winter overcoat was speaking quietly and calmly, though in a voice thickened with rage, to a rather pretty woman, apparently his wife, who wore a red cloth coat with black buttons and a white scarf. Her face wore an expression of shock. The woman was kneading her hands together at waist level. They were both middle-aged. As Christina passed them, she heard the man say, "I always thought I could trust you, but then you . . ." Christina slowed down to hear how the sentence would end, but she couldn't make out his words. He had grown quiet for fear of being overheard. She would have to finish the sentence for herself.

Outside, the plows had done their work. She'd been hoping for a snow day to recover from yesterday's events, but the sun shone down on the snow in the mall's parking lot with a puritanical intensity.

Inside the bank, she was hanging her own tattered overcoat up in the cloakroom while the phrases unreeled: *I always thought I could trust you, but then you fucked my best friend*. No, that wording was too coarse—and too straightforward—for this region. Did people make such accusations to each other out on the public sidewalk? In Europe they might, but they rarely did in America and never in the Midwest. In Paris, Christina had once witnessed a public quarrel between a young man and woman on the Rue Madame. Their obscenities were so eloquently and loudly vehement that Christina had felt the blood draining from her face as she listened. She had once spent a summer working on a French farm and thought she knew all the colloquialisms for sexual insult, but there on the Rue Madame, across the street from the Hôtel de l'Avenir, she had learned a few more, the sorts of personal verbal assaults that no one could ever forgive and that preceded murder.

The two lovers in Paris had shouted at each other as if they themselves were Passion Monsters. The odd detail was that the young man had a clubfoot and advanced down the street like an insect. His limp did not end with his leg. It caused the entire left side of his body to give way, slump, and then recover.

In America, especially here, public denunciations would be dull and muted, if they happened at all. Minnesotans distrusted passion and seldom knew what shouting was good for.

So boring, these locals. Outbursts were not part of the repertoire in the upper Midwest. Everyone seethed and simmered instead. Returning to her station in the bank before the doors were unlocked, and carrying her cup of Americano, Christina caught a glimpse of herself in the front window and felt uplifted for a split second by the sight of her face before she turned away from it. She didn't particularly enjoy being looked at, especially by herself. She felt she lacked the right sort of vanity, the kind that went hand in hand with a successful career.

After getting out of the shower today, she had tried on a touch of Orgasm blush, matched with Springtime lip gloss, to counteract her natural pale color. She had a kind of fragile voluptuousness that occasionally excited the envy of other women, though she was rarely conscious of it herself and didn't like it when customers ("guests" was the preferred usage) entered through the front door and caught sight of her, even though her job was to greet them. Men involuntarily smiled, and often women involuntarily frowned; she almost always had an effect on whoever was seeing her for the first time. She'd never known what to make of her appearance. It was a distraction from changing the world. Revolutionaries, she thought, should look seedy and uncompromising and implacable, with stringy unwashed ratty hair, without makeup and in rags that smelled of paint thinner.

All through high school and then in college, she had found herself surrounded by eager boys, then eager men, most of them sweet and well meaning, but slightly oblivious to who she actually was, as if all they could see of her was this image, this goddess-effect she had on people. But who *was* she really? She didn't know, not yet. A moderately angry person, for starters, but angry with privileges.

All she really wanted was to do some good in the world. But how? She had a gift for acting and was a good musician and a real whiz at math and the sciences, but nothing seemed to define her in the minds of her classmates except her looks. The mean kids had called her "the Snow Queen" and "Little Ms. Brainiac," though not to her face, because they feared her beauty and wit. Sometimes Christina envied the plain girls whom everyone left alone—the invisible ones who could walk down the hallways, lost to themselves, unremarked and untouched. They were the ones who would end up running things.

Her first real love in high school had been for writing; she had written articles for the school newspaper and at home had completed the opening chapter of a children's novel employing the style of Roald Dahl. The book was about a sinister clockmaker who knew how to make time run backward, causing unwary children to disappear. The site of their vanishing would be marked by bright green poisonous mushrooms. She liked the chapter but couldn't figure out what would happen in chapter two. Somebody had to eat the mushroom; she just didn't know who.

And she'd had boyfriends, one in particular who said he loved her. Amused and flattered by his desire for her, she had let him cure her of her virginity one summer night in the bed of his truck, with the radio playing country-western. It hadn't hurt as much as she thought it would. Lying there on a scratchy blanket, on her back, she counted the stars in the night sky while he panted and moaned over her. On the radio Faith Hill sang "Mississippi Girl." By the time he came, with a groan she'd never heard from a boy before, she had gotten to thirty-six.

He said he'd write to her once they both were in college, though of course he never did.

In college she'd been written up in the school's alumni quarterly as a "Woman of Note": the Ivy League college she'd attended had been

in the center of a decaying industrial city plagued by drug use, un-
employment, and crime, and she'd spent hours doing fieldwork in
the local bars and pool halls talking with the townies, who were at
first suspicious of her and then, very gradually, accepting of her presence, because she was a pretty good pool player who didn't mind
being hustled out of a few dollars now and then. She noticed how
gregarious and angrily despairing these men and women were, and
sometimes gruffly funny, though she often had to fend off the advances of the men with jokes and the claim that she already had a
boyfriend. She was respectful with them, and polite. Occasionally
she brought along a guy to act as her beard. Eventually the men gave
up making passes at her. They accepted her presence among them,
which pleased her. They called her "the little professor." What they
said behind her back, she never knew.

She was curious about their politics. Why, considering their situation, didn't they believe in revolution? What had happened to their
sense of injustice, their knowledge that the plutocrats were grabbing
every last dime for themselves and killing the planet in the process?
Where was their rage? Where had it gone? Why all this stoicism? Why
did they accept their own defeat? Their raucous despondency struck
her as a form of cultural depression, a collective anger that had turned
inward, as if the workers felt their condition was their own fault. This
was a soul-error, though she never got up the nerve to tell them.
That wasn't her job, to be in a workers' vanguard. Besides, all the
vanguards had failed.

She had learned the hermeneutics of suspicion and skepticism,
and now . . . now here she was, working in a branch bank in a Minneapolis suburb, paying off her accumulated student loans. Every
morning she felt her ideals disappearing into a remainder bin. After
all, you couldn't package and merchandise a revolution. The revolution was not for sale, everyone said.

In those days, in graduate school in Chicago, she had a kind and
thoughtful but occasionally bad-tempered boyfriend named Farrell,
who'd started as a graduate student in math but had branched out
into computer programming with a bit of high-end drug dealing on

the side. He was a student in name only. Mostly he helped small businesses on the Near North Side with their inventories and their HR accounts, and he used his contacts to sell a bit of weed and other boutique concoctions whenever the moment seemed right. Farrell was the one who had introduced Christina to Blue Telephone. He knew personally its gnome-like inventor, who was Farrell's second cousin once removed. The first time she'd tried it, she had a vision of her future, and Farrell did not appear in it as her lifetime partner, not that she thought he would. In this vision, which consisted of four discrete scenes, one of them set in a Greyhound bus station, she was beaten up and then murdered—stabbed—in the second scene, a black-and-white noir thriller, by someone who looked a lot like Farrell. She considered it a subtle warning sent by the future not to hang out with Farrell anymore and certainly not to sleep with any Farrell look-alikes, those seedy but handsome intellectual guys with staring eyes and oversize sweaters.

When she broke up with him, over dessert in her apartment in Hyde Park—for the main course she had served pot roast—he picked up his steak knife, to which were still attached tiny shreds of meat, and waved it at her threateningly. He called her a monster whose specialty was lighthearted cruelty, the kind that only intelligent people could manage, which hurt because it was almost accurate; then he got down into the gutter and called her a sexist name, and a freeloader on his drug supply, which seemed anticlimactic. He called her other names as he put on his shoes and socks and sweater before storming out of the apartment. Through her upstairs window, she watched him walking down Fifty-seventh Street to the Metra station. He was shouting at no one and waving her steak knife—one of a set of four!—in the air. She murmured a prayer of thanks to fate and the Blue Telephone for warning her about him before he had had a chance to kill her. The steak knife was a minor sacrifice.

Then a few weeks later, she had seen a play while under the influence of BT, gotten a little obsessive about the lead actor, and so now here she was in Minneapolis.

Having taken up her station at the bank, Christina checked her iPhone for messages. She had heard it ding in her pocket. One text—*Matilda gave birth last night to 5 puppies! But one died. So sad*—was from her sister, Matilda being the family's rescue dog. Christina texted back, *Congratulations Mom but 2 bad!* She went to her Facebook page and posted a message about last night's snowstorm. She checked her Instagram account. She pulled out a hand mirror and gave herself a once-over.

ONE NIGHT, POST-FARRELL, AND VERY, VERY HIGH ON WEED, BT, AND a German mood-enhancing drug, EZ Straße, floating up there in the ionosphere, she'd gone to a Chicago professional theater company to see a production of Brecht's *The Resistible Rise of Arturo Ui: A Gangster Spectacle*. The lead was to be played by someone named Timothy Brettigan. The play started, and in the fourth scene of Act One, the young man came out made up to look like the current American chief executive, A. A. Thorkelson, in a tight-fitting double-breasted pinch-back suit, the latest male fashion craze. Christina felt as if she'd been kicked in the stomach: everything else in her life fell away while she watched Timothy Brettigan–as–Thorkelson–as–Arturo Ui. He had the kind of animal sexuality that compelled attention. You couldn't not look at him. The guy radiated hypnotic charisma promising the big illicit thrills, entirely appropriate for a murderer and a seducer, a sexual sportsman who left a trail behind him of broken women and dead bodies. In his opening speech, Arturo Ui complained that his name hadn't appeared in the newspapers for two months. Like all narcissists in the public eye, what he wanted was *recognition*—favorable or not, it didn't matter. He committed murders in order to become famous, Arturo Ui claimed, and to become an unavoidable presence, the sort of character who transfixed the masses and caused everybody to talk about him in an endless conversation about what he was really thinking and what actions that homicidal thinking would lead to. But lately no one had talked about him. More murders were therefore required.

During the intermission, she felt weak in the knees and could hardly stand, and when the play was over, she stood floating at the stage door waiting for him to appear. When Timothy Brettigan came out, dressed in khakis and a plain cotton shirt, and wearing glasses, disguised as an ordinary man who had somehow in the theater been made up as preposterously handsome and dangerous, she asked him to autograph her program. "I loved your performance," she said, her voice a bit shaky, and her mind so high from the drugs that she saw herself married to him someday, and he nodded after taking a quick appraising look at her. "You were the black heart of capitalism." For once, she wanted to look beautiful. Whatever dark light he radiated while onstage, however, was now extinguished. He needed a stage to create that electricity, and here, out on the street, he seemed to be in a kind of low-wattage plainclothes disguise, just a guy, a mere actor. Maybe all he had were disguises. After he finished writing his name, she also wrote down her phone number and gave it to him. Very quietly, he asked her what *her* name was, and as soon as she told him, he took her hand in his and half-shook it, half-held it, before letting her go. "Hi, Christina," he said. "I'm Tim."

He never called. What was it about these men who never called?

Every once or so often, she thought about him and wondered where he was now and why he had disappeared from her life, considering that, on a whim propelled by a designer drug, she had moved to Minneapolis because her life in Chicago was over and was threatened by Farrell's ongoing existence there.

IN A FEW MINUTES THE DOORS AT THE BANK WOULD OPEN. CHRISTINA'S friend Eleanor, a teller, was already at her post, humming, as she usually did, and her other friend at the bank, Jürgen, a lovable and rumpled German green-card immigrant who was the branch bank's assistant manager, was picking tobacco—when not at work, he rolled his own cigarettes—off his tongue, as he lumbered toward his office. He was the perfect boss: firm when he had to be but essentially lackadaisical and good-natured; it was a wonder that their branch hadn't been picked clean by embezzling rogue elements taking advantage of

Jürgen's essential benevolence. In Germany, learning to read English, Jürgen had fallen in love with the fiction of Sherwood Anderson and had come to America in a search for those lonely, emotionally volatile, and half-innocent citizens, and he had been a bit bewildered to discover that contemporary America no longer looked like Winesburg, Ohio. Having a secondary gift for accounting and management, he applied for a green card and was now working here, though he feared being kicked out, given the erratic content of President Thorkelson's decrees concerning "aliens" and their wicked ability to get their hands on American money whenever they found it.

A solitary, watchful man whose unpressed neckties occasionally exhibited food stains, though he had a disarming smile, Jürgen habitually drove around the back roads of the Midwest on weekends in search of the historical remnants of behavior he had found only in books. "This *quality* must be out there somewhere," he had told Christina, his eyes expressing his *weltschmerzlich* German melancholy. "It is this American *quality* for which I search." With his Hasselblad camera and his iPhone, he took photographs of pickup trucks, derelict barns, old wireless wooden telephone poles collapsing sideways into swamps, and the main streets of small towns abandoned by their industries and now given over to meth labs and massive opioid addiction; occasionally he showed these photographs to Christina during their coffee breaks, checking her face for her reactions, and he had had one gallery exhibit, during which he had sold two photographs, one of a fading antique wooden barber pole standing in sunlight, the other of an old cigar box whose lid had been made into a pincushion.

He was a bit of a lost soul and a photographer of lost worlds. Christina felt protective toward him, even though technically she was his employee. She ambled down to his office to say good morning.

His head propped on his hand, Jürgen was at his desk, gazing fixedly at his computer screen, on which an Excel spreadsheet appeared, as if it contained important information, which Christina knew it did not.

"Good morning," she said. "Am I interrupting?"

"You cannot interrupt when nothing of any great importance is happening," Jürgen said, in his softly accented English. His clothes gave off a pleasantly reliable odor of cigarette smoke. "Whenever you interrupt me, you are not truly interrupting. This word—*interrupt*—is perhaps ill-chosen. Or it does not apply." Jürgen enjoyed splitting hairs for comic effect. As a student, he had studied the philosophy of Heidegger. Once in a while he would talk about being "thrown" into his current job. He put aside the desktop screen. "Since you are so kind always to explain your country to me, Christina, could you also explain to me American lane usage?"

"Lane usage?"

"On the freeways. This morning, in broad sunlight, on my way to this very bank, I nearly had an accident in my little Chevrolet. Now, later, here, I feel lucky to be alive. I will tell you how it happened: I had possession of the center lane and had signaled a movement of my car into the right-hand slow lane. Somehow I had failed to see an immense black vehicle approaching me in that very lane. As I attempted with great effort to get into that lane, the immense black vehicle, hearse-like but in actuality an SUV called, I think, a 'Subdivision,' honked at me and almost rammed into me. I have never been so frightened in my life."

"Jürgen, people in this country pass in the right-hand lane. They shouldn't, but they do. You know that."

"Yes. I have noticed. I feel that Americans lack lane discipline. This is only my opinion, which I offer to you."

"We do lack lane discipline," Christina admitted. "It's a free-for-all out there."

"Also, I fear American drivers," Jürgen said. "I worry about being fired upon by enraged motorists holding tightly to their cell phones and their multiple handguns." He leaned back and pulled his fingers through his flyaway hair. On his upper lip was a tiny shred of tobacco. "I apologize for saying so, but these large vehicles are *vulgar*, don't you think so?"

"Yes, I do."

"One should try to be more sage in rush-hour traffic," Jürgen said, tapping his fingers on the desk before checking his watch. Gazing toward the front plate-glass window, he pointed. "Who is that strange-looking person standing out there on the sidewalk, I wonder. What does he want from us?"

Christina turned and saw, in the direction where Jürgen was pointing, a man staring into the bank's front entryway: Ludlow. Well, that was quick. He had found her. How did he know that she worked here? Had she blurted out what she did for a living and had she, in a weak moment, specified the address? She couldn't remember very clearly what had happened last night or what she had told that guy, though she *did* remember the yoga and the snowstorm and the Blue Telephone and the small but important detail that Ludlow seemed to have no fixed address.

As soon as the front doors were unlocked, Ludlow came inside, looking around at the surveillance cameras and the tellers with the fixed, neutral expression of a man planning a robbery who naturally expects to be watched at all times. He seemed to have grown or expanded since she had last seen him. He had bulked up somehow. Too confidently, as if he and Christina had already slept together or had shared some other form of intimacy, he approached her just past the bank's vestibule and told her he would meet her tonight as planned at the bank's closing time. As a would-be reformer she was "needed" at a political meeting, and someone named "Why" was extremely eager to make her acquaintance, having been informed that she was a very brainy unattached political activist with ambitions to help out.

"Besides," he said, "I'm just following your suggestion that I should come out here this morning, to make arrangements."

"My suggestion? What? No, I didn't make any such suggestion. How can you say that?"

"You've forgotten. You, uh, you—you must have blacked out from that Wonderland drug you took. You don't recall? You told me all about the actor, how he transfixed you, and you said I sort of looked like him, and because of him, this actor, you sort of moved to this city even though he wasn't here maybe anymore. You gave me your whole life story. You talked *for hours*. We talked so long, they told us to leave the restaurant at closing time."

So shocked was she from these revelations that she stood quite still. She couldn't remember any of these episodes he was reporting. They hadn't happened. He was confabulating.

"I'm busy tonight," she finally told him, although she wasn't.

"No, you're not," he said. "Last night you said you had nothing going on this evening. Come on. Let's not have—I'm—don't bullshit me." He palmed her cheek, a proprietary caress that caused her to flinch. "I'll be back at five."

"Six-fifteen," she said. She saw that Jürgen was watching them both, his hands clasped together on the desk in front of him, a posture that made Christina think that he was praying for her.

"What political meeting is this?" she asked. "For what? For whom?"

"The Sun Collective," Ludlow whispered. "We have great plans." Then he smiled. "Everyone should have great plans, don't you think? In the absence of a great plan, a person is less than fully human. What are *your* great plans?"

"I don't have any," she said.

"So there you are. You should be ashamed of yourself." He thought for a moment. "We're going to alter the flow of history. Only great plans will accomplish that. *We* will give you *our* plans, and they will become yours," he said. Having announced his ambitions, Ludlow collected himself and, without a word of goodbye, made his way out of the bank and into the superficially brilliant winter sunshine. He seemed to be absorbed by the sunlight so completely that Christina couldn't tell in which direction he had turned, but perhaps his route didn't matter, since he was a homeless transient anyway. Christina looked over at Eleanor, standing at her teller's station, and Eleanor smiled thinly while simultaneously raising her eyebrows, half with admiration, half with scorn.

- 9 -

THAT EVENING, WEARING AN OVERSIZE AND RATTY-LOOKING BROWN overcoat stained with blue ink on the back, Ludlow loitered outside the bank's entrance, hopping occasionally to stay warm. He had appeared magically out of the frozen dark. One minute he hadn't been there, and then he had materialized, seemingly clothed in fresh rags that very day by Goodwill. His right, ungloved hand held his backpack. The doors to the bank were locked, so he would have to wait near the fiercely illuminated ATM until Christina came out. Eleanor walked from her teller's window over to where Christina was gathering up her purse, phone, and water, and gave her a nudge.

"Who's that guy?" Eleanor asked, nodding her head in Ludlow's direction. "I saw you talking to him this morning." A dour woman with a humorless chuckle that punctuated many of her statements, Eleanor wore drugstore perfume and gave off a scent of raspberries, making her seem friendlier than she actually was. For some reason, her brown tattered hair had always reminded Christina of asbestos. The hair had a vaguely carcinogenic appearance.

"Oh, him?" Christina did her best not to look in Ludlow's direction. "Just someone I met yesterday at my yoga class. He's . . . well, I gave him a ride home through that snowstorm. He had asked for a ride and so I gave it to him. I *think* that's all I gave him. That's it. He's very political. He said he wants me to alter the flow of history. You know: just a small request on our first meeting. He's got some gathering he says he's going to take me to, tonight—I guess that's where history will be . . . whatevered. So I was curious, and I kind of agreed to it. I mean, who doesn't want to do some good in the world?" The business about giving Ludlow a ride home was a polite lie, of course, since Ludlow broke and entered wherever he slept, but with a white lie, on the innocent side of the spectrum, who cared?

"Um, Christina," Eleanor said, leaning in to her and lowering her voice. "Is he homeless? Just asking. Did you *really* take him home? You can't take a homeless person home. Be honest. Because he looks kind of homeless to me, like one of those panhandlers, you know? With the cardboard signs? And the grocery carts and heroin addictions, heh heh?"

"That's about right, except for the addiction." Christina was startled by Eleanor's accurate guesswork concerning Ludlow's transient lifestyle. "Anyway, I like how raggedy he is. He says he's going to teach me to fight."

"Well, how would you know what he's addicted to? I mean, you met him, like, *yesterday.* So, okay," Eleanor said, "just be careful, all right? I mean, he's cute and all but kinda on the grungy side, and so maybe he has a crush on you, but a homeless person? *Raggedy?* No, I don't think that's a good prospect even if he *likes* you. What's this political group, by the way?"

"He said it's called 'the Sun Collective.' But I don't know what they are, really. I checked the internet, and they don't even have much of a website. There's almost nothing there. Who doesn't have a website?"

"Never heard of them," Eleanor told her, leaning down to whisper, "And never trust a guy dressed in rags. I speak from bitter experience." As she turned to walk away, Jürgen glided toward Christina's desk, blinking his bright, owlish eyes.

"Your stalker awaits," he said, worriedly.

ONCE HE WAS SETTLED IN CHRISTINA'S CAR, LUDLOW DIRECTED HER toward Northeast Minneapolis. As soon as she had unlocked the door for him, he had dropped down on the passenger side, positioning his backpack on the floor, and, once the engine had warmed up, he directed all the available blower vents so that the air blasted out in his direction.

For a moment, Christina imagined that this Ludlow person was a creature of one season, winter, and would melt if he should ever be exposed to heat, like one of those Japanese creatures she'd once heard about, the yuki-onna, a person made of snow who knocked on the door, begged for a glass of water, and then departed quietly, so as not to thaw in the presence of her host. Usually the yuki-onna was a woman. Forced to take a bath in warm water, she dissolved into little bits of floating ice. Ludlow's existence here—and the mere fact that she herself was in this car and driving this guy, who was almost a perfect stranger, to a political gathering—none of this seemed properly scripted to her, and as she contemplated the peculiarity of it all, the recklessness, the possible tragic outcomes, she almost stopped and told him to get out.

But her life had been so dull lately, so . . . wispy and thin and uninspiring. She was tired of realism and its wanton monotony and wanted a life that was not as real as the one she currently had. Her dreams bored her; they looked like previews of coming attractions that never arrived. Her job was so tedious that it made her ache. All the random men in her life recently had been narcissistic, money-obsessed, poorly educated assholes. She had almost signed up for lessons in swing dancing so that she could be thrown around a little by an exuberant strange man with a good sense of rhythm; she was that lonely. Given her chilly beauty, men hadn't come calling lately. Somehow Ludlow's appearance in her life seemed propitious. She felt unmoored but also slightly ironic about her life, as if she didn't care what happened to her as long as the outcome was interesting.

"I can tell you're wondering about me again," Ludlow said, slouching down in the passenger seat, his winter knit cap pulled down so that it covered his eyebrows but not his eyes, which peered out at the evening traffic. "You're wondering what I'm all about." He did seem able to access her thoughts, which was worrisome.

"Of course, I'm wondering," she told him. "Why shouldn't I? I don't know who you are, except you go to yoga classes and break into houses in the winter and recruit people for your little political group. The only reason you're here is that I'm super-bored with my life. I really don't give a shit what's going to happen to me."

"First of all, it's not a 'little' political group," he said, his voice rising with irritation, "and you shouldn't talk to me like that. I'm the best damn thing that's happened to you lately. Your luck has changed: I *told* you that I was a bright angel. I *told* you that I was a messenger from heaven."

"Only crazy people say things like that. Well, don't quit your day job. Oh, wait: you're unemployed. If you're a messenger, I'm Joan of Arc and Wonder Woman," she said.

"You're smarter than they are."

"Wonder Woman's pretty smart."

"All right," he said, sitting up. "Wanna see me do something?"

"I doubt it. Well, go ahead."

He took his left hand out of its glove and reached up and touched her lightly on her cheek with his fingertips, and as he did, they drove past a church whose bells began to ring plaintively. His fingertips were unexpectedly warm and then hot, and she felt her entire face heating up as if he'd ignited a brushfire, and an image entered her head, that of a young man eating an apple and sitting in the upper branches of a tree. Ludlow had performed the same trick this morning in the bank, when he'd palmed her cheek. He had a genius for the unexpected and unprotected caress. She didn't like that.

"You haven't been touched by anyone for a while, have you?" he asked. "You haven't been loved."

"Take your goddamn hands off me," she said, driving a few more blocks and feeling that she was being threatened.

"Well, we're here," he told her. "There's the parking lot." She turned the car in to an open area that hadn't been plowed since last night's snowstorm. A few cars were covered in snow. Apparently those cars had been here for days; maybe some people lived here. It was the Sun Collective, after all, and they had to exist somewhere.

The parking lot adjoined what appeared to be a desanctified

church clad in brown wooden siding, with an old signboard out in front displaying a few scattered letters from a broken sentence,

Wel

me tr

t over!

and two smaller characters, ☞ ✸. The ex-church had a high vaulted roof and stained-glass windows whose images were too dark to see.

She parked the Saab and noticed that several other people were arriving and walking toward the building. She'd expected that they'd all be as young as Ludlow, and a few had the youthful look—pierced and punked-up—but others were middle-aged, and several were bent over and made slow gingerly progress across the icy parking lot. These people had little in common except their clothing, which, like Ludlow's, had the battered appearance of cast-off apparel (the punk kids wore strategically ripped skinny jeans, torn T-shirts, and unzipped hoodies), but as a group they all had eager expressions as they made their way toward the doorway over which a single light-bulb burned. To Christina they resembled mendicants or a procession of the poor—the lame, the halt, and the blind—arriving at Lourdes. She glanced up at the front apex of the building, where ordinarily a cross would be located, but instead of a cross she saw a dark sphere with lines sticking out of it, rays of the sun painted black, like an invisible star that burns only at night, radiating a deep shining darkness. Toward the rear was a steeple topped by a spire without anything at its peak.

A man standing in the doorway had eyeglasses with peculiar squarish frames, with lenses that caused the blue of his eyes to curve slightly. He had the appearance of a mean-spirited bouncer at the portal of heaven.

After reaching into her pocket, Christina clutched at a Blue Telephone and, with a furtive move, popped it into her mouth. No one saw her. She smiled winningly as she descended the stairs.

- 10 -

THE NEXT THING SHE KNEW, SHE WAS LYING IN BED AT HOME, AND HER phone was ringing. *I must have blacked out,* she thought, as she reached over to the bedside table and saw that the caller was Eleanor. After Christina answered, Eleanor, sounding concerned, said, "Sorry to call at this hour. I tried texting you. You're okay?"

"Yes," Christina said. "Why wouldn't I be okay? I'm at home. I'm in bed. I seem to have my pajamas on."

"Thank God," Eleanor said. "I was, well, I was worried about you, going off with that guy to that meeting or whatever it was. He seemed rather shabby to me. A man made of rags, if you know what I mean. *Made* of them, not just wearing them, with clothes instead of skin. Like those guys at intersections with cardboard signs. Not a good prospect." She waited. "But, okay, credit where credit is due, I guess he was pretty cute, sort of."

"I can take care of myself," Christina said. "He was harmless. *They* were harmless. I think. The Sun Collectivists." Little by little, it was coming back to her, what had happened.

"You're not sure?"

"Well, I got high before I got there. I didn't mean to, but I did. I was nervous, so. It's still kind of a jumble in my memory now." Slowly, with one detail after another downloading into her brain, she was beginning to see how the evening had come and gone. "But it's getting unjumbled."

"Christina, you've got to lay off that Blue Telephone shit, I'm telling you. It's a bad bad drug. I know you get sad and everything, we all do, and it helps, but you keep up that habit, you're going to turn into just a mess of atoms, heh heh, you know, like a horror movie? You won't even be a person anymore, just a puddle of unrecognizable molecules. I mean it. I saw this thing in the paper about how it alters reality permanently. You could turn into a tree or something."

"Reality isn't what it used to be," Christina said.

"You got that right," Eleanor replied. "I miss realism. But that's life here in America. So that guy, did he put the moves on you?"

"No." She waited. "No, I don't think so."

"You don't remember?"

"I'm beginning to," Christina said. Now she was remembering everything piece by piece, though the sequence of events had somehow reconfigured its beginning, middle, and end, like a French art house film. What she remembered best was the warmth, the *welcome* she received at the Sun Collective, as if she'd returned after a long stay abroad in a place like Italy, maybe Siena, and she'd walked back through the entryway of her family home, and everyone had rushed to greet her and had covered her with hugs and kisses and exclamations of affection, even love—love for a stranger, which was herself. They had recognized her as a fellow soldier in the army of social reform. "They were happy just to see me," she said quietly. "They welcomed me. It's a community."

"How nice," Eleanor said.

"No, I mean it," Christina insisted. "I felt as if I belonged there."

"Wow. Are you sure?"

"You should come. It's just . . . well, they said, they told me, that it had started as a neighborhood watch group, and after the world got worse after President Thorkelson was elected, that sort of transmogrified or something into a community garden collective, growing vegetables and sunflowers on a vacant lot, which is why they're the Sun Collective, and then they branched out into neighborhood Free Boxes, with clothes and shoes and overcoats for poor people, and they've been working on restoring, no, that's not the word, reclaiming . . . no, that's not the word either, homeless people, anyway there are former homeless people at the meeting, ex-addicts getting straight, and, yeah, it's kinda anarchic, with some universal basic income proselytizers and democratic socialists in other parts of the room, also they want to start a co-op bank, everybody arguing, just a bunch of chaotic subgroups including urban farmers, twelve-step groupies, you know, activists for this and that, and it's sorta unruly, but the point is that it's fun and they welcomed me in; they *wanted* me there." She sighed. "It made me happy." She sighed again. "And they were real, actual people. Human beings. Doing work in the world. It wasn't like another fucking chat group on the internet."

"Are you sure about this?" Eleanor asked. "Because I have my doubts."

"Yes. I was there."

"Well, okay," Eleanor said. "But you were high."

"It made me happy," Christina repeated. "I felt there was finally some positive work I could do. Modest advances. Don't you ever want that?"

"Fight the power?" Eleanor asked. "Little ol' me? Yeah, I guess so. Sometimes."

"Come with me to the meeting next time."

"Well, maybe," Eleanor said. "Heh heh. You're sure we all won't be arrested?"

"We're United States citizens," Christina said. "What can they do to us?"

SHE HAD FLOATED FROM ONE GROUP TO ANOTHER, FLOATING NOT SO much from the drug but from the ideas and the activism, and— yes, they were as disorganized as anarchists usually are, feverish with ideas and wandering around from room to room, but they had moments of practicality when they reminded themselves that they lived in what remained of the real world: paying rent on their meetinghouse, restocking the Free Boxes they had set up around town, doing repairs on the meetinghouse wiring, and forming a new group that advocated affordable housing and another group charged with ending racism somehow. The majority of the Sun Collectivists were white, and Minnesotan, but several members were Native and African-American, along with a smattering of Asians, and one guy who looked like an Inuit and spoke with an upper-class British accent complete with aristocratic mumbling. The Blue Telephone seemed hot and sexy for once, given her involvement with what was being said and done, making her beautiful and desired, and another odd feature to the experience was that everybody seemed to know her name and seemed to assume that, of course, she would be *one of us* or already was *one of us* or perhaps had been *one of us,* from birth. People with smiles on their faces approached her and drifted away. They were so happy to see her. They said so.

A warm rush of acceptance had washed over her, sweetly oceanic. She was beautiful. They were all beautiful.

They seemed opposed to the internet on practical and ideological grounds.

What had happened to Ludlow? He seemed to have disappeared. Who cared? He had just been her enabler, to get her here. She floated toward another subgroup, sat down on a folding chair that someone had thoughtfully unfolded for her, and immediately found herself immersed in a discussion of how to get control of the narrative, whatever that meant.

What *did* it mean? Christina leaned forward to listen. Sitting next to her was a woman about her age, dressed in a red flannel shirt and blue jeans, a blue cap on her head even though the room's temperature was tropical, wearing thick glasses over watery brown eyes. She gave off an aura of power held in check by force of will alone, and as she spoke, her jaw hardly moved, the words issuing from her like cigarette smoke but with greater mass and specificity.

The woman, whose name was Rachel, was saying that it was just extremely stupid to think that they could get control of the narrative by passing out pamphlets like some of the collectivists were doing, at the fucking mall, for chrissake; that it was equally stupid to write letters to the editor, any editor; and it was criminally stupid to think that in an age of late capitalism the control over the spreading of information would be managed by means of Facebook pages, or internet chat groups, subreddits, et cetera. Something more radical was required, political action, *praxis,* she called it, but just as Rachel began to explain what that might be, Christina found herself relocated into another group, or maybe bilocated, where she was given a manifesto, also the website link to the manifesto, and then relocated again in front of a man who said that his name was Wye.

"Why?" she asked.

"W-y-e," he said pleasantly. "Short for Wyekowski. Welcome to the Sun Collective."

"Thanks," she said. "Did you start this? Seems kind of disorganized. Is all you do, is talk?"

"No. Oh, we're getting things done, all right," Wye told her. "Just you wait and see. It's only disorganized on the surface. Down below, where you can't see it, it's like I can't tell you." He laughed. His laugh sounded like a whooping cough. "We're small but we're big and getting bigger. Behind the curtain, plans get hatched. We're like Jupiter, the planet? Big, but with a lotta gas in the atmosphere. The protective veil."

"What happened to Ludlow?" she asked him.

"Who?" Wye's glasses were thick and interrogatory.

"This guy. Ludlow. I met him at yoga. He talked me into coming over here. I gave him a ride." Thanks to the drug, she felt as if her mind was on an out-of-control thrill ride.

"Ah. Well, he's here somewhere."

"What do *you* do here, Wye?" Christina asked, forming the words with difficulty.

"Oh, I'm sort of a spokesperson now and then. I turn on the charisma when they point a camera at me. I provide useful confusion when necessary." Another whooping cough emerged from him. She turned to her right and saw Arturo Ui approaching her with a steady tread, and then her spacetime became slightly warped as she remembered seeing that very guy, that actor, Timothy Brettigan, playing Arturo Ui in Chicago, but here he was now, and here, also, was she, after blacking out and driving home and getting into her flower-pattern pajamas, remembering his face, which was no longer the face of a ruthless dictator but that of a thoughtful young man, taken in by the Sun Collective. Seeing him was like being hit in her stomach. She had tried to talk to him, but she could not, given the people who were in his way, and he disappeared as if he had never been there.

"Christina, what would you like to do for us? To help our project along?"

"What is your project?"

"What do you think it is?"

"To save the Earth. To help the poor. To reform. To fix. To right the wrongs created by President Thorkelson."

"Bingo," Wye said. "Do you know how to do any of that?"

"Offhand," Christina said. "No."

"Well, next time you come here, why don't you come in with a project? How about next week? To show us that you're serious? Because after all the point is to repair our society, our culture, before the Thorkelsons of the world take over and destroy it. Which they almost have. We may be in the End Times. It's serious business."

THEN, STILL SITTING UP IN BED, SHE WAS ASLEEP WITH ALL THE LIGHTS still on, asleep and conscious somehow that the lights were burning not with light but with fire, and wishing that she had put on her pink sleeping cap, knowing also that the Sun Collective, a harmless and maybe loony group but a *welcoming* one, was a logical and perhaps necessary response to the way things were and are, at which point a little girl who resembled Christina herself at the age of eleven approached her in the dream and said that she owned all the rights to the number eighteen, and if Christina wanted to use the number eighteen for any purpose at all, she would have to pay her, the eleven-year-old, a user's fee.

Christina said she didn't need the number eighteen right now and went on her way. She noticed her own clothing, as one does in dreams: a cowgirl hat, leather boots, and jeans, and in her left hand a revolver. *Am I supposed to kill someone?* she wondered. *Who?*

- II -

AT WORK EARLY THE NEXT DAY, CHRISTINA WAS DOING HER BEST TO appear professional—a model of smiling morning sobriety and calm, a spreadsheet kind of gal. Eleanor seemed to be avoiding her, but Jürgen, her boss, managed to find her in the staff lounge as she was brewing a fresh pot of coffee, one of her daily assigned tasks. The bank had not yet opened; they had a few minutes to chat. For a bank, the social norms were casual; it was a wonder they were still in business. By now the Blue Telephone had worn off—its effects usually departed on time with few aftershocks, leaving behind a calm midsummer mental haze that followed images of the city ravaged by earthquake, black smoke coming out of the sewers, the frightened residents running here and there—and Christina's necessary clearheadedness alerted her to Jürgen's presence and to his lonely man's need to talk. She was always pleased to see him; his essential benevolence had an element of dependable, half-comic melancholy. He was so mild, you couldn't help but like him. He seemed to be a nonstandard German.

"You are looking shipshape this morning," he observed. He smelled of tobacco and drugstore aftershave. She knew he meant to compliment her, but "shipshape" wasn't close to how she felt. Where did he find his adjectives? In a book? His sentences in English sometimes sounded like grammar exercises.

"Jürgen, that's not the right word. Not for how I feel. Not this morning, anyway."

"What word should I have employed?" he asked. "I am trying to compliment you on your hummingbird pin and your speckled scarf without drawing unseemly attention to your appearance, as a creepy person might do."

"*Nice* would sound okay," she told him.

"Okay, nice. And your date with the homeless man last night, dressed in rags, how did that go? Did he take you home to his homeless home?"

"Word gets around, doesn't it? Oh, it was fine." She dropped the coffee in over the paper filter. The ground beans poured out of their container, smelling of burnt toast. Why was this brand so famous? It was like drinking dissolved fireplace ash.

"He took me to the Sun Collective," she told him. "It's this little neighborhood group of do-gooders, you know, um, neighborhood gardens, free giveaways of clothes and shoes, helping the homeless, redistributing wealth, environmentalism. Like that. Then I lost track of him."

Jürgen looked at his reflection in the coffeemaker's stainless-steel exterior and fixed the Windsor knot in his tie. "Ah," he said. "A revolutionary cell. Marxism?"

"No. I don't think they believe in that."

"What then do they think they are doing?"

"I just told you."

"But, you will forgive me for saying, there is therefore no program here, except . . . cleansing. Cleansing of the individual conscience. These little ad hoc things you describe, they are like narrow dirt roads going through the woods and stopping in nowhere. To change the world, you need a system with sharp teeth. And the teeth must bite down hard into the skin of capitalism. Otherwise, no change."

"Jürgen, we *work* in a *bank. We* are capitalists."

"No." He shook his head. "We help out the capitalists. We are the pet dogs that run with them only. We are forced to." He listened to the coffeemaker's brewing cycle, the spurting and bubbling, with something like satisfaction. "We are mere employees. You, me. We must do our work in order to, to do, what? To *put food on the table,* as you say here. We are the children of necessity. Forgive me if I say that what you need is a mass movement, with backbone and the teeth I just mentioned. Little neighborhood groups will not, what is the expression, cut it." He made a gesture with his right hand. As a gesture, it didn't seem to mean anything. "Though I do admire the modesty, the bravery of having no plan."

"Everybody has to do *something*," Christina said, feeling a heavy cloud beginning to form over her head near the ceiling. She gave him her best dazzling smile. "I liked being there. I got it. I mean, I, well, I get it. The activities. The doing something."

"Christina," Jürgen said. "My grandmother, as a girl, saw Hitler in a motorcade, going down the street in Hamburg, surrounded by mass hubbub. Do you know what she called him, whenever she told me about it? She said he was a mesmerist. We have this word in English also?"

"Yes. *Hypnotist*."

"I did, I do not like it, that she thought she was hypnotized. That the whole country was under a spell. It takes all responsibility away."

"And your point is?"

"Not to be hypnotized by good intentions."

"This is more than that," she said.

"How?"

"Jürgen, I was only there for a little while. You can't expect me to explain them."

"Why not?"

"Because . . . they have soup kitchens, they told me. They give away clothes and food. They've been taking in homeless people. They have gardens. I mean, it's just a neighborhood group, but that's, I mean, they—" She felt herself getting flustered. "It's action. Not just intentions."

"You are a convert?" he asked, placing his index finger on his lip.

"Maybe. Only not yet."

"I want to say this." He picked up a soiled coffee cup labeled with his initials and filled it absentmindedly. "In Germany, people are suspicious of cleansing. Good intentions and practical taking care of, yes, that is okay, but cleansing, no. We did that and look what happened."

"Nobody's talking about cleansing."

"Not yet. But soon, they will."

"You're a defeatist," she said.

"Well, okay, but soon we must go to work, at our posts, so to speak. Do you know, have you heard of, the American poet Ezra Pound?"

"Yes."

"One of my teachers went to visit him, in his old age, in Italy. He was saying very little, the poet, by then. He had wanted to reform the world, Pound, and the Italians put him on the radio, in Rome, during the war. He was advocating cleansing, the elimination of Jews, 'kikes,' he had always called them. He had other ideas. He was a man of ideas and the ideas were all bad. He liked cleanliness and purity. Social credit. He was lucky they didn't hang him for treason. They said he was crazy. That saved him.

"So my old teacher went to see Pound. They spoke Italian, but Pound didn't say, well, he didn't say much of anything. And my old teacher, who had taught me English, came back to Germany, and he told me, he and I were having coffee, and he said to me, about Pound, 'He's seen too much. His eyes are burnt out, like Oedipus's.'"

"Jürgen, they're opening the doors. Why are you telling me this?"

"Because I fear this will all end in violence," he said. "By the time this is all over, I fear you will have seen too much, and you will be like him."

"Now you're exaggerating."

"Wait and see," Jürgen said to her.

THAT NIGHT, IN BED, HALF UNDER THE COVERS, HER LAPTOP SET TO
the Sun Collective's manifesto page, she found herself getting bleary
and decided to read the paper copy instead. Manifestos interested
her, with their rage and storm clouds and fists aimed at the outdated
criminal heavens. But what an ugly typeface they had chosen for this
one! Already the pages had started to yellow. The book seemed to
have been printed by hobgoblins. And who wrote this thing?

THE SUN COLLECTIVE: A MANIFESTO ☞ ✳

Note: the following is a statement produced by the Aims &
Observations Sun Collective Subgroup and is not necessarily a reflection of the thinking of our members. It was
crafted by the subgroup but, after lengthy discussion, was
never brought up for an affirmation vote and thus does not
reflect the views of the Sun Collective as a whole. We offer
it as a general outline but do not endorse its claims or
necessarily agree with its proposals; nevertheless, it has
a right to exist. The Sun Collective is in no way liable or
responsible for consequences of the following paragraphs,
and no Sun Collective members are to be recognized as its
authors. Read at your own risk.

We offer the following ideas in a spirit of humility.

A specter is haunting America: the specter of millennial uprisings, of anti-consumption.

What would our current lives look like, given a just distribution of goods and services in an environment providing the greatest possible happiness of the greatest number? What if every person had (1) meaningful work that served as a source of pride, (2) sufficient leisure to pursue a hobby or an art, (3) noninterference by the state apparatus, (4) loving relationship with others (if desired), and (5) an inner life that acknowledged and did honor to the sacred? How would these goals be met without damage to the planet and without damage to the individual or to our own natures? Would the end of racism and sexism also follow?

These questions and collective hopes for their answers have led directly to the bloodletting of history and its arterial spray.

She was enjoying the manifesto, but she really wanted a drink. After getting out of bed, she went to the kitchen, poured herself a glass of white wine, and brought it back to the bedside table.

The gods are dead and with them their heavens and promised lands, leaving us the remnant-dump of our current reality. We live in the ruins of Valhalla, rehabbed as a flea market whose tiny gods are on display and for sale. Our era is therefore one of unrealism.

All that is airy solidifies into dogma.

We exist in a post-ideological age and have no choice but to reside there.

Every day is a birthday whose celebrant is Death.

Therefore, we state our first principle: No more utopias. The path to happiness lies elsewhere, in the middle kingdom, here, in our neighborhoods.

Individual action without political or social organization cannot alone produce positive social improvement, as history has shown. To quote a noted American writer, "One guy alone ain't got a chance." The solo warrior working to correct societal wrongs becomes a comical, dangerous, and absurd figure (cf. Don Quixote, Kaczynski, et al.), and the solitary individual's pent-up frustrations logically have their consequences in mayhem.

A bomb explodes with the energy of meaninglessness and meaning mixed together. Meaningless in itself, the bomb creates a fugal nothingness as a by-product of suffering, dismemberment, and death. That must change. We will find the articulate, eloquent bomb, if we must.

She took another sip of wine, a delicious Sancerre. She was tempted to ingest a Blue Telephone but refrained thanks to a massive effort of willpower. Those pills were ever so slightly addicting. But you couldn't live in two places at once all the time. It wore you down.

How do we undo our current unrealism, our ruination, without imagining a paradise?

It can be assumed that anyone who is paying attention must feel a sense of outrage, a gasping breathless anger. We live in shameful times. Thorkelson is a symptom, not a cause, of collective shame. We wish to shed our shame. We feel this need for change as a flower feels the need for water, nutrients, and the sun.

What is to be done about the hungry man or woman standing at a street corner and holding a cardboard sign saying, "Homeless. Anything helps. God bless"? The disheartened, the discriminated, the disinherited, the insulted and injured, must be solved.

"The disheartened must be solved"? Alone in her bedroom, Christina expelled a laugh. Who *wrote* this? Someone with an uncertain grasp of English, an Eastern European, apparently, or some madcap whose convictions outstripped his eloquence. And the logic! All the same, she continued reading.

First must come the diagnosis of the contemporary.

Everywhere we see the Triumph of the spectacle. Thorkelson is a creature of the screen and exists only there. No one has ever experienced him as an actual. He is flimflam incarnate.

The great tidal forces of technocapitalism and of Big Data stored in machines that cannot themselves be accessed threaten to overpower every political movement by multiplying those very movements through chat rooms, websites, Twitter feeds, Instagram, subreddits, and other forms of social media, a constant meme-scream. The end point of this process is a single person in a room yelling at the top of their lungs.

Thus arrives the necessity of being unplugged, the necessity of anti-consumerism.

Instead of asking, "Are you committed?" we must ask, "Are you unplugged?"

We must begin, again, with print, with pamphlets. As a group, we must produce converts one by one. We will emulate the termite. In this one way we will also emulate the Jehovah's Witnesses and the early Christians, termite-believers, while rejecting their "heaven." We must engage in individual persuasion through speaking and writing and the sunlight of reason, and we must alter the conditions of our daily lives so that we consume less, and then less than that, and lesser still. We shall thus all be Hunger Artists.

The most radical action in our time is to turn off the TV and to throw away the iPhone. Whoever can do both is one of us.

We shall rely not on faith nor on ideology, but on the truth of our spiritual recognitions:

- Start with helping your neighbor; then take care of your neighborhood. Begin with gardens.
- Charity in all things, always, until it hurts
- Intercede for the poor
- Technocapital—digitized, tidal, opaque, supranational— is coded to be above the law, a Sphinx with an unanswerable riddle; do not collaborate with it but kill it
- We make the point that capitalism's logic of inequality, waste, and spectacle lies at the heart of Thorkelsonism
- That we are desperate and our remedies are desperate
- That computers, the Internet, and all forms of cybernetic data warehousing that locate, target, and characterize the online person must somehow be vandalized or evaded or both
- That communities of every kind must be reformulated and reinstated
- That loving-kindness is our highest ideal and our only hope; we must say "No" to the narcissism of celebrity and beauty and accumulation and sexism and racism
- That not-wanting by necessity must be the path forward; we will be defined henceforth by an emancipation from acquisition, an activist asceticism especially tailored for women and people of color and LGBTQ persons
- In the absence of theory, we will still act
- State power must be placed in the hands of ordinary people
- That we shall freely offer our love to almost anyone, at any time, a love without desire
- That we shall be invisible, always
- We call for the end of capitalism without any claim as to what will replace it
- If not this, then violence—but not the hyperviolence of the state; we will invent a new form of effective termite microviolence. Such violence will be articulate and lyrical.

As our guide, Marsilio Ficino, writes, "Now our own soul
beyond the particular forces of our members puts forth
a general force of life everywhere within us—especially
through the heart as the source of the fire which is the
nearest thing to the soul. . . . The world's body is living
in every part—

It went on for several more pages with more practical suggestions.
She agreed with most of it but thought it was rather ho-hum, being
a kind of vulgarized Buddhism combined with a Pop Warner School
for Revolution tone, and in certain parts the manifesto was just waving a white flag of surrender, though the effective microviolence
interested her. What was that? How did you manage it? Exploding
wristwatches? Bugs painted with anthrax? Tiny explosions of nitromethane on the subway? At least it didn't attack the bosses with the
usual Marxist shitstorm of unresolved oedipal difficulties. She looked
up from the manifesto: her cell phone appeared to be ringing. When
she answered, she heard Ludlow say, "Christina. It's me. Listen, I
almost got caught. I thought no one was home, but they were." She
could hear him panting.

"Are you okay? Where are you?" she asked.

"I've been running. They were about to shoot at me. I think maybe
they did shoot at me. This guy. He had a gun, a revolver. Uh, actually,
I'm outside the door to your building. I looked up your address and
I got here."

"My address? How did you find it?"

"Never mind. Could I please crash in your place for the night?"

"Well."

AFTER SHE BUZZED HIM IN, SHE PUT ON A BATHROBE AND WENT TO HER
entryway, hearing him clumping up the stairs, and after his knock, she
unlocked and opened the door, and even from the distance between
them she felt his winter condition from the cold that radiated out
from him, and she saw how red his cheeks were, but what she no-

ticed about him—she quickly realized—was secondary to what she noticed about herself.

She was glad to see him. That came as a bit of a shock. There he was—lumpish, clueless, homeless, just another guy—and he was no one's idea of a good prospect, much less a good human being, but there he was anyway, entertainingly earnest, shaking the snow off his cracked shoes and then stomping them on the floor, poor but sexy, and the truth was that if he actually believed the Sun Collective Manifesto, he probably had certain resources of sympathy, and idealism, and—who could say?—some other interesting qualities, so she reached out and took his hand and led him into where she lived.

"That's where you'll sleep," she said, pointing to the sofa, and he nodded.

- 13 -

SHE CALLED IN SICK THE NEXT DAY AND SPENT MOST OF THE MORNING
with Ludlow, feeling a variety of hot peacefulness as the sun traveled
across the sky, entering through the south-facing window and eventually landing on the living room carpeting. She was deciding about
him—whether this man might possibly be a path to some sort of
better life. She doubted it, but. By late morning they had both calmed
down enough from their conversation to go to the kitchen, and while
she brewed coffee, he stood behind her reading his iPhone. Maybe
he hadn't read the manifesto. Without warning, she felt his lips on
the back of her neck, and she said, "Stop that. You know, I have to go
back to work tomorrow," and he nodded, raising his head so that his
chin rested lightly on her hair. She had a residual cramp in her left foot
from the moment last night when her leg had straightened involuntarily during a dream and knocked against the wall—the dream was
about bliss, about having a purpose in life.

In the afternoon they went out. Her mind had cleared sufficiently
so that she could try to reconfigure her future, creating a space in it
that he might occupy. She had decided that he had a kind of generic
attractiveness, and despite his ragged appearance she liked his hands
and blue eyes. She and Ludlow were both hungry, and they headed
down the snow-encrusted sidewalk holding hands through her mittens and his gloves, eventually approaching a greasy spoon from
which a hamburger smell—emanating from the one exhaust fan—
could be detected hundreds of feet away.

Once they were inside, sitting at a booth across from each other, Ludlow shook the snow off his hair. "This is the second meal we've had together," he said quietly, not looking at her.

"I paid for it last time," she said.

"Uh, right."

"Just teasing," she told him.

"Okay. May I say something?" he asked, with a serious expression. "You won't mind?"

"How can I mind if you don't tell me what it is?"

"Right."

"So?"

"Well, I think you're kinda beautiful, and I'm grateful that you took me in last night, and I like talking to you."

"Uh-huh."

"I might as well be direct," he said, picking up the saltshaker. "I'm not good at the sweet talk. It bores me. Life is too short. The thing is, and I'll just say it, it's— well, I want to fuck you."

"Well, we'll see. Give it time." So he was just a guy after all. She could see that he meant the statement as a compliment. It wasn't love, but it wasn't anything else, either. "I'm not even sure I like you," she said, taking the saltshaker out of his hand and putting it back on the table. "I don't know who you are. But I appreciate your friendly attitude."

"You don't have to," he said. "It's not about appreciation." He picked up his paper napkin and dabbed at his mouth.

"It isn't? I mean, I'm confused. I'm really confused here."

"About what?"

"Okay, for starters, what was that actor, Tim, doing there last night? I thought I saw him. But most important, who are *you*? Every time I think I've got a handle on you, you slip away."

"I told you: I'm an angel."

"Oh, please. I hate talk like that."

"Take it or leave it." He leaned toward her. "I'm just saying, I think we should have sex. It'd be the right thing to do. I'm attracted to you. We're wasting our time otherwise."

"Jesus," she said.

"I didn't know you were a Christian," he said, as the server, a young woman with streaked mascara, and who was wearing a stained apron, approached them for their order. Chewing her gum, she took a ball-point pen from behind her ear, shook it twice, and grimly asked them if they knew what they wanted. Christina ordered a bowl of soup, and Ludlow ordered something else, but Christina didn't catch what his order was because her full attention had been sidetracked by the presence of a large white dog standing alone on the sidewalk outside the restaurant window. The dog had no collar and therefore no tags, but it seemed to know exactly where it was, unlike the abandoned or lost dogs that looked around and sniffed wildly to find some place or some scent that they recognized. This dog seemed almost like a sentry: planted firmly in its spot, it slowly moved its head in the direction of the restaurant window, and when it had finished turning, it fixed its gaze on the window and, through the window, on Christina, who found herself exchanging a glance with the animal. It seemed to be asking a question for which she might have an answer.

". . . and the other thing we need to do is," Ludlow was saying. "Wait. You're not listening to me."

"Yes. Sorry. There's a dog out there."

Ludlow turned in the direction where she was gazing. "So?"

"I don't know. It looks like a stray."

"The city is full of stray dogs. Every city is full of stray dogs. I'm a stray dog."

"I know. But this one is asking a question."

"Christina," he said. "Dogs *don't ask questions*. They beg, but they don't ask questions."

"This one does."

Ludlow sighed. "Okay. I'll play along. What question is it asking you?"

Just then, the server, whose name tag said her name was Lucille, returned to the table with Christina's soup and Ludlow's order. "Ah," he said with a W. C. Fields accent, "my ham-bur-zhay," but by now almost all of Christina's attention was focused on the quizzical dog.

"It wants to know something," Christina said tentatively. "It wants to know who I am."

"I see. A serious dog, apparently. Are you high on that drug again?"

"Anyway, you were saying . . . ?"

"I was saying that we have to start at the bottom. We can't use the social media, with those goddamn posts and memes and chat rooms and subreddits and all that. They lead back to the NSA computers that will track us down and disable us. We gotta get to the phone zombies, the PZs, staring at their little screens. We've got to go out to places where the darkness is . . . *darkest,* like the Utopia Mall, and we have to drop our pamphlets out there, and, you know, create a stir that will spread out, you know, a contagion, and then we have to enlist people into our cause, and we—"

"Ludlow, would you explain to me how come you know Timothy Brettigan? I mean, you know him, right? What's he doing here?"

"That's for later." He took a bite of his hamburger and commenced to chew thoughtfully, playing for time. "For right now, we have to get our message out, especially to those people who most need to hear it." He was speaking as he chewed. "Those *consumers.* We have to make our way up the chain until we reach the President of the United States. We have to use our rage positively and not squander it in stupid, meaningless action like those fake revolutionaries in the 1960s and those creepy New Left people now with their stale academic neoMarxism and talk-you-to-death boring theories. Or like Occupy with their drum circles. All they do is chatter and argue. What did you tell the dog?"

"What?"

"Just now. You said the dog was asking you who you were."

"I didn't say anything."

"Yes, you did. You said—"

"Stop telling me what I said or didn't say."

"Don't be like that. Please." Now his expression had changed, so that, with the light coming in through the window, he didn't appear to be quite awake, in fact just barely conscious, and once again Christina had the unpleasant sensation that many of Ludlow's sentences were practiced, pulled out of a bin of preconstructed sentiment, and as she was wondering why he had insisted on himself as an angel, an identity claim that no man—in her experience—had ever asserted for himself, a customer dressed in a blue parka entered, followed by the white dog. No one else in the restaurant seemed to notice the presence of the animal or to care. The dog trotted over to their table and sat down in the aisle, keeping its gaze fixed on Christina, who looked up in the direction of the server, who happened to be giving a menu to the customer in the blue parka, who had seated himself at the counter.

"Somebody get this dog out of here," Christina said. "Somebody should call the health department."

"What do you suppose it wants?" Ludlow asked.

"Maybe it's the restaurant owner's dog. Maybe it lives here. Maybe it clears the tables."

"Why don't you answer its question?" Ludlow suggested. "Why don't you tell it who you are?"

Paying no attention to the dog, the server came by and refilled their coffee cups. "Uh, miss?" Christina called out, as the waitress returned to the kitchen. The dog growled, as if it were growing impatient. All at once she heard hamburgers sizzling on the restaurant's griddle as a dense cloud of greasy smoke and steam rose to the ceiling, and Ludlow leaned toward her, and something in the air or in the room or the sunlight made her skin prickle, as she felt herself lifted up, just as if she were about to give a speech. "I'm just so fucking sick of my life," she began, "I mean, really sick of how meaningless it is, and I want to act and to be strong and to put my hand into the river, and I want change, real change, and I want to bring down the machines that are killing us. The way people are suffering has to end, and even though I'm nothing, just a dot on the landscape, I've got to become somebody who helps, you know? Because sometimes I feel that I'm not even here, that I'm already gone. Because really the only point is to change the course of history, and you have to have power to do that, and I know . . . I know that we have to make the right decisions, because the Earth depends on it, and we have to do what no one else has ever thought of doing. *And I'm willing to give up my life for it.*"

What she had just said hadn't made any actual sense in the real world, she knew. She felt herself turning red, shamed by the verbal garble she had just spoken. But it felt right and had made some kind of emotional sense, like an eloquent speech in a dream, and Ludlow had nodded.

She breathed out. The dog had been gazing at her while she spoke, and when she was finished, it stood for a moment before bowing to her, lowering itself with its front legs extended and its chest and head resting on the floor, its rear end still in the air. Holding this posture for a few seconds and then straightening up and barking in agreement, it then turned and ran down the aisle between the tables toward the front of the restaurant, where it skidded before changing direction and racing back again in a kind of animal joy, a happiness so infectious that Christina thought she heard the sun itself laughing. Ludlow began laughing too, whereupon the dog altered its direction again and headed toward the counter, where the man in the blue parka tore off part of his hamburger and handed it down to the dog, now beginning to run in wild circles interrupted by its stops for handouts, everyone else in the restaurant dropping food down into the animal's mouth until the dog's running became so fast that it was almost a blur, an abstraction.

"You know, these other people at the collective want us to shadow the Brettigans, Tim's parents. There's something about them that they want. Or need. I sorta remember that from the meeting." It was all coming back to her.

"Yes," Ludlow said. "They told me. I know."

When the next customer came in, the dog pushed its way outside before the door closed completely and, full of new purpose, raced down the sidewalk away from where Christina could see it while Ludlow put his hand on her thigh and said, "You're different now, aren't you?" He leaned over and whispered in her ear. "I would kill for you," he said. "And for the others, too. Believe me."

"I believe you," she whispered and simultaneously thought: *We're going to become a couple, and we're doomed.*

☞ Part Three

- 14 -

SITTING ON A BARSTOOL IN THE HIDEAWAY LOUNGE AS HE WAITED FOR his friend Elijah, the pediatrician, to arrive, Brettigan felt the initial liftoff of early-stage inebriation. A genial, alcoholic warmth washed over him, beginning in his chest and radiating outward in all directions until he himself was a small friendly star shining in the night sky. Booze made you feel as if you were always welcome in a place where they were permanently happy to see you, and where, because they liked you without qualification, no mistakes were possible until later when the warmth departed, taking the good times with it.

He nursed his second scotch and appraised the patrons behind him. They were visible in the huge mirror framed in mahogany on the north wall, and, watching their reflections, Brettigan thought they had the appearance of a painting by one of those American Ashcan School Realists—somebody like John Sloan, whose bartenders were little sources of luminescence in the taverns where the genteel drunks stood or reclined. In Sloan's paintings, drunks just dissolved into the comforting background woodwork. Getting intoxicated was like that in those days. You slid right off the map into darkness, the little star that was you lighting the way.

By contrast, these patrons, the ones who had just come in from the street, were shrill, triumphant capitalists full of themselves and their successes. They weren't dissolving into anything. Alcohol just made them louder. The inaccurately named Hideaway had been filling up with them—division managers, project managers, low-level executives, and assorted lawyers and accountants—everybody fit and sleek from their workouts, and they were bellowing with earsplitting victory-laughter as they grasped their artisanal craft beers.

What had happened to the low murmuring of alcoholic intimacy, the friendly mumbles of the guy sitting on the barstool next to yours whose wife had left him for a younger man? They were all extinct, that species, gone the way of the dodo. The quiet, sad bars of Brettigan's youth, whose tables had been polished with the tears of the clientele, had been replaced with sports bars like this one, where the noise level resembled that of an ongoing ordnance blast. In these locales, everywhere you looked you saw a TV set depicting politicians or sports heroes, accompanied by commentary, under the din of surrounding real-time revelry.

Brettigan set his gaze on the TV just above and to the left of the glass shelves; it had been tuned to a twenty-four-hour cable news outlet. The President of the United States, Amos Alonzo ("Coach") Thorkelson, was on the screen, sitting on a chair in a charter school second-grade classroom and reading from *Tommy the Runaway Truck* to a collection of fidgety children who kept sneaking glances at the camera. Brettigan tried to hear what the president was saying. It was mostly unintelligible, but he could make out the general outlines. The truck, it seemed, had a mischievous streak, along with a parallel urge for freedom, and nothing, including speed limits, seemed capable of holding it back. Although its out-of-control behavior brought the Chief Executive to a high pitch of happy excitement as he read aloud, the children appeared to be frightened by the truck's misconduct and President Thorkelson's delivery, which included spastic flapping movements of his right hand as he held the book aloft with his left. One child was sucking his thumb, and another, a little girl with pigtails, had put her hand over her mouth in a gesture of fear. Watching the screen, Brettigan realized that the truck's impulse to go seventy miles an hour in residential neighborhoods and to plow through work zone barriers was meant to convey mechanical bravery, a pushing-the-envelope, out-of-the-box sort of thing. Even though the little truck slammed through a guardrail and tumbled down a hill at the story's climax, rolling over several times, it landed right-side up, still smiling, and, a day later, was given a medal by the mayor of Paradise Valley for daring. Nobody arrested it or issued a citation for speeding. It was an über-truck and was maybe beyond good and evil. The End.

Then President Thorkelson spoke up to editorialize on the story's meaning. Brettigan still couldn't hear exactly what he was saying, but the closed captioning at the bottom of the screen, all of it in capital letters, reported his words to the children. "ISN'T THAT AMAZING KIDS?" he was saying. "JUST AN INCREDIBLE TRUCK WHOSE FANTASTIC ATTITUDE CAN BE A WONDERFUL MODEL FOR BOYS AND GIRLS WHO WANT TO TRY OUT THEIR TERRIFIC COURAGE AND DON'T WANT TO EMULATE ALL THE OTHER FOLLOW THE LEADER WEAKER TRUCKS."

The president's toupee was slightly off-center. "Weaker trucks?" Brettigan turned away and stared down at his drink. Why in God's name had the doctor chosen this bar as a place to meet? Conversation would be impossible here, given all the background noise, which also included piped-in music that sounded like a health club aerobics class.

After another few minutes, the front door opened, and the doctor waddled in and removed his overcoat, hanging it on a hook near the bar. Brettigan felt the autumnal chill from the street as Dr. Jones dusted off the barstool next to Brettigan's and, with great deliberation, lowered his considerable weight onto it, simultaneously motioning at the bartender for his drink order. The doctor's appearance and his unhurried motions were reassuring—he gave off an aroma of mellow fruitfulness, a scent of ripeness; and his wide face, benevolent and wise behind his tortoiseshell glasses, beamed at Brettigan as if Brettigan's presence alone, his merely being there, brought him happiness.

"It's good to see you!" the doctor shouted over the background noise as he patted Brettigan affectionately on the shoulder. "Sorry I'm a little late! I had to run an errand for my wife! Susan needed some aspirin! And we didn't have any! She gets these headaches!"

"Oh, that's all right!" Brettigan shouted back, before realizing that his words of comfort might be misconstrued. "Elijah, I was just sitting here drinking and watching our current president!" He pointed at the television screen. "He's always entertaining!"

"That's not a word I'd use!" the doctor said, just before ordering a draft beer. "He's a criminal! That's not entertainment! It's indoctrination!"

"Yes, of course! But you shouldn't say so in public!"

"Why not? We don't have a police state, not yet! Let them arrest me if they want to! What are they going to do, torture me? What do I care! I'm untorturable!"

"It's your family!" Brettigan said. "They'll go after your family!"

"What?"

"I said, *'They'll go after your family!'*" Brettigan shouted. He took a sip of his scotch. "That's what they do! They have ways to harm people!"

"Oh!"

The background noise, which previously had been at din level, had risen louder, to an unwholesome pandemonium. One woman near the front plate-glass window seemed actually to be screaming at the man she was with, in conversation. It was a conversational scream. She was wearing designer jeans and a T-shirt with the words TOO GLAM TO CARE in stencil lettering across her breasts, and she had two fingers on the man's coat lapel, while the man, for his part, smiled indulgently at her and was nodding as he touched her face tenderly.

"We can't talk like this!" Brettigan said. "It's too loud!"

"They have a back room!" the doctor said. "I know the owner of this place! It's okay! We can go back there and talk!"

"Good!" Brettigan nodded. "Let's go!"

After paying, they took their drinks and made their way through the clusters of young people to a hallway at the back. On the hallway's left-hand side were the restrooms, and on the right-hand side, behind a heavy door painted black but with a red line running down the center, was a darkened meeting room. Brettigan flipped a switch, and several fluorescent lights flickered on as if reluctantly awakened. The room had scattered tables and a central circular table for banquets on which rested a dead African violet in a circular green metal pot. The room gave off a distant smell of spilled food and Lysol, and an even more distant smell of mold. Brettigan found a place to sit under an electric clock on the wall; the clock was running but showed the time to be three-fifteen. Brettigan checked his watch: the time, the actual time, was twenty-three minutes past eight.

After closing the door, the doctor dropped himself down on the other side of Brettigan and sighed. "Well, that's a relief," he said. "What is it with young people and noise?"

"Makes them feel less alone, I guess," Brettigan said. "The more raucous the party, the happier they are."

"Yes."

The two men sat quietly for a moment, staring off into space. There is a kind of friendship that thrives on conversation but does not require it; Brettigan had discovered several years ago that he and Elijah had an elective affinity that permitted them to be in proximity to each other in a condition of peacefulness unsullied by anxious chitchat. If they wanted to talk, they could talk, but they didn't have to—their friendship didn't depend on it.

After what seemed like an extended period of meditation, the doctor asked, "How's Alma? How's her recovery? That stroke, or whatever it was?"

"They say it wasn't a stroke. Your colleagues in the practice of medicine have done all the tests. There aren't any signs of it. But the trouble is that she's not herself, and I'm not sure exactly who she is. Ever since her episode in the park, she's been different." Brettigan was careful not to detail his participation in that episode, with the mirror in the water; there was no point in confusing matters.

"How come?"

"Well, she's been talking to the dog and the cat. I mean, people do that, they talk to their pets, but these encounters she's been having are *conversations*. It's not a one-way deal. She thinks *they're answering her*. I asked her what they were saying, and at first, she wouldn't tell me, you know, privileged conversations, and then finally she said that they're very thoughtful creatures who consider what their place in the world is and the point of life, what that is—well, okay, but what's the meaning of life *if you're a dog*? I'm not a dog, but I'd say it's food and alerting the household if there's a stranger at the door, and, yes, according to Alma they say all that, but it's more than just food and strangers and other dogs. I mean, the cat doesn't say anything about strangers because she doesn't like them, and that's her sole opinion about them. But Alma keeps telling me that the dog has *other* opinions. The dog has views. The dog makes *judgments*. For example, get this, the dog thinks I should worry less. In the dog's opinion, I should be more amiable, more easygoing. The dog thinks that all the worrying I do week after week is bad for my health. It puts, the dog thinks, bad vibrations into the air."

"The dog is correct," the doctor said. In the background, from behind the closed door, Brettigan heard more yelling and screaming from the main room. Those young people were staging a riot in there.

"I don't know," Brettigan said. "It's creepy, these conversations Alma has. The cat is more philosophical, but she is in general agreement with the dog. The cat's contribution to this general conversation is as follows: it is a mistake, she believes, to care about much of anything. In the cat's considered opinion, you should just let things happen, because they *will* just happen no matter what you do or say. The cat is a determinist. Of course, there are mice and birds to torture and kill, but that's just in the cat realm, not the human realm. According to the cat, God is in charge."

"The cat thinks about God?"

"That's what Alma tells me."

"And what does God say to the cat?"

"'You are in my hands.' Those are God's very words, according to her."

"I'll be damned," the doctor said.

"Could be," his friend replied.

"So the cat is a theist?"

"Yes."

"Monotheism or polytheism?"

"One god, the cat claims," Brettigan answered. "And Alma reported. Oh, as I said: the cat also has observed that everything is predetermined, predestined. That's why cats act the way they do. For them, free will is a myth. Forget about decisions. Just act. They all believe that."

After another long moment, during which Brettigan heard the humming of the inaccurate electric clock over the ruckus in the next room over, the doctor spoke up. "This is all very interesting, but you've got to remember I'm retired. I don't like these large generalizations about life, to be honest, from human beings or from the animal perspective. They hit too close to home. Don't forget I was once a scientist—medicine is approximate, but it's still a science—and I don't like to philosophize. I'd rather not worry about the meaning of things."

"These animals do."

"I wonder why," the doctor said.

"Because they sit around all day. Pets have a lot of leisure time. There's nothing else to do but think."

After a long pause for meditation, the doctor said, "You know, you could do worse than to talk to animals. That's not so bad an activity, when you consider it. You worry too much about Alma. If she wants to carry on a dialogue with the dog and the cat, why not let her?"

"She goes to churches, too, you know," Brettigan said. "Churches, synagogues, assembly halls, neighborhood meetings, political groups, affinity groups, you name it."

"What for?"

"She thinks Timothy will be there." Brettigan did not like to talk about their misplaced son and rarely raised the topic when he was in the doctor's company. He felt that the entire subject highlighted his failures as a parent and could leave the impression that he should have done more than he had been doing to find Timothy "He's been seen around here, and he's living here in the city somewhere, but he won't tell us where." Brettigan took another slug of his scotch in an effort to intensify and reverse the now-diminishing effect of warmth and well-being. "She's been visiting activist groups. Ecological and environmental groups. Sun worshippers. Did I tell you about the Sun Collective?"

"No, I don't think so. But I've heard about them."

"They meet in an ex-church. A local neighborhood action outfit. They have strong beliefs in . . . *something*. I don't know how Alma found them, but she really likes them and has sort of joined up. She tells me that they have a manifesto, but I haven't seen it yet."

"I'd love to see it."

"Me too. She's hidden it, just as if it were spiritual pornography that I shouldn't see, toxic materials. They have an interesting way of propagating the faith: they drop pamphlets around town. I actually saw a couple of those collectivists going out to the Utopia Mall to leaflet, and I brought one of their pamphlets back home. It was about surviving and not being greedy. They're against greed."

"No kidding. Good for them. But it's a tragic position to take."

"And they're anticonsumerists, and they hate computers and social media and the internet. They call it the New Enemy. They're against racism, of course. Two Sun Collectivists were in the park when Alma had her episode, her nonstroke. Funny coincidence, that they were there. You ask me, they're bad pennies; they keep turning up. She wants to bring them home with her. She thinks I should listen to them."

"Alma wants to bring them to your house?"

"Yup. For dinner or whatever. Maybe we'll have pizza night with these clowns, right in front of the TV. We'll talk about the evil of commercials. We'll make New Year's resolutions not to buy anything."

"That reminds me," the doctor said. "Speaking of leaflets and pamphlets. Have you been reading about the murders?"

"What murders?" Brettigan asked. "The usual murders?"

"No. These are not usual murders."

"What are you talking about?"

"Oh, it's all just urban legends. Folklore. It's not true, exactly. From the internet rumor mill. Twitter stuff and like that." The doctor sat up to emphasize the seriousness of what he was about to say. "Funny that you haven't read about it. It's also in the local free community newspapers, You can go to the web, HeardThisOne.com, et cetera, and look at the posts people are putting there. You didn't read about this?" Brettigan shook his head. "It's all about this group called the Sandmen. Rich young men in their Mercedes and their Audis. The story is, they come in from the suburbs to one of those overpasses where those ragtags hang out and sleep. They beat up the poor. Sort of an upscale gang. Like fraternity guys." He waited. The doctor had been looking down at his drink, but now he turned his gaze upon his friend. "I mean, it's just a story. Just a rumor."

"Yes?"

"And the Sandmen leave notes, according to the urban legends. These notes are pinned to the clothes of the injured and deceased."

"What do they say?"

"'Worthless,'" the doctor said. "'You were a zero,'" the doctor quoted in a monotone. "'You will not be missed. A parasite has been removed from the body of society. This is a War on Poverty. You are nothing. *You have been erased.*'"

"Interesting rumors. No one's more anonymous than a homeless guy."

"Right." The doctor took a sip of his beer. "According to these internet sites, the Sandmen beat up and assault the homeless. Just for fun. That's all they do."

"And they leave notes?"

"Always."

"Are the notes signed?"

"According to these stories, they are. Signed by the 'Sandmen.'"

"What? Are you kidding? *Who* do they say they are again?"

"The Sandmen."

"Like, 'Mr. Sandman, bring me a dream'?"

"Yup."

"That doesn't make any sense. Maybe it's an acronym."

The doctor shrugged. "I didn't make it up, and I didn't write it, so I can't help it if it doesn't make sense. But it's all over the internet. Just go look."

15

THAT NIGHT, BRETTIGAN LAY AWAKE ONCE MORE, BROKEN OPEN BY THE same antique visions in which he stood accused of murder, his soul drenched with the blood of his victims. Maybe his unconscious needed some R & R. In the dreams, he felt pride for the slaughter he had committed, standard dream-slaughter, but as soon as he awakened, he came homeward to his habitual self and tried not to be undone by what he had cooked up while asleep. He thought of his daughter, his son-in-law, and his two grandchildren and of how he loved them, believing himself to be, outside of the kingdom of nightmare, an ordinary decent guy. He tried not to think of his family; he didn't want to contaminate them. Still trying to calm himself, he observed the shadows on the ceiling cast by the streetlight outside the bedroom window. The shadows, like Brettigan himself, were, for the moment, harmless. Down the block, a dog barked. Brettigan did his best not to move so that he wouldn't disturb his wife. The scotch ebbed in his bloodstream; he could still feel its effects.

With great stealth, he rose from the bed, checking the bedside clock: 2:04. In the dark, he put on yesterday's clothes hanging on a chair, and he descended the stairs, avoiding the squeaky step five steps from the bottom. In the kitchen, after drinking a glass of water to fortify himself, he still wasn't sure where he was about to go. But he had a feeling that the dying were instructing him to take a walk of some kind, an excursion: outside, tonight, he was meant to be a witness. The dying wanted him to be awake.

The dog padded into the kitchen to observe him. The animal

seemed noncommittal about the nocturnal walk Brettigan was planning to take, though he did lick Brettigan's hand in greeting before
returning to the living room, where the dog's bed was located; the
cat typically slept curled up next to the dog. For the most part, the cat
was indifferent to Brettigan's daytime or nighttime projects and rarely
got up to greet him; Alma had reported that the cat believed Brettigan
was not long for this world anyway and therefore did not want to be
emotionally attached to him, or, for that matter, to anybody, people
usually being more troublesome to the cat than they were worth.

Outside, the late summer air was still warm, and the night winds
blew almost soundlessly through the maple trees lining the block.
Here and there, lights were still on in the upstairs windows of the
neighboring houses, probably for the sake of the insomnia-ridden
homeowners who were reading long novels or watching late movies or hatching plans for tomorrow's business day. The crickets were
making a racket from the bushes, almost as if they were on fire.

Brettigan glanced up as he walked. Through one upstairs window
two blocks from his own house, he saw a woman in a dressing gown
standing between side curtains as she gazed toward the sidewalk in
an attitude of watchful attention. Standing there, she was the very
picture of loneliness. He didn't recognize the woman—she presented
only a dark outline, like someone's mother standing in a nursery
doorway—and he didn't know who lived in that particular house,
which, like most of them in this Minneapolis neighborhood, had been
constructed around the turn of the century and would be drafty in
winter and difficult to heat, with large screened front porches. Seeing
Brettigan passing by on the sidewalk, the woman raised her hand to
wave but then seemed to think better of the gesture and lowered her
arm to her side.

Brettigan waved at her, a gesture the woman did not acknowledge,
though she did lower the window shade, and then he continued on.

The street curved slightly to the left as it descended into a flat area
with few trees and no wind, before the street and the sidewalks rose
in the distance to a hill, and as Brettigan made his way toward it, he
thought of the street fondly: on this very incline, he had watched

Timothy accelerate and jump over curbs on his skateboard. How long ago was that? Another era. In this same street, where it flattened out, he had taught both his children how to ride their bicycles. Before that, his daughter had made her unsteady way down these sidewalks on her pink-laced roller skates. Decades ago after a snowstorm, his son had pulled his sled up this hill on his way to Kenwood Park, all the streets blocked with snow, the city having gone silent except for the distant occasional noise of trucks plowing the freeways. Both the street and the hill had a comforting domesticity for Brettigan. Although they were public spaces, he felt that they belonged to his family and to the neighbors and to no one else. He owned part of this street; he was a shareholder. No, more than a shareholder: the sole proprietor, the lamplighter, the night watchman, the one who calls out to anyone who will listen that it's two a.m. and all's well.

At that moment Brettigan felt so weighed down with the past and its memories that the present had almost dried up and disappeared on him. Everywhere he looked, he saw spectral remnants, his own and his family's. He brought so much of the past to what he saw, he could hardly see what was actually there.

He heard footsteps behind him. When he turned around, he saw a mangy dog following him with some sort of intention, but when the dog saw Brettigan observing him, it stopped and peed nonchalantly on a fire hydrant.

Befogged by sleep and melancholia, Brettigan was startled from his personal reveries and from his curiosity about the dog to discover that someone a block away was approaching him on the sidewalk—a man wearing trousers too large for him, the pants' cuffs flapping back and forth above the spindly exposed ankles, the trousers themselves held up by what seemed to be a necktie in a pattern of polka dots. The man wore scuffed saddle shoes with no socks. He was clearly not of this place—he shambled like a tourist-vagrant with no particular destination in mind. The man's T-shirt had sentences on it that Brettigan couldn't make out, though he could discern a faded *M*. The other letters had washed out, as had the man's face in the half-lit dark. As they approached each other, Brettigan tried to see the markers of identity, but the man's face had the unfinished quality of someone whose birth had been incomplete and who had never loved anyone who could love him back, and whose face, as a result, had no emotion in it except dismay when he gazed at an inhospitable locale, this particular Earth to which he had been consigned. He had probably staggered through life in solitary confinement and was still staggering. The guy had several days' growth of beard, and eyes emerging out of the darkness that fixed on Brettigan with a kind of melancholy indifference.

The guy stopped in front of Brettigan, blocking his way. Looking off in no particular direction, and almost frail, he was not physically imposing, though he also seemed to feel no obligation to step aside, and Brettigan felt no particular alarm for himself, just an idle nighttime curiosity. The man gave off a smell of burnt wiring and dirty motor oil, creating around himself an entire atmospheric zone of rancid chemical odors. He swayed as if pummeled by a strong wind, but here there wasn't a breath of air.

"Hey," the man said, still being careful not to look directly at Brettigan.

"Yes?"

"You got a menthol cigarette?" the man asked.

"I don't smoke. Sorry."

"How about a buck for a beer?"

"The bars are closed," Brettigan told him.

"But not the all-night groceries," the man said. His voice had the distant inflection of someone who isn't thinking about what he's saying, and whose sentences come out of the mouth without anything behind them.

"You really have to drink?" Brettigan asked. Too late, he realized how patronizing he sounded.

"You from AA?" the man asked.

"Sort of."

They stood together on the sidewalk, neither one moving. A stranger, seeing them from a distance, might have thought that they knew each other and had met here by arrangement. Still trying to see the man's face, which seemed both broken and inhospitable, and noting that the man didn't appear to be headed anywhere, Brettigan decided to engage him in conversation. Behind him, the dog trotted away.

"How come you're still up this late at night?" Brettigan asked.

"I don't like the homeless shelters," the guy said, shaking his head. "So here I am."

"How come you don't like the shelters?"

"There are bad people in there. I don't feel safe. Besides, they don't let me in, usually."

"Why?"

"Because I'm a drunk." The guy breathed out: an impressive sensory blare of brutal wine, whiskey, and other industrial fluids. "You show up at the door drunk, they don't let you in."

"Why don't you quit drinking?" Brettigan asked.

"I can't," the man said, firmly.

"Why not?"

"Because I'm crazy."

"Oh. Well, that's too bad. What did you say your name was?"

"Albert."

What an odd name for a homeless guy! "Albert, where do you sleep at night?"

"I *don't* sleep at night. I walk around. Like this here. And then during the day, I get on the light rail and I go to sleep there. Or I sleep on the benches outside the library. Could you please give me a dollar?"

"Why don't you sleep at night?"

"You sure got plenty of questions. At night I stay alert, because of the Sandmen. They'll come and get you and kill you. Wipe out the poor people. They call us 'poverts.' I've seen their gangs. Didn't you say that you would give me a dollar? I'd like that now, if you please."

"The Sandmen?" So it really was a rumor. Brettigan reached into his wallet and in the streetlight's dim illumination tried to see what was in there, but the only bill he had was a five, which was too much money to give away to an uncompliant stranger. Shrugging to himself, he pulled it out and handed it to the man anyway.

"Thank you," Albert said. "I'll say an Our Father and a Hail Mary for you." He spoke the sentence grudgingly, as if he didn't really mean to invoke God but was required to do so by convention.

"Could I ask you a question? How'd you get here?"

"I walked," the man said.

"No, I didn't mean that. I mean, how did you get to be a person who has to walk up and down the streets all night and who lives the way you do? What did you do? What happened to you?" Brettigan waited. "I mean, you don't have to tell me." After another moment's wait, he added, "I'm sorry I asked. But I did just give you five dollars. What's your story?"

"Me? I didn't do nothin' ever in my life. My daddy, he used to drunk himself up and beat on me, broke my arm once. So I dropped out of school before I graduated and then signed up myself into the Army. Got my GED there. Even went to Afghanistan. I wasn't a shadow like I am now. I was a warrior back then, twice my size. The Army turned me loose but I didn't care for Afghanistan and you could say I lost my mind over there after I killed this guy in hand-to-hand combat when his sweat fell into my mouth, which poisoned me, and also saw my best buddy die, shot through the head, so they had to discharge me because I got so lunatic. I came home to nothin' and nobody. You want a guy who's got no skills, you're looking at it."

Brettigan realized from this little outburst that the man was young, though he didn't look it. Youthfulness had drained out of him. "You could learn."

"Learn what? No, I can't. I've learned everything I'm ever going to learn."

"What about the VA?" When the man looked puzzled, Brettigan said, "The Veterans Administration?"

"I tell you what: they ain't no good to nobody. They just boiling up the red tape over there in a vat, making more of it. They tried to mend me. They couldn't. I'm too busted to fix."

"What's this you were saying about the Sandmen?" Brettigan asked. The man's reek was intensifying and becoming more emotional somehow, an odor that somehow conveyed an entire lifetime of loss and despondency. Brettigan tried to breathe through his mouth in order to lessen the effect.

Albert looked up and down the street. "You shouldn't talk about them. Or say their name either."

"Why not?"

"Because they're devils," the man said in a tone just above a whisper. "They come at night in their cars, real stealthy, quiet-like. They creep up on you and kill you for fun, and they take your soul and sell it on the soul market downtown, in those sheds they've got. Like I said, they're devils. You speak their name, they come for you. You been warned. I gotta go now."

"Oh, that's just an internet meme," Brettigan said.

"No, it ain't."

With one last look at the street, the man—Albert—pocketed the five-dollar bill and shuffled rapidly, getaway-style, down the sidewalk, throwing furtive, guilty glances from side to side as he scurried along until he was absorbed by the darkness. Brettigan, now that he had a moment to think about it, felt that he had met this man somewhere before, but, no: the man—he had to keep reminding himself that the guy had a name, which was "Albert"—was just a standard-issue panhandler, down on his luck, someone in constant contact with misfortune and its delusions, and was no one familiar and certainly no one he would ever have to call by name again.

In this genteel neighborhood, you could be arrested for walking around the way Albert was doing, creating a public nuisance by simply being alive.

Maybe he was hoping for jail. After all, they sort of took care of you behind bars, in their own way.

Standing under the streetlight, casting a shadow that seemed thicker than usual, Brettigan heard a car approaching from up the street, a gray Escalade with red clay mud splashed across its fender. As it approached, the car slowed down, and from behind the smoked glass someone seemed to be taking a long gangster-movie appraisal of Brettigan before speeding away. At least no one would mistake *him*, Harry Brettigan, for a vagrant: his light windbreaker, though slightly soiled at the elbows from gardening, was a product of a famous brand-name haberdashery firm headquartered in New Hampshire, though the clothes it sold were made in China by factory workers earning pennies per hour, and his beautifully tailored blue chambray shirt and pressed chinos and Ecco shoes constituted an impressive ID card in this or any other American neighborhood. His flat-brim hat from Old Navy was a tasteful marker of his respectability.

The evening's stroll had cleared his mind of nightmares, but instead of turning around and heading back home, Brettigan set out again down the block before walking east toward the freeway and its overpasses, where the homeless, the ones who hadn't been taken in anywhere, gathered to sleep. He wanted to see them. He felt he had the right.

AS HE APPROACHED THE FREEWAY, THE RESIDENTIAL HOMES GAVE WAY to apartment buildings, including one from which music emerged: something with heavy orchestration, Brahms, maybe, feeling inconsolable. From another window, he heard a woman shouting, "Carl, are you over there?" and, in response, a male voice shouted back, "No." The night air was full of voices. Brettigan heard the increasing background noise of the freeway, and when he looked off to his right, he saw, two floors above a mom-and-pop corner grocery store, another figure standing at a window in a thoughtful posture, again a woman, her left arm supporting the right at the elbow, the right hand cupping her chin, surveying the street. She seemed to be wearing a wedding dress. When Brettigan looked more closely, however, he saw that this figure wasn't a human being at all but a mannequin, standing there in front of the window, a fully gowned dressmaker's dummy sporting a tiara.

Brettigan increased his walking speed. This excursion would be good for his heart. His cardiologist constantly badgered him to drive less and to stroll more. Brettigan reminded himself that the Thundering Herd would be gathering the day after tomorrow at the Utopia Mall, where he would report on the Sandmen. Surely the drug dealer would know where the Sandman story came from. He was acquainted with all the local stories.

Up ahead, on the other side of the street, Brettigan saw a clutch of homeless people, Victims of Capitalism, four or five of them encamped together under the prestressed concrete highway overpass. They looked like a ragged platoon that had been through a terrible winter battle in Russia and were now in retreat after having traveled hundreds of miles through snow. They were huddled together for shelter. Some sort of fire guttered nearby inside a barrel, the fire itself invisible though it gave off sparks that shot upward.

Gazing in shadow from across the street at this raggedy human assemblage, Brettigan felt transported to all the world cities where threadbare cast-off men and women gathered under public structures for protection, return-to-sender subterraneans, the clustered hollow-eyed irregulars who . . . but wait: as he drew closer, he saw that the five individuals were seated on the ground, not crouching, passing around a bottle of what was probably vodka. On the left was a tattered young man wearing a shabby red flannel shirt too heavy for late summer, seated next to someone with long, greasy, stringy hair identifiable as neither gender, possibly not gendered at all, this person in turn located next to a young man who was leaning back on his elbows and whose clothes were slightly cleaner than those of the other wasted vagrants, in fact *so* incongruously clean that he seemed to be in costume, an actor pretending to be a homeless drifter, and as Brettigan drew closer, he saw that the young man was, even at this distance, alert enough to return his gaze, and as Brettigan's eyes came into focus and his mind cleared, he thought that he was looking at his own son, sitting there like a guard or protector of the others, and Brettigan called out to him, crying his name, before the young man stood up and ran out from under the bridge and down the street toward the sidewalk, disappearing into the distance and the night.

16

"I'VE MET THE MOST WONDERFUL YOUNG COUPLE," ALMA SAID AT THE dinner table, repeating herself. "And I think you should meet them. I've told you about them, and we need to make some plans. Pass the salt, please."

Brettigan pointed his fork downward at the roast. "Really? It's very tasty. It doesn't need salt."

"Well, it *might*." She sat back. "Please, Harry. Don't be a trial to me."

"I thought we had agreed on this point. No more added salt? Your doctor warned you about salt and high blood pressure and all that, didn't he?" He smiled pleasantly, somewhat against his will and better judgment. But when he looked up, Alma's face had taken on an expression of familiar dismay and a sadness that she was trying to disguise with an uncertain, tired nod. Dismay: Where had he seen *that* emotion recently? On Albert, the walking vagrant last night, that was where. How strange to see a homeless man's facial expression on your wife's face at the dinner table! The succession of life's small jokes at every human being's expense seemed to have no limit.

"Harry, why do you think you know what's good for me better than I know it?"

"No, I don't think that. I didn't say I did." He put down his fork and tried out yet another agreeable countenance on her.

"Of course you did. *Salt*. You were badgering me about the *salt*. I asked you to pass the salt and you started to scold me. I am *not* a child. All I had was an episode of fainting, and suddenly everybody knows what's best for me. And by the way, where were *you* last night? Middle of the night, I woke up, and you were gone. Have you acquired a mistress, at last? I can't wait to hear about her. Does she drink? Is she a gold digger?"

"No. I told you," he replied. It was going to be one of those evenings. He would have to explain and justify everything he did and said and everywhere he went. "I couldn't sleep. So I went out walking, that's all."

"Why couldn't you sleep?"

"How should I know? I couldn't sleep because I couldn't sleep. Now you're the one doing the badgering."

"You're a man with a bad conscience," she said, with an innocent, beatific expression. "And you have bad dreams. I *know* you. So. Where did you walk?"

"Around. Around the neighborhood. I talked to a vagrant."

"I'll bet." She stood up, reached across the table, grabbed the salt-shaker, and vigorously scattered salt on her portion of the roast. Brettigan prayed for her to stop, and eventually she did. Then she cut into the meat. After one bite, still chewing, she asked, "Why can't you sit downstairs and watch TV or read like every other old insomniac in town?"

"Sometimes I do. Remember when I saw *Outward Bound*? But sometimes, my love, my dearest heart, I can't. I'm . . . restless. You know?" She nodded ironically. "I am *unsleeping and unsleepable.* Rest does *not come to me.* Sometimes I feel as if I'm going to jump out of my skin. That's how I feel."

"Poor Harry," she said. "You're a queer one." She sprinkled more salt on her meat to spite him.

"I wish you wouldn't use that adjective. It belongs to gay people." So far, he had not mentioned seeing their son at the vagrants' encampment the night before. Telling her that particular piece of information would involve making reassurances that he wasn't prepared to articulate; he didn't feel reassured about anything. He hadn't figured out how to break the news to her. Besides, why *was* their son among those homeless characters? It *had* been Timothy, hadn't it? Of that, he felt relatively certain. What had he been doing there and what was his mission? How could anyone know? "What young people?" he asked, though he knew the answer, to change the subject.

"What?"

"A minute ago, you mentioned a 'wonderful young couple.' Who are they? Where are they? *What* are they?"

"Oh, those two? The ones in the park. And I met them at this meeting, this . . . well, they call themselves a 'collective' but they don't live together or anything, they're just people who are working for equality and justice and so on."

"What collective is this?" He was playing dumb.

"The Sun Collective," she told him.

"Oh, right. Them. Right. Now I remember. You told me. Zoroastrians?"

"Not so far. I mean, not literally." She cut into another piece of salty roast. "Not the *sun* sun in the sky. More like the eternal light, if you know what I mean. They're against buying things you don't need and they're for being modest and advancing up the ladder spiritually and social reform and I don't know what all." As she finished the sentence, the dog and the cat padded into the dining room, the dog leading the way. Together, as if synchronized, the two animals sat down near the door to the kitchen, the cat a few feet away from the dog, both of them focusing a concentrated attention on Alma, who dropped her hand at her side so that it reached toward the floor. The cat walked up to her hand and put her head under Alma's palm. Alma cocked her head to listen.

"Behemoth says that you're thinking bad thoughts. Really *terrible* thoughts. About what?"

"The cat lies," Brettigan said.

"Not this cat. What bad thoughts are you thinking, Harry?"

"Since when did a cat get the right to set the conversational agenda?"

"Today. That's when. Just humor me."

"I can't." After a long, unpleasant pause, he said, "So you like this nice young couple who rescued you."

"Well, they're very friendly and so unassuming. Just a couple of kids. Between the two of them, they really make an effort. Their names are Christina and Ludlow, and they've called me, and I went to their meetings twice. You never listen. I went to a meeting a few days ago, remember? Total chaos over there, very much fun. And I must say, I liked them, and I agreed with them and their ideas. That's who they are." She bit into another small square of roast and chewed thoughtfully. Because it hurt him to watch her consuming so much salt, he thought he probably still loved her. "Oh," she said, "I think you'd like them. They gave me some of their literature. They even have a manifesto. They want a quiet revolution. They've got different projects. Fine with me. Harry, I'd like to invite them over here. We don't know enough young people."

"We don't know *any* young people. Knowing those two is not the same as knowing young people."

Abruptly, the cat and the dog left the dining room, the dog making an audible dog-groan as he departed.

"I want to have them over here. I want to befriend them, Harry."

"Why? I don't get why you want them here, in our house. What are we to *them*? They're going to pick our pockets."

She put down her fork, and in a sudden rage balled up her cloth napkin and threw it at him, though she missed, so that the napkin opened and fluttered to the floor. The effort made one sprig of gray hair get loose and fall down almost to her eyebrow. "Pick our pockets? Listen to you!" she shouted. "What a doddering, complacent old man you've become! Here we are sitting at this table eating our very nice dinner, while more and more people in this country go hungry and homeless because the rich suck up all the wealth for themselves, and people just go around mindlessly buying things and shooting at each other with their concealed weapons as if it were the Wild West and open season on every citizen, and the minorities get stomped on over and over while the rich waddle around on their golf courses, and that idiot in the White House gambols and prances around like Marie Antoinette, and our son gets chewed up by all of it and you don't give a shit!"

"That's not fair," he said with enforced placidity. "I do. I do give a shit."

"It's all collapsing!" she cried out. "The trail of blood leads straight to this house! I can't bear it. I can't *bear* being the cause of so many people suffering. The *injustice* of it. The *madness*. And I say that if they want to start bombing the malls and the . . . everything, well, let them! Blow it all up!" By now, the tears were running down her face. "This country is in a slow-motion catastrophe, and *we're* in the slow-motion catastrophe, we're part of it, and you just sit there in your chair, telling me not to salt my roast! It's unbearable."

"All right," he said.

"All right what?" The dog and cat, attracted by the noise, had reappeared in the doorway and were watching both of them.

"All right: invite them over here. All right, go to their meetings. Go to the Sun Collective. Do whatever."

"Now you're trying to placate me. I know you." She waited for a moment to compose herself. "I'm sorry."

"You aren't about to go out and buy ammonium nitrate, are you?" he asked.

"For what?"

"For the bombs. They make bombs out of ammonium nitrate and fuel oil."

"No," she said. "I'm too old. Let the youngsters do that." She dabbed the tears off her cheeks with her sleeve. "They should start with the country clubs and move on from there. I can't stand it. I can't stand any of it. I'm turning into a middle-aged nihilist. Did you really talk to a vagrant last night? That's not like you."

"Yes, I did."

"And what did he say?"

"He talked about his life. He said he walks around at night because he doesn't like homeless shelters. He worries about the Sandmen."

"Who worries about *them*? I never heard of them. I'm sorry I ruined our dinner."

"Alma, do you still want to stay married to me?"

"Why do you ask?"

"Because you were just now talking like a woman who doesn't want to stay married to her husband anymore."

"I *said* I was sorry." She dabbed at her eyes again. "I'm just being crabby. I already apologized."

"Okay, I accept your apology. The Sandmen? It's internet folklore. This guy last night—he said his name was Albert—told me that they're rich kids who go around killing homeless people." He waited. "Those panhandlers are mostly anonymous anyway. You kill them, nobody misses them." Reacting to his last sentence, she glowered at him. "Alma, that's not *my* view; it's what *they* think, according to the homeless guy I talked to. They're—the Sandmen—are creatures of the internet. On the internet, they beat up the poor."

"Just my point," she said. "That's what I'm telling you."

"Which was what?"

"I wish you'd pay attention to me now and then. You make me repeat everything because you don't listen. You said 'Nobody misses them,' and what I just said to you is that if we had a good and just society, anybody's death, even a homeless person's, would diminish the rest of us."

"You didn't say that. I don't remember your having said that at all."

"Anyway," she said, "I want to have that nice young couple over here. I feel as if I owe them something."

"Okay," he said, putting down his fork. He had finished his meal a long time ago, and now he watched his wife cutting up and chewing and swallowing her salt-saturated meat. The worst part of it was that she didn't seem to be enjoying her display of exasperated passionate irritation but continued simply because she wanted to follow through with what she had started. It was in her nature to take self-destructive steps to justify the steps she had already taken, no matter how many losing hands she was dealt.

Brettigan contemplated his wife with what he knew to be becalmed, blind, and loving impatience. The delicate negotiations between married partners had all the subtlety and complexity of high-level global diplomacy, even when the stakes were so small as to be invisible to outsiders. Nothing would have mattered if they hadn't loved each other, but, because they did, the wounds were reopened every night with each touch and each application of pressure, and the resulting infection had set in without either of them noticing until inflammation created this low-grade fever in both of them.

When she had finished, he picked up his dinner plate and hers, along with the cutlery, and with a serving tray brought them to the kitchen. Still sitting at the dining room table, Alma opened a book where her napkin had been, a history of Tasmania she had taken out of the neighborhood Little Free Library. She was pretending to read it. Or maybe she was actually reading it; Brettigan wasn't sure. Either way, she wouldn't budge from her appointed space until Brettigan had done all the dishes and dried them; her immobility was a form of spousal surveillance. At the sink, he ran hot water halfway up his arm, added dish soap, and began scrubbing. His motions were so unnecessarily vigorous, escalating to aggrieved violence against the place settings that the first plate, his own, quickly broke into pieces under his assault. Reaching down, he picked up the remnants and dropped them into the garbage.

"I heard that," Alma said. "We should both try to calm down."

THAT NIGHT, SLEEPLESS AGAIN AT TWO A.M., SPORTING A CLEAN PAIR of blue jeans, and a windbreaker over his T-shirt, but with the same straw flat-brim hat he had worn the night before to give himself the appearance of genteel refinement, Brettigan put the leash on the dog's collar, and together the two of them, man and dog, went out the front door and down the block, the dog nervously glancing up from time to time to inquire about the purpose of this nighttime stroll.

"You'll see," Brettigan told the dog quietly, so as not to rouse his neighbors. "I thought dogs liked adventures."

I was sleeping, the dog said. *You woke me up.*

"You can sleep during the day if you want to," Brettigan said, sotto voce.

I still don't get it. What are we doing out here?

"Well, I was curious about Albert. I'm curious about the Sandmen."

"Talking to yourself?" And there she was, Alma, his wife, who had caught up with him and now put her arm in his. She was wearing anything that she had found in the dark bedroom after he had left: a T-shirt, jeans, and sandals. Here in the shadows, she was oddly sexy in a comfortable, middle-aged way. Together, arm in arm, they proceeded down the sidewalk, and she said, "I woke up, you were out, and I was curious about what depravity you were up to." She bent her head toward him affectionately. "Are you still feeling rotten over me, Harry? I *did* apologize."

"And I accepted your apology. I don't feel all that rotten."

"What an ill-tempered old broad I've become." She leaned against him sleepily. "What are we going to do about ourselves?"

"Just get along, I guess. The way we always have. We're too old to get a divorce. And it's too expensive, all those lawyers."

"I s'pose so. You go your way, I'll go mine? I don't even know what 'my way' is anymore. Isn't that sad? I don't know what I'd do without you, and I don't say that as praise, either. It's just a fact. What's that up there?"

Ahead of them, several blocks down, a small group of police and emergency rescue workers, lit by a group of flashing red, blue, and white lights, were loading someone or something onto a gurney. Two attendants, one on each side, lifted the person onto the gurney and then unfolded the wheels underneath it. At such a distance, Brettigan couldn't discern any identifiable features, but as he and Alma approached, they could see that the patient was a man wearing scuffed saddle shoes but no socks that poked out from under the covering fabric; Brettigan didn't need to see the face to know who it was.

"Poor fellow," Alma said. "What do you think happened?"

"I don't know. Maybe it was the Sandmen." The flashing lights were flickering over Alma's face and over the dog's as well; as if in response to the scene, the dog had planted himself with a wide stance, making it difficult to pull him forward, and he had started to make a low, guttural growl that sounded like a complaint about some imminent evil. "Here," Brettigan said to his wife, handing the leash over to her. "Do me a favor. Stay back here."

When he approached the scene, the attendants had already closed the doors to the EMS vehicle, which seemed to be in no hurry to speed away, and from the group that remained, Brettigan singled out a policeman whose name tag read LUCAS and whose face gave the impression of toughened, unsentimental curiosity about everything of a criminal nature that might happen within his line of sight. When he saw Brettigan, he checked him out in a professional manner and then quickly observed Alma and the dog a block away, waiting there, and, having taken in the three of them—husband, wife, and leashed dog—he lost interest in the lot of them. *Well,* Brettigan thought, *we wouldn't harm a fly.* Several other local homeowners had gathered on the other side of the street and were gawking.

"Officer?" Brettigan began.

"Yes?"

"What happened here?"

"Sir. Do you live nearby?" The cop glanced in the direction of the departing EMS vehicle and then returned his inquiring gaze downward to Brettigan's creased trousers and shoes; the very edges of irritation and impatience were appearing on his face, as if something important had just happened, and now another, less important, event had interrupted it. In any case, everyone knew that cops did not like dealing with the bourgeoisie, with their terrible, subtle crimes. They preferred riffraff, whom they understood perfectly well. Brettigan immediately realized that his own questions, whatever they were, would probably be considered impertinent and would therefore be deflected and answered by other questions.

"A few blocks away," Brettigan said, having almost forgotten what he had been asked.

"And what are you doing here? Now?"

"My wife and I couldn't sleep. We decided to walk our dog."

"Ah." Officer Lucas threw his shoulders back and turned toward his squad car. He now seemed to be rather intensely uninterested in Brettigan. Not only was Brettigan a person of uninterest; he was simply in the way. "Well, we received a report of a homeless man in a state of collapse. And we responded. He was passed out." There was obviously more to say about this particular situation, but Officer Lucas was not about to say it, and Brettigan knew he would not volunteer any information, germane or otherwise. A chatty cop was of no use to anybody.

"Yes," said Brettigan. "I could see his saddle shoes when you loaded him onto the gurney."

Officer Lucas now seemed to be struggling inwardly; boredom and a newfound suspicion were both somehow gaining ground with him. "You saw his *shoes*? The saddle shoes? Did you know this man?"

Brettigan thought for a moment before saying, "No, I didn't." With a small, almost imperceptible shock, he noticed that Officer Lucas's fingernails were jagged and bitten.

A cop who bit his fingernails! That was one for Ripley's.

"Never saw him here before?"

"No, not here."

"But somewhere?"

Brettigan thought for another moment. "No." Then: "I don't think so." He had never felt that he himself was a skilled or effective liar. "Did he have an ID?" Brettigan asked. "What was his name?"

"No," Officer Lucas said, "he didn't have an ID. We don't yet know his name. We're unacquainted with the individual. However, I'd appreciate it if you'd write down *your* name and phone number for me in case we need to get in touch with you. Or if you should happen to see anything suspicious in . . . this neighborhood. After all, you say that you live close by."

"Okay." Brettigan took out a pen from his shirt pocket, while Officer Lucas handed him a sheet of oddly tinted blue paper, on which Brettigan wrote "Albert Tauber" and a false local phone number.

"Thank you," Officer Lucas said, eyeing the name and phone number with an expression of distrust, at which point Brettigan worried that he would be asked for his driver's license.

135

. . .

"WELL," ALMA SAID, STEERING THE DOG BACK TOWARD THEIR HOUSE, "what was the situation?"

"The guy was passed out. Or he'd fainted. Officer Lucas did not elaborate."

"The poor man. As for Officer Lucas, he seems to have made short work of you."

"Short work? No, I wouldn't call it that. I was very forthcoming with him. He didn't care to tell me anything, that's all. I was a mere aggravation to him." The dog was pulling Alma forward, eager to get home. Something about the evening seemed to be getting on the dog's nerves and was causing him distress. "I noticed that Officer Lucas's fingernails were bitten. You don't see that very often. Well, I suppose it's a high-tension job."

"Well, aren't you the Sherlock Holmes tonight? I hope you didn't comment on his fingernails to him. He'd think you were a racist. You could be arrested for a microaggression."

"What do you mean by that?" Brettigan asked.

"What do you mean, what do I mean? I meant what I meant: you can't go around telling Black cops that you've noticed that they're biting their fingernails. It's not polite. It's not done."

"I didn't tell him that. You mean it's a political thing? He was African-American? I guess so. I really *hadn't* noticed, to be honest. Well, he was tall. I did notice that."

Alma snorted. "You're so funny. Of course you saw that he was African-American. How could you not see that?"

"No. Really, I didn't. He was a cop. What did I care what color he was?"

"Don't be smug. What did you write down for him? He was making a list and checking it twice, which I saw from way back here, and you were adding to it."

"My name. I gave him my name."

"Why would you do a thing like that? Why did he ask for it?"

"I don't know. Well, yes. He did ask. I was there, you know, show-ing up at the crime scene and all that. If there *was* a crime. I gave him a name because he asked for one. Anyway, you shouldn't worry. He won't be appearing on our doorstep anytime soon, the reason being, I didn't give him my real name. I gave him an alias. I said my name was Albert Somebody."

Alma didn't register any surprise. "Harry, you gave him an alias?" It was a rhetorical question. "I must say, you're getting stranger and stranger all the time. You alarm me." She did not, however, sound particularly alarmed; her voice was quiet, subdued, resigned. "The poor man," she repeated, and for a moment Brettigan didn't know whom she was referring to.

"Because . . ." he said, to fill the silence. And there, only a few feet away from the front of their house, Harry Brettigan stopped, while his wife walked on ahead of him grasping the dog's leash, momen-tarily oblivious to her husband's hesitation behind her and having seemingly forgotten her own question, and at that moment Brettigan felt as if he had become invisible, or at least as invisible as the dead were, watching his wife go on up the street without him, not paying attention to the answer to what she had asked. He felt diminished and evasive, shielding Alma from the real story that was sinking down into his interior and that he kept trapped there. "Because I'm not myself," he said aloud. "Because I'm not myself anymore."

In the distance a dog barked, a sound followed by a second answer-ing bark, and then a third, a canine chorus rising, and Brettigan tilted his head back. Overhead he observed a sky without stars but also without clouds. Where had the stars, all those pinpoint suns, disap-peared to? He couldn't remember the last time he had seen them.

- 17 -

"THE USUAL, HARRY?" THE BARBER ASKED.

"The usual."

The west wall of Franklin Avenue Barbers displayed a collage of variously colored male paraphernalia: a fishing net with several lures and rods and reels attached, and, behind the net, a picture of a speckled trout with an outraged expression, a hook in its mouth, leaping into the air. On the opposite mirror side, the wall facing the fish, there was—attached somehow with double-sided adhesive tape, next to the implements of haircutting and the jar of combs immersed in liquid green disinfectant—a collection of military patches prized by the barber, Elliott, who was, at this very moment, trimming Brettigan's hair and passing on news, most of which was barbershop rumor concerning the neighborhood.

Tuned to a classic rock station, a radio had been placed next to the cash register, the barbershop being a cash-only business, the last of its kind, and Brettigan couldn't be sure that he had heard Elliott correctly over the tinny racket of the music. The barber seemed to be saying that the internet claimed there'd been trouble on the streets, but the trouble, Elliott said, had been invisible, and directed at what he called "invisible people." "They've been disappearing," Elliott said. "No one knows how. But"—he shrugged—"they don't exist anyway. It's just a story."

Meanwhile, in the next chair over, another man with thinning brown hair and a genial pockmarked face, who was being tended to by another barber whom Brettigan didn't know, had started a loud monologue of sorts on the raising of children and homeownership. The man with thinning hair was saying that two years ago in late spring he had been up on a ladder, replacing the storm windows with screens. The storm windows, he said, were of the old-fashioned kind: rather heavy and difficult to hold on to, consisting of a wood frame and a large sheet of glass, but they were necessary to install for the winter months to protect the house from drafts. Besides, he had always taken considerable pride in completing householder tasks, the man asserted, because he possessed few handyman skills and could not repair plumbing or wiring problems; whenever he *could* do some practical chore, he did so with zest. Replacing the storm windows reinforced his masculine role in the family, so to speak, and would impress onlookers. His son, who was nine years old, had been standing at the foot of the ladder, holding it in place.

It had been a hot day, the man with thinning hair said, sitting up straighter in his barber's chair, one of those early-spring hot days, and the winter storm windows really *had* to be removed, and so he had placed the extension ladder—not a stepladder, which wouldn't have gone high enough—in front of the house, close to the shrubbery, beneath the first front window he had to reach. If you leaned the ladder against the house, you could climb up and pull off the storm window from the hook-hinges that held it in place at the top. You pulled the window out at the bottom, grasped it on its sides, lifted it off the hooks, and climbed down the ladder with it.

Everything had gone well with the removal of the first storm window, he said, but he hadn't been able to get a good footing for the ladder beneath the second upstairs window, so when he climbed up, he could feel the ladder shaking with each step he took. The ladder this time was almost straight, hardly tilted against the house at all. So when he reached the upstairs window, he pulled and then lifted the storm window off its hook hinges at the top, as before, but more precariously.

At that moment, after pulling the storm window out, he lost his balance and felt himself falling backward. He also realized that the window was falling with him, since he was still grasping it, and that he would land on the ground with the sheet of glass on top of him, and it would shatter all over him. But what was odd was that after the first moment of terror, he felt himself relax into it, into the act of falling, and as he fell he saw through the glass the sun and the sky, and though he feared falling on top of his son, he knew somehow that his son had moved away from the base of the ladder, and was safe.

"It felt peaceful, that falling," the man said, "one of the most peaceful moments of my life," before adding that he hadn't landed on the lawn, where he might have broken his back, but in the shrubbery, which had lessened the impact, even though the glass did indeed shatter all over him, but miraculously leaving very few cuts, nothing terribly serious, no stitches needed. What had upset him the most was not the broken glass, or the bruises left on his forehead from the window frame, but his son's sudden hysterical crying, really closer to a scream, at the moment he landed.

The other, funny thing about it, the man said, was that what upset him were not the cuts and the bruises or even his son's loud outburst, but his failure in his role as the man of the house, in this case, being the man who performs a job incorrectly, incompetently, and dangerously, endangering his own son, and therefore appearing to be not so much the man of the house after all.

The stories you heard in barbershops! Brettigan thought. You could be personal and anonymous here, and no one would care.

WITH THAT, THE MAN WITH THINNING HAIR LAPSED INTO SILENCE. THE only sounds in the barbershop were now emanating from the radio tuned to the classic rock station and from the electric shaver that Elliott was using on Brettigan's hair. "Well, I don't know," the barber said quietly. Meanwhile, the man with thinning hair looked at himself in the mirror, his haircut having concluded, and he nodded, evidently pleased with the job. He rose from the other barber chair, the one closer to the door, paid for his haircut, and left.

Brettigan began to feel drowsy, as he always did when his hair was being cut, but he felt that he needed information and that Elliott might be in possession of it. "Elliott," he said, "have you ever heard of the Sandmen?"

"The Sandmen? What makes you ask?" the barber said. Like Officer Lucas and Socrates, he answered questions with other questions.

"There was a thing that happened in our neighborhood last night, this guy told me about these Sandman people. I'm not sure who they are."

The scissors behind Brettigan's neck stopped moving. "Cops tell you anything?" the barber asked.

"Not really."

"Nothing about the notes the Sandmen leave behind?"

"No." Ah: the notes again.

"Well," the barber said, "okay. What I've been hearing, and this is all secondhand, of course, just hearsay, is that the notes are *statements*. You know, like editorials. Why they're doing it."

"What do they say?" Brettigan asked. "Are the police telling you anything?"

"What do I know?" the barber asked. "I don't know anything. You should go to the internet. That's where the stories are. Not here."

Elliott stopped to examine the length of Brettigan's hair.

"You checked the internet about this?" Brettigan asked.

"No," the barber said. "Why should I? I just hear things that people tell me. These guys, they're called the Sandmen because they got inspired by this novel, you know, *Prometheus Unchained*? By Sally Ann Surely? I understand that that's her pen name. It's got this hero, Ben What's-his-name. They get their ideas from him."

"From that novel?" Brettigan asked.

"That's what I heard."

"No one reads novels."

"They read this one. And it's like *a thousand pages* long. Okay, I think we're done." He gave Brettigan a hand mirror so that he could check out the haircut, and Brettigan nodded. The barber removed the cutting cape from around Brettigan, shook it out twice to remove the hair, and smiled. "So like I said, those are *their* ideas. They aren't *my* ideas. I just cut hair, you know? That'll be the usual seventeen dollars, Harry."

Brettigan handed Elliott a twenty, as he usually did, and, as usual, said, "Keep the change."

"Thanks," the barber said, with an affable smile.

SALLY ANN SURELY'S IDEAS HAD BEEN SPREADING. SEVERAL MEMBERS of President Thorkelson's cabinet were members or former members of Sally Ann Surelyesque Rationalist Societies, as was the bodybuilder Speaker of the House of Representatives, "Little Bill" Hemble, who had once announced in an interview that the most influential book he'd ever read had been *Prometheus Unchained,* which had changed his life by presenting him with arguments on behalf of self-reliance and against self-sacrifice. Charity was a sin in this novel because it encouraged losers. Nothing was more sacred than a dollar. Brettigan suspected that Little Bill Hemble had probably never read Ralph Waldo Emerson, that tricky thinker who despised charity in most of its forms, but you could never be sure what anybody had read or left unread these days, President Thorkelson having a made a now famous speech in which he cited "too much reading" as a form of trespassing compared to "looking into matters and places where you don't belong." He had proposed a forty-four percent tax on books, the same as on cigarettes.

"Some things," President Thorkelson had added with his trademark grin, "don't bear very much looking into."

WHEN BRETTIGAN ARRIVED HOME IN THE LATE AFTERNOON, THE DOG and the cat greeted him in the foyer with uncommon enthusiasm, the dog lapping his tongue against his hand, and the cat, Behemoth, curling herself against his leg in a pantomime of cat sensuality. They were pretending to be affectionate as a mask for their disquiet; both of them looked worried about something that was going to happen.

Brettigan smelled a meal being prepared in the kitchen—cinnamon and clove, which probably meant Indian cuisine—and he saw that the dining room table had been set for four. There would be surprise guests, though he knew who they'd be; the surprise was that Alma had invited them for this evening without consulting him. Pulling himself away from the two animals, and feeling for a moment as if he were falling backward off a ladder clutching a storm window that was also falling a few inches above and over him, Brettigan approached the kitchen, where Alma stood at the sink, peeling cucumbers. The late-afternoon sun was shining slantwise on the kitchen floor, creating an oddly chilly light.

"The dog," Brettigan said, "told me we'd be having guests tonight, people he says he doesn't know."

She did not turn around. "Quite the chatterbox, isn't he? Woland told you that?"

"Yes. Was this occasion going to be a secret? This dinner?"

"I explained to you that those two young people would be coming. I *invited* them. You just forgot. Like you forget everything."

"Oh, I remember: The Sun Collectivists."

"Yes," she said. "Them. We need to have more friends, you and I. People whose ideas aren't identical to ours."

"Ah."

Still she had not turned around. He had a good view of her back and of the knot tying her apron. "I think you'll enjoy them. They're people with principles. Anyway, I've met them and liked them. You haven't."

"I've seen them. I just haven't met them. And don't worry about me. I always enjoy having strangers-with-ideas over for dinner," Brettigan said. "It sharpens my wits. Just think of the excitement of trying to find common areas of interest when you're conversing with principled strangers, people you know nothing about but are forced by circumstance to admire. Nothing better in life. Nothing better than a cozy, sociable evening with prospective friends. We can ask them about their ideals."

" 'Sociable.' Haven't heard that word in a long time. Where'd you dredge that word up from? Your crossword puzzles? Harry, don't be like that. Are you going to be like that?"

"Like what?"

Now she turned around to face him, the peeler clutched in her right hand. "Oh, you know, making clever mean remarks, using words nobody's heard of, editorializing on what everybody else is saying from your great Olympian height. Like a Brit in the House of Lords, or someone."

"My height isn't so Olympian as all that," he said. "More like the height of, I don't know, an outhouse."

"Harry," she said. "Please be nice. Put a limit on the irony. Do try to make a social effort with these kids, all right? For me, please? If you love me, you'll do this for me."

"What are their names, again? You know how I always forget names."

"Hers is Christina," she said. "And his is Ludlow. They're revolutionists."

"Yes, I got that part. So I should expect some speechifying. And I can assume that they're a couple?"

"Sure. I mean, who can assume anything about anybody these days? I like your haircut, by the way."

"Thanks. Actually, you should thank the barber. He was very talkative today."

"About what?"

"About the internet rumors. The campaign to eliminate the homeless by, you know, killing them off."

"Oh, that. Another everyday atrocity we have to take in our stride."

"How do you know about it?" he asked. "I thought it was a secret."

"You're so senile. You told me about them, remember? Now you go upstairs and shave. Make yourself presentable. I'll be up in a few minutes. Okay? Get on with it."

He turned and trudged up to their bedroom, followed by the dog and the cat, both of whom appeared to be shadowing him and studying him. On the landing, he glanced at the photograph of Timothy in which the boy, wearing his high school graduation robe, was smiling and frowning simultaneously as he watched some activity outside the frame. A smile and a frown: Timothy had always been adept at projecting compounded and contradictory emotions: he could be the very picture of amused despair, bored joy, excitable lassitude, and— his real specialty—restless calm. He typically gave the impression of someone who wanted to be somewhere else even when he seemed to be perfectly happy right here. With Timothy, the compass was always pointing in two directions at once. No wonder he was such a good actor. With consummate tact, he kept you from knowing what he really felt or thought whenever he was being torn in opposite directions and didn't want to trouble you with his own suffering.

And the picture of Virginia, their beautiful daughter. Older than Timothy, and always, from his birth onward, in his shadow.

As the dog watched sympathetically, Brettigan felt the tears threatening and wiped his eyes with his shirtsleeve. Indifferent, the cat glanced away. Brettigan felt the necessity to compose himself. In two hours, when the guests would be here, he would have to serve up a façade of hospitality. Maybe he wasn't so different from his son after all. Anyway, now he had to clean himself up.

18

SOMETIMES WHILE SHAVING, BRETTIGAN SAW HIS FATHER'S FACE returning his gaze in the mirror. There he was, his old man who'd died young, encased inside the glass and gazing out with the wry paternal skepticism that fathers sometimes bestow on their sons. Older friends of the family who had known Brettigan's father said that Brettigan looked—uncannily, alarmingly—like his dad: similar facial expressions and hairline, same blue eyes: uncanny, they said. Brettigan's father, an insurance salesman, had died when his son was a few months old, and even now Brettigan missed him in the way that you could miss a place you've heard about, such as Madagascar, without ever having been there. Brettigan didn't believe in an afterlife but hoped if there was one that he'd have a chance to have a conversation with his father, an odd prospect, since Brettigan was now thirty years older than his father had ever been. He was his father's elder.

If you met people in the afterlife, how old would they be? No one had ever satisfactorily answered this important question.

He wanted to ask his father's ghost certain questions about revolution. The ghost would have opinions. Minneapolis had once been a hotbed of progressivist politics, an outpost of Trotskyists, full of radical socialist ferment that had left an almost invisible collective memory in the city's psyche, as had another faction, corporate defenders of the status quo, the "Citizens Alliance," so-called.

What had it been like to see open warfare in the streets of this midwestern city during the Minneapolis General Strike in 1934? To have witnessed the melee when police and hired thugs wounded sixty-seven strikers and killed two of them? To have had a socialist governor in Minnesota, Floyd Bjørnstjerne Olson, who had grown up among Jews in North Minneapolis and who spoke fluent Yiddish when conversing with them and campaigning in their neighborhoods, a man who had had to call up the National Guard to restore calm? Olson had once said, "I am not a liberal. I am what I want to be—a radical."

The downtown battles in 1934 were pure class warfare out in the open, when workers fought managers over political principles. Brettigan felt that he was entering another such world, beginning with this evening's dinner party, but without instruction or guidance from anyone about who the combatants would be and how their battles would be staged. And none of it would be out in the open. Insurrection was invisible now.

Returning home during his freshman year from college at the Christmas break, Brettigan had come in through the front door after having taken a taxi from the airport, and his mother, startled, had looked up from her chair and said, "Oh, *hi*. It's you. Welcome, weary traveler. Take off your coat and stay awhile." And then she displayed her characteristic forced grin, which showed her lipstick-stained teeth. Still in her chair, she picked up her newspaper to resume her reading.

The stepchild syndrome, the superfluous offspring: it occurred to him that most revolutionaries probably had backgrounds similar to his.

Really, if the only problem was that he was not welcome anywhere or by anyone, then he was still given permission to live. He was permitted to eat, and to sleep, and to work. But then, half a century ago, there came the day when Alma had said to him after a bout of soul-stirring lovemaking in his dorm room that she loved him and then touched his face tenderly as tactile proof. They were both naked and sweaty. Of course, her claim seemed implausible, quite possibly a con, and it wasn't until several months later, after she had repeated the claim of her love for him so often and had touched him so often and so sensuously that her love had become a joke in the face of his disbelief, that he felt she meant it, after all. It was as if he had successfully robbed a well-protected and thoroughly alarmed bank that contained love instead of money. He could not resist loving her in return; every minute he was not with her seemed like wasted time.

He would never let her go, not for anything in the world. Nothing she could say to him would ever change his feelings about her, that she had been his rescuer, just as he had rescued her, that indeed they had rescued each other from their separate deserted islands where the unloved and uncared-for waited out their time.

FROM DOWNSTAIRS, HE HEARD THE DOORBELL RING, A TWO-NOTE chime, the guests apparently having arrived thirty minutes early, Alma's Sun Collective youngsters, anarchists or insurrectionists or whatever they were, who probably had abolished the clock or could not tell time or just estimated what time it was by glancing at the sun's path in the sky. Startled by the doorbell, Brettigan felt his hand twitch, causing the razor to dig into his skin, which provoked a cut that immediately began to bleed enthusiastically down his cheek. There in the mirror was his father bleeding, poor guy. If he had been his father, or any man of that generation, he would have reached into the medicine cabinet for a styptic pencil to sting the wound shut. Having none, Brettigan mashed a wad of toilet paper against the cut, letting the tissue hang down slightly from his face for effect, as if he were an unhinged curmudgeon.

He rushed into the bedroom, grabbed the first clean shirt and trousers he could find, put them on, and hurried downstairs. How he hated to welcome guests into the house! It was against his nature to warm up to strangers, mostly because he had never learned how.

AT THE BOTTOM OF THE STAIRS, ALMA, WHO SEEMED GIDDY WITH HAP-piness and anxiety, was keeping up some patter about how, no, they hadn't come too early, not at all. Brettigan remembered them slightly from the park, and his impression of their dinner guests as he approached them was that Christina, standing there under the over-head light, wearing blue jeans and a man's collared white shirt, was an attractive young woman who gave the impression of never having been inside anyone's living room before—she stared at the furniture with a sullen, watchful sensuality as if she were a voluptuary observing tribal customs. And something was wrong with her eyes, though Brettigan found himself unable to guess what it was. The lids were halfway down, sleepy bedroom eyes, possibly in a drug-induced torpor. Or maybe she was always like that, fresh from lovemaking, her hair a bit of a mess, all the senses distracted and flushed.

As for Ludlow, he had a good-looking, vague blankness, the unthreatening handsomeness of a catalog model, although from moment to moment he took on the astonished, blank expression of a crash-test dummy. His blue jeans were ragged, with threads hanging down from the cuffs. He wore a plain black T-shirt and had a tattoo saying YOU'RE WELCOME! on his left arm. Interesting: he expected gratitude from others for his mere existence. For comic effect, he wore a blue striped necktie over the T-shirt. When he exhaled, he gave off an odor of breath mints. And now that Brettigan examined his guest more closely, he saw that Ludlow's left cheek had a bloodstain on it very much like his own. Different face, similar wound.

Just as the guests shuffled toward the living room, the dog and cat trotted in, the dog sniffing and measuring Christina, the cat sitting at her characteristic distance and staring at Ludlow.

"Who's this?" Ludlow asked, indicating the dog.

"Oh, him?" Alma said. "Pay no attention to him. He's very friendly."

"Woland," Brettigan said. "The dog's named Woland. The cat is Behemoth."

"Funny names," Ludlow said.

"Aren't they, though? My wife named them. She found their names in a book, a Russian novel, if I remember correctly. Isn't that right, dear?" They were still standing in the front hallway the way strangers do in close quarters when they're unsure of themselves and are feeling shy. Alma was wearing an apron over a rather formal black taffeta skirt.

"Yes," Alma said, touching Christina on the back to herd her toward the living room. "Please come in. Our pets are . . . remarkable creatures. They're both quite, um, telepathic. Jesus, Harry, what happened to your face?"

Out of what seemed to be a very thick fog, Christina said, "Excuse me, but who's Harry?"

"My husband," Alma said, nodding in his direction. "This guy. Didn't I introduce you? Where are my manners? My husband is Harry, well, *Harold* Brettigan, and of course I'm Alma, and naturally I know both of you from the park and et cetera, but for heaven's sake, Harry, what did you do to yourself? You look like a horror movie monster, toilet paper hanging down from your skin, just like that creature, that scary undead personage, who is it—?"

"The mummy," Christina offered from her great distance.

"Yes, that's it, the mummy," Alma agreed nervously, "staggering around in his funeral wrappings, and quite unpresentable. Did you cut yourself?"

"Yes," Brettigan said, "the doorbell rang while I was shaving and I cut myself. You"—he pointed at Ludlow—"are just as disfigured as I am. You've got a scab or something on you. If you don't mind my asking, what happened?"

"Oh, this?" Ludlow touched his jaw. "We were having sex this afternoon and she scratched my face just before she came. She does that. You should see my back. It's like somebody whipped me."

"And the sex wasn't that good, either," Christina added, frowning. "There's the irony."

In the expressive air pocket of silence that followed, Brettigan showed the guests to the couch, where they sat gingerly, leaving the impression that they believed the cushions would give way and land them on the floor. "Ah," Alma said, taking an hors d'oeuvre for herself and popping it into her mouth. "What fun to be young."

"Yeah," Ludlow said. "Check under her fingernails and you'll find blood and my DNA."

"Would you like drinks?" Brettigan asked, hoping to normalize the conversation. "We're having Indian cuisine tonight, and the bar is open." He smiled in an effort to present a festive impression. "Putting on the Ritz tonight, so to speak. And, just imagine: it's all free!"

"Whiskey," Christina said. "Scotch, please, on a rock."

"One ice cube?" Brettigan asked.

"Yup."

"How about you?" Brettigan asked Ludlow. "Wine, beer?"

"How about a martini?" Ludlow said. "What do you mean," he asked Alma, "about those pets, the dog and the cat, being telepathic?"

"Oh," Alma said airily, "they're just like animals anywhere. They can sort of tell what you're thinking. They can grasp what's going on. They're knowers. They know."

"Alma thinks that they talk to her, don't you, dear? What can I get you? Oh, and help yourself to the hors d'oeuvres, kids." He pointed at some cheese and crackers on the coffee table in front of the sofa, the ones that Alma had been sampling.

"Wine, Harry."

Again out of the fog in which she seemed to be permanently residing, Christina asked Alma, "What are they saying to you? The dog and the cat?"

"Oh, them?" Alma laughed. There followed a long moment during which the sound of ice being dropped into glasses and liquor being poured came distinctly from the dining room, where Brettigan was fixing drinks. "Well." She gazed in the direction of Woland, who was sitting stiffly near the window at a safe distance from the guests, eyeing them suspiciously. The cat sat beside him in a similar skeptical posture. They didn't like being talked about. "You see, when you helped me in Minnehaha Park, after I fainted, I mean, after that, when I came home, I felt I could converse with them both. Animals are quite alert creatures, you understand. They're very communicative."

"But what are they saying?" Christina asked again. "I'd really like to know."

At this point, Brettigan reentered the room carrying Ludlow's martini and Christina's glass of scotch with the single ice cube. He had been careful to make both drinks generous in an effort to get the conversation going. He was handing the drinks to both guests when Alma said, "The dog says you two are in love. He says you're both desperate. He says you're planning something."

"That's interesting. And what about the cat? What does *she* say?"

"Oh, the cat?" Alma waited for a moment, tossing her head back slightly, as Brettigan placed the stem of a glass of white wine delicately between her fingers. "I'm sorry, but I can't tell you."

"Because she's silent?"

"No," Alma said, with a thin smile. "Because it would be against the rules."

"She doesn't like us?"

"No, it's not that."

"Excuse me," Brettigan said, "but are we really having a conversation about what the cat did or did not say? Please, let's change the subject. We've all just met, or at least I have, met you, I mean, and we don't want our guests to think . . ." Another silence, like an interior fog bank, hung in the living room air. He could tell from Alma's expression and from the way she was sitting that she believed the cat had communicated something quite dire to her. "Please bring me up to speed. I know that you, Christina, work in a bank, but, Ludlow, I don't know what you do. Did I hear correctly that you're a medical student?"

"No. If you did hear that, you heard wrong. Doctors are such shits."

"Ah. My mistake." Brettigan waited for Ludlow to offer a piece of information in response to his question, and when the boy said nothing, Brettigan began to speculate aloud: "From your diagnostical looks I'd say you were a med student. Or maybe a graduate student in political science. Or a project manager somewhere?"

Ludlow sat back, took a long, hearty swig of his martini as if it were a beer, and gazed up toward the wainscoting. "Nope. Sorry. Wrong on all two, or is it three, counts. I'm a professional revolutionary for a revolution that hasn't happened yet." After Brettigan's single yelp of a laugh, leaving yet another silence behind it, Ludlow continued, "It's what I do, and I'm sorry if you think it's funny. I undermine the economy by . . . well, it's complicated. I'm part of a movement, and it's spreading, but I . . . you wouldn't know about it unless you knew where to look, the silent secret places." Ludlow turned toward Brettigan and gave him a measuring glance devoid of friendliness. "We're like termites. It's a termite revolution. Termites can bring down a house, you know. If you have enough termites, the city itself will fall. We termites want to get out from under our rocks and into the sun. That's what we'll do."

"When I met him," Christina said, studying the cheese and crackers in front of her as if they might be poison mushrooms, "he was living from house to house."

"Evictions?" Alma asked, reaching for a cracker and popping it into her mouth. "You were evicted? Rents are so high these days."

"No." Christina wiped some invisible crumbs off her lap. "No, he was breaking into houses and staying there while their owners were gone. You know, like off-the-books house-sitting? He didn't burglarize anything so it wasn't burglary. Anyway, that's what he was doing *then*. Real solidarity with the insulted and injured and poverty stricken and the desperate bottom dwellers. You have to know how they feel if you're going to rise up. Or rise down. And he was going to SC meetings, organizing and recruiting. He recruited me. He lives with me now."

"So," Brettigan said with a smile, "no more breaking and entering?"

"No," Ludlow replied, tilting his head in Christina's direction before turning to exchange a glance with her, "not with you. I entered you voluntarily, didn't I?"

"Was that a question?" Christina said, after taking another gulp of her drink. Then she grimaced, nodded, and took his hand and dropped it into her lap before noticing that her hostess, Alma, seemed slightly aghast by the turn the conversation had taken, whereupon she retrieved her own hand and removed Ludlow's. "So, Alma," she said, "I know we've spoken before at the SC meetings, but as long as we're on the subject of, um, *occupations,* or being *occupied,* I don't think I know what you do. Or *did*. In life, as your job. Because maybe whatever it was that you did, you probably *don't* do it anymore. Being retired, and all. I mean, if you *are* retired, because I don't know *if* you are. I'm sorry. I'm not saying this very well. I'm a little nervous. Parties with older people make me nervous. I'm just trying to be friendly, with, you know, what do they call it? Chitchat?"

"Oh, that's all right," Alma said, gulping down the last of her wine. Brettigan hadn't been paying close attention to his wife and felt the first twinge of alarm that she was drinking so rapidly. He was growing certain that the young woman, Christina, was high on some drug or other. "I was a music librarian before I was a principal in the public schools," Alma said. "At the university library. I did that for years. I was once," she said, standing up, "a little piano prodigy. Just like Mozart without the genius. I played one of his concerti. I wore a gray dress with a Peter Pan collar, and I had black patent leather shoes. And I had a teacher, Señor Batista, who smoked cigars during my piano lessons. He played piano with the lit cigar between the third and fourth fingers of his right hand, like Glazunov. Didn't hinder him at all."

"Really," Christina said. "How wonderful."

"No, it was awful. His studio stank of cigars," Alma replied, leaving the room. Brettigan heard her rapidly pouring herself another glass of wine. From the next room, she said, almost shouting, "I wouldn't wish it on a dog. I just sat at the keyboard while other kids were out having a good time and making friends while I was practicing octaves and those goddamn Czerny exercises. Anyway, I quit. I was tired of being a performing seal. Goodbye, Bach. Goodbye, Beethoven. And good riddance to the lot of them, those Germans." She reentered the room with a full glass of rosé and sat down, holding the glass carefully so as not to spill. "I played in cocktail bars for the money, and I was a rehearsal piano for a synchronized swimming team. They couldn't use a tape player because they had to stop so often. Then I sang in a chorus for a while, just as a hobby. I have a pretty good soprano voice. *That* was fun. I still have a respectable range. And perfect pitch, even though I loathe music. I can still hit the A above the staff."

"Well, why don't you?" Christina asked.

Brettigan, sitting on the other side of the coffee table, watched as his wife sat back, put down her drink, hummed a tone to herself, and then opened her mouth. He was about to say, "Wait, don't," when from somewhere inside her, her deepest interior, a sound came out that might have been a note or a scream, though she hadn't projected her voice for an audience, and the sound was too soft really to qualify as a scream. It was more of a screech.

"There," she said. "That was an A."

"You're flat," Brettigan told her. "That was an A-flat." He went into his Russian accent. "Is like fork in brain."

"Nonsense," Alma said. "Harry, my sense of pitch was always better than yours. Much better. You're only fooling and pretending." She smiled at the guests. "Pay no attention to my husband. He's not worth the trouble."

"We met, Alma and I," Brettigan said to Christina and Ludlow, who didn't seem particularly interested, if their facial expressions were any indication, "at a college mixer, a dance, and then we both discovered that we were musicians. She majored in music, and I played the trumpet in the school orchestra and in a jazz combo. It wasn't my major. I was more interested in the sciences, in physics."

After taking a swig of her scotch, Christina leaned back and stared at the ceiling, indicating her boredom with this topic of conversation, and at that moment, Alma, with what appeared to be a sudden inspiration of emotion and breath, opened her mouth again, and what came out was a sound, this time steadily on one tone that, for all Brettigan knew, was probably A and not A-flat after all. This time, however, she held it for several seconds, longer than was really polite, and behind the sound of her voice was every emotion—passion, desperation, rage—that she'd been holding in for . . . who knew how long? Just when he thought she'd stop, she took another breath, and out came that note again, sustained, saturated with an indescribable emotion, and loud enough for the neighbors to hear it through the front screen door, and the neighborhood dogs, too, one of whom, from somewhere down the block, began to bark. It was as if she had reached the climax of an opera, a mad scene, of which she was the tragic heroine.

When Brettigan turned away, he noticed that both the dog and the cat had left the room, apparently wanting no part of what was about to happen.

"You wanted an A," Alma said, smiling in her triumph. "*That* was an A."

"I'd call it an A-plus," Ludlow said, shaking his head with enthusiasm. "Oh, man, that was crazy. Wowza. I didn't know that we were going to be at a party like this. You could really put that to practical use, you know. I mean, you could go out and round up all the strays and runaways and the homeless, you could go around singing your A or A-flat or whatever the fuck it was, and they'd cluster near you, just like that guy, the Pied Piper." He nodded with glee. "You could take people to their doom behind the mountain. That would be so cool."

"Darling," Brettigan said, obviously shaken, "please don't do that again."

"You could test me," Alma said, "just by going over to the piano and playing that A, the A above the staff. You'll see how accurate I was."

"No," Brettigan said. "I don't think so. Do you want another drink?" he asked Ludlow and Christina, as he stood up. Having apparently forgotten what he had just said, he walked over to the baby grand piano and lightly touched the A above the staff, and when he did, Alma nodded in triumph.

"You see?" she said. "That was the note. I hit it, didn't I?"

"Yes, please, another drink," Christina nodded, before closing her eyes. "God," she said, "there's really something to be said for bourgeois life. Right now, I feel so . . . *entitled.*"

"Me too," Ludlow said, holding up his martini glass. "Privileged." He smiled. "The thing I always forget about parties is that all the drinks and the food are free, just like you said."

"Dinner will be served in a momento," Alma told them, as she rose and smoothed down her apron, "in a few minutes, and, yes, it's free. No charge." Brettigan had taken their glasses into the next room and was busily refilling them. Everybody including himself was getting a little tipsy. "Ludlow," she said, turning to the boy, "I hope you won't mind if I ask you a few questions about something you said earlier. You were talking about a termite revolution. I don't think I understand what you mean. Am I a termite? And I really do want to understand. I think we're all trying to figure out how to live, what to do. Could you help us out?"

"Yes," Brettigan said from the other room. "Because we've been thinking about the internet stories, about the Sandmen, those goons who go around beating up the homeless, you know?"

"The Sandmen?" Ludlow asked. "Well, it doesn't matter. Besides, yes, I can tell you how I came to it. Because, here's the thing: what the Sun Collective is all about is *imagining a future.* We're not a religion because we're not praying to anything and because we don't want an apocalypse and the end of the world and all that. We want love and respect and kindness. And the thing about termites, about us, is that we're all the people who have been invisible to everybody else, all the submerged populations, and we're not just what Marx and everybody else called the 'proletariat,' because this isn't just an economic revolution of workers, doing factory jobs et cetera, because there aren't enough of those characters anymore, it's something else, it . . ."

"Yes," Brettigan said, coming into the room with more drinks. "What is it?"

Ludlow sat quietly, apparently thinking about what he would say. Brettigan handed Ludlow his second martini and noticed that the boy seemed to be both perplexed and slightly bedraggled by alcohol. He had the appearance of a loquacious character in Dostoyevsky who might fall off the chair and land on the floor, where he would have a seizure. Christina's hand had dropped back again onto Ludlow's thigh, seeming to take up residence there a few inches from his genitals, and she opened her mouth as if to help her boyfriend through this difficult logical puzzle, at which point he gazed toward the ceiling, and, following his own upward trajectory, stood, though for no particular reason. Christina's hand fell off his leg back into her lap.

"Termites," he said, "eat out the house from the inside. They don't knock it down. They undermine it. I mean, read our manifesto. We . . ."

"I *have,*" Brettigan said, having sat down again. "I have read it. You

believe in a more loving future, sharing everything you have com-
munally, not wasting the world's resources, getting rid of ideologies.
You're like the early Christian ascetics."

"No, we aren't," Ludlow said a bit too loudly, from where he was
standing. A fly flew over to his arm, and he irritably swatted it away.
Alma had retreated to the kitchen, and Brettigan could hear her putting the dishes on the table. Eventually this evening would come to an
end. "They thought the world was apocalyptoid. They believed that
the Kingdom of God was somewhere else. We think it's here, now."

"Oh, okay," Brettigan said, nodding. "I get it. What about the
microviolence? The microviolence in the manifesto?"

"I'll get to that," Ludlow told him. "Christina? Uh, Chris?" Christina appeared to be thinking or had fallen asleep: her eyes were closed,
and she had leaned back against the sofa's cushions, giving the impression that she didn't like the direction the conversation had taken and
would sleep through it until the talk arrived at a topic of her liking.
"She's dozing," Ludlow said. "She doesn't like it when I talk about
politics. She's talking on the Blue Telephone."

"I'm not asleep," Christina said, her eyes still closed, her head tilted
back. "I'm completely aware of everything that goes on. I can see
through my eyelids. You know, like a lizard? In fact, I know exactly
what's going to happen. I'm right here in the future. You're going to
tell the story of the guy whose life you saved, and when we get to the
table, Alma is going to tell a story, too. You see? The Blue Telephone
keeps me up-to-date on everything and has a call-in to what's about to
happen." She smiled, showing her front teeth, though her eyes were
still closed. Brettigan flinched slightly at the sight of her eyes-shut
smile. When she did it, she was both beautiful and homely.

"The blue telephone?" Brettigan asked, suddenly curious.

"Don't ask," Ludlow said. "It's a pill."

"It's more than a pill," Christina asserted. "I can assure you." She
waited. "It's a way of life. It bends time and space."

"Dinner is served," Alma called from the dining room. "Come
and get it."

As Brettigan herded the young couple toward the dining room, the sight of Ludlow and Christina together, along with the talk of the drug, produced a time-machine effect that transported him momentarily to a small farm in Wisconsin where he'd once lived for two months in a rural commune after graduation from Holbein College and before he'd entered graduate school. During that time, he'd been separated from Alma, who was then working in the Minneapolis Central Library. The two of them, Ludlow and Christina, were replicas of youngsters produced by that period, the late 1960s, weighed down with idealism and revolutionary intent and powerful illicit drugs, and he wondered, as the faint breeze from the past blew across his face, whether Christina and Ludlow were two contemporaneous incarnations of Alma and himself.

STANDING THERE, HE REMEMBERED THE CHURRING LOCUSTS ANNOUNCING the late-summer heat and invisibly clinging to the trees, as he remembered the telephone poles with their sagging wires leading away from the farm and following the county road down to the horizon flatly untroubled by hills. A tame crow whom they had named Bucky hung around the barn. Wind preceding a thunderstorm knocked the roof off the toolshed, and a bolt of lightning electrocuted the commune's mascot, Nelly, a goat. At times the place seemed under a curse. The farm spread itself out on just over one hundred acres, hardly enough for sustainability, and only one of its members (the one who'd grown up in Iowa) actually knew how to plant, cultivate and harvest, pack and sell the fruits and vegetables they grew. Their only real source of steady income was the U-Pick apple orchard alongside the driveway. In August, their car wouldn't start, and they couldn't afford to buy a new battery for it. They didn't know how they would get through the winter. Day after day, as the commune members grew poorer and more quarrelsome and sicker and hungrier, Brettigan watched the disappearance of their good intentions until, near the end of his stay, the beauty of their ideals, which had given them all an initial shine of attractiveness and energy and humor, turned to bad-tempered, moody despairs: no one was sleeping with anyone else; sex had become inconceivable, as had square meals; conversation had given way to remarks; and even the commune's dog, Lila, had run away.

He remembered their names: Opal, Sarah, and a girl who had once been Barbara but had renamed herself SkyAir; and Big Mike, Little Mike, and Ben, a former philosophy major who rarely spoke. Brettigan himself was not a charter commune member, just a visitor who had been tolerated because he was willing to work on their plumbing and wiring and had brought some money with him (he had befriended Little Mike at summer camp when they'd both been counselors a few years earlier). When Brettigan left, no one had bothered to say goodbye. He felt like a defector. He had had his first lesson in loving what people were trying to do without being able to love them as individuals.

And yet there had been moments now and then in the late afternoons and early evenings when he had finished his day's work and rested on the front porch's swing, and a peacefulness took him over, a calm spiritual ease that he had rarely, if ever, felt before in his life. A physical sensation, it began in his chest and moved outward. The churring of the locusts was like the pumping of blood through his veins and arteries. Somehow he knew that his heart brought him life and was a tree itself with roots and branches. No tasks pressed upon him; he had worked so hard all day that his face and hands were gritty with the evidence of his labor. All he had to do now was watch the red-winged blackbirds flying toward reeds surrounding the little pond out in back or listen to the sparrows under the eaves. In front of the house, the driveway, gray in dry weather and patched black with dirt after rain, went out to the county road, where the telephone poles traveled off lackadaisically toward the west horizon, and Brettigan thought that if he'd been a painter, he would have painted that driveway, making it beautiful, desolate, and calm, and he would put the telephone poles in the background as a reminder of distances. He would paint the peacefulness he felt. He understood the joy of inactivity. On that porch, Brettigan sat in the late afternoons with his glass of sun tea, his mind empty of anxious thought, and when the sparrows, who were used to him, flew down onto the edge of the porch, he would reach into his pocket for bread crumbs and toss them down. He was so inwardly calm, he was like St. Francis, and the birds knew it as they approached him.

In those moments, he felt the peace that passes all human understanding, and he thought: *This is what everybody wants. The Kingdom of God is on Earth.*

"IT'S CURRY," ALMA SAID, SEATING LUDLOW AND CHRISTINA ACROSS from each other, and Brettigan and herself at the two ends of the table. The guests sat and appeared to be surprised by the place settings, the candles at the table's center, the matching forks, knives, and spoons, and the folded cloth napkins, as if all this propriety were some kind of exhibit at a trade show.

"This is so pretty," Christina said, still with her eyes half-closed. "Where did you get all this?" she asked, apparently referring to the plates and the silverware.

"Wedding presents. And at the store," Brettigan said, lowering himself into his chair at the head of the table. "The store where they sell these appurtenances."

Christina nodded, while Alma flashed a don't-be-like-that and don't-say-those-words expression at her husband as she served the guests. "I hope you like curry," Alma said. "There's saffron rice and chutney and bread. And couscous. I used to serve this meal to guests—I suppose it's my travelogue meal."

"Were you ever in India?" Ludlow asked.

"No."

"Then how'd you learn to cook this?"

"Cookbooks and practice. And somebody showing me."

"Because it's really good," Ludlow told her, his mouth full, spraying several grains of rice down toward the saltshaker, the boy having started the meal before everyone else had been served. Brettigan watched with mingled admiration and horror as Ludlow daintily picked up two of the grains of rice from the now-stained tablecloth and popped them back in his mouth. Across from him, Christina seemed to be watching her boyfriend through those same half-closed eyelids; she gave off, Brettigan thought, an odd aura of timelessness and immobility. When he turned back to Ludlow, he saw his dinner guest wolfing down the chicken and rice and papadums like an orphan who was desperate to eat before anyone nearby snatched the food away from his plate. The young man's hunger had entirely eclipsed his good manners and deactivated his personality altogether. He ate like a peasant.

"So somebody showed you to do this?" Christina asked her. "Um, sorry. I meant anybody ever show you *how* to do this?" She giggled. "When I have a drink, sometimes I get confused. *I* know what I mean, but not everyone else does." Her speech subsided into a half-muttered whimper.

"Well," Alma said, "I can tell you in a minute, but, speaking of drinks, do you want anything more? The bar's still open."

Both Ludlow and Christina shook their heads slowly, and Brettigan noticed that his wife was relaxing into a storytelling mood that was expansive and rare for her, possibly from the effects of the alcohol that she had already consumed.

"When I was a young woman, right around the time I met him," Alma said, pointing toward Brettigan, "I had another friend, this guy whose parents had been diplomats. He'd been all over the world. India, Pakistan, Tunisia, Morocco. The hot weather countries. He loved them, he loved the people. He loved heat. Loved to sweat, made him feel alive. He went to their schools, this child of diplomats, and made himself a polyglot. Everywhere he'd been, he learned the language first, and then how to cook the local cuisine—curries and kebabs and merguez, asida and couscous. He was the first man I ever knew who could prepare food in a tagine, the first non-Arabic person I ever knew who could speak Arabic. He had a smattering of Hindi, too. He spoke so eloquently, even the pleasantries, in any language. He'd invite me over to his little apartment, and you could smell the spices from the sidewalk, kind of exotic for Minnesota, and then going up the stairs, you'd just be moonstruck by all the aromas he had cooked up and concocted. When you saw him in person, he was just *beclouded* . . . enveloped in those delicious . . . smells. He was almost succulent. You can't say that about a lot of men."

"He was never her boyfriend," Brettigan said.

"He was never my boyfriend," Alma affirmed, with a nod, "because by this time, *he* was"—pointing at her husband—"even though he was off at that commune in Wisconsin, and besides, the guy, this world traveler I'm talking about, had an attraction to me that was always kind of abstract and conceptual. It wasn't really physical. At that age, a woman wants a man who's a little bull with a ring through his nose who wants all of you, the whole package, all the time, and this guy, the tagine guy, wasn't like that. He was always one step away from you, just a little remote and ironic and removed and displaced. You know: adrift. I didn't like that. I had reservations about him as a man."

"Maybe his world travels had created that effect," Brettigan said.

"Yes, maybe his world travels had done that," Alma continued, "but you could never tell with him. Still, I . . ." She couldn't quite finish the sentence.

"You loved him, a little," Brettigan said, once again finishing her sentence for her, the words emerging like stones.

"I loved him a little. He would invite me over, and he would cook a wonderful dinner for me, dishes and preparations that were new to me, and in return, I would sing to him. Well, you know. That was the price I paid: singing. You pay the piper with a meal, a meal that's come straight to the dinner table from North Africa, well then, the piper plays for you. Among the languages he happened to speak was German. So I sang and played German songs to him, at the piano he had, this old broken-down spinet. 'Erlkönig,' songs like that. We were very high-toned in those days. German art songs. We were sick with culture, having gorged on it in college. Nothing but the best."

"'Mein Vater, mein Vater,'" Brettigan said, quoting Goethe's poem, "'und hörest du nicht—'"

"Oh, stop. This isn't school, but, yes, correct, that's the one." Alma nodded irritably again at her husband down at the other end of the table. Her two guests were now looking carefully at her. The story she was telling seemed to be treading down a weedy, overgrown path, with marital land mines nearby. Something, very subtly, was going wrong. "You have to forgive my husband. He likes to show off his German."

Brettigan kept his eyes on his plate. He had stopped eating by now.

"Well," said Alma. "The years passed, the calendar pages fell from the wall." She took a forkful of curried chicken, held it up to examine it, then put it down. "And I forgot about him, that boy who smelled of spices, though sometimes I would read about him in the college alumni magazine, one diplomatic posting after another, because, as time passed, he himself went to work for the State Department. Like his father, he'd gone into the diplomatic corps and had been sent to Egypt, stationed in Cairo, I think. Then countries in North Africa: years in Morocco with side trips now and then to Algeria. Did he also speak French? I don't remember."

"He did not speak French," Brettigan said, still studying his dinner plate. "That was a language that he did not speak. Odd, for a diplomat."

The room, despite their voices, seemed to have gone quite silent. "No, you're wrong. I think he did. And so the years passed," Alma continued, "and one day I received an email from him—oh, forgive me, I haven't told you his name, let's call him Stepan, Stepan-the-diplomat, and the email informs me that he's going to be in town for a meeting of former foreign service employees, though why these retirees would meet here in Minneapolis was a mystery then and now, but anyway they were going to gather together in one of the big hotels here, and he wondered if he could stop by on one of those days when he didn't have a meeting, catch up on old times, which caused me a bit of . . . *puzzlement,* because I wasn't sure what he was talking about, and I didn't actually feel that we shared old times, all we had had was a passing acquaintance that involved cooking and singing, nor was I inclined to tell him about my life if that talk was going to include conversation about family. About children."

Brettigan turned his head to see what Christina was doing: she had gone rigid, and her eyes had opened wide, and now she was staring at Alma fixedly.

"But I said okay, we could meet somewhere, perhaps a restaurant of his choosing, and he replied that, no, he'd prefer, for reasons that he would make clear eventually, to drop by here, at our house, this one, right *here,* a request which seemed unusual, a person inviting himself into a friend's house, but anyway we set up a time when we might have lunch, and Harold would be around, because after all Harold had known him in college, too, though I wouldn't have called them friends."

"No," Brettigan said, in the quiet that followed. "I wouldn't have said we were friends, Stepan and I." He smiled. "But not enemies, either."

"So," Alma said, pressing forward, "there came the day that we had assigned to ourselves when he would drop by, let's say for sandwiches, luncheon sandwiches for the diplomat, sandwiches free from their crusts. I had no idea what subjects we would find to talk about except for those memories of college umpteen years ago, and I couldn't imagine why he had . . . *Anyway,* I made some sandwiches ahead of time, and I brewed a big pot of Darjeeling tea, and I'd broken out some white wine and sherry in case he wanted either one of those, and I'd set up all these amenities by the time the hired car, one of those black hearse-like limousines, pulled up in front of the house, and Stepan got out from the backseat passenger side hardly able to walk, supported by his cane."

"He got out, supported by his cane," Brettigan repeated. "And his appearance . . ."

"His appearance," Alma said, almost simultaneously with her husband's last two words, "was enough to give you a chill. He looked *awful,* unrecognizable. He walked into the sunshine, this pale creature, this remnant. I wasn't sure it was him. *Was* it him? Really? For one thing, he was wearing a brown suit. You'd think a diplomat would have had better taste. Brown suits are bad enough—they have an almost inherent trace of cut-rate shabbiness and bad taste, but this one was a couple of sizes too large, like a brown suit draped over an unsuccessful scarecrow, which was exactly how he looked, a scarecrow in decline, but without a field, without crops to guard."

"Sparse hair standing up like hay," Brettigan remarked.

"Yes. And his white shirt, also too large for him, had a collar that went around his neck with space to spare, along with a bedraggled necktie with food stains on it, a heartbreaking effect."

Christina at last spoke up. "He was dying? Of what?"

"I shudder to think," Brettigan said.

"Please, Harry, for god's sake don't be like that. So. Up the sidewalk came my former friend, the retired, sickly diplomat with that cane beside him like the only companion he would ever have to lean on until he toppled into his grave, and when he saw me standing on the front steps, he held his arms wide as if for a hug, a gesture that must have been difficult for him, considering his bad balance, the cane et cetera. But he held his arms wide, as I said, in what I suppose you might call an invitation, which is how I read it, and so I descended the steps and took him in my arms, with Harry standing back there at the front door and smiling down at the two of us, I'm sure. And you know what? The man we're calling Stepan still smelled of those spices, of cumin and curry and cardamom. He had an odor of the world, and that was how I knew it was him."

Alma's eyes were beginning to fill with tears, though her face remained sociably neutral, a hostess expression.

"But it was like hugging a scarecrow too: nothing there but skin and bones. HIV, of course. We brought him inside and sat him down at this very table, and the sandwiches were brought out and offered, all of us getting through the awkward moments somehow, talking about current affairs or whatever it was and trying to pretend that what we were doing was normal, like an everyday lunch when one of the guests is only eating nibbles and crumbs, speaking in a croaking voice that sounded like a phone line to the tomb. And outside on the street, the children playing, and the sound of an ambulance in the distance, first coming and then going away. And the wind, too. The wind had picked up. You could hear it."

"He was quite sick?" Ludlow asked, breaking his own silence.

"So we ate our lunch. Well, I ate mine. He admired his but didn't bite into much of anything. The conversation began to flag. And then he managed to get to his feet and with his cane helping him, he went toward the fireplace mantel where we had some peacock feathers in a vase, and he turned around and said, 'Didn't you know? *Don't* you know? Peacock feathers in the house are bad luck. They're just *terrible* luck. Didn't anyone ever tell you? It's a curse to have peacock feathers inside the house.' And I said, no, no one had ever informed me of that. He returned to the table, having made his point about the peacock feathers. I threw them out later that afternoon."

"I wish you wouldn't tell this story," Brettigan said. "I wish you would just stop. Please stop."

"What? And then," Alma said, pushing onward, "as we neared the end of the lunch, he asked about Timothy, and I told him what I knew, this and that about his acting, and when I got to the end of my recitation, he stood up again and said that he had always wondered how a person should live, and he had never really been told truthfully what the secret was, and he wished someone had told him, he wished someone had told him how a person should live, now that he was *near the end of his time, the last roundup,* as he put it."

The little dots of sweat on Alma's forehead seemed to match, somehow, the little dots of moisture around her eyes, and if Brettigan noticed his wife's sorrowful hilarity, he gave no sign, having put down his fork and folded his hands into his lap.

"And you know what I told him?" Alma asked, first turning to her right to size up Christina's reaction, and then to her left, for Ludlow's. "This is exactly what I said. I said, 'The only entrance requirement for Heaven is that you must be so spiritually refined that you will never be bored once you get there. Because in Heaven nothing happens forever."

"You said that?" Christina asked, her mouth staying open, her eyes glistening.

"That's what I said. It just came to me. It just popped right out of my mouth."

"What did he say then?" Christina asked.

"He told me that I hadn't answered his question. And then he thanked both of us and wiped his mouth with his napkin and hobbled off toward the black hearse-like limousine that brought him here and that took him away."

DOWN THE BLOCK, SOMEONE'S CAR ALARM WENT OFF, AN INTERMITtent but regularly spaced set of horn honks that interrupted the silence at the table following Alma's story about Stepan the diplomat, the man who smelled of exotic spices. Brettigan resumed eating, satisfied that neither Ludlow nor Christina had spotted the unanswered questions in the center of his wife's story.

"I think I know what he was asking," Ludlow said confidently. "He wanted to know how to be a revolutionary when there's no revolution, nobody out there to tell us that we should change our lives. *But I have it all figured out.*"

"You do?" Christina asked suddenly, now fully awake, her eyes wide open.

"Yeah, I mean, for example, if there was one thing you were going to do to make this life on Earth better for poor people, what would it be? What would you do?" He studied his right hand. "How should a person live?"

"Guaranteed basic universal minimum income," Brettigan said, at the same time that his wife said, "Affordable housing. Urban ecology. Stewardship in every one of its forms."

"Oh, those solutions." Ludlow shook his head, an ironic smile, faintly condescending, aimed at his host.

"They aren't old," Brettigan told him. "They haven't been tried."

And at that moment Ludlow stopped eating and stood up, brushing bread crumbs and rice off his lap and straightening his blue-striped necktie over his T-shirt as if he had been led to the dais for an after-dinner presentation. He began speaking in a torrential jumble, and Brettigan, not understanding at first what the boy was saying, also couldn't be certain what had set the tirade off. This particular outburst couldn't have been caused by the drinks, because even alcoholic speech had a certain variety of logic that this verbal eruption lacked. He seemed instead to be blowing out words in a great propulsive rush, extruding them like steam escaping from the spout of a teapot. He gave the impression that if the words hadn't escaped from him, he might have exploded.

Gradually Brettigan put some of the fragmentary sentences together. You had to assemble Ludlow's phrases like jigsaw puzzle pieces or the contents of a do-it-yourself kit. Ludlow seemed to be saying that the country was being led by a craven, slippery fish of a man who was broadcasting and tweeting to promulgate a vulgar form of Supermanism in which the powerful exult in their power and are eager only to increase that power, never to share it, while the system, the one they all inhabited, was breaking down from power's unequal distribution and that it, the system, was not sustainable and everybody knew it, and that information was being ruthlessly privatized while computers tracked your every move, and the resulting current culture was greed-driven and murderous and racist and that the mythical Sandmen were not merely beating up the homeless vagrants living under freeway overpasses in the city, no, they were *killing* them in not hypothetical but actual economic pogroms and agendas of murder to eliminate the poor through liquidation, because, the Sandmen said—writing in their semi-secret hiding places on the internet—*the poor had only negative economic value* and therefore it was the duty of the high-spirited and proud producers of wealth to eliminate negative value, as Nietzsche had insisted, since life should only be lived in the plus column, and since the only morality the high-spirited producers of wealth recognized was power, joyful power and domination, tit-for-tat justice, the solutions of groups like the Sun Collective, he now recognized, were doomed to failure, poor passive creatures that they were, and so, Ludlow continued, still standing up, his necktie flapping against his chest, murder had to be answered with murder, and against the liquidation of the poor there would be commando squads, guerrilla groups, sent out to the suburbs, targeting the reptile rich, creeping up on them in their backyards as they bent over their propane-fired grills, where their marinated tenderloin steaks were being seared, or they would be found out as they bent over to attach their lawn sprinklers to green retractable garden hoses; they would be set upon as they planted their pansies and petunias in their mulched gardens or, clutching their sweating drinks, their Arnold Palmers, as they lay back on a waterproof chaise longue poolside; or, strolling out to the boathouse, thinking about Claude Monet's haystacks, they would be approached from behind, and it would be quick: throats cut, stabbings, garrotes, a form of violence such that the other reptilian capitalists would have the shit scared out of them, no wall would be high enough, no security would suffice, so that the formerly jolly plutocrats and oligarchs would no longer be capable of enjoying their markers and manifestations of wealth: the Waterford crystal, the Persian ponies munching imported oats in the stables, the Manolo Blahnik shoes positioned properly on canted shelves in the shoe closet, or the sun setting in a picturesque way on the Florida room: no, fear would grip the mansions of the rich; pain and anxiety and terror would begin to nest in their cookie jars and in the spice rack, and peace, the peace that money could buy, would be theirs no more.

And then the system would collapse.

"WELL, MY GOODNESS. YOU DON'T MEAN THAT," ALMA SAID, SMILING uncertainly at her dinner guests and worrying her napkin. She reached up to straighten her glasses. She patted her hair. Outside, the sun seemed to have set. "You're can't be saying what you're saying. That's not what the Sun Collective believes, not a word of it. And furthermore, I'm not sure I understood you. You seemed so placid until now. Peaceful. Just like a sheep, chewing grass. What brought this on? What do you mean? You can't mean what you said," she repeated, "that is, if I understood you correctly."

"What if I *do* mean that?" Ludlow replied, sitting down and looking very pleased with himself. "What if I've already started meaning that? What then?" He waited. "Will you join us? We mean business."

"This is why I hate politics," Alma retorted, glancing at her husband. "When someone says, 'Do you mean business?' the words always lead to murder, one way or another."

Meanwhile, Christina had straightened up, and what had started as a slow private smile had broadened to a radiant expression of love, or what might have passed for it. She reached over the table and touched Ludlow on his outstretched hand. "What happened to the story of the guy whose life you saved? What happened to *that*?" she asked. When Ludlow didn't answer her, she said, "You're a mess, but I love it when you get all revolutionary and homicidal in polite company. When you get that way, you're so transgressive. You're so beautiful, you could melt the furniture."

"So. Is that your idea of microviolence?" Brettigan asked Ludlow, lowering his fork to his plate. "Killing rich people in the suburbs? That's absurd. It's just plain nuts. What's the matter with you?" The air seemed to be thickening in the room, Brettigan noticed, making it hard to breathe, now that the conversation had turned to political murder. Everywhere you went, people seemed to want to talk about that very thing. The late-summer breezes carried a whiff of homicide everywhere. People were signing up for death cults.

Murder was in the air. Everybody wanted to get into the act. No one wanted to miss out. Even President Thorkelson had been recommending murder, in a joking manner.

Gazing at Brettigan, Ludlow said, "Come on. Please. Don't say you haven't thought about it. Don't say you've never had murder in your heart. It's a subject that interests everyone. The Great Terror. Well. We have to go," he announced to Christina, who nodded submissively. They rose together on cue and joined hands. Christina, seemingly remembering that good manners define character, thanked Alma for the meal, and then, without any other expression of gratitude or farewell but saying that they would skip dessert, the two of them headed for the door.

·   ·   ·

ACROSS THE TABLE, BRETTIGAN AND HIS WIFE STARED AT EACH OTHER with the expressive blank looks of longtime partners as, through the doorway, the dog and the cat padded in, now satisfied that the guests were gone. The animals sat expectantly in the corner, waiting for the next show. The dog, who was more compassionate than the cat, seemed worried, however, almost agitated; the cat's expression was one of smug amusement. At last Alma sighed. "All those good intentions we once had," she said in a trembling voice, "and yet the fuse has been lit."

"The fuse had always been lit," Brettigan said. "The fuse is eternal. So is the bomb it's attached to."

"No, Harry, you're wrong. They . . ." She seemed to forget her own thought. "I think what happened was, we invited murderers into the house. Sweet-looking murderers. And then we gave them dinner. And they ate it."

"It's their world, not ours, you know," Brettigan said, walking over to the space behind her chair. He put his hands on her shoulders and massaged her gently. "We don't have much of a say."

"I've loved this world so much," she said. "I hate to see it end."

"Young people take over the world. It's what they do. The kids inherit everything. You get old, you lose your vote."

"Do you think . . . do you think they'll let *us* live?"

"For a while."

"I want to see what happens next."

"I know you do," he said. "Everyone does. Well, at least the dinner was good. Delicious. Thank you."

"You think so?"

"Yes."

"I worked on it for a long time. Preparing. Chopping."

"I know. But they didn't eat your rhubarb pie."

She turned and tilted her head. "No, no, they aren't," she said, in response to something.

"What?"

"Oh, just a little telepathy. My usual." She pointed at the dog.

"Woland just told me that those two kids were bad people, and I said that, no, they weren't, not really. Despite the plans. No worse than we were, at that age. Full of ideas and big plans."

"The dog is a good judge of character."

She sighed. "Yes, I'm afraid he is."

"Do you want to go to bed? I can clean up."

"Oh, maybe I'll read for a while. You don't have to wash all these dishes."

"No, it's all right. I'm happy to do it. It gives me a chance to think."

"Think about what?"

His hands stilled on her shoulders. "What I should do. And whether I should do it."

"Harry, don't leave me."

"I won't. You think I would?"

"I'm a little frightened."

"Oh, don't worry. I'll be right here, doing the dishes. Well, I mean: at the sink. The kitchen."

"Don't run off."

"Why would I ever do that? I can't run at my age. Besides, where would I run to?"

"I just had a fear, that's all."

"Everyone has a fear," Harry Brettigan said.

"Mine is worse than everyone's."

Near the doorway, the dog made a sound like coughing.

"Do you think about Timothy?" he asked.

"Oh, sure." She waited. "Because he's out there somewhere."

"He'll come back to us. I'm sure of it."

"I know," she said. "But who will he be when he returns?"

19

SLOWLY, FROM THE CORNERS OF THE NEWSPAPERS AND APPARENTLY AS afterthoughts on the broadcast news, came scattered reports that some deaths described as "mysterious" had recently befallen the citizens of the wealthiest west suburb of Minneapolis. One investment banker had been impaled when he'd fallen or stumbled onto the gnomon of his backyard sundial. Another, a VP in charge of international relations at a privately held grain milling company, had died when his high-end crossover vehicle had slipped out of park and rammed into him as he had tried to unstick the frozen lock to his gated community. Still another, a graduate of Vassar and Harvard Law, had drowned after having been tossed into the water when her sailboat, during a regatta, had turned about unexpectedly, and the boom had knocked her overboard. She had not been wearing a life preserver, and her boat had sailed on without her. There were instances of food poisonings at salad bars, strains of E. coli traced to the Bibb lettuce, and anomalous asphyxiations caused by cars left running in closed garages. A retiree had drowned in her five-inch-deep serenity pool; a CEO had had a fatal encounter with a band saw while making a small display case for his jade and ivory carvings; and a matron known for her garden club activities had had a fatal accident when, barefoot, she had switched on her electric treadmill, the one with faulty grounding.

No malicious intent was assumed to be the source of these calamities, but the citizens of Wayswater collectively grew doubtful and pensive, and when the chief financial officer of Intaglio Bank Corp was struck by lightning on the green of the eighth hole at the Wawa-tosa Country Club (after raising his putter to the skies in triumph) and another vice president for international corporate relations had choked on his cocktail, a Bootleg—"Minnesota's signature drink"—in the Wawatosa Country Club bar, the *Wayswater Gazette* ran a head-line story about the apparent epidemic of misfortune afflicting the well-to-do. In the story, the reporter quoted a citizen as saying that accidents seemed accidental when there were a few of them, but when there were this many, a multitude of accidents, they didn't seem accidental anymore. They seemed to be planned. Wherever a plan exists, there must be a cause.

"What do the gods have against us?" one man asked the reporter. "Who or what is behind this?" On the internet, in a subreddit devoted to the subject of the epidemic haphazard deaths in Wayswater, anon-ymous contributors theorized that the citizenry of the town had been drugged, somehow, and were in a collective stupor. Another argued that the God of Righteousness had been punishing the rich and prof-ligate, the worshippers of the Golden Calf. Still others claimed that distraction caused by iPhones had led to a kind of massive attention deficit disorder. A disgruntled Marxist prophesied in *Town and Coun-try Pages* that what had happened to Wayswater would soon hap-pen to Greenwich, Connecticut, and Westport, and Palo Alto, and Scottsdale, and the Hamptons: "They have it coming," his irony-laced article asserted (later he claimed that he'd been joking—everybody seemed to be emulating the Joker). Others editorialized that the vic-tims were privileged white people, so who cared? And one anony-mous contributor argued that a small group of anarchists, the Sun Collective, noted for their hatred of the rich, must be the ones pulling invisible strings behind the curtain. A spokesman for the group, a Mr. Wyekowski, denied this particular accusation.

"We have nothing against the rich," he said, in a printed statement. "We have nothing against anybody. Everyone is a child of light."

And that was the end of it for a while.

· · ·

FOLLOWING THE DINNER FIASCO WITH LUDLOW AND HIS GIRLFRIEND, Alma was determined to cheer up her husband when his birthday arrived in four days. He deserved it; as he aged, he had grown more, rather than less, lovable. He'd become sweet and distracted. He needed kisses just to get by. He didn't like presents or gifts generally, claiming that he had more than everything he needed; every object was a burden, a weight on the soul, and after all what did he look like—a king who required tribute? She was determined to get something for him anyway. He deserved *something*. Perhaps a shirt. A plain patterned shirt, short-sleeved, for summer. He might like that.

Parking her car in a downtown lot, Alma took an escalator up to the Minneapolis Skyway and began walking through its corridors toward a shirt outlet-store. Built above the city streets and connecting one building to another, the Skyway always reminded Alma of those plastic tunnels constructed for hamsters, Habitrails or whatever they were called. All the professional-managerial people did their business up here, coatless in winter, laughing at the weather conditions outside, and rarely deigning to descend to the sidewalks below, where the street-creeps bided their time selling drugs, asking for handouts, spitting on the pavement, foraging in the trash cans, and in general making a nuisance of themselves. Sidewalks were for losers and junkies, the Skyway for the gentry. It hadn't been intended that way, but that was how it had worked out.

And there they were, the gentry, in front of her, striding forward, their corporate ID tags hanging by alligator clips to their pockets, beautiful and young, smiling forcefully, raucously alert, sexy and fragrant, while below, on the street, a hatless man sat at the corner with his derby upside down for passing change, and his cardboard sign— **HOMELESS ANYTHING WILL HELP GOD BLESS**—on display out in front of him. Alma stopped to look at him through the plate glass. He had the characteristic slumped posture of the truly forlorn. Gazing up, he saw her standing there in the Skyway studying him, and he winked at her and waved his hand in a festive manner. Panhandlers, those Morlocks, weren't allowed up in the Skyway, which was private property devoted to the Eloi. She waved back at him, trying not to smile or to be pointlessly cheerful. Some Chopin piano music—she couldn't remember which piece—was going through her head, an earworm, ta-ta-ta-tum-ta. She frowned, dropped her hand, and continued walking.

Somehow, somewhere, she had picked up her husband's obsession with the poor, along with his inability to know what to do about them, which in turn was accompanied by the conviction that if no action were taken to help them, the omission would be at the cost of one's immortal soul. Maybe the Sun Collective knew what a person should do. She liked having found them. She liked their earnestness. Well, after all, that was what political action was for, devising strategies for public well-being. None of it had seemed personal until her son had dropped off the radar screen and had taken to living in the streets, or rented rooms, or whatever space it was that he occupied now. Otherwise, she might not have cared so much; she might have been like everybody else, blithely planning dinner parties, trips to the south of France, to the Dordogne, acquiring more kitchen accessories.

Studying a Skyway storefront display window, she picked out an attractive and vaguely nautical shirt patterned with intersecting blue-and-red horizontal and vertical lines, but when she went inside to check its price, the salesperson told her that they didn't have that particular item in her husband's size, though they could order it. She thanked him and headed back out to the Skyway again, going north, where the passage led her away from the piped-in music, an instrumental version of "My Way." In this section, the background noise consisted of a low, throbbing hum. She was beginning to feel slightly lost. Some of the windows here had been boarded up, and she didn't recognize the structure she had entered. Thinking that another men's clothing store was located on the other side of the old Commercial Exchange Building, she proceeded in that direction, but when she did so, she found herself in a corridor of the Skyway she didn't recognize and where no other pedestrians accompanied her. The passageway had an abandoned, distressed appearance, sorrowful somehow, like a dream-hallway proceeding to an antechamber that in turn led to a rather specific nowhere where terrible outcomes were likely to occur. In the air was a distant scent of lemony cleaning fluid. The hum intensified, and Alma thought she heard someone weeping in the distance. A doorway opened automatically in front of her, giving the impression that it had been patiently waiting for her, and she found herself in another dimly lit corridor with forest green wallpaper, with shapes meant to resemble the leaves of trees, maples and elms, behind which, here and there, incongruously appeared the floating faces of circus clowns advertising a clinic for children, now closed. A dead potted plant whose black, brittle leaves sagged toward the floor had been abandoned in the corner.

On the wall to her left was a corporate logo shaped like a parallelogram whose lines ended with arrows pointing to the left and right, up and down. Below it was the single word *QitterCo,* and below that on the floor, in front of her, on all fours like a beast, was a human shape, someone groaning, smelling of excrement, moving forward. The shape turned its head to look at her. It was barefoot, wearing soiled blue jeans and a torn T-shirt, or pajama top, with several yellow spotted stains. The man's hair stood up in all directions like pins in a pincushion. For a single instant, shocked into blank fear, Alma thought that the human being down there on all fours was associated in some way with QitterCo, an employee managing a complicated prank, a thought that she recognized a moment later as crazy. Out of the creature's mouth came a growl or a groan, and, without thinking, Alma turned and fled in the direction from which she had come.

A few moments later, without knowing how she got there, she found herself down on street level at the light rail stop. At the corner stood two policemen, their bulletproof vests beneath their blue shirts artificially thickening their chests. She approached them, but as soon as she tried to explain what she had just seen, a man on all fours in the Skyway, she found herself unable to say what she meant. The sight had been unspeakable. The cops looked at her with the skeptical, appraising expressions characteristic of their profession, and at that moment the train heading for the Utopia Mall arrived, and the doors opened, and Alma found herself backing up until she was inside one of the cars.

The exterior of the train, sheathed in translucent advertising, gave the light a brownish blue cast, so that the backs of her hands, folded in her lap, seemed mottled and bruised. In the seat two rows in front of her a woman was speaking aloud to the air; then Alma saw the woman's Bluetooth earbud. The woman said, "Yes," then, more firmly, "No," then, "That's an exaggeration. I've never done that willingly. And I sure won't do it with you."

And what was that woman referring to, the unspecified action she had never done willingly? These overheard conversations tormented Alma, since she regarded herself as a person with a natural curiosity about the human species, someone who had been around the block a few times and was not easily shocked, but she felt herself shaking still from the sight of the crawling man in a remote part of the Skyway, so that the cityscape passing by outside the window—a paint factory, a colossal football stadium in the shape of a Viking ship, a biker bar with multiple Harleys parked outside—seemed like a stage set for a play that she had entered after the first act was over and all the essential information had been laid out. She felt a residual trembling.

For a single moment, she had the sensation that her life had been lived behind a screen and not sheltered, exactly—she had her family, after all—but artfully mismanaged and too carefully guarded from the base realities on the other side of the curtain.

From inside her purse, her phone rang. She could never get used to the new technologies, and whenever the iPhone began its tiny impish xylophone chiming, she startled. Reaching in and pushing aside a hankie, her change purse, a tube of lipstick, and a ticket stub for some past concert or other, she finally managed to grasp the phone and pull it out.

When she answered, she heard her daughter, Virginia, saying, "Mom?"

"Oh, hello, dear," Alma said. "How nice that you called. I'm on the light rail. I'm going out to the mall to get your father a birthday present. A shirt. How are you? How are the kids?" She knew she must sound breathless and distracted.

"Mommy, are *you* all right?" her daughter asked, with the light, recently acquired southern accent that Alma could never get used to.

"Yes. Why do you ask?"

"I don't know," her daughter said. "I mean, this morning I was at work, and this *thing,* I don't know what all to call it, this *event* concerning you hit me, and I thought: *I gotta call my mommy.* I cain't tell you what the thing is. I just knew I had to call you from the hospital." Alma's daughter was a veterinarian.

"Well, if you were worried that I had died, I haven't. That's very nice, that you called." She decided not to tell her daughter about the creature on all fours in the Skyway. "The fact is, I'm all right. How are the children?" Alma braced herself for her daughter's report, which would be, as it always was, a summer rain shower of beautifully sweet clichés, interrupted by odds and ends of southern locutions that Virginia had picked up after several years of living in North Carolina, just outside of Asheville. She and her husband, Robert, had two children: Bobby Jr., a red-haired boy, eight years old, and Sally, four years old, whose nickname was "Goobie." Alma saw her grandchildren two or three times a year, and they talked to her via Skype every week or so. Alma loved her adult daughter in a slightly absentminded way, and she admired her daughter's solid husband, a high school biology teacher, and she loved the two grandchildren without any effort or strain, although it nagged at her that they were all so ordinary, so normal, so lovely and fine; with such a surfeit of blandness, you almost didn't know what to say to them or about them. You didn't have to intervene with help and succor. You just had to skate conversationally back and forth on the surface of their pleasantries.

Two years after getting married, Virginia had had a four-month affair with another veterinarian in the clinic, with whom she had fallen in love when she saw him gently examining a cat. Ecstatic, prideful, weeping when not giddy, she had called her mother to confess, and later, to confess again, apparently believing that she wasn't the sort of person who went to motels in the afternoon to have sex, even though that was exactly what she had been doing. Having sex was bad enough. What was worse was that she enjoyed it; she admitted as much to her mother. She was burning up with it. "Sheer bliss," she told Alma, who had never heard her use that noun before. Alma thought it peculiar that her daughter would confide in her on such a private manner. She would have never done so herself in Ginny's place. Whatever had happened to discretion, to secrets? She herself had hundreds of them.

During those calls Alma had tried not to be judgmental and had done her best to comfort her daughter. Alma knew the affair would end fairly quickly, and it did. Love like that didn't have much staying power. Virginia's magnanimous husband forgave her, and together they got on with life. Given her temperament and her love of gentility, Virginia would never again get carried away by love or the fundamental animal passions. Secretly, very secretly, Alma wished that her daughter's flame would burn a bit brighter and hotter than it usually did, and she was touched that Virginia's heart had been broken that one time by love-mania. To be fully human, Alma thought, you have to have been heart-singed. For that brief period, Virginia didn't speak in clichés. Now she did, again, in rubbishy little phrases. Still, she had always been a low-temperature child and no trouble at all; it was Virginia's brother, Timothy, whose flame never cooled; he was the family's fever carrier.

"I tell you what," her daughter began. "Bobby here's been a holy terror lately, kind of ripping up around the house without any reason except to attract attention and, you know, to get a rise out of people and create a mess and scenes, but, bottom line, he's got a heart of gold, that boy. I don't know what bed he got out of the wrong side of these past few days, though, I surely don't. Still and all the other day he told me that when he grows up he wants to be a minister of God. So I asked him in what church, and he says the Church of Jesus. He says he knows already that he'll someday be able to perform miracles and bring corpses back from the dead, fresh as babies, full of that new-car smell. What ambition! He'll be faith healing in no time. I do wonder how he's going to practice his miracles, though. And on who. Goobie's got that new stuffed silver unicorn you sent, just takes it everywhere she goes. Last night she sang to her daddy when he came home from work, just the sweetest 'You Are My Sunshine' you ever heard, accompanied by her music box, which is broken a little. They're fine. We're all fine. But something's going on. I mean how come I was sure something happened to you this morning? I had this strong premonition like a ghost was talking to me. Oh, I just remembered. Will you wish Daddy a happy birthday for me?"

The light rail had almost arrived at the Utopia Mall. When the sun fell all over Alma's face, she turned toward it. *Ah, Sunflower, weary of time, who countest the steps of the Sun. I'm that sunflower,* she thought. Always have been. Just opposite her, a pale, stumpy passenger with an insolent expression was staring at her. She had to be brief. "Oh, well," she explained to her daughter, "I had a bit of a shock this morning, just a little confrontation with a . . . panhandler, that's all, one of those heartbreaking hopeless cases, but it's so sweet of you to call to check on me. I worry so about your brother."

"Tim? Of course you do. But, you know, he sends postcards. To me and the kids."

"Postcards?"

"Yeah. And he calls sometimes."

"He *calls?"*

"Yes, Mom, he does. I've told you this before. He's not a missing person, he's a found person. He's finding himself."

"Well, he doesn't call us, your father and me."

"He can't. He needs his space, I guess, for just now. Tim's kinda unique. With him, they broke the mold, broke it in half, lost the other half."

"Is he all right? Coping?"

"Oh, sure. Mom, I gotta go. I've got an appointment in five minutes with a Dalmatian who's got a broken leg. Anyhow, Tim's a survivor. He'll show up on your doorstep one of these days, no kidding, bright and cheerful, safe and sound. He will. You can kill the famous fatted calf when that happens, I promise. He says he's been researching life."

"Researching life? He's not in trouble?"

"Oh, no. No more than you are. No more than me. He's just adventuring, going places, doing things. I'm glad you're okay, Mom. I was a tad worried. Listen, I've sent Daddy a birthday present, and I'll call him on his birthday, okay? I love you, Mommy."

"And I love you, Ginny."

With the call ended, Alma collected herself, stood up, and headed into the mall from the train platform. When in the past had Virginia ever told her that Timothy was "adventuring" around the country, or wherever he was, as she claimed? Alma had the abrupt sensation—it wasn't a thought so much as a feeling—that her son was everywhere and nowhere on the planet, and he might be, at this very moment, observing her in a scientific study whose purpose was to profile the behavior of mothers who had lost or misplaced their adult sons and daughters.

Or maybe she was being told important information and was forgetting it, day after day. The thought made her shiver inwardly.

Rising on the escalator into the first-floor shopping area, she observed the other consumers headed in the same direction as her own, and she noted how, once they reached the top of the moving stairway, they hurried off unsteadily, already intoxicated with a longing to acquire something that they didn't yet have or hadn't even known existed until they would see it for the first time, at which point they would desire it. For them the Utopia Mall was a carnival of consumable wonders. It just took you away, made you forget yourself. The shoppers were obeying an instinct, like insects eating their way through a leaf. Ahead of her, an obese ponytailed woman in sweatpants and a T-shirt, holding hands with her daughter, waddled off in the direction of a department store. On the back of the T-shirt were the words

BEER

*It's not just
For breakfast
Anymore*

I shouldn't be such a snob, Alma thought, straightening up and dusting herself off, catching a few hairs from Woland and Behemoth in between her fingers. *I'm no better than anyone else here,* she said to herself. *I'm as off-kilter as they are.*

She passed an audio store, Unbound Sound, in whose window was a statue of Prometheus, wearing headphones. Inside, someone was playing a recording of Stravinsky's *Firebird,* the sad parts. Ahead of her, near a corner of the mall, was some sort of commotion: in the middle of the walkway, a wild-eyed man with a widow's peak was shouting with lunatic conviction and ferocity about Death Squads. What Death Squads? *They've started the killing,* he was saying, *they've started on vagrants and street people, and they've got an agenda set by the Eclipse Global Group, which hired people called the Sandmen, and they're planning to liquidate the rest of the poverts, all of them, using gangs of robots and drones. It's a War on Poverty where they actually kill the poor!* but at that moment three security guards arrived on the scene and hauled the bearded man away, advancing through an exit door that Alma hadn't realized was there. The wall had opened to a secret passageway and absorbed all four of them before closing and becoming a wall again. As soon as the door shut behind them, the shouting stopped, and the mall's customary bustle, its casino tumult, resumed.

Alma's legs took her into a store, Shirtz-and-Shooz!, where the salesclerk led her toward a selection of what she remembered had once been called, in another era, "dry goods." Collared shirts in joyful colors were lined up on a counter in soldierly array. Still feeling slightly dazed, she asked the clerk, a young man with a disarmingly angelic face with one perfectly placed dimple, whether he had heard the man outside shouting and speechifying.

"No, ma'am," he said, shaking his head and chuckling. "They don't let them do that here. It's illegal."

"Excuse me?"

"You can't do that here," he repeated. "Public speaking. Editorializing. They put a stop to it in no time flat."

"Put a stop to what?"

"Free speech. This is private property. You try to speak up, they'll take you away, never to return. You have a thing to say, you gotta go somewhere else to say it, like in the middle of the highway or the street corner on your soapbox. Now here's a nice shirt," he said, holding up one with a pattern of vertical lines. "What'd you say your husband's size was?"

"Fifteen and a half, thirty-three," Alma said, the words coming out of her mouth automatically. The angel-clerk nodded. The day seemed to be made up of one tectonic earthquake after another, and the angel seemed to be conscious of it all and able somehow to live with the tremors and the shivering beneath his feet. Well, some people could tolerate poison by taking little doses of it day after day, increasing the dosage until they had an immunity. Then Alma was clutching a patterned shirt and paying for it at the counter with her credit card. Following her purchase, which was nestled in a Shirtz-and- Shooz! carrying bag, she drifted on automatic pilot back to the light rail, where she took a seat before the doors chimed shut.

A man wearing a trilby hat walked down the aisle toward her. He was conventionally well-dressed in a three-piece suit, and he carried a pointed umbrella with a carved mallard's head for a handle. He had the appearance of someone on a stage, a character actor. He wore glasses, but some property in the lenses concealed his eyes behind them, giving him the appearance of a well-tailored rabbit. Or maybe a bug: Alma couldn't decide. After sitting down on the other side of the aisle from Alma, lifting up the crease in his trousers in an old-fashioned gesture, he settled himself and blew his nose with a handkerchief that had popped up spontaneously from the pocket of his sport coat. He nodded in her direction as if to confirm that they were two of a kind, recognizable people-of-quality and identifiable as such to each other. He then lightly doffed his hat to her before gazing down at her shopping bag. The duck's head umbrella was propped up to his right and angled so that the duck was looking at Alma.

"I see," he said, in a light southern accent, in its gentility very different from Ginny's broad drawl, "that you have made certain *purchases*." He smiled companionably.

Alma nodded. "A shirt," she volunteered. "For my husband."

"And what, if I may be so bold as to ask, would be the occasion of this particular gift?"

"It's his birthday. Two days from now."

"Aha." The man nodded agreeably. "What I have always liked about birthdays," the man said, "is not the acknowledgment of aging but the validation of the wish, any wish at all, prior to the blowing out of the candles. Every wish is an investment in the future. As we all know, the person whose birthday it is can extinguish the candles on the cake and make a wish. But these conditions are *not* the most propitious ones to make a wish come true. There are other, much more powerful means." He paused for effect. "They are not well known," he confided to her in a near whisper.

Oh, God, he's going to be one of those types, thought Alma, *those talkative characters you run into on buses and airplanes and passenger trains, those people with demonic agendas, and theories and conspiracies expressed in a cloud of terrible, toxic bad breath reeking of wine and the despairs.*

"Well," Alma asked, as the train's doors closed, "what conditions are you thinking of? How does a person make a wish come true?"

"It pleases me that you have asked me that question," the man said, reaching into the other sport coat pocket and withdrawing a business card from it, which he then passed across the aisle to Alma, who, at the moment she grasped the card, felt a headache like a bolt of vertical lightning instantly streak through her brain before it vanished as quickly as it had appeared.

DR. ARVER L. JEFFERSON, M.D.

PSYCHOANALYTIC AND
ASSOCIATED THERAPIES

Member: Midwest Institute of Proton-Analytics

"What are proton-analytics?" Alma asked. "I've never heard of them."

"Very few people know how to make a wish come true," the doctor informed her confidently, "unless they convert the wish into a prayer, but I am happy to pass on the secret to you as long as you are willing to believe in me."

"Believe you?"

"Believe *in* me," the doctor corrected her.

"Like Jesus? All right. Sure."

"Here is what you do," the doctor said, growing suddenly agitated and sitting up straight. "First, you must shut off the clocks and cover the mirrors in your house with clean cloth. Recently washed bedsheets will work perfectly well as long as they camouflage the images. And then—and this is the hard part—you must cut off *two* of your eyelashes with a pair of small scissors, just so, and place those *two* eyelashes on the back of your hand, and when eleven minutes past eleven in the morning comes—and you will have to make a good guess about the time, because your clocks will be stopped—you must make your wish. I give you my personal guarantee that this technique will work. There is literature to this effect among my people. It is proven. It is so."

"Well," Alma said, "I imagine there's no harm in trying."

"Indeed not," the doctor affirmed. "The wishes that we make for others are the most effective ones of all the major types. A wish in that form constitutes a prayer to the all-powerful and all-consuming power of love, which coils within the membrane that interfuses all things and provides us with the spark of divinity. I pledge this truth. Now can you tell me," the doctor asked, "what form such a prayer will take? *What is your wish?*"

"I thought a person wasn't supposed reveal that."

"You can tell me." He smiled at her. "After all, I'm a doctor."

"All right," said Alma, suddenly emboldened. "I want everyone I love to be safe."

The doctor settled back in his seat. "That is exemplary," he said, "though it is slightly conventional." With his right hand on the umbrella, he thrust his arm forward twice, giving the impression that the duck was nodding in agreement. "I don't suppose one can expect originality when it comes to wishes. All the same, yours has the virtue of being honorable."

"Who cares if it's honorable?" Alma said. "All I want is for all the people I love to be safe and to be cared for, and I'd wish that for everybody, even though I'm quite aware that that's too much for any one person to ask." She closed her eyes and began to weep quietly and unobtrusively. "I want everyone I love to be safe," she blubbered. Outside, the landscape passed in a descending rattle of click-clacks from the rails underneath the train. Now they had stopped at the Veterans Administration hospital. A bearded Iraqi War veteran on crutches hobbled out of the train car. It had been one of the most upsetting days of her life. Dear God, where was her son Timothy on this Earth? And why was he hiding from her? The wooden mallard leaned down to watch her tears fall.

 Part Four

20

LYING IN BED ON THE MORNING OF HER HUSBAND'S BIRTHDAY, WHICH had dawned with a racket of song sparrows warbling outside the bedroom window, Alma watched the ceiling fan rotating slowly, and she remembered the evening a few weeks ago when she had flipped on the light switch and had seen a bat circling the fan's moving wooden blades. Feeling no particular alarm, she had shut the bedroom door, opened a window, popped the screen, and left the room, hoping that the poor winged creature, the Fledermaus, would depart through the window into the night, which it eventually did. In the meantime, the opportunistic mosquitoes had flown in and for the next few hours had buzzed her ears while she was trying to sleep, her husband tossing back and forth restlessly beside her. She'd never been frightened of bats or mice, but she had a deep, intractable fear of spiders that a reading of *Charlotte's Web* years ago to her children had done nothing to diminish. You couldn't choose your fears, after all.

Once at the outdoor courtyard of a museum in Arkansas, she'd seen a Louise Bourgeois sculpture, *Maman,* representing a giant spider thirty feet high, with tennis-ball-size eggs held in an ovular cage underneath her, the most frightening artwork she'd ever seen in her life.

Her husband, lying next to her and pretending to sleep, did not like elevators and as a young man would climb up several flights of stairs rather than get on one. The dog hid under the bed during thunderstorms. The cat, like many of its kind, was aquaphobic. Virginia hated to fly on airplanes and usually drank several martinis before she had to go anywhere. She'd show up at the baggage claim area tottering back and forth as she peered at the suitcases with a drunken smirk. "A successful flight," she would say, "is one that does not crash."

Only Timothy had no fears. As a boy he'd climb any tree, talk to any stranger, ride any vehicle, skateboard down any incline and try any jump, and throw himself in front of anything powerful, animate or inanimate, that got in his way. He had advanced rapidly in the martial arts, particularly tae kwon do. He was fierce and loved fighting. Once, visiting the Pacific Ocean with his parents, he had thrown himself at the waves as the waves, in turn, threw him down. Again and again, he would stand, half-drowned and happy, like an adolescent sea god, and rush back into the surf. If you had a brave son, you had to do all the worrying for him.

Now in bed under the rumpled covers, Alma turned toward her husband, the birthday boy. Filtered by the venetian blinds, the sun threw thin strips of parallel light onto the rumpled bedsheets, and the morning light rose, ladderlike, into dust-flecked air. Today, probably before either of them rose out of the bed, the two of them still in their pajamas, she would have to tell him that Virginia had been getting postcards and phone calls from Timothy. The postcards signified that Timothy was okay, maybe even thriving. He just wasn't anywhere in particular. For them, he wasn't locatable. He had chosen to be nowhere to them.

His absence from their lives had a quality, Alma thought, of simmering rage that children sometimes felt toward their parents when a grievance couldn't be spoken aloud or even described. But what was the grievance? Despite his fearlessness, or because of it, he'd always been a fierce, agreeable boy. But somewhere down in the depths of his soul, he harbored a certain homegrown, undifferentiated rage. That must be it.

Now, in bed, with a chickadee singing outside—*phee bee, phee bee*—each time sounding out the descent of a minor third in notes way up there above the staff, Alma flinched involuntarily, thinking of her own carefully planned cruelties as a young woman. Her misbehavior had been decades ago, and she still flinched. *That's very odd,* she thought.

Well, everybody's past was often dark with malice and error, and in youth those feelings are usually directed at the nearest target, the parents.

So what had she and her husband ever done to Tim to make him invisiblate himself?

Her husband tossed on his side of the bed. What time was it? A few minutes before seven. "Are you awake?" she asked him softly.

It was a trick question. Without turning or opening his eyes, he said, "I'm always awake. You know that. I never sleep." His eyes shut, he rolled over to face her and put his familiar hand on her shoulder almost as if the move were involuntary, done without thinking. He gave off the scent of the dreams he'd been having: she knew him so well, she could almost enter his dreams as a tour guide. One of his persistent delusions was that he had a murderer's psyche. She had told him many times that his dream-homicides were fallacious and products of his vanity: he was completely harmless, an appraisal that he did not like.

"Happy birthday," she whispered.

"Thanks." He didn't sound grateful.

"How old are you, little boy?" she asked, mussing his hair a little.

"One hundred and two years old," he said, "give or take a few decades. As old as Methuselah."

"I thought it was a hundred and three. But you don't actually look your age. You don't look a day over a hundred."

"Thanks. I owe it all to the baths I take in formaldehyde."

"There's something I have to tell you," she said, feeling the weight of his hand and grateful that his eyes were still closed. "I talked to Ginny. She said her brother's been sending her postcards. Tim even calls her sometimes. Can you imagine that? They *chat*. So I guess he's not gone and disappeared after all."

"I never thought he *had* disappeared," Brettigan told her. After a pause, he said, "*He* always knew where he was. *We* just didn't. Besides, I think I saw him a little while ago. I just never told you."

She let that information settle in as she decided whether to be angry. "You *saw* him? And where was this?"

"Where was what?"

"That you saw him. Timothy. Our missing son."

"Oh, a few blocks from here." He was almost whispering. When he spoke softly, his voice began to crack; he sounded like an old AM radio.

After she repeated his phrase as an enraged question, Brettigan sighed and said, "Yes. Right here. In town. He was . . . it was at night. You know: when it gets dark, and I was Mr. Insomnia, and I was walking around, and I got to the freeway overpass, where the homeless congregate, and there he was or at least someone who looked exactly like him, and I called out to him, but before I could talk to him, this person scampered away. I asked the vagrants if they knew who he was and they said that they did. His name, they said, was Tim." He gave her another moment in which to process this news. "So it was probably him."

"I wonder if we should start calling his friends again, see if he's contacted them—you know, let them know where he is."

"Maybe if he has, they won't tell us."

"I keep wondering what we did to get on his shit list," she said. "Or if he just went crazy for a little while."

"I think the latter."

Alma sat up slightly so that she could look down at Brettigan, whose eyes were closed. "There's something I want you to do," she said. "That boy, the one we had over for dinner, that kid full of purpose and nonsense, Ludlow, that one. The Sun Collectivist. I want you to hire him, Harry. I want you to call him up, you know, on the *phone,* and get him to find Timothy, because . . . because somehow I believe they know each other. Don't ask me how I know. I just do. Something tells me that they're acquainted. Something tells me that they're in cahoots."

"What makes you say that?" he asked sleepily. He didn't seem particularly surprised by her request.

"I don't know. They're alike, somehow. You know: like reflections. Mirrors."

He ignored this observation by choosing not to reply to it or to interrogate it. "And what if he does find Timothy? What then?"

"What sort of question is that?" she asked.

"The sort of question I ask, *that's* what kind. I mean, the point is, Timothy doesn't *want* to be found. He's not a missing person. He's never *been* a missing person. He's something else. If he wanted us to know where he was or is, he'd have told us by now. He's hiding away. He's the J. D. Salinger of sons. After all, he's living on the streets. People do that."

"If they're on drugs, they do. Please don't use that tone on me. And please do this," she pleaded.

"Why don't *you* call him, this Ludlow, if you want to talk to him so badly?"

"A man should do it, not me."

"Do you think Timothy's in the Sun Collective?"

"I haven't seen him over there."

"How many times have you been?"

"A few times." This was a lie. She'd been there multiple times.

"All right," he said. "I'll get in touch with him."

AT THE BREAKFAST TABLE, SHE GAVE HIM HIS BIRTHDAY SHIRT AND A funny birthday card with a grinning dog wearing a party hat on the front; the dog looked like Woland. Brettigan said he had to go out to run a few errands and would call that Ludlow person once he got back. After he kissed Alma on the forehead and thanked her for his birthday gift, he ambled out to the garage and started the car and drove off to wherever he was going. She had meant to tell him to pick up some tomato juice and a faucet washer, but she forgot.

Alma sat at the breakfast table in the kitchen alcove and let the morning sun shine on her face. She had a moment of contentment, of pure mindless happiness, and as she shut her eyes, the dog padded in, his paws clicking on the linoleum, and put his head on her leg, with just an eyedrop of slobber, and the cat jumped up onto her lap and began purring. Outside, from down the block, she heard a lawn mower. Absentmindedly, she stroked the dog's head with her right hand and scratched the cat with her left.

Cover the clocks and the mirrors, then cut off two eyelashes, the man on the light rail had advised. *How preposterous! We do not live in an age of miracle cures,* Alma thought with an unconscious throat clearing, and we never have since the dawn of reason and the dark era of superstition: we have no evidence of miracles themselves, or magic, or of ghosts and hauntings, or of any of the side effects of divinity, including resurrections or walking on water or moral redemption or healings or telepathy or clairvoyance or transubstantiation or prayer. Wine didn't turn into blood; it stayed wine, despite what the priests all claimed. And blood, usually shed for no purpose, didn't turn into anything else as it flowed downward into the ground, fertilizing it with nutrients. The bread didn't turn into flesh—who's kidding whom? Who wants to eat the flesh of God? Miracles constituted the hope chests of the credulous and the insane. Priests were in the business of keeping everybody stupid and ignorant, and they kept busy by abusing the children in their care. She had been to all the churches and storefronts and synagogues and temples and cathedrals, and every one of them had promised miracles, and none of them had delivered or ever would, because they made promises as long as you gave them plenty of money and granted authority to their clerics, but none of them promised the return of her son, and none of them promised a cure for poverty or the salvation of the wretched of the earth, the door to heaven, which was nowhere, unless it was everywhere. Heaven! What a concept! So low you can't get under it.

Unless it was here, now.

The dog looked up at her. *Well, you could try it.*

Try what?

What he suggested. The clock thing and the mirror thing and the eyelash thing.

Don't be ridiculous.

Just a suggestion. What do I know? Scratch behind my ears, okay?

Alma looked down at the cat. And what about you? What's your opinion?

I'm supposed to have an opinion?

Just asking.

Do whatever you want. I don't care. You want caring, ask the dog.

She checked the driveway for the car, stood up so quickly that the cat had to jump out of her lap and the dog had to lift his head abruptly away from her, and, both giddy and bent over with her burden, Alma climbed the stairs to the bedroom, feeling that her heart would break.

No one really understands a mother's love, its furnace blast. Not even her husband; not even him. No man. No power on Earth could equal it. She didn't understand it herself or how it had control over her, like music played at full volume, which did not stop for rest and never seemed to diminish.

Once upstairs, she unplugged the bedside digital clock, went into the two other bedrooms and did the same for the two electric clocks beside the now-unused beds, and after pulling out a flat bedsheet, she covered the vanity mirror above her dressing table by hanging the sheet over it. Searching in the drawer, she found her old-fashioned fingernail scissors flecked with tiny dots of rust, and, almost without thinking, lowered her left eyelid and clipped two eyelashes from there, holding the cut lashes in her fingers, feeling their unusual thickness, not like hair from the top of the head. Would Harry notice the missing eyelashes? No: he hardly glanced at her anymore or gave her a second thought, even when they made geriatric love. She wouldn't wait until eleven minutes past eleven, or whenever it was that that crackpot doctor had instructed her. Whatever she had to do, she would do right now.

After sitting down on the edge of the bed, which sagged slightly— really, they should shop around for a new mattress—Alma placed the two eyelashes onto the back of her left hand, and she closed her eyes and thought about her son. She waited for something to happen.

Sometime later when she'd lost track of the time, she was startled to hear the doorbell ring and someone screeching for help. The voice was pitched in the frantic upper octaves. Alma collected herself and went downstairs, and at the front door, she saw her neighbor, a widow, Grace Wispely from down the street, peering in through the screen and making desperate cries.

"Grace? What is it? Come in."

"Alma," Grace cried on the other side of the screen while making little childish hops and holding her arms tight to her sides, an unlit cigarette in her right hand and lipstick smeared to the right of her mouth. Her coiled gray hair spewed out in all directions. "My house is on fire, and my phone doesn't work! Its batteries are dead or something. Can I use your phone? Please help. Nobody else is around."

"Yes, of course," Alma said, her eyes suddenly tearing up with fellow feeling for her neighbor. "Please, Grace, come in." She held the screen door open, took Grace Wispely's hand, and led her to the kitchen, where the landline phone, beautiful relic, sat on the kitchen counter next to the lime green Mixmaster. While her neighbor called the fire department in a trembling, rushed, and too-loud voice, giving information that she had to repeat, Alma returned to the front door and with the equanimity of a child gazed across the street, where Satanic black smoke flowered up and outward from Grace Wispely's downstairs window, and the usual pedestrians gathered on the front sidewalk, hands on chins, thoughtfully offering commentary.

Five minutes later, the welcome sirens wailed, and there was Grace, her friend and neighbor, sitting on her own front lawn as the firefighters strode quickly across the grass, unspooling their hoses. Sitting on her lawn? Apparently in shock, she had lost the ability to stand. Alma poured a glass of water and, crossing the street, carried it to Grace, who took it with thanks and drank it with one hand while simultaneously wiping her eyes with her other sleeve.

"I don't even know how it started," Grace said, as Alma helped her to her feet, getting her out of the way of the firefighters and the pushy videographers from the TV news crews, and at that moment a sensation flooded over Alma, uninvited but nevertheless quite welcome: a feeling that, despite everything, she, Alma Brettigan, was a lucky woman and that God, who did not exist and in whom she didn't believe, loved her. Or, if not God, *something:* something loved her, loved her for no reason at all.

21

BRETTIGAN PRIDED HIMSELF ON HIS PATIENCE, BUT A WALL THAT STOOD against his worst thoughts had crumbled somewhere inside him, and now he was speeding across Northeast Minneapolis, past churches and bars and single-family lots, the houses and buildings visibly rushing away on both sides as he advanced toward the headquarters of the Sun Collective, whose address, 4201 Roosevelt Avenue NE, he had found on Alma's dressing table.

In the middle of that night's tableau of dreams he'd realized that that place, those people, were the key to his son's disappearance, to his wife's absentminded despairs, to the deaths of the homeless perpetrated by the Sandmen, and to the seemingly accidental deaths of the plutocrats out in Wayswater. *The Sun Collective was responsible for everything,* the dream informed him, including his own aging; this dream-insight had come to him while he was asleep, when he saw Alma, whom he loved, swept up by a huge wave that transported her away from the beach on which she had been standing, as she gazed out at the sea where the moon, shining and dead, was rising. He saw President Amos Alonzo Thorkelson pointing a finger at Alma and himself in the dream, saw a banner across the sky that read in Gothic script, **THE SUN COLLECTIVE IS EVERYWHERE AND CASTS NO SHADOW**, and now, this morning, when Brettigan glanced out of the car window at yet another Catholic church whose weeping Madonna stood in front, downcast, her palms open on both sides, inviting the little children inside to suffer, he turned to his left to see a wine store, and then a riverfront restaurant speeding by, as if the car were stationary and the landscape were moving, and he thought of his night terrors and the way that Alma had touched his back around two a.m., knowing that he was drowning in that oneiric tidal wave, and she had said, "Harry, wake up. Harry, it's not real. You're dreaming."

No, it wasn't, and neither was he. Accelerating on the residential side street, Brettigan felt that he had somehow walked through a doorway that he hadn't known was there, with the result that he had been ejected from the real, from realism generally. As this idea entered his head, producing an effect of dizziness, he understood that he had to calm down, *right now*. Was this feeling an effect of aging? Poor circulation, in every sense? Or retirement? No doubt it was. Or was he having a stroke? Perhaps that too. After turning the car toward the curb, he parked in a vacant spot in front of a modest two-story house with a cream-colored stucco exterior, a steeply pitched roof, and a storm door with glass that revealed a front hallway leading back toward someone's living area. Upstairs he could see two sash windows with shades pulled halfway down. A black cat sat on the front stoop, eyeing him while licking its paw.

The small lawn in front of the house had been recently mowed. Cut green grass, unraked, lay here and there at the lawn's south border. Purple pansies, red petunias, and phlox had been planted underneath the house's front window. Brettigan clutched at the padded steering wheel of his car and waited for the sensation of disorientation, or whatever it was, to pass. After putting the transmission into park, he turned off the ignition before leaning back and closing his eyes.

He counted to twenty before he opened his eyes again, and as he came back to himself, he noticed that he was scratching his own knee while he examined the house in front of which he had stopped. The morning light of summer outlined the roof and gutters with the crisp certainty of a Dutch realist painting, but Brettigan, still waterborne behind the wheel, felt that this stranger's house, with its green lawn and flower garden, was a stage set, not an actual house but a mock-up on a sham street populated by counterfeit men and women who did not live here but merely pretended to do so.

Did other people ever feel that the world had turned into a facsimile of itself, a carefully constructed labyrinth of appearances?

Watching a mailman advancing down the block, pushing his little trolley sack of letters before turning to drop some advertising brochures into a mail slot, Brettigan broke out into a cold sweat. He felt old and sick. Chills and fever burst into blossom gently along his spine. The doorway that had opened for him led into the Land of the Unreal, where most young people, their eyes fixed on their screens, lived nowadays. Realism was over. It had crumbled. *This* was the world we had now—this duplicate, the realm of unlikeness, even here on Haas Street where nothing solid remained, and bogus birds shrieked in the cardboard trees.

"Hello? Pop? May I help you?" Someone was knuckle-knocking on the driver's side window. Brettigan rolled the window down.

"What?"

A young man in a T-shirt and jeans stood there, leaning over, his hand on the car door. His thick forearms, tattooed with slogans and sayings and a Coptic cross, were speckled with dirt, and he sported a full blond beard. On his face was a calm, concerned expression. In his right hand, he held a plastic water bottle.

"I saw you pull up here. I was upstairs."

"Oh, I'm all right," Brettigan said.

"The thing is, sir, you've been sitting there behind the wheel with the motor running for fifteen minutes now."

"I have?"

"Yup. Here. You might want to take some water."

Brettigan reached out and took the plastic bottle from the man's beefy hand. "Thank you." He took a sip of the water, then another. He felt himself swallowing.

"Do you want me to call 911 or something?"

"No, I'm okay."

"You don't look okay. Why don't you at least turn off the ignition for a minute?"

"I did turn it off."

"Maybe so, but the engine is still running. Could be you only thought it."

"Oh, all right." Brettigan reached down to the key and switched off the engine again. The car had apparently started itself.

"It's actually been closer to half an hour you've been sitting there. That's not good. I saw you holding on to the steering wheel. Are you really sure that you're feeling all right?"

"I think so. Well. Come to think of it, I'm not. Sure."

"You want to come inside my house for a minute? And, you know, sit down? Cool off?"

"No, I think I'm fine out here."

"Reason I asked, you look like you been hit by lightning. So therefore my invitation. Do you remember where you were headed?"

"The Sun Collective," Brettigan told him. "I was going to talk to them." He took another sip of water.

"Oh, right. Well, you *almost* made it. Their building is only a few blocks from here. They're great. They're totally great. I can sing their praises. Are you sure you don't want to come inside, Pop? Because actually I think you should come inside. You know: to, like, cool off."

"Oh, no. I don't want to impose."

"Naw, it's nothing. See, I'm babysitting my daughter, she's in her playpen right now, and my girlfriend is out right now running an errand, buying diapers, and . . . so I have to go back inside, where my daughter is right now, and why don't you come in? I don't think you should drive, to be honest."

Brettigan felt himself looking down at the young man's tattoos. One of the slogans said, NEVER RETREAT. On the other forearm were the initials USMC. You had to trust a Marine, Brettigan thought; somehow they required it. "All right," Brettigan said, and then said, "No harm done," without knowing quite what he meant or why he had said it.

·   ·   ·

INSIDE THE MARINE'S HOUSE, THE MAN'S DAUGHTER, WHO, UNLIKE HER father, had dark skin, was lifting up and dropping her stuffed animals in the playpen, pretending to count them. She saw Brettigan, then glanced at her father before going back to her inventory. The man picked her up and carried her over to a chair, where he sat down after motioning Brettigan toward a sofa on which, at its opposite side, slouched a large, blankly staring stuffed giraffe. Toys were scattered here and there on the floor, little plastic horses and dollhouse furniture. Between the living room and the kitchen, a Jack Russell terrier ran back and forth, stopping to sniff Brettigan before returning to his OCD tasks. The room had the customary controlled chaos of a household with a toddler and busy, harried parents, and Brettigan could tell that some dish that smelled like stew was simmering on the stove, visible through an entryway opposite him. A pack of cigarette papers lay open on the coffee table. On the wall to the side of the flat-screen TV was a studio photograph of the man and his girlfriend—who appeared to be African-American—and their baby daughter, dressed up in a pink frilly outfit. She was clutching a little stuffed unicorn. They were all smiling, even the unicorn.

On the opposite wall was a large framed poster of Prince, an expressionist painting complete with the musician's purple hair and purple skin.

"Yeah, that's my family," the man said proudly, seeing Brettigan scrutinizing the studio photograph. "Typical Americans, is all we are. By the way, my name's Peter Schemp." He took out his phone and began texting someone with his right hand, as he held his daughter with his left arm. "I'm just telling Shonda that everything's fine, and we got ourselves a surprise guest here, which is you."

"I won't be long," Brettigan said, before giving his own name back to Peter Schemp. "Nice picture of your family," he said. "You have a beautiful daughter." A mistake not to have mentioned the man's partner? "A beautiful girlfriend, too." Trying to find a conversational connection, Brettigan said, half in a panic, "I have a daughter, too. She's a veterinarian, lives down in the South. Two grandchildren. And . . .

a son." The Jack Russell returned to Brettigan, and, displeased by his presence there, barked at him once irritably, as criticism, and ran back to the kitchen.

"Quiet, Jack. Um, your daughter has a son, or you do?"

"She does, but I do, too. But my son's gone missing."

Schemp showed no surprise. "Uh-huh," he said. "Some people do that. Do you want more water? Ice?"

"No, I'm fine."

"Something to eat? Piece of toast?"

"No, thanks. Really, I should be going."

"Stay one more minute. Wait until the color comes back into your face. You're, like, *too* white." He smiled at his own joke. As Peter Schemp began bouncing his daughter gently on his knee, Brettigan had a sudden thought: the man, his daughter, and this entire household were deeply in the real world from which he himself had recently been ejected, and they didn't realize it and wouldn't begin to understand what he was talking about if he raised the topic in conversation. Of *course* they lived in the real world. Where else would they be?

Brettigan glanced over at the playpen, then at the toys on the floor, the newspapers piled up in the corner, the electronic vape cigarette on the coffee table next to the cigarette papers and a library book on child care, *How to Be Your Child's Best Parent*. On the book's cover, a little white girl reached up happily toward her parents' outstretched arms.

"What's your daughter's name?" Brettigan asked, indicating her with a tip of his chin.

"Rai-Ellen."

"Never heard that name before," Brettigan said. "It's nice."

"That's how come we came up with it," Peter Schemp told him. "Sure you don't want toast?"

"No. Thank you. Mr. Schemp, if I could, may I ask you something? Actually, two things. I don't want to be intrusive. It's just . . . well, I suppose I *was* feeling faint in the car, and I had this weird sensation that I won't go into, so my question is, do you ever feel that the world,

I mean the reality of—" When he saw an expression of early-warning bewilderment break out on the young man's face, Brettigan switched topics. "I'm sorry. So . . . what do you do, if I may ask?"

"Me? I'm a lineman for the power company. How about you?"

"Retired. Maybe you can tell. I was a structural engineer."

"And you were headed over to the Sun Collective? What for?"

"Yes. Well, my wife is interested in them. Have you been there?"

"Totally. I mean, when I got out of the Marines, before I was married, they found me. They were like giving away free food and clothes. They set me up. They helped me get a job. There are people over there who will help you do that. It's just what they do. And they've got a co-op food store near here, and they tell me they're going to start a co-op bank, and they've got, like, gardens around this part of the city where you can grow your own vegetables. They're sorta like angels if angels were practical and actually showed up to help you. So I mean, they also have other plans, trying to get their people elected to government. They aren't crazy but they want more power. Whatever. I don't care. I even met my girlfriend over there. Every neighborhood should have one. They saved me, did I say that already?"

"Oh, well, that's good. No, you didn't say that."

"Well, you must have heard something. I mean, there are rumors, too. Maybe not everything is on the up-and-up." He carried his daughter back to her playpen and gently let her down into it.

"Rumors?"

"So, what I heard was, and this is only a rumor from my neighbors, and what they say, is that over there at the Sun Collective some of the members, they want to neutralize the Utopia Mall."

"'Neutralize' it?"

"Yeah. Like it was some sort of sinful place, *entrapping* people with stuff that they force them to buy. Criminal mind-control capitalists operating in the retail world, like that. Which is loser-thinking. I mean, it's not like people are being *ordered* to go out there to the Utopia and buy the shit they're selling. You can always, like, stay at home if you want to, plant tomatoes, fix the plumbing, play with your kids. It's a free world."

"How would they neutralize it?"

"Anthrax is what I heard."

"No kidding."

"Yup. You get some anthrax or some other airborne poison from somewhere, and you take it out there to the mall, and you get like an aerosol spray on a timer to blow it into the air, and that's it, that's the end of the Utopia Mall." After a pause, he said, "Also the end of all the people in it. I'm not saying that I would do it, just that I heard that *they* might. So I mean they've got a light and a dark side. All I ever saw was the light. Maybe they're keeping the crazies under wraps. You want another glass of water?"

"No, thank you. I should be leaving now."

"Okay, you're looking better." He glanced down at his daughter. "Say goodbye to the man, Rai-Ellen."

The little girl turned around at the mention of her name, and through the playpen's webbing she exchanged a glance with Brettigan before raising her hand to wave at him, and she said, "Bye bye," in a clear voice, giving the impression that she had heard and remembered everything that had just been said and could comment on it if she wished, as long as she didn't have more important matters to attend to.

BRETTIGAN PARKED HIS CAR IN THE LOT OUTSIDE THE SUN COLLEC-tive's building, which had the appearance of a deconsecrated church clad in brown wooden siding, with an old church signboard out in front displaying a few scattered letters from a broken sentence,

Wel

me tr

t over!

and two smaller characters, ☛ ✸. The ex-church had a high vaulted roof and stained-glass windows whose images were too dark to see even in broad daylight. Somehow the sun itself could not penetrate that glass, or its light was wholly absorbed by it. The glass produced an unwholesome effect.

"Mr. Brettigan! What brings you here?"

It was that young guy, Ludlow, of all people, from the other night's dinner, approaching him. He held a pair of hedge trimmers on to which a few cuttings hung, and he wore a sunhat whose visor rose in the front and dropped in the back. Dark glasses with enlarged lenses gave his face an insect appearance. His expression was that of wary, goofy friendliness mixed with earnest theatrical embarrassment, as if he'd been caught out in the midst of a shameful activity and was doing his best to pretend that he wasn't who he seemed to be and wasn't doing what he appeared to be doing.

"I wanted to see what you guys were up to, over here," Brettigan said. "Some hunch sent me. And there's something else." Brettigan took a deep breath, as he often did before lying, and said, "I wanted to see where I could sign up. Incidentally, I didn't know that you *worked* for them. You didn't mention that fact, last time we saw you at dinner. Did they hire you for maintenance? And, by the way, as long as I'm asking, where do I find the big cheese? Your maximum leader. Is he inside?"

"We're anarchists. We don't have a maximum leader. But I think Wye's around. His specialty is speaking. Aloud." Ludlow put his hedge clippers down and wiped the sweat from his face with a red handkerchief that he had snatched rapidly out of a side pocket of his jeans, both the jeans and the handkerchief stained with dirt and grass. With his other hand he pulled out his phone, apparently to read the messages there. The two actions seemed to be constructed as a means of giving him time to think of what he was about to say after having been caught unawares.

Watching him, Brettigan had two recognitions: first, that in his day, generations ago, people pulled out their hip flasks and surreptitiously emptied them when relaxing or anxious, hoping to stop the flow of overwhelming events; now, post-alcohol, they pulled out their phones to take a drink from the internet. His second recognition was that Ludlow, in his smilingly innocent way, had somehow entered a police state and was carefully monitoring himself for possible speech crimes. He seemed like a different person from the one Brettigan had seen at dinner.

"Oh," Ludlow said, "you just go in there." He pointed to a doorway with a Gothic arch.

"You work here?" Brettigan asked again.

"Sure," Ludlow said. "Sure. I do. You could say that."

"Is that recent?"

"Oh, for sure. Just a few days now." Ludlow smiled briefly before the smile broke apart into a smirking frown. "You go in through that door," he said, in a tone of excited gloom, while he pointed again at the doorway. "Follow the signs and then just keep going. And don't be discouraged. It's a little bit of a labyrinth down there."

INSIDE THE DOOR, IMMERSED IN THE SUDDEN DARKNESS, BRETTIGAN grasped the handrail and descended several steps that led to a corridor on whose right-hand side was another stairway downward. Over the stairs, lit by a single incandescent bulb, was a joke miniposter that said *"The World is Yours!"* in fun-house script. Wasn't that the phrase from *Scarface,* that ode to cocaine-fueled appetites, world-gobbling egomania, and Miami chain saw bedlam? I'm so behind the times, Brettigan thought; maybe the sentence was harmless and had been set out for Sunday Schoolers.

The corridor veered slightly to the left, apparently curved. The building was, indeed, a funhouse of sorts, and at the next doorway, he stepped into an assembly hall, what had once apparently been a modest Protestant sanctuary, with a cross-shaped floor plan, and, on either side of the aisle in the spaces where the pews had been, in the dim light cast by the sun through the thick stained glass, he saw card tables laid out symmetrically, and behind them, toward the back, other tables and a few folding chairs in no particular pattern, the room silent except for some buzzing static coming from a small radio plugged into an electrical wall socket, and, above him, a live bird, probably a sparrow, chirping and frantically flying back and forth over and under the roof's support beams. No one seemed to be around, or tending to anything. That contemporary deity, the God of Neglect, lived here. In what had once been a locale for prayer and reverence and even joy, there was only this gray air emptied of comfort, filled with static, desolation, and the cry of a frightened bird.

On one table Brettigan saw some Tarot fortune-telling cards spread out, showing the Magician, the Hierophant, and the Sun; on another table were some playing cards scattered here and there, disarrayed, it seemed, from a game of solitaire.

"Those Tarot cards are a window to the future and to the past. May I help you, Mr. Brettigan?"

The voice came from behind him, and when he turned, he saw a tall man, wearing a dark brown corduroy suit and what seemed to be a midnight-blue necktie, smiling beatifically. This expression seemed to light up what Brettigan could see of his face, but there was something provisional about the smile, as if the man were testing out an apparent friendliness that could be withdrawn in an instant. Also, he had a Mexican bandito mustache that looked glued on. On his head he wore an African shako.

"Wye, I am, yes," the man said. "Welcome to the Sun Collective. I believe the reason you're here, this is a reason I know."

"Oh? You do?" Brettigan said nondirectively, trying to see the man's eyes.

"Why don't you, down to my office, come? Just follow me. I apologize for the enforced gloom in our . . . *facilities*. My eyes are to the light somewhat sensitive. If you need to see where we're going"—he laughed—"you may grasp onto my coat."

"Oh, I won't need to do that," Brettigan told him, wondering over the man's inventive manipulation of English syntax, perhaps for comic effect.

WHEN THE MAN STARTED TO WALK AWAY, HIS FIGURE, IN THE CORDUROY suit, seemed to dissolve into the air behind him, as if he had pressed a button on a disappearance machine and had vanished from sight. He opened the darkness in front of him and closed it behind him as he walked. Brettigan followed his lead, stubbing a toe on a small box on the floor that seemed to have been nailed there, and after a moment he found himself descending another flight of stairs lit by Christmas tree lights, above which was a sign with the Sun Collective's symbol, a pointing finger and a dark star: ☞ ✸. The stairway led into yet another corridor also lit by Christmas lights, but the lights here were so helpless against the surrounding obscurity that they lit only themselves. Brettigan navigated mostly by sound, following Wye's shuffling feet in bedroom slippers.

At last Wye opened a door to a room that was apparently his office. Like the preceding hallways, the room was dimly lit, and Brettigan's eyes took a moment to adjust to the greater darkness that was not only visible but palpable: he could feel it, as if the air were threaded and woven with black cotton against which he might lay his head and rest. On the other side of the room Wye sat or slumped in an easy chair upholstered in a faded-flower fabric. Above him, a framed poster of a Bonnard painting had been hung on the wall, but the room's lighting contained so much murk that he couldn't discern any of poster's colors, though he could make out that the painting depicted a window opening to another window, and another one beyond that, with an indistinct figure resting on the window frame. Wye's room itself had no windows and was a bunker of sorts.

"And so here we are," Wye said. "You have come here for Tim?" He flashed Brettigan a sour smile full of easygoing condescension.

"Yes. How did you know?"

"Yes. Essentence is what we call the holographic radiance in us that shines outward. That's how I knew."

As he spoke, Wye made a gesture that Brettigan had never seen before in his life: clasping his hands together just above his lap, Wye rapidly lifted his elbows up and brought them down rapidly and repeatedly, fluttering his arms in the air like birds' wings.

"Please tell me: Where is my son?"

"Beyond essentence is luminarity and beyond that, occasionally, is pain, like the extraction of teeth. And if we—"

"Oh, for chrissake," Brettigan said. "Just please tell me where my son is, if you know."

"You are angry," Wye observed. "That is the wounded ego speaking, the damaged and frightened bird on the sidewalk making its little chirps."

At that moment, Brettigan felt a pair of hands on his shoulders, pressing down gently. Turning his head backward, he saw, looming over him, his bearded son, Timothy, smiling serenely. "Dad," he said, "here you are."

- 22 -

IN MOMENTS OF DEEP EMOTIONAL SHOCK, BRETTIGAN SOMETIMES FELT his surroundings giving way and becoming insubstantial, the world's materiality crumbling. Of his wedding to Alma he could remember only the notes of an out-of-tune piano, Alma's voice saying, "I do," and the cascade of summer sunlight on the sidewalk outside. From that day, he also remembered the newfound sensation of the gold wedding band encircling his ring finger. When Virginia was born, he retained a single memory of his wife's groans of pain during her contractions, followed by his daughter's first piercing cries in the delivery room. From Timothy's birth he could now recall nothing except a surge of emotion so powerful upon seeing his son for the first time that a nurse or someone wearing hospital scrubs had touched him on his back and bent him over so that he would not faint after he gave evidence of a light-headed unsteadiness.

A voice from somewhere had said, "This happens to a lot of new dads."

The passage of time had not insulated him. In contrast to several of his contemporaries who had been hardened by life, he had been softened. He felt this change as a weakness. His manhood was being revoked piece by piece. These days, everything got to him in its relentlessness, and Alma knew it. Sometimes he felt like a chick just hatched out of the egg.

Now he felt his son holding him up and then dabbing away his tears with a handkerchief and saying, "It's okay, Dad," followed by sobs, apparently Brettigan's own, that broke out from somewhere deep and untreated inside himself. Who was the child here, and who the man? Timothy Brettigan held his father with his right arm as they made their way up a flight of stairs out to the parking lot and to Brettigan's car, and after Timothy deposited his father behind the wheel, having fished the car keys out of his father's pocket, Brettigan said to his son, "Forgive me, it's just that I—" followed by another emotional seizure, inside of which the car and the parking lot and the rest of the world desolidified and took on the insubstantiality of a stage set.

After a minute, Brettigan said, "I'm okay now." He wiped his eyes with his shirtsleeve. "I'm fine."

"I'm sorry, Dad," Timothy said. "I guess I didn't know—"

"You don't have to apologize."

"I know, but you're sorta wrecked."

"I'm okay. Really."

"You don't look it."

"I'm just so glad to see you," Brettigan said, looking up at Timothy, standing next to the car door and blocking the sun so that he was outlined in light, all detail gone from his face. "That you're doing so well." Again he was embarrassed by his emotional excesses. "That you're here—"

"I was mostly always here."

"Maybe. Do you want some breakfast? Or lunch? I've lost track of time."

"Sure, Dad. Whatever you want." A pause. "Can you drive?"

"Yes. I think so." Brettigan's heart was both pounding and fluttering, but at least he was still alive. Timothy opened the passenger-side door and dropped himself in.

STICKING TO ROUTES THAT HE KNEW WELL, BRETTIGAN DROVE TO THE nearest restaurant with which he had some acquaintance, The Egg and I. He parked his car in the adjoining lot beneath a billboard that read, YOU'LL LAUGH, YOU'LL CRY, YOU'LL BEG FOR MORE! next to a smiling 1950s-style waitress. His hands were still trembling as he turned off the ignition. Fearing destabilizing emotions and another outburst of tears, he gradually felt himself calming down into a condition resembling adulthood and maturity.

His son, during this brief trip, had not spoken a word, quietly observing the pedestrians and the houses passing by with the greatest attention, as if he'd never seen their like before, though he did touch his father's right shoulder from time to time as if to reassure him. Timothy had always been an observant boy, but his fixed concentration on the neighborhood they were passing through seemed, this time, an act of charity and kindness toward his father, allowing the old man several minutes to compose himself.

As soon as they entered the restaurant, Timothy glanced around and sniffed. The restaurant smelled of bacon grease. "A breath of fresh air," he said with the thinnest of smiles as he sat down in the closest booth, motioning toward his father to sit on the other side, opposite him. Elsewhere in the restaurant were clumped groups of customers, and against the wall opposite theirs, a pair of lovers sat on the same side of their table, feeding each other scrambled eggs, the girl's right leg over the boy's left leg, a sight that made Brettigan feel old. Lovers in public gave you a window into happiness, but what they did was always slightly theatrical, as if they were performing their love for someone else's benefit or envy, or perhaps their own.

Timothy glanced over at them before sitting down, raising an eyebrow with studied neutrality before taking out his iPhone to check for messages. With nothing there to occupy him, he put it back, picked up the menu, glanced at it, and handed it to his father, who was pretending to read his own menu but who was really absorbing the presence of his son into himself, incorporating him into memory so that if he ever disappeared again, he would have him there, internally.

"I'm under a curse, you know," Timothy said with a half-smile, glancing at the restaurant's wall clock. "But I almost forgot to ask: How *are* you, Dad? And how's Mom?"

"You can see how I am by looking at me. As for your mother, you'll see, soon enough," Brettigan said.

"But I'm interested in you telling me."

"It's hard to summarize." Brettigan instantly regretted the tone he was taking and tried to backtrack. He was so loaded down with emotions that he was almost speechless. "I'm fine, I guess," he said with a dismissive shrug. "My ticker isn't everything it could be. The valves and the flutter." The server came by, asked him if he wanted coffee, and filled his cup. Meanwhile, the lovers on the other side of the room, having completed their breakfast, were kissing. "Your mother had a little stroke a while ago, but she's okay now. She goes around the city looking for you."

"I know."

"How do you know?"

"People tell me."

"*Who* tells you?"

"Ludlow and Christina."

"Oh, those two? The Sun Collectivists?"

"Yeah," his son said.

"You're one of them?"

"One of them? If you put it that way, yes, I guess so. They have projects. I go over there sometimes. I help out. I saw Mom once. I hid from her. I wasn't ready."

"Why?"

"I don't know. I just wasn't."

"You said you help out. Where?"

"At their co-op. In the gardens. Other work. It's a long story. I wanted to do some good in the world. And they found me. That's what they're all about."

"And why would you want to do that?" Even as he asked it, Brettigan knew that the question was nonsensical. It was simply the sentence that had come into his head, and because it was there, he said it; that was all.

"Because I'm under a curse."

"You said that already," Brettigan told him. "What sort of curse?"

The server came over, took their orders, and left them there. Meanwhile, the restaurant had grown quiet. The lovers were obliviously kissing, waiting for their check. Seeing them, Timothy grimaced.

"It takes some explaining. Remember when I was in Chicago? Playing Astrov in *Uncle Vanya*?" Brettigan nodded.

His son began to talk: the theater Timothy had been working for, the Stage Players on the Near North Side, had given him a furnished apartment where he'd stayed while the Chekhov play had its two-month run. The director of the play, a witty, goateed, manipulative character with a small but easily detectable mean streak, had urged Timothy to push his characterization of Astrov to the edge: usually, Dr. Astrov is played as a weary, alcoholic country doctor obsessed with the ecological damage being done to the Russian countryside where he practices medicine halfheartedly. The director, Simonson, had wanted him to put, as he said, "more broken nerves on the stage": to present Astrov as jittery and unkempt, alcoholic, half out of his mind with overwork, a male hysteric. Exhausted and solitary, Astrov is susceptible to a hopeless infatuation for Professor Serebryakov's beautiful wife, Elena, and is meanwhile oblivious to Sonya's desperate love for him, a classic triangle. All this plays out on the professor's estate. Sonya, the professor's daughter, is plain and attracts no one's notice. In the play, everyone wants what's not available, and, given the gift of eloquence, Sonya herself confesses her wretched condition to anyone who will listen. "You'll be a walking nervous breakdown," the director had said, smilingly. "Sonya and Astrov, you're both wrecks. The audience won't be able to keep their eyes off the two of you. It'll be like driving past a head-on collision on the freeway with the bleeding bodies still groaning and twitching."

Another one of the director's ideas was to cast a beautiful woman as Sonya and to "frump her down," and to cast a homely woman as Elena and to "glamour and glitter her up" against type. The part of Sonya, one of the greatest roles in Western theater, usually taken by actresses who were eager to make themselves unlovely for the occasion, had in this case been cast with a woman who had typically been given dewy ingenue roles. Her name was Hazel Stearns, and she was a graduate of Juilliard's theater program. She was beautiful—thick brown hair and deep, haunted eyes like the young Kim Novak—and she enthusiastically made herself as plain as she could for the part.

"Sonya's a beautiful woman who has been convinced that she isn't," Simonson had told her in front of Timothy as they were blocking out their scenes. "She's been worn down by her daily work. You can look like that, can't you, Hazel dear? Of course, you can. A little more stooped over, please. When you walk, remember to shuffle. No hand gestures, though. Sonya is Russian but not like that."

From the first table reading through the rehearsals, Simonson had done everything he could to push Hazel Stearns and Timothy together, teasing them and buying them drinks in the evening, arranging a love affair between them, and before long that possibility had become a probability and then given way to its inevitability: Hazel, channeling Sonya, had fallen in love with Timothy, but he, somehow, couldn't reciprocate. He felt no love, just a dull and moderately insulting low-voltage heterosexual attraction to her. Astrov's spirit had taken him over and swamped him. He was possessed by inappropriate longings, but not for her. One night, before the dress rehearsal, Hazel, leaning into him, had told him, "I'm getting so I'm in love with you," and, without thinking, either as himself or as Astrov, he had blurted out, "Well, I can't say the same." Nevertheless, trying to be decent, he'd taken her out to dinner after the rehearsal, and, then, after the dinner, he'd driven her back to his apartment near Lincoln Park for a drink. He brought out the ice and the whiskey bottle and the half-soiled glasses from the kitchen. On his living room sofa, she'd gotten drunk and pleaded with him.

Out of the great repository of my bad impulses, Timothy told his father, those that proceed from pity are the worst.

One thing had led to another. "I hate directors," Timothy said. "Those Svengalis, I hate the effect they have." All through the run, Timothy and Hazel were having low-down, dirty sex, usually after each performance. On her side it was desperate and sordid and crazy; on his, dutiful and mechanical and cruel. He even splashed cologne on himself as a repellent. Nothing worked. "I knew it was wrong," Timothy told his father, as the server arrived with his cheese omelet and English muffin. "But I couldn't stop myself." He had degraded Hazel and found himself remorseless. She was compliant and would do anything he asked her to do and would do it repeatedly. You only think you're in love with me, he had told her. No, she replied, I know I am. You're in my bloodstream.

"You know, I think maybe there's such a thing as sin," he told his father. "I didn't think so before, but I do now."

On the opposite side of the restaurant, the lovers had paid, picked themselves up, and left.

The relationship Timothy and Hazel Stearns were having had produced a static-electricity aftereffect onstage, just as Simonson had hoped it would. When Sonya gave her heartbroken curtain speech in the last act, even the stagehands wept night after night. After the final performance and the cast party, Hazel and Timothy had returned to his apartment and had sex for the last time. They fucked in a sad valedictory way. Lying there in the dark bedroom afterward, she had proposed marriage to him, and he laughed and told her that, after all, they'd just had a plain old showmance, familiar to all actors from high school onward.

In the bed, he could feel her stiffen. "You're a shit," she told him.

"Yeah, I guess so. I'm forced to agree."

"I love you and you're walking away."

"It happens."

She drew in a breath. Then, sounding slightly like Sonya but in a dead calm, she said, "No one will ever love you. You'll go to the end of your days, trying to love others, and *no one will ever love you back*. They'll offer you a token friendship, but you'll want more, and you'll never get it. They won't even care about you. Ever. I promise you, you'll be solitary to the end of your days. You will live and die alone. And in your desert you'll feel your solitude and be homeless everywhere."

"That's a very impressive curse," Timothy mumbled, naked, next to her. He rolled over and entered her again.

"I feel like killing myself," she whispered, just before she came.

·   ·   ·

HOURS LATER, SHE ROSE OUT OF BED, PICKED UP HER CLOTHES FROM the floor, dressed herself quickly, and let herself out.

He was so tired from the performance and the sex, which was also a performance, that he didn't get up to see her go.

She killed herself the next week, throwing herself out of a sixth-floor downtown hotel room window. She didn't leave a suicide note. She didn't have to.

"WHAT HAPPENED TO ME AFTER THAT," TIMOTHY SAID, FINISHING HIS omelet and taking his first sip of coffee, "was that I became, I don't know, spellbound, I guess you'd say." He'd gone to the memorial service in her hometown, Bar Harbor. The director hadn't shown up; maybe he was busy somewhere. At the memorial, Timothy met Hazel's parents, who, beyond an initial politeness, would not speak to him. One of her friends from high school approached him to say, "You're the boyfriend? I've heard about you. You shouldn't be here. You have a lot of nerve, coming to this thing." She gazed at him with steady, eager hatred. She was quite beautiful and radiant with loathing.

He returned to Chicago. He was offered the role of Estragon in *Waiting for Godot* at a theater in Minneapolis but initially refused it after informing the theater director that Estragon was a toxic role that wounded, sometimes permanently, the soul of the actor who played it; it was common knowledge among actors, a role that was worse luck than Macbeth. He would have to research it. Besides, he was impaired already; words and music were beginning to echo in his head all day long. He packed up his necessary belongings into his car, stored everything else in a friend's basement, and took off for no particular destination.

Avoiding the interstate highways, he made his way through one small midwestern town after another, stopping to eat at no-name diners and to rest at seedy motels without corporate affiliations, where the mattresses sagged and the TVs rarely worked and stray mongrel dogs sat out sunning themselves in the parking lots in front of the rusting metal porch chairs where no one ever sat. During the day, the trees and farmlands rushed past his car, not in a blur but as specific instances that he would remember each night: one hill after another plowed in parallel lines, every cornfield and individual haystack, every anonymous individual seen at a distance as if painted there, unmoving, but returning his gaze with fixed expressions.

He felt himself searching for forgiveness. At night the familiar stars slipped further and further away.

He found himself outside Iowa City in Coralville, where he lived in a Motel 6 for two weeks, walking around the University of Iowa campus and along the Iowa River on the jogging trails, and reading magazines and German philosophy in the library before he resumed his wanderings. Soon after, he landed for a week in Fort Collins, Colorado, where a bachelor friend from college, a high school teacher, put him up in the basement on an inflatable air mattress. He walked around the Colorado State campus and drank cheap draft beer in the student bars. He felt penitential and was beginning to see the elaborate abyss that was being prepared for him. In it, eyes without a face examined his soul and turned away with distaste. Forgiveness might be everywhere, but it was for others, not for him.

The battery in his cell phone died; he threw the phone into a restaurant dumpster before he took off again and found himself in Las Cruces, New Mexico, and then Austin, Texas. He was comfortable for a while in these and other college and university towns where no one ever seemed to notice him or to mind his increasingly bedraggled appearance. With his backpack, shabby sweater, jeans, and running shoes, he fit right in. He began to talk to himself in a low, eloquent mutter. As his money dwindled and his credit cards maxed out, he considered his situation dispassionately, as if his life were being lived by someone else. He felt himself expanding into invisibility. Soon, he imagined, no one would be able to see him at all. He would just fade away and vanish before taking up occupancy in the spirit world where he would be as unwelcome as he was here.

Outside Bentonville, Arkansas, the home of Walmart, his car wouldn't start. He had it towed to the nearest garage, where the mechanic told him that the ignition switch needed to be replaced. After being given the estimate, Timothy asked the shop to go ahead and do the job, signed the work order, and while the car was being repaired, he walked to the Greyhound station and bought a ticket to Kansas City, Missouri. In Kansas City, he bought another ticket to St. Louis, where, for the first time, he stayed in a homeless shelter, on Tucker Boulevard. By now it was autumn. There, he was given a clean set of clothes and a dinner of beef stew, broccoli, and applesauce. Looking around the dining area, he saw men who were either silent, or, if they were talking, talked only to some inner part of themselves, interrupting their own monologues with gallows laughter.

"People don't realize how a curse can work," he told his father, as he finished his third cup of coffee, and the restaurant's other customers paid for their meals and departed. "A curse can be very effective, if you do it right."

In St. Louis he made his way to the basilica on Lindell Boulevard to see whether the collective power of the Catholic Church could ease the weight of the darkness falling in thick layers over him. Darkness, this particular variety of it, had considerable weight attached to his back; he could feel it. All day he sat in a pew, studying the ceiling mosaics and the Sacred Heart Shrine. People came and went, lit candles, went to confession, and prayed. He heard a disquieted background murmuring—the sounds of perpetual contrition sent upward, to the highest reaches of the ceiling and beyond that to God. The basilica smelled of incense and blood. Toward evening, a priest, who introduced himself as Father Walling, came down a side aisle before sitting beside him and asking in a voice of practiced compassion whether there might be anything he could do. It had been noticed that he had been sitting there for several hours. Was anything the matter? Timothy shook his head. No. "The matter" wasn't the matter. Well, Father Walling asked, in that case, what might be the trouble? Because I suspect that you have a troubled soul. How may I help?

Timothy opened his mouth, intending to say that he had a problem but didn't know how to name it or what it was, but nothing came out.

Yes? asked Father Walling.

Timothy opened his mouth again, but whatever brought words out of the mind's reservoir of language had severed. Nothing came to him, and he felt darkness and its sister, silence, overtaking him completely, the heavy soundless darkness and its attendant speechlessness floating down lazily from the sky where they had originated. Looking at the priest's brown eyes, blinking behind a pair of wire-rimmed glasses accompanying his kindly expression, Timothy tried one more time. "—" he said, waiting for a sentence of his own to come to him. "—" he tried again.

Do you speak English? the priest asked him. Timothy nodded. Well, then, why not say just anything?

"—"

You would be better off, the priest said, if you stood up. You've been sitting here for too long. You look like an educated man. But I have to tell you that you can't spend the night here. What has happened to you? Something terrible must have happened to you. Would you like to see the front of our basilica? The baldachin? I believe that you must be a visitor from somewhere. What's the matter with you? My goodness, even your hands are sweating.

Timothy opened his mouth one more time, and this time, words that were not his own came out. "'I haven't had much time to myself,'" he said, as Astrov. "'I've grown shabby, and why not? Life drags you down, and you're in the company of characters and crazy people . . .'" The voice wasn't his; it was Chekhov's doctor speaking. Somehow he'd gotten locked inside the part and couldn't get out, just as Hazel had been locked in hers. The only sentences he had left belonged to Astrov, who'd gotten them from Chekhov, who'd gotten them from Russia in the late nineteenth century.

What? the priest asked.

" 'This quiet,' " Timothy-as-Astrov recited. " 'The pens write, the crickets chirp. Warm, cozy . . . I don't feel like leaving here. There, they've brought the horses. All I need to do is to say goodbye to you, my friends, to say goodbye and . . . soon I'll be gone.' "

I think you need help, the priest said. More than the help that we can give you. I'm going to call somebody.

Without any sensible transition, Timothy found himself in another location with institutional walls and beds, and nurses at first who took his temperature and his pulse and his blood pressure, and other male attendants who bathed him and asked him who he was. "Michael," he said. "Dr. Michael Astrov," he managed to say. One morning when he woke, his wrists were tied to the side rails of the bed.

They had no record on any of their databases of any such Dr. Astrov. He carried no other ID with him because he had discarded his own somewhere back there in Kansas City. Eventually when they thought he was marginally lucid, they let him go, and he dipped downward onto the streets.

"THAT'S THE LAST SOLID MEMORY I'VE GOT," TIMOTHY TOLD HIS father, "before I came back to myself a few months ago." He had clasped his hands together, both elbows on the table, and propped his chin at the top of the triangle formed by his arms. "I seem to have made my way back here, and the Sun Collective people put me together after I was in pieces."

Brettigan took a final sip from his coffee cup.

"A middle-aged woman found me one day on the street and said she recognized me. She took me to the Sun Collective. They gave me a meal and a clean set of clothes. I remember taking a shower. I was there for several days, and it was as if I was waking up. I woke up there. They acted as if I wasn't cursed. They acted as if I was forgiven. They forgive almost everybody. That's their thing."

By now, it was early afternoon, and the restaurant, which served only breakfast and lunch, was closing up: two employees were mopping the linoleum floors and putting the chairs upside down on the tables near where Brettigan and his son sat alone, while seemingly random sounds came out of the kitchen as the cooks yelled in Spanish to each other over the background noise of water spray on the dishes and the clattering of a pail that someone dropped on the floor.

"I guess we have to go," Brettigan said. "And where are you living now?" he asked his son. "There's so much I want to ask you." He waited. "I've missed you."

"I know."

"Well?"

"What?"

"Please tell me: Where are you living?"

"They brought me back to life," Timothy said. "The Sun Collective. They found me. They gave me a purpose. They told me who I was. And they have a *program*. 'Reclamation,' is what they call it."

"So you're living there?"

Timothy nodded. "No. I have a little apartment. And I have a job. I'm working as the assistant manager of a movie theater, the Alhambra. It's uptown."

"What should I say to your mother? Will you come home with me and have dinner with us?"

"Not just now."

"Why?"

"All I want is an ordinary life, as myself," Timothy said, looking straight at his father. Brettigan felt himself shrinking backward. "I don't want to do great things." He waited for his father's reaction. "And, oh, I meant to ask: How are *you*, Dad? And how's Mom?"

"You already asked," his father said. "Several hours ago. I told you that I was getting by and that your mother had a small episode." He waited a moment. "You know, I missed you."

"I missed you too, Dad. It's too bad about Mom."

"You did?"

"Yes. Sometimes I saw your face. You were smiling. You were proud of me."

"Yes, I was. Are you telling me that you don't remember living on the streets? Because I think I once saw you."

"Yes," Timothy said. "I was out there, with them, that society of souls. But it was like living in a dream. The thing is . . ." He stopped to think. "The thing is, out there, something happens to you, and you don't remember it. None of it gets remembered. Nothing registers. Nothing." After smiling for no reason at all, he stood up. "Those people found me, and they reclaimed me. And I awakened. Do you know their motto? *'What's been done can be undone.'* Those words saved me. And now you have to take me back to my apartment."

"No," his father said. "I'll take you there, but first you have to see someone else."

BRETTIGAN PARKED ON THE DRIVEWAY OF HIS HOUSE, SEEING ALMA'S car nestled in the garage. His son, slumped down on the passenger side and knowing where they were, kept his eyes closed until Brettigan said, "You know, you really have to do this. You have to see your mother."

"I don't want to. I can't. Shouldn't we warn her?"

"Why?"

Timothy squirmed for a moment, then said, "She's going to collapse or something when she sees me. And she won't forgive me, either, for what I've done. For disappearing for so long."

"How long has it been? Since you've seen her?"

"Months. I don't know. I mean, I don't— Years."

"You just have to do it. She's been worried about you for so long now."

Timothy's eyes were still closed. "The house looks the same. The lawn looks the same. Everything looks the same. Even the sky is the same. I feel about five years old. Jesus, I hate homecomings."

"I know."

"Oh, all right." With a gesture that seemed violent even though it was slow and measured, Timothy opened the car door and got out, blinking at the afternoon sun that had acquired a hazy reddish tinge from distant forest fires to the west. He bent down to touch his toes and then stood straight, turning his face toward the sky in a gesture that reminded Brettigan of prayer, specifically of supplication, and he sniffed the air. "Smoky," he said, "like everything's burning down. Maybe it's not all the same."

"Well, you know, climate change. Global warming. Last rites."

"Let's get this over with," Timothy said. "I mean, I love Mom and everything, but, you know, I'm just—" He seemed to be temporarily out of words.

They walked toward the front door, directly across the lawn, and Brettigan pulled out his key chain and turned the lock. The two men crossed the front entryway and the living room, Brettigan going first, followed by his son, and Brettigan called, "We're home." The dog and the cat came over to examine them. The cat, who did not like strangers, retreated from Timothy, running up the stairs. Something was cooking: the air held the smell of onions, garlic, and tomatoes. The dog, who was more hospitable, wagged his tail.

"We?" Alma was in the kitchen.

"Come see."

"Christina?"

"Well, not exactly, no," Brettigan said, as Alma came out of the kitchen wearing a red bib apron stained with blue and brown streaks. With the back of her wrist, she pushed a strand of hair away from her forehead. Seeing Timothy, she froze, six feet away from where he was standing.

"Hi, Mom," Timothy said, his voice higher than usual from the strain. Neither he nor his mother rushed across the room to embrace each other.

"Timothy? Tim?" she asked, blinking, before she jerked back, as if she'd been kicked in the stomach. "Is it you?"

"Yup," he said, "it's me." He gave her an uncertain smile.

The blood having drained from her face, Alma turned to her husband. "This isn't him," she said. "That's not Timothy. It *can't* be."

"Yes, it is, honey."

"But look at him!"

"Well, he's changed." Brettigan put his hand on his son's shoulder. "We're all older, you know," he said, a bit helplessly.

Alma walked toward Timothy, never taking her eyes off him, and, holding her hand out, as if to shake his, reached for his right hand and examined his wrist, where a faint scar in the shape of an inverted V seemed to be outlined in pale scar tissue.

"Oh my God," she said, gazing up at him, "oh my God oh my God." She closed the distance between them, leaning and then caving herself into her son, wrapping her arms around him as he, more tentatively, took his mother into his arms. "Oh ramcist munerobt," she said, her face pressed against his chest. She seemed to be speaking in tongues, in her grief and joy.

Before her legs gave way, her son had the presence of mind to lock his hands behind her back so that she would not fall. On his face was an expression that somehow mingled tender love, pity, and stark terror.

- 23 -

DAYS AND WEEKS PASSED, SUMMER TURNED INTO AUTUMN, AND FROM her desk at the bank, Christina watched the sun cross the sky as it marked the hours, the sands in her mental hourglass falling almost audibly as Ludlow became indefinable and distant, full of projects that he would allude to but not explain. Something in him had slowly curdled and turned sour. By November, Christina found herself waking up next to Ludlow and wondering who he was, exactly. Was he unknowable or just secretive? Perhaps both. On top of the usual opacity of men, Ludlow had added to the mix a kind of furtiveness, like someone in a spy organization under orders to keep his mouth shut. And she was beginning to think that he might be operating some kind of confidence trick with her. Where were his parents, for example? His siblings? Why didn't they ever call? His last name, Schmitz, struck her as bogus, and his behavior was becoming, well, erratic: occasionally now he would lean back on her sofa and talk at length about what he called "necessary violence," though he never specified what form the violence would take or against whom it would be directed. Then he would stand up and dance a little jig, sit down, and resume his monologues about the coming End Times. How do you get rid of a man like that?

She had wanted to steal his wallet to check his driver's license, but he didn't carry a wallet.

Dumping him would be difficult because he had nowhere to go. She believed she would need help doing it—someone to lean down with her, pushing hard on the crowbar to pry him loose. You needed at least two people for that. He was like a used car with a thirty-day warranty, which had run out; there was no getting rid of him now.

He gave her bad dreams. He *was* a bad dream. Of course, Amos Alonzo Thorkelson was making everybody crazy these days, but Ludlow's craziness was more personal and apocalyptic than that of most of them. Even his lovemaking had a subtle undercurrent of violence, although he never hurt her. His orgasms were like psychic calamities during which he made noises as if an explosive device had detonated inside him, requiring first aid.

But if he had loved her, she might have managed somehow. On that score, he'd set her straight. Her car had been in the shop for repairs, and they had decided to take a night off for dinner and a movie. To get there and to return, they would have to take public transportation. When they were a block away from their local bus stop, the Number 4 pulled up and disgorged its passengers. Ludlow let go of Christina's hand and sprinted toward the bus, squeezing on just as the doors were closing and the bus pulled away. She was left behind, watching it roar down the street. He got off at the next stop, but even so, she knew from the way he had abandoned her there on the sidewalk that he had never loved her; he did not love her now, and he would never love her.

Also he had started to complain about her kisses. He seemed to have developed an aversion to her tongue and the way she used it during sex. He would stop the show, turn on the bedroom light, and lecture her about what her tongue should and should not do. He took obvious pleasure in humiliating her. How many more warning signs did she need?

In the middle of his lengthy disquisitions he seemed to be looking through her, not at her; she felt that she was gradually eroding away in his eyes. Soon she might not be there at all.

But that wasn't the real problem with him. The real problem lay elsewhere. He had an unkempt and disorderly soul.

IN THE MEANTIME, THE SUN COLLECTIVE HAD MOSTLY BRANCHED OUT as a group, though they occasionally met together in Northeast Minneapolis, occasionally in secret. For greater political efficiency they had divided themselves into smaller cells using the models of the early Christians and the Comintern. Reluctantly, they had gone online to combat the internet chatter about them. One group appeared to be engaged in legislative lobbying, while another, filled with refugees from the business world, was starting the co-op bank and operating a co-op grocery and food shelf; while a third seemed to be engaged in rehabilitations of homeless street people and converting civilians to Sun Collective principles through the manifesto, persuasion, and free food and clothing. The less visible you were, the more you could do. Termite actions.

One new motto they had was "We're not a group, we're an idea, and we're doing good works everywhere." Another motto was "We're implausible. Believe in the implausible." A third was "You can't see us, but we're here."

During her time away from the bank, Christina had taken on the semi-ironic title of Minister for Propaganda for the collective and was posting her very own ten-step program on her blog, titled "Happiness in a Corner," whose goal was the quiet serenity that she claimed was within reach, once you realized that whatever you possessed already would be enough to sustain you. You didn't have to buy much of anything. You could *de-consume;* there was no such word, but soon there would be. She herself felt no serenity whatsoever thanks to Ludlow—his dead eyes, his boredom with her, his distaste for her kisses—but believed that if she made the effort, eventually happiness would arrive on her doorstep somehow. Joy would take her over like a benevolent bout of flu she might have caught by breathing.

The collective had designated Wye, not Christina, to be its spokesperson. She felt she would have looked better on TV than he did. He still believed in visibility and publicity. "We are not Fight Club," he claimed. "We can talk about ourselves. We are not afraid of ourselves." He went around quoting everybody and anybody. "All of humanity's problems," he intoned on Channel 5's evening news, "stem from man's inability to sit quietly in a room alone." He was a sententious son of a bitch.

Still, something had to be done. If you watched TV and saw the news, or if you noticed what people were posting on Facebook, and what they were tweeting about, you would see President Amos Alonzo Thorkelson ("Call me 'Coach'") issuing edicts—securing the borders, temporarily closing down the Supreme Court by using the New Executive Army, and issuing personal "consumer vouchers" through the Commerce Department (ten dollars per adult-age individual, fifteen dollars for those on Social Security, thirty dollars for those on Medicare) to be spent only in certain friendly retail outlets whose CEOs had supported Thorkelson's most recent presidential campaign. "We're getting America back to work again! And we're spending like there's no tomorrow! Because, who knows, maybe there isn't!" he said with his gameshow grin. His rallies ended with twenty- and fifty-dollar bills fluttering down from the ceiling to the supporters below, all of them roaring with happiness and holding out their hands turned upward as the Chief Executive beamed at them with his arms crossed, surrounded by his bodyguards.

You had to apply to get into his rallies. "Many are called, but few are chosen," President Thorkelson said with another trademark expression, pointing at the camera like Uncle Sam.

The real problem was what people were saying on the internet. A new rumor had started to the effect that the Sun Collective was a front organization secretly invented and funded by Amos Alonzo Thorkelson himself to create a convenient false-flag enemy. They weren't just a local activist group that had started up in a neighborhood, these rumors said; no, the word was out that the Sun Collective was an invention of President Amos Alonzo Thorkelson himself, a man who needed idealistic enemies to mock and belittle. On Twitter, the president had suggested that the Utopia Mall itself might be in danger, menaced by local "crazies," as he called them, and commentators were quick to name the Sun Collective as exactly that: an unhinged, untethered political group whose agenda was one of terror and whose goal was to bring down the Utopia Mall. They hadn't said so, but you could just tell.

After putting up notices about workshop sessions in co-ops and independent businesses, and posting other notices on social media, Christina would return home to her apartment unsure whether she wanted Ludlow to be there, but he had his own schedule by now and usually didn't return until after midnight. Tired and unclean, he would climb into bed and curl himself around her, and when she asked him where he had been, he would say that he had been out there in the big, wide world. He had projects, he murmured.

"Where?" she would ask sleepily.

"Here and there."

"You smell funny." She sniffed. "Are those chemicals?"

"Go to sleep," he said.

So there she was, working at the bank by day, volunteering for community action in the evenings as a consumerist-addiction counselor, trying to combat the internet rumors spreading about the collective's various projects, and trying, really trying, to figure out how to get Ludlow out of her life. He was hanging on to her like grim death. And because she usually knew what he was thinking without his having to say anything, she knew that he was contemplating newsworthy trouble and its lethal practical applications.

IN THE MORNINGS, LUDLOW WOULD OFTEN BE GONE AGAIN, ENGAGED, he said, on secret projects he would not disclose to her, though in his absentminded manner, he left notes and drawings on the kitchen counter and the living room coffee table.

Ck. on poss. of timers & sl. powder plus remstn

Those *boys*. The boys ruined everything! You'd go to work, organizing urban neighborhood gardens and meetings on constructive, achievable happiness, and you'd march down to the streets and to the new SC homeless shelters, and you'd institute programs and procedures to help people get back on their feet, setting them up in affordable housing and work-training programs. Meanwhile, as you were doing all that, in the back of the room, the boys (you couldn't really call them "men" when they got like that), including Ludlow, were talking, huddled together, whispering, hatching their little plans of revenge and ruination.

And what they wanted to do was blow things up. Disintegration and de-creation were in their nature, buried in their hiding places underground, where their boy bomb-love could fester and grow. What she and her co-workers built up, they would tear down. She knew how these boys thought. All her life she'd watched them. Men looked at women, but women *watched* men; that was the difference.

On his right shoulder, on the other side of his body from the YOU'RE WELCOME! on his left arm, Ludlow had acquired a tattoo with a death's-head, signifying that he had become a soldier in some new private army dedicated to bloodletting, and she imagined him as a horseman with a skull's face galloping down toward Earth where fuses were lit here and there for bombs that would put down a marker, it hardly mattered where, to send an underlined message, a notice in boldface type, that things would not go on any longer in the way they had. The pillars of the temple had to be knocked down. Force was required. The mass murderers also had to be put in their place, at least temporarily. Each week brought news of another unsociable boy who had opened fire on a bar or a nightclub where people were dancing—the mass murderers seemed to have a special hatred of dancing—and where the partiers were intolerably happy, the particular happiness that enraged solitary and lonely men. Mass shootings, however, were the wrong way to bring about the revolution. A mass shooting was a statement, all right, but an unintelligible one. You needed more firepower to make a genuine statement, one that everybody could agree with. Such was Ludlow's thinking.

Somehow the sunshine part of the Sun Collective hadn't managed to shine down on those guys. What they wanted was the fusion part of the sun, a little manageable core of the H-bomb lit by a fuse before the perpetrator scurried away in his pickup. Nitromethane was more their style.

She would have to talk to somebody about Ludlow, who was growing eerily calm, more detached and zombified, as if he were thinking constantly about something unspeakable. He was behaving like a man who is carrying on a clandestine affair—not with a woman but with an idea, one that he loved and that was probably, technically, criminal.

To whom could she talk about him? Timothy Brettigan? Maybe not yet. What about Wye? Or someone. Just last night, when Ludlow came home, she had met up with him in the kitchen. She was seated at the kitchen table and he stood at the back door with that innocent look on his face. He had been beautiful once, when she still temporarily loved him. Now that the love was gone, he had become quite ugly.

"Where've you been?" she asked. She was trying to project indifference.

"Around. Doing stuff."

"Care to tell me?"

"No."

"Are you seeing somebody else?"

"No. Why? You mean another woman? No. I'm not like that."

"I think you're planning something. I think you're planning to hurt some people."

"What makes you think that?" he asked. He was actually grinning.

"I know you."

"Not *that* well. I have curtains and screens. They make me invisible."

"You want to scare everyone. You've said so."

"People need to be scared. It wakes them up. You gotta break their heads open."

"Ludlow, you talk in your sleep, speaking of which. I hear what you've been saying."

He seemed startled. "Well, I don't, I never—I don't talk that much. And besides, it's, um, better for you not to know what I'm about to do." He thought for a moment. "It's world-historical. I got the vision-goggles on."

"What the fuck does that mean?"

"You have to, well, I have to wake people up, like I said. By any means necessary. I'm the person to do it."

"I wish you wouldn't talk in clichés. I wish you were an ordinary guy. I wish I could love you. I wish you would just go away." She was gazing at the floor, at her own bare feet.

"You don't mean that. Besides, there's no getting rid of me. I'm here to stay."

"I'm not going to sleep with you anymore," she told him, still looking down.

"Okay," he said amiably.

"Someone should turn you in," she said, "before you start hurting children, or whoever."

"Nobody will turn me in because, guess what, I haven't done anything. Yet. Good night." And he crossed the kitchen and headed toward the living room sofa.

SHE WAS SITTING AT THAT SAME KITCHEN TABLE TWO MORNINGS LATER on a Saturday, following a sleepless night when she realized that she would have to talk to somebody. When you were dealing with anarchists, no one was in charge, so she might as well talk to Wye. Conversation with him was like listening to an oracle, but sometimes one had to put up with his platitudinous wisdom. When she called him, he told her that they should meet in the little public zoo on the other side of the Mississippi, not at Sun Collective headquarters. "Too many eavesdroppers here," he said with a mirthless chuckle. She could hear his accompanying scowl over the phone. He often scowled when he laughed. The zoo was open 365 days a year, he told her, and the public was always welcome there, no matter what. The animals would also be pleased to see them. The animals were bored and lonely this time of year.

"But it's November," she said, glancing out the window. "There's already snow on the ground. No, wait." She heard a tapping on the pane, as if someone were tossing pebbles. "It's snowing now."

"The zoo is open *every day of the year,*" Wye repeated with an odd intensity. "Wear your overcoat and your boots. The zoo animals get forlorn when winter comes. Whenever the snow is falling, they overcome their distaste for human beings and welcome us. We should always talk to lonesome, deserted animals. In a snowstorm, they particularly need company."

Sometimes he could sound so . . . what was the word? *Moralistic.* Even though he was usually correct.

"Oh, all right," she said.

"Let's meet in front of the wolves," he suggested.

THE SNOW WAS FALLING SO THICKLY THAT HER CAR'S WIPERS AND THE hot-air defrost blower couldn't remove the flakes before they melted and refroze, and by the time she was a mile away from the zoo, her windshield had curved striations of ice blocking her view of the street. The weather reminded her of the first night she'd met Ludlow, months ago, last winter—the snow falling, the spectral playground inhabited by ghost-children, the tear in spacetime. She pulled over, parked the car in front of a boarded-up restaurant, The Serpent, swore to herself, and took out the ice scraper. Feeling the flakes of falling snow dropping like tiny cold insects inside her collar and forming little melting clusters of water that dripped down her back, she swore again as she removed the ice, chip by chip. She could feel her fingers inside her gloves burning with cold, and the tips of her toes deadening with incipient frostbite. She wished she had worn her thick gray woolen socks, the ones with the crisscross pattern. Why in God's name did anyone live in a frigid climate like this one? You had to have a mind of winter to live here.

Behind the wheel again, she skidded down a side street, the car fishtailing while the windshield wipers made horrible death rattles as they pulled themselves over the quickly reappearing snow-impacted ice, and when she finally pulled up next to the zoo and the little amusement park that stood out in front of it facing the street and the parking lot, she couldn't see more than two car lengths ahead of her. To the side, the Tilt-A-Whirl ride was quickly being buried, obliterated, under layers of soft snow, its individual cars covered with blue protective plastic tarp gradually growing whitely indistinct, the ride standing next to a shuttered popcorn-and-donuts stand on top of which a solitary crow, apparently in charge of its surroundings, first surveyed the scene and then flew off after spotting Christina and uttering a single admonitory caw.

The sounds of traffic—the sounds of everything—were muffled by the snowfall. Even the few cars passing by seemed to have been silenced, the only noise they made being the soft crunch of tires and the occasional anguished whine of spinning wheels.

Lifting her feet to get through the drifts, she made her way toward the indoor botanical conservatory, and, once inside, she stamped her boots free from snow as she breathed in the warm, humid, artificially tropical air. The plant rooms—the ferns, the orchids, the flowers, the pools with goldfish—had a few visitors, refugees from winter, and in one of the sections of the conservatory, she saw a couple being married, the high glass dome over their heads darkening from the storm outside.

The bride wore white, a gown resembling the snow falling onto the glass above them, and the handsome groom, wearing a dark blue tuxedo, red cummerbund, and tennis shoes, was now stumbling through his homemade improvised vows as he held the bride's hands in his. "Edie, I promise you that I'll always for sure be there for you, in like sickness, and, um, health also," he said in a nervous monotone, staring into her eyes. "Because I love you and the love we have for each other is, like, cement." *Cement?* Behind the couple was a ragtag group of friends and relatives, wearing flannel shirts and jeans, witnessing the vows.

Christina felt herself tearing up. Those two were just strangers. She didn't know them, and they were so young, they could be teenagers. They hardly knew each other, probably. Who cared what they were doing here, what vows they were making? Apparently, *she,* Christina, did: she wiped a few tears off her cheeks. The heat and the tropical air must have once inspired those two to get engaged; that must be it.

She could imagine the scene: they'd been walking through the

Fern Room a year or so ago, and, overcome with the indoor heat and humidity, the catalysts for love and lust, he'd gotten down on one knee and proposed to her.

Christina despised love junkies but, standing there in the conservatory's humid air, she wanted just a portion of all that for herself, and someone to love her.

BRACING HERSELF, AND INVOLUNTARILY BUNCHING HER SHOULDERS together, she walked forward out of the conservatory and into the snowstorm outside, following a path that led into the little zoo. Almost no one was here. She saw one maintenance worker clearing a path on the sidewalk, and, ahead of her, a tall forlorn solitary man, though certainly not Wye, wearing a stocking cap, a red scarf, and a long brown winter overcoat, approaching her. The guy was walking with his head down, his hands in his overcoat pockets, past the primate cage. *Another lost soul,* she thought, somebody killing time by wandering through the zoo in November. Seeing Christina, he turned toward her and waved, a gesture of pure loneliness. Snow covered the lenses of his eyeglasses and was nestling in his eyebrows, though he must have seen her somehow, because, after all, he had waved at her. He coughed.

What the hell: she waved back.

Putting her hands back into her pockets, Christina plunged ahead, the snow now getting under her cap into her eyes and sticking to her eyelashes, as she walked into the Primate Building. Inside, the little monkeys, or whatever they were, were crouched in pairs grooming each other, and after studying their solicitous behavior, she walked out the other side of the building toward the western edge of the zoo where the wolves were caged.

THEIR OUTDOOR PEN WAS ABOUT HALF THE SIZE OF A FOOTBALL FIELD. The wolves, like the snow, were white, and one of them was pacing back and forth at the edge of the opposite side near the high fencing.

Each time the wolf reached the corner, it would turn and head back in the direction from which it had come. It seemed to be trying to solve a problem. The animal appeared to be thinking. What, Christina wondered, was it worrying about? Maybe the problem it was trying to solve was *What am I doing here? How did I get here? And how do I get out?* Christina projected her thoughts into the wolf's mind, and thoughts from the wolf came back to her. *There must be an answer,* the wolf believed, in wolf-thought. In wolf-world, everything had a purpose, except being in a zoo. All caged and imprisoned creatures were forced to mull over such questions.

For a moment, looking at the height of the fencing, Christina imagined herself inside the enclosure, and the wolf outside, free.

On this side of the cage, only half-visible in the storm, stood Wye. He wore a bright blue parka matted with snow, thick mittens, and a woolen cap on which snow had already accumulated. His dark glasses, the ones that he customarily wore, had a curtain of snow over them, and more snow was accumulating in his scraggly beard. He looked like a sage in disguise, a snow-bespectacled shaman. As Christina approached him, she heard him muttering instructions to the wolves.

"This is where the magic happens," Wye said, studying the pacing wolf.

"What? What magic?" Christina asked. "I don't see any magic."

"You have come here," Wye continued, still not turning around to acknowledge her—it was one of his gifts to know when people were nearby him, given his creepy extrasensitive human radar—"you have come here to ask about your boyfriend, Ludlow, and about the other one, Timothy."

"Yes. How did you know?"

"Wolves don't like human beings, did you know that?" Wye asked. "They detest and avoid us. They can't stand the way we smell. Our smell offends them. Even when starving, they will not come into a city. If they come near us, it is against their nature." All at once he let out a whistle, followed by a high keening cry, an *ai-ai-ai* that made both wolves regard him slowly and suspiciously, as if he'd spoken the password but mispronounced it. In response, however, the two wolves ambled toward Wye and Christina, on their side of the metal fencing. On the back of each wolf was a layer of snow. Wye reached into his pocket and pulled out a piece of candy, a Skittle, but instead of feeding it to the wolf, he popped it into his mouth. It was a territorial gesture.

"Wye, I think Ludlow is in some kind of trouble, and I—"

"Oh, he's not in any *trouble,* Christina dear. Don't you worry. Anyway, I wouldn't call it 'trouble.'"

"I think he's constructing a bomb or something." One of the wolves was still approaching the two of them, seemingly not afraid. "He won't talk about it. I don't know for sure, but I have this intuition. It has me worried. He talks in his sleep."

"Did you know that the Aztec god of the sun was Huitzilopochtli?" Wye's voice was phlegmy. "He was also the god of war, and so he did double duty. Tlaloc was the rain god. Both bloodthirsty gods required human sacrifice. It was the source of their power." His narration grew soft and tender, at a bedtime-story level. "Thousands upon thousands of men, women, and children. Those being sacrificed— well, their beating hearts were sawed out with an obsidian knife and then burned, right at the top of the Aztec pyramid. Imagine the flow of blood down the steps, the great pools of blood at the bottom! Children, too, were sacrificed, their little hearts cut right out of them. The gods require terrible, unthinkable actions from us. They give themselves that particular permission. That's why they're gods. Gods don't make requests. They make demands. You know: Abraham and Isaac. The Old Testament God was like that. Implacable."

"I wonder if there's a god of winter."

"Ullr," he said. "In other mythologies, Boreas."

"Wye," she asked, as both wolves edged closer, "why are you telling me this? Why are we here? I'm freezing out here."

"Because, my dear," he said, turning his dark glasses toward her, "the gods are about to ask something terrible of you, some actions that traditionally would cause fear and trembling, but now, in the modern age . . ."

His voice trailed off, or perhaps he was still speaking, and Christina couldn't hear his words because the snow continued to fall even harder than before, muffling his voice, and she was growing inattentive because, to her astonishment, the wolves continued to come nearer to them, as if Christina and Wye were their prey, but what was most odd about their presence before them was that their white fur had been camouflaged, subsumed, by the thick snowfall, producing a moment when, looking through the lattice-pattern fencing, all Christina could see of the wolves were their gray eyes seemingly floating in midair and fixed directly on her.

It was the strangest sight, those eyes in the midst of the snowfall, focused on her like suspended beams of light asking her a question to which she did not yet have an answer.

"What will be asked of me?" she said, still watching the animals. "What am I being called to do?"

"That would be telling," she thought she heard Wye say, but when she turned toward him, he seemed not to be there any longer.

24

WHEN ALMA OPENED THE MORNING PAPER, SHE SAW ON THE FRONT page two major stories, one national, the other local. The national news was that President Thorkelson had released his Monthly Poem, a practice he had instituted several months ago while claiming that he was treading in the footsteps of the great poet-presidents, Thomas Jefferson and Abraham Lincoln. Smiling crookedly at his news conference—one of Alma's friends had called it a "grim grin"—he had said that these United States suffered from a dearth of poetry and that he, Amos Alonzo Thorkelson, would fill that particular gap. America, after all, had a history of great poets. "Poetry is the heart and soul of the nation," President Thorkelson claimed. "No great country can long survive without great poems. Even our enemies recognized that simple fact. Chairman Mao wrote poems. Saddam Hussein wrote poems."

January's poem was on the subject of welfare cheats, and the poem was entitled "No Free Lunch." The president had recited his new poem at a news conference, and the paper had printed the entire poem in a sidebar.

NO FREE LUNCH

At the local supermart I saw
A sight to make me weep:
A woman buying tubs of slaw
With her eyes closed, half-asleep.

At the cash register she paid
For junk food with a wad
Of food stamps, and this made
Me very very very sad,

For she was superfat and didn't need
More food of any kind
Paid for by taxpayers. Her breed
Of food hound you will find

Waddling down each grocery aisle
Past the fresh produce and the fruit
To grab a fistful and then a pile
Of popcorn, chips, and candied loot.

Ounces, pounds, and lbs. to spare
Loaded in the grocery cart
For the Winner at the Fatty Fair
Who pays with food stamps at our
supermart.

No more! No more! The voters bray:
Fat lady, you have been sacked!
For we have heard a wise man say
The times they are a-changin' back.

"That's absolutely and without any doubt the worst poem I've ever read in my life," Alma said to her husband, who was sitting at the other end of the table eating a banana, whose peel was green at one end and overripe at the other. He was taking careful bites. He had already finished his cup of coffee. Alma was clutching her brown mug of chamomile tea with both hands. Steam rose from it and clouded her glasses. "And vicious. Plus stupid. He's such a shameless know-nothing. People go around reciting this trash."

"Hmm," Brettigan said. He was eating his banana quickly, from the unripe end downward until it got soft, because the Thundering Herd would be exercising out at the Utopia Mall in an hour, and he didn't want to be as late as he usually was.

On the other side of the front page, the paper reported a gas-line explosion in downtown Wayswater, at a women's clothing store, F. Christianson & Co., which specialized in elegant, high-end fashion for the yacht club and country club set. Forensic teams were investigating.

"Did you see this report?" she asked. "About the natural gas explosion? In Wayswater? At the F. Christianson?"

"Anybody hurt? Killed?"

"Doesn't say. Probably not. Seems to have happened after closing time."

After exhaling, he brushed away crumbs from his sweater and smiled halfheartedly. "Want some more tea? By the way, when was the last time you saw Tim?" The question was preemptive. He knew the answer, because Alma's depressions and fears had abated, now that their son had been rehabilitated by the Sun Collective, and she was happy to tell Brettigan about all the lunches she'd had with Tim downtown, and how *good* and how *happy* he had now seemed. He had dinner with his parents every two weeks or so, a bit dutifully, but he was a recovering adult, after all. Sometimes she thought he was *too* good, *too* happy, for comfort. Still, he was back in town; he was sober; and he was taking his meds. He had a job at the Alhambra Theater in Uptown as the assistant manager, and he had an efficiency apartment nearby. God bless the Sun Collective, she had said. Now if they could only find him a nice woman, everything would be fine. Still, watching Alma at the breakfast table, Brettigan wanted to hear her repeat her news of Tim. He was curious about the tone she would take.

"A few days ago," she told Brettigan. "He and I had lunch downtown. At Chez Antoine? Don't you remember? I *told* you. I had a Cobb salad. Tim was . . . fine. You never remember anything I tell you," she said, with some odd darkness creeping into her voice. "You don't pay me much attention. I could be dying here and you'd never notice. I should get used to it, but I never do."

"Oh, I'd notice if you were dying. Well, I've got to go," Brettigan said. He stood up halfway before sitting down again.

"What?"

"I have a question for you," he said, without asking it.

"Don't you have to get to the Utopia Mall for that senile exercise gang of yours? So ask," she said, biting into a piece of cold toast. Still chewing, she rose and went over to the stove, where she was making hard-boiled eggs. The timer buzzed, and she turned off the heat.

Brettigan coughed, then said, "Has he, do you know, I mean . . . these difficulties and so forth, and . . . so I'm wondering what Tim's been doing with the Sun Collective."

"He isn't doing anything with them." She sat down again, taking an extended look at her husband.

"How do you know?"

"You always make them sound like wackos. They're just plain citizens. Listen, Harry, they're working for community gardens and improving urban environments and encouraging people to stop buying what they don't need. They're *helping* people, and is that so bad? Come on. You can see what they've done with your own son. Rehabilitations—they've stepped up when no one else has. What's the harm? They're idealists. Who doesn't want a better life?"

"Well, for starters, I don't. Let's start with me. I like the life I've got. I'm grateful for it. Harmless *sun worshippers*? There's no such thing as harmless. You don't know how or why they're rehabilitating anybody. You don't have a clue about what they're doing over there. Nobody does, except them."

"I've gone to their meetings."

"That's for the public. That's just a sideshow. You gotta get into the inner circle."

"Oh, Jesus." She slammed her fist on the table, making the forks rattle. "I can't *stand* your cynicism! So what makes you the great expert? Do you actually *give a damn*? About anything? About Tim?

They're fighting for *better human beings*—and they want to rehab the insulted and injured, I mean, they're not just a bunch of complacent fatheads sitting at the bar and drinking beer and watching football like most men your age. They want to improve the world. What's wrong with that?"

"Alma, dear, you're sermonizing. I hate it when you get like this. I *like* the world the way it is." He had the beginnings of a cold, and when he took out his handkerchief to wipe his nose, he sneezed. "I don't want better human beings than the ones they have now. Even if I did, you wouldn't get them."

"Yeah, I bet you don't." The measuring expression on her face was both unsympathetic and direct. "Pretty soon you'll be writing monthly poems yourself. I can't wait. An ode to your reclining chair? A sestina about the microwave? A sonnet on the subject of fresh vegetables in the produce section?"

They sat in silence for a moment staring at each other. "You know, I had ideals once," he said.

"And? So?"

"A bunch of us once broke into a Selective Service office during the Vietnam War. We opened the files and poured pigs' blood onto the records. We almost got caught."

She leaned back and closed her eyes. A theatrical sigh came out of her. "That tired old story. It makes its appearance one more time. Okay, here's the Applause sign." She raised her arm in the air and pulled an invisible cord. "I *know* that story—I know *all* your stories. I know your entire *history*, Harry, for chrissake, every little botch and twig and stone in it, every little success and failure, every doodling up and down, every snicker. Anyway, by now your history is, let's call it, *ancient* history? Yes, let's call it that. Okay, there we go, the Dark Ages way back there, in your *youth*, back when you had *values*. Yes, those were the days. The difference is, I'm talking about right now. I'm talking about Tim. Who is alive. And working. And sane. At last."

"Alma, listen to yourself. You're getting to be a blowhard. Every sentence out of your mouth is a cliché." He smiled, then raised his arms in song. "Ah, white liberals, where would we be without us?"

"And Harry, I love you, but now that you're old you're getting to be such a shit, and you're going to be the death of me. I mean it."

"Please don't shout."

The orange peel she threw at him sailed past his right ear and landed on the floor. She wouldn't throw the saltshaker: he was sitting in front of the alcove window, and it would have broken the pane. In the meantime, the dog and the cat, Woland and Behemoth, had come into the kitchen and had taken up battle stations: Behemoth jumped up onto the window ledge, where she could see Alma, and Woland sat several arms' lengths away, near the dishwasher, as if he were afraid of domestic violence and could run to the basement if the situation warranted it.

"They're worried," Brettigan said, observing them. "They're like children. They think something is really going to happen."

Alma studied the dog's face for a moment. "Those animals are smarter than you think they are. They can smell your fear."

Finishing his banana, he removed what was left of the center and threw the peel in her direction. She caught it with one hand and threw it back. He let it fall to the floor.

"I don't love you anymore," she said, with something like a smile.

"You don't mean that, but I don't love you, either," he replied calmly, getting into the spirit of things. "Anyway, make up your mind. You said you loved me a minute ago and just now you said you didn't."

"You're impossible. I can't stand the way you talk. I can't stand the way you *are*. You're not even my type."

"Woe is you. I know."

"And you're wicked. And complacent. You disgust me."

"That's as sad as it can be. Isn't it awful?" he asked. "They should just come and haul me away."

"I already called them. They'll be here any minute now. With their paddy wagon."

"They don't haul humans with paddy wagons anymore. They have all the new devices. It's trucks now, with electric cages inside. Handcuffs. Up-to-date torture equipment."

"You're just laughing this off," Alma said, sounding disgruntled.

The dog had been watching both of them, turning his head back and forth like a spectator at a tennis match. Now he appeared to be bored.

"Laughing? Do you see me laughing? I haven't laughed once. You don't put words in my mouth, but you do put other stuff there."

She pointed down at the floor. "You should pick up that banana peel before someone slips on it."

"Alma, you threw it there. *You* pick it up. And I'm the disgusting one?"

"I thought you'd catch it. Harry, do we sound like an old couple? The Bickersons? I think we do, actually."

"Yeah, I guess so. How come you called me 'wicked' just now, by the way? Were you just fooling and pretending?"

She sighed. "We don't even fight the way we used to. The fun's gone out of it. It used to throw you for a loop when I told you I didn't love you anymore. You'd get hysterical and sad and tear up. Now you don't even notice when I say it. You don't care. You don't raise a single eyebrow."

"Sure, I care. My eyebrow went up an eighth of an inch. I asked about your use of 'wicked.' If that isn't caring, what is?"

"Harry, how long have we lived together?" she asked. "How long have we been married?"

"You're being evasive."

"Decades, that's for how long." With her elbow on the table, she propped her head on her palm. "No. *Centuries.* Before recorded history. I think I've been married to you all my entire life, and maybe before that. I was married to you before I was born. In the pre-universe. Since before the Big Bang."

" 'Wicked.' I hate to repeat myself, but why did you use that word?"

"I can't remember."

"Well, try. Think back."

"I didn't call you 'wicked.' That's for witches."

"Don't deny it."

"I never called you a 'witch,' " she said. "I would never do that. A warlock, maybe."

"Could we please get to the point? 'Wicked'?"

"You didn't mind calling yourself 'disgusting' by the way."

"I'm an old man. Old men are disgusting by nature. I can carry that burden. But 'wicked'?"

"You're going to miss your geezer group out at the mall."

"Well, I'm late already." He checked the kitchen clock.

"You let things happen. You just let the world slide along. Slipping and sliding, slipping and sliding: that's you."

Brettigan sat up straight, took out his soiled handkerchief, and glanced at the ceiling. Then he blew his nose. "Why can't we just be happy that our son is back in town? I guess we can't. Anyway, one time," he said, "there was this one time, and because you think you know everything about me, I'll tell you a story that you *don't* know. I never told you this story, because . why? Well, I just didn't. Anyway, this was, oh, maybe two years after we were married. You and me.

"So anyway there I was, two years after we were married in that backyard, out there at the world's end visiting my very own mother on a Friday night, and you were home in our apartment, not accompanying me on my trek to visit my mother, whom you did not like and who was, let's be honest, and sad to say, in her cups that particular evening. She was sitting on the sofa, my mother, smoking her cigarettes and slurring her words the way she did once it got dark outside and after her cup had brimmed over a few times. And because she often liked to order me around, even though I was an adult married man, she asked me to go over to the shelf where the family photographs were perched in their standing frames, because I would find a little private something behind one of those photographs, a little something I should see. And, sure enough, when I did as I had been instructed, I found, behind a photograph of me as a little boy wearing my sailor hat, a stash, a stash of what seemed to be newspaper clippings.

" 'Did you find them?' my mother slurred, and I said, 'Yes,' because indeed I *had* found them and brought them over to where she sat, and what they were, as I went through them . . . were these pictures of babies, little human creatures, infants, ten or twenty or thirty photographs of babies that she had clipped out of magazines and newspapers, just for my benefit, or should I say, *our* benefit. Why had she clipped out these pictures of babies? Well, subtlety had never been my mother's strong suit. The idea was, you and I should get cracking, get busy, get it on, get you knocked up, pregnant, pronto, so there would be a child and then a whole host of grandchildren for her to dote over, or whatever. She didn't *say* anything, my mother. She just looked with her watery shining eyes at me as I sifted through these newspaper and magazine clippings of these cherubic offspring in their little cribs and cradles.

"So of course I got the point, the request moment achieved itself, and then the evening was over, and I kissed my mother good night on the cheek and got in my car and drove away, out of the suburbs and back into town. I *had* had a drink or two but wasn't drunk—fortunately, as it happens. Because my idea was to take the back roads, and when I was just outside of the town of Hopkins, I came upon an accident, which had obviously occurred a mere few minutes before I got there, because only one other car was in attendance, actually a pickup truck, and this was before cell phones, and so somebody would've had to have gone somewhere to call the police and the emergency squad, for the EMTs. And my heart began beating fast, because the wrecked car, which had swerved off the highway and lost control, and then come swerving back on the highway and hit another car, was an old gray Ford, just like, I almost said 'identical to,' your old gray Ford, the one you had back then, and I thought, Oh, Jesus, it might be you. On the pavement you could see broken glass and green antifreeze fluid, and rubble. Enclosed inside the wreck was a woman still behind the wheel, in shock, I think, or at least not getting out, talking loudly to herself, and I couldn't see her clearly, just her hair, same color as yours. So I was saying as I got closer, approaching her, 'Alma, Alma,' like a prayer, but, as we both know now, that wasn't you. She was somebody else.

"I stayed long enough with that car and that woman and the pickup truck guy to comfort her until the police and the ambulance arrived, and once she was ambulanced away, I got back into my car and drove back home. To you. I walked in and maybe expected to see you sitting up reading or watching TV, but, no: you had turned in early. For the night. I came in and closed the apartment door, and I heard you call from bed, 'How was it? How's your mom?' and I said 'Okay,' and after I drank a glass of water, I headed into the bedroom. The light was off, and there you were. You hadn't worn your nightgown that night, so you were splendid in your winter nakedness, and after I undressed, we made plain old homespun love that night, no fireworks, nothing special.

"And that was the night we made Virginia. That girl, that woman, exists because of my mother's alcoholism and her newspaper and magazine clippings, and because I saw a woman who had just been in an automobile accident and who looked like you, and because you weren't wearing your nightgown once I got home. That's why Virginia is on this Earth." Brettigan leaned back, his story concluded, and closed his eyes. "I never told you that story."

Alma rose and walked over to where her husband was sitting, avoiding the banana peel on the floor on her way. Positioning herself behind where he sat, she put her chin on the top of his head. She put her arms down over his chest after wiping away the tears from his cheeks.

"Don't go to the mall," she said quietly.

"I need exercise."

"For what? No, you don't."

"What are we going to do? If we stay here?"

"We're going to go upstairs and lie down and hold each other."

"That's sentimental."

"Well, okay, I don't care," she said. "Come on. We just have to."

Together they went upstairs, the cat and the dog padding behind them.

25

TIME AND SPACE WERE GETTING MIXED UP AND MULTIDIMENSIONAL,
Christina noticed, particularly after the ingestion (by her) of several
tabs—in the psychological undertow following the zoo episode, when
Wye, or somebody like him, had been on both sides of the wolf
cage, those pills were really getting quite necessary, you could say
"urgent"—of Blue Telephone from a new improved batch concocted
by that genius misfit albino living in Memphis, making daily life like
something out of a quantum mechanics experiment, so that what was
going to happen seemed already to have happened, and you could
be in two places at the same time, and the task that life was about to
put onto her dinner plate was getting much closer to where she was
actually located at the table, so to speak. As predicted by Ludlow, she
was living a quantum life like Schrödinger's cat. She was both particle
and wave. She was *here* but also *there, now* and also *then.* For starters,
certain informants now claimed that the Sun Collective had moved
into its second phase, "Phase Two," they called it, the "certain informants" and "they" being Ludlow, who wanted to make his personal
initiative sound as bland as possible, and they, or he, announced that
in the past, it, we, she, you, had been going in the wrong direction,
the direction of compassion and little urban improvements, vegetable
gardens on vacant lots and the restoration of street-dwelling human
wreckage such as Timothy Brettigan, free clothes and food, universal
basic income, that sort of thing, humble ameliorations, but now the
right direction would be toward rage and pitilessness, so that violence, which had once been micro, would henceforth be macro. It

would leave a strong impression. Nerves would be shattered. Death was implied, multiple deaths. Humanism and terror: one would morph into the other because, it, they, had to. No one would be spared, the custodians of white privilege, especially. Would the white privileged children be spared? The answer, apparently, was also "No." Why should they be? You had to have courage to wrest control of the narrative. It took real nerve. If white children were not immune, then no one was safe.

Because now Ludlow was not sleeping. He was awake all night, like the fire department. He was talking and being a little more tartly conversational about the making of Tovex sausages, for instance, which Christina had to look up on Google, and you would *not* like what you found there if you didn't admire big-time explosives, several floors up from homemade pipe bombs—no, these new bangers were the world-shapers that altered history and about which Ludlow seemed uncommonly happy and enthusiastic. "The point," he said, "is not to float down the river of history but to alter its direction," quoting Lenin or Nietzsche or maybe Dr. Phil. *Someone* had said it.

And he was being sly, Ludlow was, about the garage, "My garage," he called it with proprietary delight, somewhere on the other side of Minneapolis, though he didn't say exactly where, a rented and possibly imaginary garage where he was assembling his explosives, which, he said, would turn the tide against President Amos Alonzo Thorkelson, the current Chief Executive; but how would that happen? you might ask. When you were living a quantum life, your mind included a radioactive atomic pile, a critical mass, flaring up now and then, often in two places at once, surrounding your bed while you tried to sleep following the episodes of crying and begging and arguing with Ludlow during which you tried to persuade him not to do what he planned to do. Tears, many idle tears, had been shed by Christina, in an effort to change Ludlow's mind. You could report him to the police except, no, you couldn't, because he hadn't done anything and maybe the garage and the explosives were all, *where, exactly? What?* Imaginary. Just a garage in his head. You couldn't tell with him.

He belonged maybe in either a prison or a lunatic asylum or

another like-minded gated community, but you couldn't get him into any such place voluntarily. He was one of many whom President Thorkelson had made mad, in the sense of crazy. He was also quoting from everybody and anybody, he had turned into a quote-machine, an open-pit mine of allusion, spewing words out. He said, "Listen to this: 'Every act we take now is a response to crisis.' Oh, and this, too: 'Spirit is thus self-supporting, absolute, real being. All previous shapes of consciousness are abstract forms of it.' That's Hegel. What he means is that scientific analysis of our contemporary history demands that we alter it radically so that Spirit, which is us, overthrows the previous, um, historical situation."

Also he had a black eye from a fistfight he had had with Timothy Brettigan, who in defense of all human beings everywhere had argued with him and tried to get the location of the garage out of him, which effort had failed. They'd been drunk, both of them, and there had been yelling that had been so loud that even Christina heard it, in her imagination wired to the Blue Telephone, although she had not been there, witnessing the fistfight, at the time. She didn't have to be. She heard everything he said wherever he was. She had a switchboard connected to Outer Space and to all Earthly points. And to make matters worse, or better, she was maybe falling in love with Timothy Brettigan (again), a man who wanted to save the lost, the unrewarded, the inconsolable, the abandoned, the forsaken, the unglued, the untethered.

And Christina found herself bilocating and sometimes liking it: seated, or standing, in the apartment living room listening to Ludlow pace back and forth as he talked about the necessary historical changes that involved mayhem directed at the innocents (an event that would go viral, really control the internet chatter and help bring about the revolution, topple the old hierarchies, also maybe Thorkelson too, nicknamed "Coach," because in Ludlow's opinion there actually and in fact were no innocents, with the result that there would be massive introspection, nerve storms, and stocktaking), and at the same time, she would be, simultaneously, speeding in her old clunker car, the old blood-clot-colored Saab, with no passenger airbag, toward a tree. The tree would stop both history and Ludlow, who had, somehow, mysteriously, turned from being an ordinary guy who practiced yoga to being evil.

Because for an absolute certainty, although she hadn't done it yet, she had already injured Ludlow. It was going to happen and had happened already; it *had* to happen, Blue Telephonically, but now she was getting both ahead and behind of herself, or so it seemed. She was in that car headed toward that tree, having forced some tiny pebble grit and a dime into Ludlow's passenger-side seat belt clasp so that it would jam and would not work, but she was also and at the same time in the living room listening to Ludlow talk in monologue form about how only violence could alter consciousness, a fact that authorized the history-smashing bombing of, it appeared, an elementary school, which was imminent, as planned by him.

With what person could she possibly consult? She, Christina, was high all the time these days in fear and terror on behalf of those children, and, yes, on behalf of herself, so that now she found her own body standing at the bank, which was her employer, and then forthwith inside the tobacco-scented office of her friend and boss, Jürgen, that gentle man, and being careful not to tell him exactly what her boyfriend, or whoever he was, planned to do, she was nevertheless and broadly speaking inquiring plainly how a person like her should act and behave as a citizen and a decent human being, *What should I do?* et cetera, given this situation, and after all why not Jürgen, whose family had witnessed history with blood all over its teeth and claws and now could give advice, being an avatar of civilization, and German? He stroked his mustache, and his smile diminished into a frown. Overhead the fluorescent light flickered, as if in sympathy, and the room seemed to tilt, a bit, like a fun-house room or a Mystery Spot.

My dear woman, he said, if you know someone who means to do such harm to children, even if he is crazy, you must try to stop him, by any means necessary, *notwendig* and *ehrenwert,* he muttered under his breath, as he shook his head at the thought of her boyfriend, this shabby character who intended harm. And even at the same time as she was speaking to Jürgen, she also, past and future, found herself in Timothy Brettigan's basement apartment, consulting with the former actor, who said, *You must talk Ludlow out of it and if you can't talk him out of it you must injure him somehow, or I will, again, but, no, I don't know how you can injure him without assaulting him. Sorry.* She kissed him because he had tried to give advice, but angels, the true ones, are helpless in the face of malice; they don't understand it and have no response to it because wickedness is not their department. If they understood it, they wouldn't be angels, would they? He had also invited her out for a date, but that would come later.

And so there she, Christina, was, back in her own apartment, and Ludlow was breathing on her and telling her to get off the Grid of Addiction, and, "Have I mentioned this already, you, Christina, should stop taking those BT pills, because they're fucking you up so bad? And they're doing this other thing: they're making you sort of transparent, and on some days I can't even see you when you're right there in front of me." She nodded at him, even though she was also elsewhere, bilocated in a classroom of seven- and eight-year-old children using their scissors and paste to cut out pictures of endangered animals. The pictures of the animals went into a scrapbook. Then they were labeled: Bengal Tiger, Giant Panda, Indian Elephant, Snow Leopard.

What did he have against children?

She was under a spell. The wolves at the zoo had approached her against their better judgment and with their pale gray eyes they had said that they were endangered, as wolves, and she was endangered also, as human, unless she took some immediate action. The little grade school children were seated at their desks in their classroom cutting out pictures of wolves, who, on the other side of the fence, had said in no uncertain terms that like all animals they had glimpses of the future, and she had better do whatever was necessary, because, *look:* There were the children, sweetly cutting and pasting their pictures, and there was Ludlow, still sleepy but defiant at the breakfast table, child mayhem on his mind, his orange juice to his right and his hot steaming coffee to his left, and his scrambled eggs with paprika right there in front of him, his bedheaded formerly cute hair standing straight up, the YOU'RE WELCOME! tattoo visible underneath his T-shirt, his bombs hidden away, and as he consumed the scrambled eggs he said (because he liked to mansplain at the breakfast table) that life had once been very simple before the industrial revolution, when everyone lived on farms in feudal conditions, but those conditions did not obtain anymore, and it wasn't enough to live simply and to practice loving-kindness and to renounce grudges. That was first-world discredited Buddhism, the dumbbell acceptance of everything that is. After God died, so did the Buddha, and Buddhism, which, in the end, was less powerful than greed, could not meet a spiritual payroll anymore, on account of its love for . . . well, everything. Quality had died, too. God took it with Him when He left. Now we all had to do the unthinkable, quote unquote, unthinkably opposed by Timothy Brettigan, a lifelong child admirer and charismatic (to Christina) ex-actor and guilt tripper, who would have none of Phase Two. Fuck him.

We have to put holy fear into the rich, claimed Ludlow as he gulped down his scrambled eggs, unchewed. Terror is our friend. Terror is the friend of reform. Humanism plus terror is the ticket. We have to stop being donkeys. The Donkey Era is over! The donkey and the Buddha had ambled away together, not as Two but as One. Fear and terror were our tools now, and, man, what is it with you, Christina, because you've gone into, like, a thin place, and I can see right through you. You gotta stop taking those pills. What was I saying? The unthinkable had to be thought right now, the planet was being killed off by the rich, the rich were in their plutocratic money bubble, their dim oligarchic haze, they had turned the planet into a vast Utopia Mall, and, surrounded by their money and the trinkets that cash and credit can buy, they were consuming the Earth, they were *eating* the Earth, chomping and chewing it up like slugs, and they were even now as we speak devising rockets for leaving the poor wasted post-apocalypse planet behind on their private rockets, they had a Mars or Bust! agenda, but for the rest of us the task is to do a wake-up call that would get the attention of the ruling klepto privileged class and the way to do that was to perform some unthinkable violence against Hilltop Elementary School because if that didn't wake up the rich not only here but everywhere, nothing else would.

What he was talking about was violence. Violence, he was saying, quoting Engels or Lenin or somebody, was the midwife of historical change. Christina didn't have many settled ethical principles, but she did have a strong position on that one. Nothing—nothing—on Earth justified harm against children. Which was why she had sort of fallen in love with Timothy Brettigan all over again, post-actor and post-Chicago, and in one of the quantum fields that she was living in now she was walking with him, and it was springtime, and their hands found each other, and they were holding hands, fingers entwined, which was more tender, and sweet, and life-sustaining than when Ludlow's dick had been inside her doing its nasty business, way back when. At the breakfast table, she had made up her mind, and in another spacetime continuum she had persuaded Ludlow to go out of town to a movie about superheroes and to get into the passenger side, the suicide seat, of the old blood-clot-colored Saab, and the snow leopard, and the Bengal tiger, and the giant panda in the children's scrapbook quietly and slowly turned their fond animal gazes toward her, and they told her to fasten her seat belt and to get ready to be hurt, because she would be, when, together, they hit that tree, head-on.

THEY ARE HEADED DOWN A DARK ROAD AT NIGHT. THEY ARE IN THE present tense in a both/and dimension. They have left the city. The panda and the tiger and the snowy owl are whispering to her, and the children, who have stopped cutting out pictures from magazines, are singing almost inaudibly to her that they love her (she's in the car, in the classroom, at the zoo, staggering down a hallway, clutching at the wall, and in a city park, holding hands with Timothy Brettigan), and words in a foreign language, or, no, her *own* language, English, words that she has recently read spin through her head about an ideal state being one in which the absolute and relative complement each other, and objects are themselves so constituted that they contain in themselves an essentiality and are not merely the accident of a particular moment, and now the wolves are nodding silently, all the verb tenses have changed from past to the immediate present, the story-clock has run out of time and the calendar pages fall from the wall, and now the children stop singing their song, and Christina accelerates toward a tree that's hardly visible because one of her headlights is out, and Ludlow says, "Hey, what're you doing?" and then says, "Slow down," and then he says, "Oh, fuck me, holy shit," and those are his last words that will ever be spoken as they approach that single, solid oak tree, the gateway spring for a catapult out of the Earth he does not love, because the injury-project has somehow gone overboard beyond injury, into the other condition, the one from which no one ever returns.

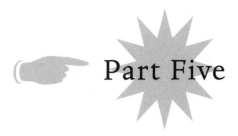 Part Five

- 26 -

HER FRIENDS CAME BY TO SEE HER IN HER APARTMENT AS SHE RECOV-
ered. A few were simply curious about her, but most were compassionate and sympathetic. Eleanor and Jürgen, from the bank, brought
her flowers and a cooked chicken. As they sat in her living room,
while she reclined stiffly on the sofa, they told her the bank would
welcome her return "with open arms." Because of her cracked rib, it
occasionally hurt her to speak, and it really hurt when she laughed;
still, despite her injuries, her mood was good. She realized that she
had to be careful about her inappropriate high spirits. Harry Brettigan and his wife, Alma, came by with flowers and a salad, having
been informed of the accident by their son, who came a day later, in
the morning. He brought her sandwiches and a selection of DVDs
to watch, mostly old movies. Other friends from the Sun Collective
came by, sweetly inquiring how she was.

Time was still slightly mixed up in her head. It was located on a
Möbius strip of some kind.

Her parents never called, but she didn't expect them to call.

When Timothy Brettigan arrived, he came in through her door
looking like all the colors of the rainbow. He sat down next to her and
inquired softly about what she'd been through. She loved the sound
of his voice. He seemed to have a good bedside manner—the sort of
person you'd want to wake up next to. Out of nowhere, he promised
to take her to Spain in a week or so. His peacefulness was so sooth-
ing that when he asked her whether she'd like him to do anything
for her, without thinking she asked him to paint her toenails because

she couldn't bend down. He went into her bedroom, grabbed her nail polish and some Kleenex to separate her toes, and proceeded to do exactly what she had requested. As he bent over her, she leaned back. Guiltily, she couldn't remember when she had been happier. He said he'd be back in a few days. He touched her hand in farewell. She asked him to call; she wanted to hear his voice again soon.

Because of her injuries, she'd been under observation in the hospital, in the yellow room she shared with someone named Sahlee, a brilliant, cheerful woman who was reading a long book by someone named Oshofsky, occasionally making comments about it. The doctors had told Christina how lucky she'd been: there'd been little damage to her lungs, kidneys, or spleen, though the pain was its own universe for several days after the accident, and she'd been lucky to have lived. In the universe of pain, the white fluffy clouds and the sun were furnished courtesy of the opioids they'd given her, and only after the sun hid behind a cloud did she know that it was time to press the button for the morphine drip or to take another pill. Which she did, days later, now at home, another one of those pills, in her now-empty apartment after Timothy Brettigan left, taking his beautiful voice with him, the living room empty except for her, sitting in the sofa, watching the twenty-four-hour news cycle and the game shows.

Well, that was luck. Another stroke of luck was that, for reasons that were still unclear to her, they hadn't found the Blue Telephone in her bloodstream, maybe because it had been designed by the albino genius in Memphis not to be detected in the standard blood tests. The drug consisted of stealth compounds and molecules never seen before by laboratory science. And they had determined, they told her in the hospital, that accidents will happen, though there would be some residual questioning, particularly by Detective Dennis O'Connor of the Placid Grove Police Department, who had not been there at the accident scene but wanted to talk to her soon or now, just to make absolutely sure that something, somewhere, was not fishy.

And it seemed they were asking all these questions because, well, another problem: no skid marks.

She hadn't met Detective Dennis O'Connor except over the phone, but on the fourth day after she found herself back in the apartment, he rang her bell at ten in the morning, and she let him into the building after he announced himself on the front door intercom. She heard him dragging himself up the stairs: a large, heavy man. After he knocked, she unlocked the bolt, and there he was: overcoat, sport coat, trousers with snow at the cuffs, necktie with food stain, hat. Also, he was African-American.

"Miss Lobdell?"

"Yes?"

"I'm Detective Dennis O'Connor. May I come in? I just have a couple of questions to ask you."

"Yes, sure, of course."

He lumbered into her living room, quickly took in its contents—sofa, semiwilted peace lily in a clay flowerpot, newspaper scattered on the floor, TV set, IKEA chair to the side of the coffee table with its green, chipped ashtray still littered with Ludlow's chewing gum and cigarette butts, and audio equipment in the corner—and asked, "May I sit down?" She noticed that he overenunciated his vowels and consonants, as if he'd gone through life chronically misunderstood. In all this time, he hadn't taken off the overcoat, a sign that he didn't plan to stay long.

"Please."

He lowered himself with a huff-and-puff exhalation and shook his head. His thinning hair was turning gray. "Those stairs," he said. "Don't they tire you out?" He didn't wait for her to answer. "How're you feeling? After the accident, I mean?" He pronounced both c's in *accident*: "ac-ci-dent," with a heavy stress on the first syllable. Maybe he had come to law enforcement after teaching elementary school.

"Oh, I'm a lot better," she told him. "My ribs don't hurt so much. I'm recovering. And they gave me some painkillers." She noticed that she wasn't thinking very clearly thanks to the drugs and hoped that she wouldn't say what she didn't mean, or, for that matter, say what she did mean.

"That's good. Pain isn't much good for anything, is it?" He laughed quickly, "Ha, ha," humorlessly and without conviction. Eleanor sounded like that when she laughed. He raised his left hand to scratch his ear. His pad and ballpoint pen were in his right hand. "Well, I won't be here long. I just have a few necessary questions for you, sorry about that. Whenever there's a death, there are questions? The ac-ci-dent . . . well, it was certainly, um, regrettable, what with the unfortunate death, you could say, of your boyfriend. Didn't stand a chance without his lap-and-shoulder belt, blunt force trauma to the head and so on. A real shame."

"Yes. Alas, poor Ludlow," she said. *Alas?* She had better watch her vocabulary; she was sounding, even to herself, excessively phony. For Ludlow, she could not grieve. Her heart simply had no room for him. Outside, from far down the street, came the distant sound of a jack-hammer. Thinking to deflect the direction of the conversation, she said, "Over the phone, you identified yourself as Dennis O'Connor, and, I don't know, I guess I was expecting somebody Irish. That's an Irish name."

"You don't say." He was taking notes on his notebook pad and raised his eyebrow. "First time I ever heard about that."

"Oh my God. You must think I'm a racist or something."

He let the silence pass. "Speaking of which and by the way, that's not his name."

"What? Ludlow? It certainly is his name. That's exactly what he called himself."

"Maybe so. Maybe that's what he did, with you." Detective O'Connor flipped back the pages of his notebook. "But he was using an alias. Real name was Mark Atherton Bagley."

"That's impossible. That's a ridiculous name."

"Well, I can't help you there. You can take it up with his parents. Don't argue with me. *They're* in town, the Bagleys, incidentally. I guess you must've never looked into his billfold or checked his driver's license, huh? Or met his daughter?" Detective O'Connor leaned down to pick up the newspapers scattered on the floor, folded them into an orderly array, and dropped them onto the coffee table next to the chipped green ashtray. "Sorry. I like a neat house. Drives the wife crazy, how I'm always picking up." He glanced at Christina. "Like

I say, the parents, these Bagleys, are in town from North Dakota to claim the body. Which is also where the daughter lives. They're pretty broke up, as you might expect. The ex-girlfriend and the daughter are still in Fargo, in case you're interested. You can probably meet the parents if you want to. I happen to have their cell phone numbers right here. They want to meet you. Have they called you?" He waited for a moment, and when Christina didn't say anything, he consulted his notepad. "So anyway, I have just a couple more questions, if you don't mind. This Mr. Bagley, this Ludlow, your boyfriend, he was working for . . . ?"

"Ludlow? The Sun Collective. He was a community organizer."

"And before that?"

"I don't know what he did before that. He was a student, I guess. And he was a housesitter."

"I see. Do you know where he lived? Prior to when you met him?"

"Around. He lived here and there. He didn't own much of anything when I first met him."

"Kind of a nomad, huh?" Detective O'Connor was writing something, but his handwriting was illegible, especially from where she was trying to read it, upside down. "And you worked for the Sun Collective, too?"

"Yes. Volunteer work. And I work for the Thrid Merchants' National Bank. I mean 'Third,' not 'Thrid.' That's where I work."

"Thank you. And may I ask you, were you distracted at the time of the accident, do you remember? Drowsy?"

"I don't know. It's all kinda hazy. It's really hard to picture what happened. I think I must've blanked out." She gave the sentence a sorrowful inflection. "You mentioned his daughter."

"Yes. Astrid, her name is."

"Oh." She couldn't decide what expression to put on her face.

"I mentioned you being drowsy. Were you sleepy? Because, as you know, we didn't find any skid marks."

"Yes. My cell phone was off. I wasn't texting or anything."

"That's correct. We've confirmed that. Did you lose control of the car? And *how* did you lose control? Do you remember?"

"Well"—she smiled—"I told the officers at the scene about all this, like what I remembered. It was an old car. A Saab." She waited, and Detective O'Connor waited with her. "With bad steering? I think I was adjusting the radio. And I'm pretty sure I hit a patch of ice."

"Ah-huh. Ad-just-ing the radio," he overenunciated. By now he was giving the impression of being perpetually bemused by what white people said, this white lady in particular. After a moment, something up at ceiling level seemed to interest him. "You were getting along with this Ludlow fellow? No recent arguments?"

"Nope."

"Do you remember what was playing on the radio?"

"Nope. Well, possibly Rod Stewart? 'Maggie May'?"

"No wonder you lost control. What'd you change it to?"

"Can't remember. Talk radio, I think."

"Ah-huh. Any idea how the all that dirt grit and a dime got jammed into the clasp of the passenger-side seat belt?"

"Oh, it was an old car, lots of junk in it."

"Ah. Thing I can't figure out, is how that grit and a dime got into that clasp so the clasp wouldn't work and the lap-and-shoulder belt was unusable."

"I can't either," she said.

"Well, maybe it's a mystery," he said, without conviction. "You weren't angry with him, this Ludlow?"

"No," she said. "I loved him."

"Is that right," he said, the three words not sounding like a question.

"He was a sweet guy. We had a lot in common."

"Such as . . . ?"

"The Sun Collective. Community organizing. We had great sex," she lied.

"I see." He was writing it all down. "You two were living together. Here. And this organization, the Sun Collective, that you were a part of and et cetera: get people standing up for their rights, help the poor and the homeless, bleeding-heart, save-the-world crusade? Like that?"

"Yeah, well, okay. That's one way to describe it. Say: You want coffee or anything? I should've asked."

"Oh, no thanks. I wouldn't put you to the trouble. But listen, don't get me wrong, I understand it, all that positive social action. We certainly need young people with ideals, what with the world on its steady downward path." His irony was almost impenetrable. With effort he rose and walked over to the corner of the living room where the audio system was, turning his back on Christina to examine the CDs and the vinyl on display. "Phonograph records!" he said, picking up one album sleeve. "I love vinyl. Still got it myself. And here's *Sketches of Spain*. What a great musician that guy was. A real badass. Miles Davis and that bunch." Still with his back turned to her, he said, "How come if you remember that Rod Stewart was playing on the radio, you don't remember how you hit that tree? That doesn't quite make sense to me, that you remember the one thing but not the other."

While she tried to think of an answer, Detective O'Connor put down the sleeve to the Miles Davis record and picked up something else, although Christina couldn't see what it was. She hoped it wasn't one of her Beyoncé CDs. She had Kendrick Lamar and Frank Ocean and Nas and Solange lying around, too. He might not like that. Several moments ticked by, and in the midst of the room's guilt-stricken silence, she said, "I'm sorry. That's the part that I don't recall. I mean, I think there was ice on the road, and maybe I was still adjusting the station or the volume, you know?"

He turned, and what she saw on his face was a complicated expression: compassionate disbelief, by a man who understood criminality but didn't really like it. "Okay," he said. "Did this Mark Atherton Bagley leave a will? We haven't found one, and his parents don't know. Because of the daughter, and so on."

"No," Christina said. "He didn't own anything, that I know of." She had made several missteps already, she realized, and she felt herself getting sweaty from nerves. "He was sort of a vagabond."

"Oh, this particular vagabond had something, all right," Detective O'Connor informed her, without elaborating. "So anyway, if you'd like to talk to his parents, who by the way are eager to talk to *you*, here's their number." He wrote it on a page of his pocket-size notebook and ripped out the page before handing it to her. "I've also included my phone number there in case you happen to think of or remember anything relevant."

"Why haven't they called me? Ludlow's parents? The Bagleys?"

"I don't know," Detective O'Connor said. "You should ask them that question, not me. But if I had to hazard a guess, I'd say that probably since your driving was the cause of their son's death, they don't care to make the first move in your direction. It's kind of typical in cases like this one."

"Oh," she said softly.

"Have you ever made a soufflé?" he asked, pocketing his notebook and pen before fixing his gaze on her. He was still standing on the other side of the room. "Cheese soufflés are the best, in my opinion. They don't take too much in the way of ingredients: eggs, which you gotta separate, whites over here, yolks over there, Parmesan cheese, cream of tartar, flour, and a bit of nutmeg. Me, I like me some nutmeg, a dash, but it's not to every taste. You need an electric mixer, and, um, I don't see one of those over there in your kitchen. You a member of Costco? They sell mixers cheap. Anyway, you could look up the recipe on the web, but my point is, you put the mixture into the preheated soufflé dish and you put that into the oven, about 375 degrees, of course. Then, after about twenty-five minutes, the soufflé rises, and it's ready. No big noises in the kitchen, or it won't rise, so they inform me, though I've never had a problem with that."

"Why are you telling me all this?" She noticed that he was now staring at her, but not as if he found her attractive.

"Because sometimes a soufflé doesn't rise, Ms. Lobdell. And this soufflé, the one you made and have presented to me, hasn't risen, but . . . well, so I've got one question before I go. Did you want this fellow dead? For any reason?"

"No. How can you say that?"

"Reason I ask, you don't seem all that heartbroken."

"I don't? Because I am."

"No kidding. You seem, what's the expression, dry-eyed to me. I haven't seen a one single tear since I came through your door, and no sort of weeping and carrying on, that business. I'm not charging you with involuntary vehicular manslaughter, but, hey, I almost might."

"I did all my crying already," she said with firm conviction.

"Did you really? Is that the Kleenex, over there?" Somewhere a clock ticked several more seconds away. Detective O'Connor nodded. "Well, that certainly settles it, doesn't it?" For the first time she noticed that he was wearing glasses, and behind the lenses his brown eyes were watery. "What we have is an accident, pure and simple, a moment of fatal inattention, and a death." He exhaled deeply. "No probable crime appears to have been committed. You have my phone number on that sheet of paper. Give me a call if you think of anything that I should know."

"Okay," she said, without getting up. "Stay warm," she told him, a standard Minnesota winter farewell.

He did not say anything in response at first, but when he was halfway out the door, he turned and said, "No problem," before closing the door quietly behind him.

ON THE OTHER SIDE OF THE DOOR, CHRISTINA TURNED THE LOCK. SHE felt a trembling begin in her right hand, which rose through her elbow and her shoulder to her chest, as if an earthquake had migrated out of the ground and moved inside her, so that the spasms, or whatever they were, took possession of her body, shuddering in waves through her. She felt herself shaking and trembling so violently that she had to sit down on the floor's tan-colored carpet outside the closet entryway. It hurt. She hurt all over. *She was responsible for someone's death.* It was a one-way gate: she would never get back to where she had been and would never be free from that. Remorse could be a physical thing. It could bite into you. She clasped her hands around her knees, her legs pulled tightly into her chest. But the involuntary painful movements did not stop, and when she loosened her fingers to lie down on her back, the stucco ceiling's pattern seemed to flicker between light and dark, and as she watched it, the daylight ceiling turned into the night sky, constellation after constellation of stars, and she felt herself swept up into it like a god, though only for an instant, on fire, burning, and she felt herself becoming a stellar entity, an emissary of light.

When she came back to herself, her face was wet with tears, and once her sobbing subsided, she rose and made her way to the kitchen sink, where she'd left two saucepans to soak. Picking up a scouring pad, with nothing in her head but the sorrow she felt, she washed them until they were clean, and behind her she felt Ludlow's restless spirit watching her.

27

LUDLOW'S PARENTS WERE POLITE AND SHY. FROM THE MINUTE SHE first saw them, she guessed that they suspected her of nothing. Having arranged to meet them for breakfast at a neighborhood restaurant, Mookie's-on-Hennepin, close to their cut-rate hotel, she recognized at once who they were: Ludlow's father wore a feed-store hat, red flannel shirt, and blue jeans under his overcoat, and his mother wore a shapeless plus-size flower-pattern dress under her blue cotton winter coat and matching blue scarf. Entering the restaurant, they blinked at the fluorescent lights like underground creatures, moles, unaccustomed to city life. They had the uncomfortable demeanor of a middle-aged couple who were not versed in conversation with strangers, didn't even have iPhones, just flip phones, and were therefore unable to text, were app-less and un-Twittered, pre-postmodern era, agrarian, and they approached her with makeshift half-smiles. They were going to do their best to make a social effort with her, but every word would emerge with a strain.

They had already decided to cremate their son's body and take the ashes back to North Dakota to be scattered somewhere on the farm, they told her. "Mark was our little brilliant boy," Ludlow's mother said sadly, and Christina had to think for a moment to remember whom she was talking about. For her, he would never be "Mark." He would always be "Ludlow"; it was more than a name. It was him. Mrs. Bagley continued to talk: her son had always been good at everything, so smart, the class valedictorian at South Branch Consolidated Schools, free ride at the university, he could have been anything he wanted to be. They did not ask Christina whether she wanted to attend the scattering. They did not ask her anything. They seemed frightened of her, or perhaps they weren't used to asking questions of strangers.

Fully five minutes into the conversation, the mother remembered to introduce herself as Violet Bagley, and her husband as Henry. Henry and Violet Bagley. Across the table, they all shook hands. With shaking hands she reached into her purse and drew out a photograph of Ludlow's daughter, Astrid. "I'm sure he showed you some pictures," Violet Bagley said. "He was so proud of her." A pause. "Right after she was born. Not so much later."

Ludlow's father had ordered the Mexican omelet, which was served with an immense helping of sour cream on top, a toxic mixture of cholesterol and saturated fat, which he then sprinkled with hot sauce, accompanied by a critical mass of ketchup on his hash browns. Christina sat transfixed as he wolfed it down, a heart-attack country breakfast, leaving the conversational side of things to his wife, a habit, Christina guessed, among rural couples. Well, you shouldn't generalize about people. Ludlow's mother was tearfully reciting the list of prizes Ludlow / Mark had won in high school and college: debate team, band (clarinet), captain of the basketball team, homecoming king (she still had the crown stored somewhere), and now what was he? Nothing but ashes. Clothes and shoes.

Her voice seemed detached from her, Christina thought, floating in the air somehow, the way voices come to you just before you faint.

It makes you think sometimes, she said, that it was no gift to be the smartest person in the county, or even North Dakota. Being smart had never really helped Mark one little bit. It was like a problem he had to solve.

Her husband, Ludlow's father, Henry, had not said a word during this time; he seemed to be dedicated to eating his omelet instead.

Mark, so good-looking, had always liked girls, his mother said now, trying to smile in Christina's direction, her voice still floating in the air, since Christina was the last of that blessed parade of girls, and of course those previous girls had always clustered around him like bees on a flower, and we, his father and I, were hoping that he'd choose one of them and settle down back in South Branch, but after Astrid's birth he and his girlfriend broke up—the way people did now—and he got agitated and instead of being a good dad he had followed the "siren song" of city life and had just disappeared from their lives as if he didn't care for the place he'd been brought up in, "almost as if he'd had no regard for us or his daughter or anybody," she said, "even though we knew he loved us anyway," and thank goodness his two brothers hadn't been like that.

"He had brothers?" Christina asked, involuntarily. The question came out of her mouth before she had thought of saying it. She was still feeling dizzy from the photograph of Astrid, who, even as a baby, had Ludlow's features. A moment or two after she uttered the question, both of the Bagleys stopped what they were doing— Henry with his omelet, Violet with her oatmeal—to examine Christina. Yes, the mother said, her surprise unconcealed, two brothers who still lived near the farm. Thomas and Benjy.

"I guess you didn't know," Ludlow's father said, the first thing he had said in the past few minutes. "Modern times, not to know about family. Cone-of-silence thing. Not to care."

"Oh. We forgot to say grace," Violet announced, touching her own cheek and interrupting the moment of Christina's embarrassed ignorance of the Bagley family. Violet took her husband's hand in her right hand and Christina's in her left. Christina leaned over to take the right hand of Ludlow's father, feeling a residual pain in her ribs, and once they were all holding hands, their heads bowed, Violet prayed, "For these and all Thy blessings, Lord, make us truly grateful. Amen." When Violet released her hand from Christina's, she said, "Are you in pain? I saw you wincing. And I could feel your injury through your hand."

"She's psychic," the father said, nodding in his wife's direction but not looking up. "Always has been. You live with her, you get used to it. All her life, from grade school."

Christina clasped her hands in her lap while Henry Bagley finished up the last of his Mexican omelet. He had tucked his napkin into his collar so that it covered his shirtfront. His meal finished, he leaned back, took a large swig of coffee, and nodded in no particular direction before removing the napkin and folding it neatly on the table.

"You probably think we're pretty simple," he was saying. "Coming from the farm and all. But here's the thing: we're Christians, and we believe in helping others, lending a hand in times of travail, helping the poor and the weak, and we believe in loyalty, and grace, and hard work, and forgiveness, especially, and not looking down on no one, no matter what. We never had many of the advantages, but we don't think we're superior to anybody, but then nobody's superior to us, either. We're all sinners here, and we're all searching for the light. We practice humility. It's part of our religion. I'm saying this to you," he said, "because ever since Mark's death, I have prayed for guidance about what to say to you, and I want you to know that whatever happened that night, the night he died and you were driving, we forgive you, my wife and me, we don't hold it against you. We don't bear grudges. We can't. That's not us. And another thing: we aren't going to ask you how that accident happened. We prayed on it, and the prayer was answered. What I am seeing in you is a person who is suffering just like us. That is our bond with you: your suffering and our suffering. And that is all that I am going to say."

After a few moments, when the waitress came with the check—Christina grabbed it—Mrs. Bagley held out her hand again. "Could I touch your forehead?" she asked. After putting down the check, Christina asked why, and Ludlow's mother said, "There's a power I have though it don't come from me. It comes from God. I can take away some of your suffering if you want me to. I can take away the burden that you are carrying. I can tell that you have a wound, and I can even try to heal it if you ask, so."

"Yes, please," Christina said, the tears beginning to well up again in her eyes, whereupon Mrs. Bagley, this overweight woman in a cheap flower-print dress and a blue scarf, touched her callused fingers to Christina's forehead, more lightly than Christina had expected, and the effect that followed was like nothing else that Christina had ever experienced, a feeling of bad air expelled from her soul, and Mrs.

Bagley exhaled sharply and tilted her head back. More loudly than was seemly in public, Mrs. Bagley followed the exhalation with an *ah* that could be heard everywhere in the restaurant, so that the other patrons turned to see what was going on.

Christina, not quite believing what had just happened to her, glanced at the walls, the servers, the woman behind the old-fashioned cash register, a ballpoint pen on her ear, the Hispanic-looking man just visible inside the kitchen, the other customers still eating their breakfasts, and the winter sun outside, and she felt the words "the peace that passeth all understanding" travel through her body. The words themselves were things and were now located inside her. What had just happened? Whoever the Bagleys were, they were better human beings than she was, spiritually and otherwise. Something in them had been transferred to their son, where it mutated in the darkness. Of that she was certain.

"Now that we're done eating, could you do us a favor?" Henry Bagley asked. "Could you take us to the Minnesota State Fairgrounds?"

"But it's winter," Christina said. "There's nothing going on over there. I mean, the gates are open, but the fair's not there."

"Oh, we know that," he told her, "but we'd like to see it anyway. We love the fairgrounds. We go there every summer, and we've always said, we want to see it under a layer of snow."

So she took them there.

SEVERAL DAYS LATER, ON THE OTHER SIDE OF THE CITY, HARRY BRET-tigan; his wife, Alma; and their son, Timothy, were headed to Northeast Minneapolis where the Sun Collective headquarters was located, and in the car Alma was saying that they should have called or texted or *something* because after all you couldn't arrive at the Sun Collective unannounced, it would be rude, and from behind the wheel, where he sat watching the landscape pass by, their son told them, a bit too loudly, that of course you could arrive there unannounced because after all he knew people over there, and it was hardly momentous to drop in on a neighborhood community group and pick up some of his belongings, the ones he had left behind, before he moved into his own apartment.

When they pulled into the parking lot, they saw immediately that the usual Sun Collective symbols, ☛ ✹, were there on the front signboard, but below the symbols the message was new.

The Sun Collective
Is Closed but
We Are Everywhere Now
Watch for Us

In the parking lot, pacing back and forth, was Christina, talking to several other collectivists. She saw the Brettigans' car, and for a few seconds she seemed to freeze in place, apparently thinking of whether she would talk to them and, if she did, what she would say. Once they had parked, she walked over to them. "It's boarded up!" she said, before they had even rolled down the windows. "You can't go in. The police closed it. Or *somebody* did. Who the fuck decided *that*? It's all locked with a notice on the door. Anyway, they're not here. Wye's not there. No one is there. What am I going to do?"

Timothy rolled down his window first. "Why don't you join us?" he said, motioning toward the backseat. "Get into the car. We'll figure something out."

"Oh, all right." She pointed with her thumb before opening the left rear door and getting into the car. Sitting down, she brought with her a contagious cloud of cold air. "We gotta get to the bottom of this."

"What happened?" Harry Brettigan asked. "What's going on?"

"Well," she said, "what I've heard from those people I was just talking to is that we're being called 'terrorists.' All of us. Anybody who ever went to a meeting in there. So I guess that includes all of you. Terrorists? For planting gardens in the city and having seminars on limiting consumption and lobbying and what we did? You call that 'terror'? The police and everybody else—they're *all* investigating us, and President Thorkelson has personally taken a personal interest, tweeting about us, another of his conspiracies, which is as bad as it can get, and now Wye has disappeared, nobody knows where, and we're all going to be arrested and locked up." Whatever peace she had found a few days before had apparently abandoned her.

Timothy hadn't turned off the car's motor and, as Christina talked, he leaned back, giving the impression that he had heard all this before. "What does it mean, 'we are everywhere now'?" he asked, rubbing his forehead.

"It means underground. I have to hide," she said. "That's what it means." Turning to Alma and Harry Brettigan, she asked, "May I come back to your house? I'm sorry, and I hate to invite myself in, but I'm sort of desperate. I don't want to go back to my apartment right now. They'll be looking for me."

"What about Ludlow?" Alma asked. "Where is he?"

"He's dead, Mom. Remember?" Timothy examined his mother carefully. "We told you. That accident? When Christina was driving? And he wasn't belted in?"

"Oh, yes." Alma appeared to be preoccupied, thinking of something else. "I'm so sorry: I was woolgathering. Or maybe," she said gleefully, "I'm sinking into dementia. Who can say? I *hope* I am. I pray for Alzheimer's. I would just *love* to be out of it." Instantly she came back to herself and turned to Christina. "There's no real hiding, you know. Everybody gets tracked down eventually. How are you feeling, by the way? Have you recovered?"

"Oh, that? Yeah, I'm okay. I'm almost fine."

"How'd you get here?"

"The bus."

For the first time, Harry Brettigan spoke up. "The impression I get," he said, "is that through a complicated series of actions and commitments, you're in trouble. It's possible, of course, that you're not in trouble at all and that all this worrying is a product of delusion common to all reformers in a period of crisis and self-contradiction." He was enjoying himself. "Come with us, then. We have a couple of spare rooms. And there's the basement."

"Harry, please stop talking, all right?" his wife said, shaking her head.

"She gets impatient with me." Brettigan laughed.

In the backseat, Christina nodded, a gesture that Timothy took to mean that she had agreed to his father's proposal, so he put the car into gear and headed homeward.

IN THE CAR, SHE STUDIED HARRY BRETTIGAN AND HIS WIFE. HER OWN parents were long past caring about her. They had graduated from parenting. Both of them, affectively absentminded, had been married several times and left perfunctory, lightweight messages on her cell phone now and then, accompanied by pictures of themselves with their latest love partners, smiling in the brilliant fixed-income sunshine of the desert Southwest where they had both retired separately, and where they were living in gated communities of manifestly cheerful seniors. Her father played tennis, swam every day, and wrote limericks as a hobby. Her mother was in a bridge club, a book club, and a cooking class. They were smiling and pacified, so self-absorbed that it was as if they had never been parents at all. If she had given them grandchildren, the situation might have been different, but her current life had little interest for them, and whenever they talked to her, they forgot to inquire about her prospects. She was their sweet, adorable, prizewinning, blanked-out girl. She was living in someone's basement? How nice! Harry and Alma Brettigan took more interest in her than her own parents did.

And in return, during the following week she came to love them. She would take the bus to work at the bank and come back to the Brettigans. She loved their dog, Woland, and their cat, Behemoth, the Brettigans' harmless quarreling, which seemed to be their pastime, the perpetual smell of toast in the kitchen, the strange recipes that produced unintelligible meals—what *is* that, on the dinner plate?—the framed picture of the Basque coastline in the living room, the books of history and poetry scattered around the house, their frumpy discontents and passions, and their seemingly endless kindness toward her, which had no reason for existing and was therefore implausible. They had adopted her out of love. They seemed to believe that she had great potential, and potential for greatness, and they were on edge to see what she would do next. The death of Ludlow was merely a prelude for the momentous next act.

At night, in the Brettigans' basement, she felt the presence of Ludlow standing at the foot of her bed as she tried to sleep. She had no unfinished business with him, but his spirit stood there with his hidden agendas, invisibly, immaterially present, not particularly minding that he was dead and that she had killed him, but letting her know, just by his being there, that the poor were still suffering, the apocryphal Sandmen might still be around, the Sun Collective manifesto was gathering dust, the Earth itself was in jeopardy, and bombs, those social-activist alarm clocks that would wake up the sleeping conscience-stricken, were not being constructed (although they should have been assembled *by now*) with the result that America was falling deeper into its unmindful decline and would fall further, unless she, Christina, took action: radical, unthinkable action, action that no one had ever dreamed of, action that would get onto the front page of the paper, above the fold: *action action action action action* was Ludlow's unspoken, silent stutter, from the other side of Death, across the river of forgetfulness, straight to her from him, not deconstructed, and still audible.

She was, she knew, blessed and afflicted with the scourge of empathy: she could not witness anyone in poverty or pain without feeling an inward wince that compelled her to seek some remedy, no matter how inefficient or futile. That was the message Ludlow had for her: every night he reminded her.

Finally, days after she had moved in with his parents, Timothy called and asked her out on a date. Where are we going? she asked.

To the Alhambra, he said, waving his arm to conjure Spain and the Moors.

28

DATE NIGHT: SHE HAD DRESSED UP FOR TIMOTHY AND FUSSED A BIT, putting a red dress on, but, really, she thought, who goes out on dates anymore? Nobody. There was no such thing. Courtship had evolved: you could go straight to the sex and bypass the love and the get-acquainted period if you wanted to, but then you were constantly dealing with anonymous strangers and their weird quirks—psychological, medical, personal—often at the last minute. And this particular date had an additional weirdness to it: he had insisted that he would pick her up at the stroke of midnight, and then they'd go to a midnight diner, and then . . . well, he said he had a surprise in store for her. Also, she felt the strangeness of being on a date, or whatever it was, with the son of the two people, Harry and Alma, under whose roof she was currently living, another one of those ironies subtly invading her life. At the last minute she ditched the dress, put on a pair of rather tight new jeans and her snow boots, a woolen cap, and a blue scarf to match her eyes.

Promptly at midnight, his car pulled up out front. He was driving a new used car, a Chevy, on which the rust had only started to appear. She hurried out to the car so that he wouldn't come up and ring the doorbell, which would result in Woland's terrified barking, followed by the awakenings of Harry and Alma and their dazed descent on the stairs, wearing their grotesque old-people pajamas, to see what was going on. Timothy didn't even have time to get out and open her door for her. It was quite cold, for March—a frozen nighttime haze hung in the air. Once she was seated on the passenger side, he said, "Hi," and as she belted herself in, he smiled and said that she looked great.

She settled back and asked where they were going. As an answer, he pointed forward, and they began with the small talk: the weather, a slight cough he had acquired from somewhere, the closing of the Sun Collective headquarters. She hoped he wouldn't ask her about Ludlow or the accident and Ludlow's parents, if he even knew about them, and he didn't ask. She was weighed down sufficiently with soul burdens without people making their polite inquiries. Timothy had a relaxed and thoughtful ease behind the wheel, and as he headed uptown, she found that his easefulness was spreading over to her. He asked her how it was, living in his parents' basement, and she told him that she wasn't down there anymore; she had moved upstairs into his old room. The bed was quite comfortable, she said. That quieted him down for a moment or two. His face, lit by the dashboard light, was not just handsome but beautiful, and he would still have been beautiful if she hadn't liked him, but she did like him. Feeling brave, she asked him whether he might ever take up acting again. He said no.

That was his past life, he told her, an occupation that was dazzlingly horrible in its way, a playground for people who didn't know what or who they were, and he was never going back to it. "The Sun Collective saved me," he said, "and they made me real," and she felt the breath go out of her, making her ribs hurt, as she wondered how they accomplished that, how that group made *anybody* real, until it occurred to her that maybe she herself had become real in the past year, unlike Ludlow. For the first time in her life, possibly, she felt that she too had substance, a specific weight and gravity that she'd acquired by having ideals and a hope for the betterment of others, as foolish as those ambitions sometimes seemed. The weight she had didn't amount to much, but it was a start.

Of course she had helped to kill someone—had that helped the human betterment project?

The melting, dirty snow clogging the side streets crunched under Timothy's tires as he parked outside the midnight diner. The diner's interior was brightly lit in that inevitable Edward Hopper way, but the diner's customers, workers of the night, weren't hunched over in the Hopper manner but were loud and cheerful. As she and Timothy walked to their table, everyone smiled at them as fellow proletarians, nocturnal laborers, here to get a cheeseburger and coffee before starting their jobs at two a.m.

Once they had settled down on their red vinyl-covered seats, Timothy and Christina examined the laminated menus without speaking. The air smelled of hamburgers, slush, burnt coffee, and wet woolens. The old jukebox was playing something by Roy Orbison. Okay, so it was a throwback diner, its ambience a little studied and artificial, but the idea was to make its patrons happy, which was commendable.

"What're you going to have?" she asked.

"It seems incorrect to order anything here except the Midnight Burger," he told her. "If I wanted a salad, I'd've stayed home."

When the server came, she wrote down their orders while simultaneously nodding as she chewed her gum and expertly blew a bubble. "Got it," she said, once the bubble had burst, and the gum reentered her mouth. "Two burgers for the young couple in Booth Five." She turned and walked away, *the best waitress ever,* Christina thought, *to call us a couple.*

"Are you tired?" Timothy asked. He glanced at his watch. "It's half past twelve."

"No, I'm fine."

"Because I was a little afraid that you'd be sleepy, considering the hour."

"It's okay. I wasn't sleepy. I'm not sleepy now. I was looking forward to it. To this."

"Good. Me, too."

"What about you? It *is* late, isn't it?"

"Oh, I never get sleepy anymore. I'm wide awake all the time. In fact, I have insomnia."

"So what do you do, when you can't sleep? Warm milk? Bananas?"

"No," he said, taking a sip of water. His upper lip was chapped; it must have hurt him to smile. "I do category games. You know: you have a category like baseball players or football players, and you go down the alphabet, thinking of them, somebody for every letter."

"It wouldn't have to be sports, would it?" He shook his head. "You could do any category. Like, I don't know, composers. Who's *A*?"

He thought for a moment. "I don't know any *A* composers."

"Well, there's Albinoni. How about *B*?"

"Beethoven."

"*C*?"

"Chopin," he said, after a few seconds.

"*D*?"

"Um, Debussy? Don't even ask about *E*. I can tell you already that I don't know any *E* composers except maybe Duke Ellington."

"Ellington counts. Or Elgar," she said triumphantly, breaking out into a grin, as their cheeseburgers and fries and coleslaw arrived.

"Okay, you win. How about baseball players? Or rock stars?"

"Well." She bit into her cheeseburger. Who could ever be a vegan when food tasted like this? "Hank Aaron. He's a baseball player, right?"

"Yes. *B*."

Was this a real test or a pretend test? She tried to think of any baseball players at all. "Charles Barkley?"

"Wrong sport. That's basketball. You lose." He nodded to himself, as if he were entertaining the thought that women rarely knew anything about sports, which was so odd about them as a gender.

"I don't lose. We both win." He poured an extreme amount of ketchup on his hamburger. She was appalled, watching the red slurry slop downward over the sides of the meat, but also very happy to have learned one of his idiosyncrasies. When she gazed up at him again, she thought she heard a door closing somewhere. He had the particular shadowy expression of someone who has gone through a trial by suffering and has come out the other side, and the combination of his effortful cheerfulness and beauty made her almost want to cry out and take his hand to comfort him. She had been through a similar trial. But he wouldn't like that; he was working diligently to be strong, and besides, they were just in a diner.

When the bill came, she felt the slow, steady onset of something like love building up, a cloudbank on the horizon changing the air pressure. As he fished out his wallet and dropped some money on the table over the check, he said, "Now we go to the palace of the Moorish kings."

"No kidding. Where is that?"

"Just a few blocks away. We get in through the back door."

She decided to play along. As they were walking, she wondered whether he would take her hand, and, if he did, whether she would like it. His face reminded her distantly of his father's face: it had the same thoughtful asymmetry as Harry Brettigan's, with one eye slightly lower than the other, but the shrewdness she saw there, the worldliness, came from somewhere else, maybe his mother, or possibly he had acquired it from life. Out of the blue, he said, "What's the point of being alone, the streets and squares, they're always empty." She had the feeling he was quoting, maybe from a play.

"I don't know," she said. "Beats me. Are you quoting from somewhere?"

"Come here," he said. "We have to go into this alley."

The alleyway was lit by one distant streetlight that cast their shadows across the pavement, elongating them so that they both seemed like giants, winter creatures scavenging close to the dumpsters there in the semidark. Timothy took out a key and unlocked a side door of the building, ushering her inside. He said, "Welcome to the Alhambra. I work here." Where Christina stood, everything was pitch black until Timothy flipped a wall switch, and another solitary light went on, and she could see that they stood in a hallway, an emergency exit to the street.

"Walk straight down there," he said and he flipped another switch. A dim utility light with a bare bulb near the ceiling went on, and she made her way up the aisle of the empty movie theater—yes, the Alhambra—restored and decorated like a Moorish castle with various arches and mosaics, arabesque designs, crenellations, and a painted fountain on each wall facing the small auditorium. The screen was a faint white square. After flipping yet another switch, Timothy said,

"Look up," and there in the ceiling were tiny twinkling lights, stars over this plaster-and-drywall Spain, like all those other movie palaces from the 1920s and '30s, almost all of them gone. This one, perhaps because it was so small, had been saved somehow.

"I've never been here before," she said, with a trace of wonder. "What do they show here?"

"Movies," he said. "It's a nonprofit now. They're trying to keep it going before the internet kills movie theaters off. It's a small theater, so it's not too expensive to operate. It's only the Alhambra. Take a seat."

Christina examined the empty rows, chose one chair in the middle, and sat down, checking to see whether Timothy would follow her. She hoped he wouldn't go up into the projection booth just now. She wanted to sit here with him and for him to keep her company. Accordingly, he followed her and sat down next to her, both of them facing the blank screen.

"Is anything going to come on?" she asked.

"No." He waited for a moment. "Maybe in your imagination. Or, I don't know, ours."

"Like what?"

"So tell me what you see on the screen."

"I don't see anything."

"Use your imagination."

"Timothy, there's nothing there."

"Yes, there is. There's something there, and you're just not looking hard enough. Look harder, Christina."

She couldn't remember when he had spoken her name until now. She liked it, the feeling that he was calling out to her. Her name from him gave her strength. "You go first," she said.

"Okay." He leaned back, his eyes fixed forward. He put his legs over the seat in front of him, and as he did, he drew in a deep breath. "There's a woman up there, a little bit like you, but different and more, I don't know, sturdy, and the movie's in black and white, kind of noirish, water on the cobblestones, echoing footsteps, and she's on a mission, I guess, because look: she's driving that small foreign car down that small foreign street, and nobody's around except children—"

"Maybe she's headed for an assignation."

"No 'maybe' about it. She's got a lover who's in the Irish Republican Army, and he's—"

"Wait. This is *Odd Man Out*. You can't do that." She was getting into the spirit of things. "They've already robbed the bank or whatever, and James Mason has been shot. This is before Robert Newton and F. J. McCormick come into the picture. We have to start over."

"Okay."

"I mean, yes, she's up there. A little bit like me. Except she has a mole on her left cheek, which I don't. And the movie is in Technicolor, 1950s, so the colors are like Popsicles, and there she is, in her kitchen, and she's—no, that isn't me. That isn't my movie."

"What's your movie?"

"She's with her lover, but they can't be lovers because it's the nineteenth century and anyway her lover is married, so they decide to die and get on a toboggan and go down a hill and hit a tree. Only he doesn't die. He becomes a vegetable." Christina didn't know why she was saying what she was saying, and the silence that followed conveyed to her that Timothy didn't know either, but he could guess. "She's done terrible things. They . . . they weigh on her conscience."

"That's from a novel I read in high school," he said. "I can't remember its name, though. It was assigned, that's all I remember. You can't do that. It's against the rules. We both have to start over. We can't do adaptations here."

"This is the strangest date I've ever had in my life." She shifted in her seat to get more comfortable.

"A date that tests your imagination."

"All right." This time she took a deep breath. "The woman does something heroic. I'm trying to see what it is. She takes a stand for the poor, for the stupid and crazy, the people who sleep on the sidewalks, she decides not to lie down and let the big SUV of capitalism drive over her, she does something wonderful and inspirational to save her soul and other souls, and, modestly, the planet, too, and very much in the spirit of the times, which she embodies."

"What is it? What does she do?"

For a long time Christina stared at the blank movie screen. As she did, Timothy Brettigan quietly took her hand. At last she flinched as if she had received a mild electric shock, and she said, "I've got it."

"What is it?"

"I can't tell you yet. But I will soon."

"Okay. Am I involved in what she does?"

"Yes. No. I don't know. And yours? Tim? What do you see up there?"

"The same thing you do. Incidentally, what do you want out of your life?"

"I want to be normal," she said sadly.

"What a sweet thing to say. But you're lying. You want to be a total hero."

They sat there companionably in the quiet and half-dark until finally he got up the nerve to kiss her. After he was done, she said, "Ah, I get it. So *that's* how the movie begins."

29

SPRING HAD COME TO MINNESOTA, AND EGGED ON BY CHRISTINA AND Timothy, who was now the manager there, Harry and Alma had decided to go to the Alhambra to see a Saturday matinee showing of Hitchcock's *Notorious*. After the movie, they planned to walk through the Minneapolis Sculpture Garden or stop at a coffee shop. As she started the car, Harry said, "Have you ever noticed? If you're a senior, all your dates are during the daylight hours."

Most films went through actual 35mm movie projectors at the Alhambra, and the auditorium was so small that you could hear the machines humming away in the projection booth. Occasionally an old print would get stuck in the machine's aperture gate, and the frame would burn from the inside out, just like old times. The film would stop; the house lights would go on, and the audience would sit there, impatient and happy, eating popcorn, until the movie started up again.

This time, the Alhambra had obtained a new print of the film, and Harry and Alma sat near the back holding hands, while on the screen, Cary Grant's character and Ingrid Bergman's character fell in love, though his character, Devlin, wouldn't act on his love until her character, Alicia Huberman, was near death, from poison. In the last climactic minutes, by which time Harry had pulled his hand away from Alma, Devlin helped his beloved down the grand staircase and into the getaway car, out of the house where the Germans had plotted to kill her. When THE END appeared on screen, over the RKO logo, most of the audience, including Alma, applauded.

Harry sat with his arms crossed. "Well, it's great trash," he muttered as they picked themselves up and headed for the exit.

"Oh, Harry, it's better than that," Alma told him. "Don't be a grump. It's like a fairy tale. They're both sleeping beauties. He wakes up first, and then he wakes *her* up."

"Yeah," he said. "Great trash."

ONCE IN THE CAR, WITH ALMA BEHIND THE WHEEL—SHE ENJOYED driving, and he didn't—she kept at it. "He loved her. And because he loved her, he saved her."

"When was the last time you saw that movie?"

"I don't know. More than thirty years ago, I guess. Before that? Maybe in college." She shrugged, turning left and then to the right, stopping at a corner where a sunburnt panhandler, with long brown hair, wearing a T-shirt with a beer logo on it, held out a sign: HOMELESS. PLEASE HELP. GOD BLESS. The man's eyes were deep blue and disconcertingly sane.

"It was more plausible thirty years ago," he told her. "We were younger then. We believed everything. We thought love could save the world." He waited for a moment before saying, "But I don't believe movies anymore. I don't believe *in* them, and I don't believe their stories. They don't seem real to me—just fantasy. Robots in space? Superheroes? Characters who look like Cary Grant? The only person who ever looked like Cary Grant was Cary Grant. Fantasy. And novels. All of it. It *all* looks made-up now. Bunch of imaginary puppets on strings, dancing around. When did we lose our grip on reality?"

"I disagree," she said. "*I* believed it. I believed he loved her. And because he loved her, he saved her."

"And the MacGuffin: uranium in wine bottles? Please."

On Hennepin Avenue they passed a large billboard paid for by some environmental group. A drawn picture of a withered tree stood at the center, and to the side were three lines of bold lettering:

THE PLANET IS DYING
WHAT WILL YOU DO?
WWW.SAVEthisEARTH.ORG

"The MacGuffin?"

"Oh, you know. That's Hitchcock's term for the object they're all chasing after. The meaningless thing that gives meaning to everything else. It's the element in the story that has no content. It's hollow. It's meaningless in itself. A football in a football game is a MacGuffin—it doesn't mean anything but it gives meaning to all the activity around it. The hollow Maltese Falcon. The uranium. The microfilm. Whatever. Incidentally, you wouldn't ever put uranium into wine bottles."

"You might."

"No, you wouldn't. It's all made-up."

They drove for several minutes in silence, Alma glancing from time to time at her husband, who sat frowning at the springtime flowers and trees beginning to green out, to blossom and bloom. Somehow a fuse had been lit. The oddest combination of topics could ignite disgruntlement in him—speakable topics that were articulated stood in as placeholders for other hypertoxic topics that had to remain unspoken—but this one baffled her. He had placed his hand over his chest, as if his heart were hurting him.

"Explain the MacGuffin to me again," she said, to break the spell. "How it got that name."

"It's from a joke," Brettigan told her. "Two men are in a train compartment. One of them looks up at the luggage rack above them and points to a large wrapped object belonging to the other passenger. 'What's that?' the man asks. 'Oh, that?' his companion says. 'That's a MacGuffin.' 'What's a MacGuffin?' the first man inquires. 'A MacGuffin,' the companion explains, 'is a weapon used to kill mountain lions in the Scottish Highlands.' The first man objects: 'But there are no mountain lions in the Scottish Highlands,' to which the second man replies, 'Well then, that's not a MacGuffin.'"

Neither of them laughed. She could tell that the entire category was causing him some odd spiritual or psychic turmoil. Well, he would get over it.

"It's meaningless, but it gives meaning to everything around it," he repeated. "It's hollow, a nothing, and all your hopes and fears go in there."

She parked the car, and together they climbed the stairs to the bridge over the highway to the sculpture garden. She noticed that he was taking the steps slowly and with evident effort, pausing periodically to get his breath. As they crossed, Brettigan glanced at the upper-left-hand corner of the enclosed span, where a John Ashbery poem, commissioned for the bridge and whose words started at one end and ended at the other, seemed to accompany every pedestrian. "'And now I cannot remember,'" Brettigan recited, almost in a whisper, reading the words, "'how I would have had it.'"

"Please be quiet. Don't do that."

Brettigan ignored her and then resumed reading aloud.

"I never understood that poem," Alma told him, after he had finished. They both descended the stairs together in the brilliant sunshine, Alma holding on to her husband's arm, and as they made their way toward a George Segal sculpture of a walking man wearing a trench coat, Brettigan said, "I have to sit down." He seemed winded. Together, in the bright sunshine, they sat on a bench, looking toward the Claes Oldenburg giant spoon on whose tip a maraschino cherry was perched. Water sprayed out of the cherry's stem.

Somewhat off to the side, in the shade, a young couple, teenagers, standing together, were entwined in each other's arms and were kissing ostentatiously. His cap's brim faced backward, and she was barefoot, holding her shoes in her right hand behind her boyfriend's back. In northern climates, when the air finally turned warm, people like that wanted to throw their clothes off. The young couple didn't want to look at the art; they wanted to be the art, Alma decided. They were like the couple she'd seen months or years ago in Minnehaha Park. Nearby, a solitary man, hands in his trouser pockets, sauntered past, deep in thought. It was odd to see a man walking through the sculpture garden but not looking at anything. Several children ran past Harry and Alma, one of the girls wearing a bright yellow dress and a red ribbon in her hair and scuffed patent-leather shoes. Another young couple, speaking Spanish, walked past in the other direction, toward the Calder, holding hands with their two little children, all four of them smiling. The two little boys were wearing coats and ties.

"I always feel like a sculpture myself when I'm here," Alma said, glancing toward a Henry Moore mother-and-child in one direction and a Sol LeWitt structure in the other. "And everybody and every-thing starts to look like art when you're here."

He nodded. "I have something to say," he announced. Alma braced herself. Had he finally had enough of her, after all these decades of marriage? Was he finally going to leave her? Had he chosen the sculp-ture garden to announce a separation? He usually didn't preface his pronouncements with a pay-attention declaration, so whatever he had on his mind must have some weight and consequence.

"God is a MacGuffin," he said.

She waited. *This will pass,* she thought.

"And the Sun Collective is a MacGuffin." Saying these two sen-tences appeared to require enormous physical effort from him, more than was demanded by the steps up to and then down from the bridge. He slumped over, and when Alma raised her hand to his forehead, she felt cold sweat on his skin.

"I don't want to walk. I don't feel well," he said. He seemed to be suffering physically from the statements he had just made: his right hand had started to shake, and he continued to lean forward to catch his breath. Inside his windbreaker, he visibly shivered, though the day was warm. Re-collecting himself, he leaned back, then sat up straighter while Alma glanced around to see whether anybody in their vicinity had the appearance of working in the health-care professions. But instead of passing out, Brettigan began talking softly, almost inaudibly.

Under his breath, he said that if power corrupts, and if absolute power corrupts absolutely, then God is, or would have to be, the most corrupt entity in the known universe. Alma told him to shush, he was talking nonsense, but he ignored her. He was raving quietly and politely. He would not raise his voice even though something had possessed him. Traffic on the nearby highway hummed as he spoke. Overhead, Alma saw a brown butterfly. Brettigan said that he was having a vision of homelessness, of thousands of people living in their cars, in tents, on the streets, hungry, most of them, knocking at the door with their malnourished and pitifully crying children, armies of Jesuses, Marys, and Josephs. The rise and prevalence of zombie movies and books were a manifestation of capitalism's response to the homeless, to the armies of the poor, and the only way a person could cope with such a reality was by shutting it out or by trying to do something, anything. If you actually cared, while living within a structured system of indifference, if you were afflicted with empathy and compassion for the destitute, and for the plainly suffering natural environment of the planet—the fires and hurricanes and droughts, he said, were forms of planetary mania—if you cared about all this suffering, human and natural, or any of it, you would be susceptible to all the MacGuffins set up by charlatans like Wye and Lenin and Siddhartha, or, on the other side, lords of—

"Oh, Harry," she said. "Stop. Calm down. You're not making any sense."

— the lords, he continued, of complacency, of things-as-they-are, you would be in the counterarmy commanded by President Amos Alonzo Thorkelson, but you would not be safe, he whispered, there would be the knock on the door eventually, the armies of the poor would find you, and then, and forever, there would be no forgiveness, you would be eternally in the category of the unforgiven. *I am unforgiven,* Harry Brettigan said with an anguished sigh. There will be no forgiveness in this life we have led, lives of vanity and vexation. Demons have entered me.

"Please stop talking. Come on," Alma said. "Stand up."

She brought him to his feet. "Do you know," he asked her, "what the most valuable object in the city of Minneapolis is?" He fixed her with a look. Was he out of his mind? He wasn't like this. The most valuable object? For a second even his nose appeared to be askew.

"Harry," she said, "we have to get back to the car." She held on to his left arm and urged him forward, out of the sculpture garden, back toward where she had parked. The sun continued to shine; birds sang in the distance; the bells in the basilica were ringing; other families approached them; it was a perfect day otherwise.

"What's the most valuable thing?" he asked her again. They were now on the sidewalk, at the corner crossing the street. They would not go back up on the bridge.

She decided to play along. "The money at the Federal Reserve? All those dollar bills?"

"No," he said. "That Goya painting. In the Institute of Art. *Self-Portrait with Dr. Arrieta*. It's the most valuable human creation in this whole damn city. Dr. Arrieta is giving Goya his medicine, and his face is weighty with compassion, and Goya's face . . . his eyes are closed, he's in pain."

"Harry, I—"

"And behind Goya, in the dark behind his bed, there are those three demons. The demons that Goya saw in his illness. Alma, I'm seeing them now."

At the corner, they waited for the light to change. If only, she thought, if only they could get back into the car and drive home, they would be all right.

And then they *were* in the car headed up Lowry Hill toward their neighborhood, everything quite in order again, and her husband gazed out the window at someone's tulips planted on either side of the walk leading to a front door. It was a fine, pleasant neighborhood, like a tranquil setting in a *Twilight Zone* episode in the minutes before all hell breaks loose. Complain about the bourgeoisie all you want, but at least they mowed their lawns and planted their gardens. "Really, Harry," she said. "Your bad conscience is just a neurosis."

"Ah, yes. The voice of sanity," he said with self-mocking contempt. "Goya's last self-portrait, complete with demons, in Minneapolis?

Impossible. But we own those demons now. They're ours. They're here."

Well, at least he wasn't talking about MacGuffins. In her jacket, her iPhone made its customary ringtone announcing a text. She fished it out. The message was from Timothy: *Get home now,* it said. *Something has happened.*

30

IN THE BRETTIGANS' LIVING ROOM, ON THE TATTERED SOFA BENEATH the picture of the Basque coastline, Timothy was sitting, bent over Christina, who was curled up in his lap, her eyes closed.

"What's going on?" Brettigan asked. Alma stood beside him, her hands clasped together.

"She's blind," Timothy told his father. "Christina is blind. She . . . this was her doing."

Christina raised her head, opened her eyes, and Brettigan saw that something was wrong. "My God," he said. "What have you done to yourself?"

"I saved them all," she said hoarsely but with a great calm and serenity. "It's posted on YouTube. You can see it there. It's gone viral. Thousands of hits. All over the world. We won." She lay her head back in Timothy's lap.

SHE HAD ONLY TAKEN ONE SINGLE RECREATIONAL-WEEKEND BLUE TELE-phone, a habit she could not break, when the doorbell had chimed *ding dong,* and the vision-messenger stood there at last, all in white like an angel, sent from somewhere—where did they find these beautiful men, men whose beauty rivaled her own? this one as brown, however, as Detective O'Connor had been but not as worn down by daily life, this newfound particular angel sent to fetch her, an adult angel fresh and unused from the cosmic womb, as beautiful as the twilight sky? white shirt, white trousers, white tennis shoes?—and he identified himself as Michael, so that was it: he wasn't *like* an angel, no, *he was one,* he'd been tasked by someone somewhere to fetch her, because her moment had come at last. The Blue Telephone, maybe connected to the cosmos after trying one wrong number after another, was telling her that today was the day to carry out the plan she had concocted in the Alhambra. She and three others, another woman and two men, all photogenic, would be the chosen ones. There is something you need to do, the man said in a voice that originated from the other side of the universe, a voice suffused with divinity, the kind of voice that you cannot say no to. This is the last request we will ever make of you. After this sacrifice, your life will be yours, among the sky-and-earth order of the blessed.

Because: the word had gone out, some said from up high, that the Sun Collective, despite being ragtag, was practicing sedition as outlined in the Sedition Act of 1918. Countermeasures had to be taken.

The authorities had asked around about the collective's symbol, the pointing finger and the star, ☛ ✳, which the authorities said was quite possibly not a star but was a bomb, exploding. That was evidence enough. That was enough to round up just about everybody else associated with the group for friendly questioning.

The idea: four members—any lesser number would not be enough, three or fewer would have the aspect of a freak show—would have to dress from head to toe in white, don't ask why, if you had to ask, you would never know, and appear together, as a group, in Theodore Wirth Park, in a hillside clearing a week from now, where it had been arranged to have a videographer who would record the proceedings, along with a group of twenty witnesses, some SC members, and others recruited at random, when and whereupon the four would stand, midmorning, each one speaking individually first, demanding that attention must be paid, anyone's and everyone's hearts had to be converted, given the harmlessness of the Sun Collective, given its essentially benign and life-affirming and benevolent ideas, which could be found online at www.suncollectiverevolution.org, including their manifesto, and then each member would, and did, recite a line from Marsilio Ficino's *The Book of the Sun,* and, once the line had been spoken, would look straight into the solar light, knowing the consequences, creating a media event whose repercussions would cause poverty to be eradicated, and the Earth to be saved.

What they had asked to do, and agreed to do, would be a sign of their faith. She would have no trouble finding three other volunteers.

It had gone according to plan.

The first person, a woman, said, "In proportion to the strength you receive from the Sun, you will almost seem to have found God, who placed His tabernacle in the Sun."

The second person said, "This pure light exceeds the intelligence just as in itself sunlight surpasses the acuity of the eyes."

Christina said, directly to the camera, "The divine light shines into the darkness of the soul."

The last person said, "God kindles a light for us believers here which purifies and converts, before it bestows the intelligence of divine things."

And then together the four of them lifted their faces to the sun's light, staring into it. To blind yourself takes a long time, as it happens, and is an act of willpower worthy of the gods.

The cameras concentrated on Christina, because, of the four, she was the prettiest.

Besides, as the Sun Collective had once said collectively, "In an age of distraction, when nothing important lasts longer than fifteen minutes, *the only true contemporary art is the art of getting everybody's attention and keeping it for as long as you can.*"

THE EVENT HAD CREATED AN IMMENSE INTERNET SENSATION, WITH thousands of responses, some of which claimed that the scene had been faked, or was preposterous, or just plain crazy. Four people, all in white, voluntarily blinding themselves by staring into the sun? To indicate their belief in everything the Sun Collective believed and stood for? Who *does* that? No one. Well, *they* had, and they had multiple witnesses who would testify that they had indeed performed an action that the YouTube video and the Instagram stream showed, which was why it had turned into a world historic event, watched and rewatched eventually by the masses. Four people blinding themselves: it was like Buddhist monks setting themselves on fire, but on a diminished scale.

A collectivist was quoted as saying that when you considered what was being done to the Earth, and you combined that destruction with what was being done to the poor and people of color, then blinding yourself to get attention for these problems didn't seem particularly outrageous or implausible. The only category of action these days that got the attention of everybody was . . . the inconceivable. To save the Earth and the poor, you had to do what no one could believe you would do. You had to fight the power with the implausible.

On social media, arguments continued to rage about the event's effectiveness: a posting from someone in California noted that, if indeed we are in the End Times, with the planet growing ever more uninhabitable and with growing disparity between the rich and poor, and an increasing global population of the hungry and homeless, then no action to raise social and ecological consciousness should be considered overwrought or hysterical. The posting concluded, "These four people are champions for the poor and the Earth. The revolution starts here. They are secular saints. They have sacrificed themselves for us. Bless them."

And there were outraged responders, who claimed that left-liberalism had reached a new low of lunacy, that leftists and bleeding hearts were blind anyway, and that it had all been only a computer-generated publicity stunt. Just a bunch of raggedy, half-assed neighborhood insurrectionists, one person said. Reference was made to the blind leading the blind, to Brueghel.

The debate continued for weeks and months. Here and there, other social activists blinded themselves in similar ways, but the impact, having lost its novelty, was greatly lessened, given the passage of time and its diminishing effects. No longer so effective now, as part of a copycat syndrome, and therefore idiotic.

In the end, the consensus was that the Sun Collective had triumphed, and the four would be henceforth treated as heroes, but their actions were unrepeatable.

But that would come later. For now, Christina lay on the Brettigans' tattered sofa, her head in Timothy Brettigan's lap, and to Alma she seemed calm in a peculiar manner, as if she had finally found a fate that suited her and her ambitions and had answered a calling. *The peace beyond all understanding,* Alma thought. And Alma could also see that her son, Timothy, who had not loved Christina up until now, had probably not loved anybody so far in his life, had indeed become transfixed with her, almost instantaneously now that she was a martyr, despite, or because of, her blindness.

She could also see that her husband, Harry Brettigan, with his drawn face, his distanced expression, was not well, was possibly gravely ill, and yet, in spite of all that, he was interested in life again, almost smiling as he tried to help, as if all those demons that he talked about had departed temporarily.

THEY INSISTED ON TAKING HER TO THE HOSPITAL. INITIALLY, SHE RE-fused to go. After an examination, she was diagnosed with solar retinopathy, with lesions evident in the retinal tissue lining the back of the eye. The emergency room physician told her that, as far as he knew, there were no standard medical treatments for her condition. She should bathe her eyes, wear dark glasses, stay inside, and rest. Oh: and never, ever do that again.

- 31 -

ALMA BRETTIGAN HAS READ THE NEWSPAPER TWICE AND IS GROWING deeply irritated at her husband, who is late coming home from that geezer group of his, the walking club or whatever they call themselves these days, out at the Utopia Mall. They had planned to go an hour ago to a flower-and-plant nursery to buy some seedlings, if it's not too late in the spring for planting. She prides herself on her heirloom tomatoes. Minnesota has the most unpredictable of season changes: snow one week in spring, followed by hot weather a few days later. You have to be an expert to know when to plant your garden around here.

Also, she has some news: Timothy and Christina are engaged. She can hardly contain her excitement, and her irritation with Harry grows in exact proportion to her excitement. In a weird way, her son and that young woman, for all her oddities, make a good pair. Anybody can tell how they've fallen for each other, those two rescuers. Good news piles on good news: Christina has confided in Alma that she has missed her period, and soon . . . well, we will wait and see.

Alma tosses the newspaper down on the coffee table, takes off her reading glasses, and waits for the explanatory and apologetic phone call from her husband. Maybe he left his cell phone at home, as he often does. What a case she can build against him! She is preparing a bill of particulars, an indictment against which he will be humbled and defenseless. As she waits, Woland, followed by Behemoth, ambles into the living room. Both animals sit together in front of her, as they do when they're ready to chat.

Where's my husband?

Doing whatever he does, the cat answers. *You should learn to wait. Patience.*

I've been patient with that guy all my life.

In that case, be patient now.

Another hour passes, and now Alma's irritation is being mixed increasingly with worry and a glimmer of fear.

Where is he? This isn't like him.

What's like him?

To let me know where he is. If something happens.

He always returns, the dog observes. *Same time every day.*

You say that because you're a dog.

So?

I just don't know what's got into him. He never does this. He never does this. He just never does.

Maybe he got lost, the cat says. *Maybe he took off for somewhere.*

You're heartless, Alma says aloud to the cat.

No. Realistic.

The room is beginning to darken slightly as the afternoon goes on.

He'll come back. He always comes back, the dog repeats.

How do you know? Alma wonders.

Loyalty and love, the dog says. *What else is there?*

ON AN EARLY SATURDAY MORNING AT THE UTOPIA MALL, BRETTIGAN
stood outside the shuttered Unbound Sound store and watched while
the Thundering Herd power walked past him. This particular morning, after two difficult Sisyphean circuits, he had had enough and
was about to sit down on a bench in the courtyard in front of the
fast-food Slow Boat to China, now open, where they were serving
soybean milk, tofu pudding, and deep-fried dough sticks for breakfast.
So far, they'd had no customers, and the chef, a Latino, was reading
something on his iPhone.

At this time of morning, with only a handful of businesses like
the Boat already open, the mall was unlittered by noise before the
racket of eager customers arrived. Celia, the retired teacher, wearing a jaunty red cap, walking stick in hand, was leading the others in
the Herd, but the retired drug dealer, sporting a blue sweatshirt, and
slightly bent from osteoporosis, would soon catch up to her. Celia
was tough and temperamentally optimistic. She could outrace anybody despite her cigarette habit. Every day seemed to enliven her; no
challenge was too great for her concentrated, hungry will. Her high
spirits were relentless. In old age she was intact and unbroken. Her
love of every detail of life's banquet gave her superpowers that no
one else her age could even pretend to possess. Brettigan found her
almost intolerable.

As Brettigan sat down, his friend Dr. Elijah Jones gave him a qualified smile, a halfhearted wave, and a concerned, diagnostic glance as
he ambled behind the others.

The members of the Herd had been annoyed by Brettigan's frequent absences and were unenthusiastic about his recent tendency to drop out of the group and sit down whenever he was winded, as often happened. Dr. Jones had told him that he needed to have a checkup with his cardiologist, and soon. Brettigan had the feeling that if he himself should die of a heart attack, the Herd would express disappointment rather than grief. In America, with its strange pragmatism, the idea was that you could postpone death indefinitely if you simply took the proper steps and followed the self-help advice given out by paid-programming dietitians and fitness experts who could also be found expounding their theories on the internet. If you died, you would be criticized for your bad habits: too much pasta, a sedentary lifestyle, whiskey instead of herbal energy drinks, pessimism. Your death would be all your fault.

Immortality, one TV and internet doctor had claimed, was nearly within our grasp. But you had to work for it.

Sitting on the bench in front of the Slow Boat, Brettigan felt a mood of summing-up enfolding him: he complimented himself that in his long life, he had never murdered anybody, though he knew himself to be capable of homicide, and had not been an arsonist, a rapist, or a despoiler. He hadn't divorced Alma, although he'd been tempted a few times, and he had helped to raise two children who were getting by. The criminality he knew he possessed had not been enacted. His daughter, Virginia, a true American down there in the wilds of Asheville with her newly acquired southern accent, would always be sturdy and fine, a lovely human being, with her husband and children. He loved her and his grandchildren, a family that was perfection itself. And his son—

The Herd came around again, this time with the drug dealer in the lead.

His son, Timothy. When Brettigan closed his eyes, Timothy's face floated in front of him in the darkness, but the details of that face remained hazy. Some feature of Timothy's personality, or his character, would always be hidden away from his view. Fathers did not need to understand their sons, and, according to Western myths, they shouldn't try, given the risk of soul-carnage. If that son happened to be an actor whose self-presentation could change daily, he might go beyond mood swings into personality swings, an occupational hazard, and that meant that he would always be unknowable, masked, as all actors are unknowable. Besides, you could love people without really knowing them. You didn't have to carry on Russian conversations with your children about the purpose of life and the contents of the soul. Simply to survive, sons may lock up their hearts against their fathers and refuse entry. Most aging fathers were simply grateful for any charity at all thrown in their direction from their children. King Lear should have settled for a few bread crumbs. Only young men need a crew.

But, he reminded himself, his son was no longer an actor. He managed a movie theater and was a social activist. He had expressed great love for his parents. He was becoming himself.

Brettigan leaned forward, trying to get his breath. The oxygen here in the Utopia Mall seemed to have come out of a plastic machine. It was monetized, manufactured plastic air.

Timothy and Christina had been publicly fondling each other lately and were planning to move in together soon. They had found an affordable barrier-free apartment in Northeast Minneapolis, and after not being in love, their hearts had undergone a conversion, and they were now—through some kind of long-term dramatic irony— weirdly infatuated with each other. A surprise ending: Christina's blindness had altered their personal psychic relationships. It shouldn't have happened according to any progressive theory of gender dynamics, but it had. They were inhabiting a prefeminist setup: holding hands, kissing in public. Her blindness played into her unspoken wish to be comforted and to have someone take care of her, a role that Timothy was more than happy to perform; and now that Christina couldn't see him, Timothy didn't have to worry about his appearance, didn't have to be conscious of being observed, a condition that suited him, and he didn't have to pretend to be somebody he wasn't. With her, he didn't have to perform. In this way, her blindness was a kind of solution.

The Thundering Herd came around again, this time with the retired garage mechanic in the lead. The others had slowed down, given the effort of their conversation, which had taken over from the power walking. Dr. Jones trailed behind them all.

Christina, whose sight was slowly returning, had quit her job at the bank and was serving in an advisory capacity to a neighborhood ecology, gardening, conservation, and consciousness-raising group. She had started jogging again, holding hands with Timothy on the wide jogging trails alongside the Mississippi River they'd found together. She always wore her dark glasses. She had not spent much time grieving that other guy, Ludlow, whom Brettigan had not liked, and she had not spoken much about the Sun Collective, whose members were active but invisible. Maybe it was just in the nature of radical reformist groups to be shattered and fragmented.

Still, one must try. There was always a new struggle demanding a person's attention.

Brettigan had never known his son to be as happy—a fragile happiness, to be sure—as he was now in Christina's company, and Christina herself seemed to have had a burden lifted from the localized part of her consciousness that'd been weighed down by an obligation she had obviously felt toward the wretched, the poor, and the homeless: all those miserable people in rags who stagger toward you in dreams and in real life with their hands out and their eyes imploring you to help and to save them. She had paid off their pain with her eyesight. It seemed to have been a sufficient sacrifice. "We never did have a coherent platform," she finally admitted to Brettigan, "but no one else does, either."

AND WHAT HAD BECOME OF THAT GUY, WYE, THE SPOKESPERSON? ON the internet, there was speculation that he had never existed. One posting claimed that every appearance he ever staged had been a performance by an actor, one of several actors, like department store Santas, so the argument ran. This explanation accounted for the dark rooms in which Wye preferred to appear. Another school of thought

posited that Wye was not a human being at all but a hologram, projected from the other side of the universe by means of quantum
entanglement.

Charismatic figures had a habit of vanishing into thin air after they
had disturbed their communities anyway. They all did it, and Wye had
apparently read the playbook.

Meanwhile, remnants of the Sun Collective were said to be re-
forming here and there in other cities, with the most significant consequence of the Great Blinding being a revival of interest in food
pantries, urban gardens, racial inclusivity, and treatment for addictive
consumers. Inspired by the group's parting event, and Wye's disappearance, the members of the collective now wore dark glasses all the
time as their secret sign of membership. Whenever you saw someone wearing shades these days, indoors or out, you might be in the
presence of a Sun Collectivist. Besides, it made them look cool and
slightly above it all.

In every age there would be a call to arms; in every city, someone
would knock at your door with requests or demands. The armies of
the poor trudged ever onward, peeing on the sidewalk and living in
tents. And even now, the Sandmen were still around in urban legends,
creating bedlam. The more things change . . .

Brettigan gazed up at the many-colored glass dome of the Utopia Mall, staining the white radiance of eternity. The glass at the
top had the word *Utopia* lettered into it. The first time he saw it, he
misread it and thought the word was *Alma. The Alma Mall. I'm losing it,* he thought, as a storefront security gate in front of Unbound
Sound rattled upward for the opening of the business day. Yesterday
he'd come into the house and found Alma talking loudly and happily
about the possibility of Timothy and Christina getting married and
starting a family. Fine, except she was carrying on this conversation
with the dog and the cat. Alma was leaning back on the living room
sofa, and both animals were seated in front of her, listening intently,
and, for all Brettigan knew, taking it all in. The dog would welcome
the news; the cat would not. Cats did not love anything, on principle.

He and Alma had been married so long that love didn't really figure into the whole business anymore, and their tolerance for each other's eccentricities didn't matter much either—Alma was like water: you didn't have to love water when you were thirsty. You just needed it to live. That's how they were with each other. They had gone from love to post-love, where each one for the other was a necessity. Necessity was the infrastructure on which the superstructure of love rested. If he couldn't hold her in his arms at night, he would die. Well, he thought grumpily, sooner or later he would die anyway.

It was a sin against God and His creation to be tired of life, but on some days Brettigan was heartily tired of all of it, with one exception: holding his wife in his arms. He had never tired of that.

"You look like you're thinking?" Dr. Jones said, lowering himself onto the bench next to Brettigan. He huffed and puffed; his face held a thin sheen of fat man sweat. "Of what?"

"Oh, this and that," Brettigan said.

"People our age shouldn't think," the doctor opined. He was still breathing hard.

"No? What should they do?"

"Lie in the sun and accept the applause."

"You should lose some weight, Elijah."

"I should do a lot of things," the doctor said. "My point is, you oughta stop thinking and start to enjoy all the wonders. Thinking never did anybody any good. Enjoy the great diversions."

"Such as?"

"Well, you take this mall. Everything a human being requires is here. Except groceries and hardware and love. There's no love here. But almost everything else a human being wants, you can find that here, too. All the wonders of the visible world."

"Elijah," Brettigan said. "I gotta go." Brettigan stood up.

"Stay. Stay with us, stay with your aging friends awhile. We're going to drink tea, and we'll talk as we always do."

"I have to go," Brettigan said. It seemed urgent to him now that he head homeward. The feeling that he should do so was very strong, an implicit order from somewhere.

"Whatever you say," the doctor said. When the Thundering Herd rounded the corner near them, Brettigan waved at them wearily before walking away.

ON THE LIGHT RAIL HEADED TOWARD MINNEAPOLIS, BRETTIGAN LET the sun shine on his face, and once again the light had acquired a blue tint from the advertising sheath that covered the exterior of the train car. When Brettigan glanced at his hands, he noticed that they appeared to be slightly blue, as if bruised. The train burst out of the tunnel into the light and stopped at Fort Snelling, where an old woman with a prominent bald spot got on, giving Brettigan an aura of pain around his heart.

He closed his eyes and thought of a bridge he would design for her, for all of them. It would be a pedestrian bridge, formed by a slender and heavily post-tensioned concrete deck, the cables anchored to stiff foundations at either end. A stress ribbon bridge would have the shape of gently sloping catenary curves, not unlike the rope pedestrian suspension bridges that humanity had been building since prehistory. To support the deck, the post-tensioning cables would exert large horizontal forces at the abutments, suited to locations where the ground consisted of solid rock at the ends of the span. The ribbon bridge that Brettigan saw in his imagination would be well suited to a river . . . he saw all of them, the shadows, crossing over on his bridge to rest in the shade of the trees.

At the next stop, at the VA Hospital, a war-torn African-American man with a U.S. Army Iraq War badge on his jacket sleeve came hobbling in, supported by a crutch on his left-hand side. His other sleeve displayed a marksmanship medal with a cross and a circle surrounding it. On his neck was a cross tattoo, and another cross hung down on a leather band over his chest. He wore an oversize black boot over his left foot, large enough to surround the wound dressings that were surely enfolded underneath the leather. Using his crutch, his face a mask of pain that, as the old preachers used to say, would make Jesus weep, he headed toward the front of the car, where he engaged the first set of passengers in conversation.

The train continued toward Minneapolis, passing several grain elevators lit by the midmorning sun. In the distance a dog ran down the sidewalk followed by a red-haired boy on roller skates. Brettigan closed his eyes.

"Sir?"

Brettigan opened his eyes. "Yes?"

It was the war-torn veteran. "I am very sorry to bother you," he said. "This is embarrassing for me. But I wonder if you have any spare change or perhaps a dollar. Please. Whatever you can spare? For a meal?"

The pain, which had been located in Brettigan's chest, had moved out to his left arm and his neck, becoming its own universe, and with some difficulty he reached behind for his wallet, which he extracted from his trousers and opened in front of the veteran. Inside it were four twenty-dollar bills and two singles. He took them out and handed them over. "Here, take them," Brettigan said.

The veteran studied the bills in Brettigan's hand, and his eyes widened. "Please, sir, no jokes."

"I'm serious. Take them."

"That's . . . you mean—?"

"Take them. I do mean it. Here. Eighty-two dollars. It's not a fortune. It's just eighty-two dollars." Brettigan was beginning to wave the money back and forth and then stopped the motion because it hurt. "I insist."

Very gingerly, the veteran reached out to take the money.

"Here," Brettigan said. "Take my wallet, too. Take the credit card. Go ahead and use it. I don't need it anymore." He held out the wallet.

The veteran stared at him.

"I came naked into the world and naked I will leave it," Brettigan said.

"No. I ain't no thief," the veteran said, rubbing the beard stubble on his chin.

"No, you're not," Brettigan said to him. "Okay, don't use the credit card. I get it. There's just one thing I ask."

"What?"

"I want a blessing," Brettigan told him. "Give me a blessing."

"Why?"

"I'm in pain."

"You been in the war, too, I guess. It shows on you, you know what I'm sayin'? Well, all right. God bless you, sir."

"Thank you."

"But I can't take your wallet."

"Sure, you can. Where's your stop?"

The veteran glanced out the window. "Next one. Cedar-Riverside."

"Take the wallet. If you don't want it, just toss it in the trash. But I'd rather you keep it."

"You are one crazy motherfucker," the veteran said with an expression of deep pity. "What's your thing got you here?"

"This is your stop," Brettigan informed him, as the train slowed.

"Thank you," the veteran said. "I ain't gonna forget you ever. No shit."

"Yes, I know."

The man limped out of the car after the doors chimed open, and Brettigan watched as he stood pensively next to a trash container before pocketing the eighty-two dollars and tossing the wallet into the container's open mouth. The doors chimed shut, and Brettigan closed his eyes as an involuntary movement took control of his left leg. A chill rose up his body. *Abends, will ich schlafen gehn.*

THE TRAIN MADE A SLIGHT TURN LEFTWARD, PAST A PRIVATE NOVELTY museum, House of Balls, where carved bowling balls with faces of cherubs and devils were on display, and then a paint factory whose exterior had been coated with primary colors. A large football stadium in the shape of a Viking ship loomed up on the left, and the train moved through several switches, lurching slightly as it approached the stop for the stadium, where several people boarded, including a woman pushing a small shopping cart on wheels. She glanced at the man with his eyes closed and took her seat close to the door.

ABOVE THE TRAIN, A FLOCK OF SPARROWS APPEAR TO BE FIGHTING with each other or are engaged in a mating ritual, and their collective mind takes them in the direction of a small city park in which office workers are even now spreading quilts out on the grass so that they can sit down and eat a midday sandwich. Four young men are playing hacky sack on the north end of the park. A light breeze cools the air, and overhead an airplane headed southeast gradually descends for its landing at the airport.

Gazing down from the plane, a passenger unfamiliar with the city and the Midwest might spy a commuter train, the light rail, making its way downtown, toward Target Field. Is it inward or outward bound? From this distance, it would be hard to say. But the chief flight attendant has just announced that everyone must secure their tray tables and move their seats to the upright position. "We will be landing shortly," she says, so the passenger quickly gathers up his odds and ends of flight mini-garbage and hands it all to the attendant walking down the aisle and carrying a trash bag. The city looks great from the air, a place of lakes and a river, the Mississippi, that flows all the way to the Gulf of Mexico, cutting down the middle of the country like an incision over its heart.

Acknowledgments

Two excerpts from this novel appeared in *The Idaho Review* and *Fogged Clarity Arts Review*. Thanks to the editors of these publications. And multiple thanks also to the early readers of this book: Steven Schwartz, Robert Cohen, Chris Cander, Julie Schumacher, Matt Burgess, James Morrison, Sally Franson, Mike Alberti, Chris Bram, and Elizabeth Darhansoff. Daniel Baxter, P.E., was helpful with the structural engineering, and Dorothy Horns, M.D., was informative about solar retinopathy.

The beautiful poem "Storm Window," by Conrad Hilberry (1928–2017), inspired part of the barbershop chapter and is dedicated to his memory. My late beloved friend Jürgen Dierking is not the same person as Jürgen the bank manager, but there are faint echoes set up between them. The final chapter uses a device invented by Wright Morris (1910–1998) and is dedicated to his memory.

Here and there, the reader may detect traces of *Toward an Urban Ecology* by Kate Orff, *A Union Against Unions* by William Millikan, *Capitalist Realism* by Mark Fisher, Hegel's *Phenomenology of Spirit* translated by A. V. Miller (portions of which Christina hallucinates, driving her Saab while high on Blue Telephone). President Thorkelson has plagiarized a line in his poem from Tim Robbins's *Bob Roberts*. The passages from Marsilio Ficino are from a volume of his works edited and introduced by Angela Voss and published by North Atlantic Books. On page 220, the sentence "At night the familiar stars slipped further and further away" is a slightly altered quotation of a line from "The King and the Singer" by the Serbian poet Ivan Lalić, translated by C. W. Truesdale.

This book was helped immeasurably by the attention and care shown to it by my editor, Dan Frank, the best reader and friend any writer could hope for. Great thanks also to Vanessa Rae Haughton.

Thanks and love to Pua Johnson.

A Note About the Author

Charles Baxter is the author of the novels *The Feast of Love* (nominated for the National Book Award), *The Soul Thief, Saul and Patsy, Shadow Play,* and *First Light,* and the story collections *Gryphon, Believers, A Relative Stranger, Through the Safety Net,* and *Harmony of the World*. The stories "Bravery" and "Charity," which appear in the collection *There's Something I Want You to Do,* were included in *Best American Short Stories*. Baxter lives in Minneapolis and teaches at the University of Minnesota and in the MFA Program for Writers at Warren Wilson College.

A Note on the Type

This book was set in Monotype Dante, a typeface designed by Giovanni Mardersteig (1892–1977). Originally cut for hand composition by Charles Malin between 1946 and 1952, its first use was in an edition of Boccaccio's *Trattatello in laude di Dante* that appeared in 1954. The Monotype Corporation's version of Dante followed in 1957. Although modeled on the Aldine type used for Pietro Cardinal Bembo's treatise *De Aetna* in 1495, Dante is a thoroughly modern interpretation of the venerable face.

Composed by Scribe,
Philadelphia, Pennsylvania

Printed and bound by Berryville Graphics,
Berryville, Virginia

Designed by Betty Lew